LOLA MILES

Lilies in Autumn

This book contains references to eating disorders, disordered eating, body dysphoria, graphic violence, fertility, and conception. Please, take care of yourself and your well-being when reading.

Cover Design by DeborahAnne Neri

Editing by Steph White (Kat's Literary Services)

Proofreading by Vanessa Esquibel (Kat's Literary Services)

First edition

This book was professionally typeset on Reedsy.
Find out more at reedsy.com

To my husband, who is every hero in every story.
I love you.
And to my children and parents, who are never allowed to read this book.
(Seriously, mom, put it down.)

Contents

Acknowledgement

I fell in love with writing, reading, and literature when I was twelve years old thanks to Jane Austen's *Pride and Prejudice.* I definitely had no business reading that novel, and I think I understood every fifth word, but there was something about the world of Elizabeth and Darcy that called to me. I'm forever grateful to my father, who bought me the book in a Newark Airport Hudson News store because I had no entertainment for a flight to Jamaica with our family.

I remember his words, "I think this is a book for girls," and my mother's incredulous look since she knew that I would comprehend twenty percent of the book. Somehow, someway, that book directed the course of my life.

I need to thank my parents for always encouraging my writing, even when they realized that I enjoyed writing more—*ahem*— explicit material. They are my biggest supporters and I cannot imagine two more amazing people. Still, they are not allowed to read this.

My brother and sister were huge inspirations for the sibling dynamic of the book; coming from a large Italian-American family (which is extremely evident based on the number of references to food in this book), capturing the cultural nuance of familial bonds was extremely important to me. Like the relationship between Ava and her siblings, our speech is often sarcastic yet supportive, linguistically aggressive yet protective. In examining my relationships with my family, I was able to model the Gregori family dynamic in, what I hope, is an authentic depiction of the tri-state Italian-American culture, outside of the stereotypes perpetuated by media and TV.

You'll also notice that there are repeated references to matriarchal figures within *Lilies in Autumn.* In my life, two of the most important female figures are my grandmothers and it seemed appropriate to document how influential matriarchs are.

My husband deserves all the praise and acknowledgment in the world. Six months ago, after giving birth to our second little hellion, I told my husband that I finally wanted to fulfill a dream I've had since I was a young girl and write a book. Not only was he a champion of my dream, but he also ensured that I had the time, the space, and the mental capacity to achieve my goal. He has continuously encouraged me to be everything I want to be— a mother, a wife, a professional, a writer— and has picked up the pieces when I don't have the energy to do so (like washing the floors because Jesus, I hate doing it). My honey, you are the best.

Thank you to Kat's Literary Services, a literal godsend of a company. I found Kat and her team when researching literary services used by some of my favorite authors, and working with the group has been nothing short of amazing, educational, and eye-opening. Thank you Kat Wyeth, Steph White, Vanessa Esquibel, and Kelly Finley for the support, guidance, and help you've all given to me.

Thank you to Deb Neri for my gorgeous book cover and for taking my statement of, "I want a lily," and turning it into a stunning, hand-drawn design. You are so incredibly talented.

I also need to acknowledge the sorority culture presented in the book. As a sorority girl myself (one of those super involved ones who was everything from Sisterhood Development chair to Panhellenic Council President) I know that the culture could be both amazing and toxic. While *Lilies in Autumn* does show the toxicity of sororities, there are so many positives and beautiful aspects to it, as well. I think, ultimately, it comes down to the fact that some people are just really shitty, regardless of their affiliation.

For all those struggling with eating disorders, disordered eating, body dysmorphia, body image issues, and everything else under this vast umbrella: you are strong, you are beautiful, and you are worthy.

Lastly, and most importantly, thank you to my two little chickens, D and L. Everything I do, I do to show you both that you can be anything, everything, whomever, and whenever you want.

Thank you all for reading my book (which is so weird and euphoric and bizarre to say).

XO Lola

Ava

When I was eight years old, I thought the concession stand at the local football field was referred to as a "confession stand." It made sense in my young, twisted mind since food was always my coping mechanism for sin, vice, and sorrow. I treated donuts like the Eucharist and soda like the body and blood of Jesus Christ.

Like clockwork, every Sunday we would be at the football fields to support my younger brother, Rafe, while he got the shit beat out of him by other boys. Somewhere between the first and second quarter, I would sneak off for penance at the concession stand and load up on "bad" food. I always thought it was strange watching other young kids dismiss the concession stand while I would beg my mother for five dollars to secure as many ice cream sandwiches as my grubby hands could carry.

As I got older, and my pants got larger, I became more self-conscious about my chosen method of repentance. But I couldn't stop; it was like an addiction—eat as much as I can in as short a period, and then cry over the wrappers as if my tears could eradicate the calories I just consumed.

What makes me even more pathetic is that I tried to throw up the contents of my stomach multiple times, but a lack of a gag reflex and a strong disposition fucked up my bulimia attempts.

I compensated by taking copious amounts of laxatives and developing a GI infection. By the time I was fifteen years old, living on the edge meant sneaking into the teachers' bathroom to use the toilet in private.

I am better now. Sort of.

While I had a healthier relationship with food and didn't binge eat anymore,

I still struggled with my size. Maybe if I were truly plus-sized, I would accept my body more easily. My not quite thin but not quite plus-size body was an unknown question mark for me; I was undefined and struggled to fit into a box, let alone clothes.

Most of the time, I faked my confidence. Sometimes, it felt like I faked who I was, too.

I know it worried my parents, my mother especially. While most moms hoped that their daughter would stay a virgin until their wedding night, my mom panicked that I had never had a boyfriend or rarely accepted a date. She worried that I had sheltered myself for so long that I would eventually experience a psychotic break and fuck every living creature, human and otherwise, within a hundred-mile radius. I know this because she told me.

I did tell her I wasn't into bestiality, but that just brought a wooden spoon out.

When she tried to convince me to stay home for my freshman year and attend the local community college instead of a four-year university, I had to swear to every Italian saint that I wouldn't dance on tables or go streaking in the quad in acts of rebellion. It helped that my best friend, Celeste, or as I called her, CeCe, would be my roommate.

The feelings of reverence and wonder I had for the concession stand are back as I stand in my dorm room at Marymount University. Boxes, plastic bins, and clothes are strewn around the floor and small desks as we try to make sense of the massive amount of shit we brought with us.

My mom, CeCe, and CeCe's mom, Trisha, are standing in front of the small window, peering into the contents of one of my boxes. CeCe turns to look at me while I struggle with my fitted sheet.

Who the hell didn't label the sides of this cotton death trap? I'm just getting one corner of it over the mattress when it snaps back up.

This motherfucker.

"Ava, why do you have a ceramic frog in this box?" CeCe calls out.

"CeCe, I don't have time for questions. I'm a little busy." I hold the sheet up for emphasis. "Deborah, why did you buy me sheets that require a college degree? I'm here to learn how to be an adult, not put a sheet on a bed." I finally have two corners of the sheet secured onto the mattress.

My mom comes over, nudging me aside. "First of all, little girl, I'm Mom, not 'Deborah.'" She takes the sheet off the mattress and rotates the fabric. Huh, so it was the wrong side?

"Second, you bought these sheets online for fifteen dollars because you wanted to be cheap. By the way, these sheets feel like they were preowned by a prison. Do you feel that fabric? It's going to rub your skin raw." She finishes securing the sheet to the mattress and starts to arrange my pillows and comforter like a *Better Homes & Gardens* magazine picture.

She looks at me while she fluffs my pillows. "Now, please enlighten us as to why you have not only a ceramic frog in that box but three boxes of condoms and a beer funnel."

Dammit, I thought I hid those better.

"Well, Mom, the condoms are self-explanatory. CeCe and I will not be dropping out due to teen pregnancy. I found the frog at the garage sale on Willow Street last week, and the owner told me it would help me find a man, like the fairy tale of the princess kissing a frog." I let out an exasperated sigh. "And we need to practice funneling if we're going to hold our own at college parties."

Trisha shakes her head, looking like one of the bobbleheads they hand out at Yankee Stadium during championship games. "Ava, there is so much to unpack there. Let me just sum it up with this: don't be idiots, don't get trashed at strangers' houses, and don't have sex in public places."

Part of me recognizes that these are our parents and probably aren't too excited to hear about the drinking and possibility of sex in relation to their daughters. But our moms aren't prudes and are realistic about what happens in college.

"Ava, you delusional soul," my mom starts. "You would need to accept a date from someone to get a boyfriend." I see we're bypassing the conversation of sex and underage drinking and going right for the jugular.

"Yes, Deborah, I know." I turn to CeCe and watch her hold up the funnel and reach back into the box to grab the tube that attaches to it. Her gaze bounces back and forth between me and the plastic in her hands as her brow furrows. "C, what are you staring at?"

"Ava, you fucking idiot, the tube is shaped like a penis."

—

Fifteen minutes after the dick tube emerged from the box, we rushed our mothers out of our dorm room with the promise that we wouldn't use the penis funnel in public, and under penalty of death, we would not post pictures with it on social media.

"C, what the actual fuck?" I seethe as I use a Command strip to stick a frame to our wall. "Why did you announce that it was shaped like a penis in front of our moms? Between that and the condoms, my mother is going to think I'm fixated on dicks."

"Ava, you are fixated on dicks."

"I am not. I just have a vested interest in losing my virginity and finding a boyfriend before I die. These are very common goals." She acts as though I'm consumed by the need to be dick-slapped. I'm not interested in that, at least, I don't think I am.

CeCe's eyes roll so aggressively, I'm surprised they didn't get stuck. "You act like you've never been asked on a date or that a guy has never been into you, which is horse shit," CeCe scoffs. "You have been propositioned and asked on more dates than any other person I know. The fact that you are disregarding that is annoying."

"Boys don't ask me on dates. They ask me for help, or they think they can get an easy blow job."

"For someone so smart, you are very, very dumb. What do you think, 'Ava, are you free for dinner?' means?" She raises an eyebrow at me. "And before you get onto your soapbox that Matt Henderson wanted you to read over his paper, the guy was valedictorian and did not need your help reading over anything. He used it as an excuse to get you to agree to dinner."

"Okay, that was one instance, and that hardly makes me a femme fatale like you're implying."

CeCe reaches under her bed to retrieve a step stool and fairy lights, wordlessly holding out one end for me to grab. "Ava, I can name a dozen similar instances, yet you always say no, or worse, friend-zone guys without even exploring the possibility. I didn't mean to make your mom think you were obsessed with penises, but you actually kind of are."

I hold up my end of the lights, securing them to the wall with a hook I put up earlier. "C, those guys showed interest in me because they thought I'd be an easy lay. They weren't attracted to me, outside of my boobs." I glance down. I have to admit, my double-D chest is an attractive feature. "I know what I look like and I don't need a guy to make me feel like shit about it or assume I'll spread my legs easily because of my limited offers."

"You've got to be kidding me," CeCe yells, throwing her end of the lights on her bed. "Cut that shit out right now. Ava, you are beautiful, and you don't even realize how many people, guys and girls, stop and look at you. I would kill, literally kill, to have curves like yours and you condemn them like they're evil." CeCe's a literature major, and she tends to be overdramatic. "You also need to let the shit that happened sophomore year go. He was an immature asshole and we dealt with him."

"CeCe,—"

"No, don't you 'CeCe' me, you beautiful asshole. I need you to listen to me." She waits to continue until my eyes meet hers. "No matter how much I tell you that you are beautiful, inside and out, and no matter how many people ask you out, you will never accept it until you recognize your beauty and your worth. This year isn't about guys or kissing frogs..." She pauses. "Which, by the way, why the fuck would you buy that?" She shakes her head while eyeing my box of horrors. "No, Aves, this year is about you learning to love yourself and accept yourself for the beautiful, weird goddess that you are."

I look down, overcome by her speech. "CeCe, I know, I know. I'm working on it. Okay?"

She looks at me for a minute before letting out a sigh. "Fine, now give me a hand. I want to hang these lights before I decide to strangle you with them." As I said, she is a bit dramatic.

Ava

It took us two hours to hang CeCe's damn fairy lights, but the result was worth it. When we started to shop for our dorm room decor, we obsessed over Pinterest boards and social media tags; we were consumed by the need to make our space feel cozy and pretty.

I'm lucky that CeCe has the same aversion to bright colors that I do and agreed to a palette of whites, creams, and neutrals. Our twin beds, piled high with an indecent amount of pillows, look like puffy white clouds on top of the beige cowhide accent rug. Marymount University may be in New Jersey, but CeCe is a die-hard country music fan and refused to compromise on the faux animal skin.

Taking a look around the room, I can't help but feel pride over how much we transformed our space. "C, I'm not sure how we did this, but it looks so freaking good. I'm proud of us."

Walking up to me, CeCe throws her arm around my shoulder. "Me too, Aves. And we did it by being anal perfectionists with an online shopping addiction."

"You're right. You know what they say: online stores are always open."

"No, I don't think anyone has ever said that, except for maybe your mother." CeCe laughs. "I get the sentiment, though."

"Speaking of my mother, let's send our moms pictures of the room. I'm sure they're still seething into their wine glasses that we didn't let them stay to finish putting everything together."

The room, which is arguably the cleanest it will ever be all year, photographs like a catalog photo. The floral wallpaper we hot glued onto

6

canvases gives the room extra depth, complimenting the neutral comforters and plush desk chairs we purchased. In the right corner of the room, the fake ficus tree breaks up the monochrome palette and adds extra life to the space.

Walking up to the ficus, I take more pictures to send to my mother. "Look at how good Fern looks here."

"Ava, you realize that's a ficus, right?"

"Yes, but it's called irony."

"I'm not sure that's how it works, but whatever. Now, enough with the chit-chat, let's go explore the campus."

"I'm going to pretend that you didn't just say 'chit-chat' like an eighty-year-old woman in a nursing home. I promise I'm going to try really hard."

"Ava, let's fucking go."

Rolling my eyes, I start to follow CeCe but trip over the cowhide, just as she opens the door to the hallway.

Falling into the desk, I hit the side of my body, sending me sprawling on the ground. "Oh, you mother fucking piece of shit, your sister's ass!" I yell, feeling like my grandmother suddenly inhabited my body with that outburst. Lying on the ground, contemplating both my word choice and my life choices, I count the seconds until CeCe will start yelling at me for my clumsiness.

Three, two, on—

"Can we not do this here? So help me God, if you spend the majority of our four years on this campus falling over yourself, or me, I will get a new roommate. Do not test me on this." You fall on a person once, maybe twice, and suddenly, they threaten extreme action.

"You act like I did it on purpose. The corner of the rug was folded, so your cowhide attacked me." I glare at the offending rug. "And I fell on you one time; you didn't get hurt. You're fine, so get over it."

"Ava, you tripped over a piece of lettuce in the cafeteria, fell on top of me, and then almost slammed a lunch tray in my face. If I hadn't ducked in time, I would have broken my nose."

"Well, you have always wanted a nose job."

"Will you just get off the floor before someone walks by and thinks we're weirder than we are?"

"Just give me a moment. I'm trying to make sure my spleen is still attached after that fall."

"Knock, knock." CeCe whips her head around while I sit up on the floor. It's official; CeCe will never let me live this down.

Looking toward our doorway, two girls dressed in matching T-shirts and jeans are smiling at the scene before them. "So sorry to interrupt, but we saw your room from the hallway and just had to tell you how cute it is." Both girls, one blonde and the other blonder, walk into our space and take a closer look at the decor we just finished putting up. The blonder one looks between me and CeCe. "Such a cute theme. I love the colors. I'm Felicity and this is Jordan. We're juniors here and part of Alpha Nu. We're having a rush party tonight, and you guys should totally come check it out."

Still sitting on the floor, I look over at CeCe's smile and roll my eyes at her excitement. The only thing CeCe loves more than country music is organized teams; it could be lacrosse, book clubs, or a flash mob, she would join it and somehow end up president or the leader of the group. Her Type A personality is both my favorite and least favorite thing about her.

Still smiling, CeCe nearly trips over her words. "We will definitely be there. Thank you so much for the invitation. Alpha Nu is on the top of our list for recruitment; we just signed up for Round Robin next week. We cannot wait." I raise my eyebrow, not even trying to hide my surprise that she signed both of us up for the first sorority rush event of the year... without telling me. "I'm Celeste, but everyone calls me CeCe, and that"—she waves her hand in my direction—"is Ava. She's not usually this clumsy, or horizontal."

I won class klutz in high school, so that's a blatant lie. Now is probably a good time to stand up, though. Working my way to my feet, I offer a smile and wave to Felicity and Jordan. "It's great to meet you. We'll be there."

The less-blonde one, Jordan, lets out a squeal. "Awesome! The theme is dress to impress, and we're mixing with TP. Here, give me your numbers, and I'll send you the details for the pregame." Handing her phone to me, then CeCe, she saves our numbers and immediately sends us a text outlining the pregame and party's location and time. The devil works fast, but sorority girls work faster.

"Okay, just sent everything. Be at the pregame by eleven. The sober sisters will start driving everyone over to the main house around eleven-thirty. And just wait until you see these guys. TP, or Theta Phi, has some of the hottest guys on this campus, and their parties are always wild." Jordan and Felicity share a look I can't quite decipher.

"Okay, well, we need to go find dresses for tonight and finish inviting the best girls. See you tonight!" Leaving just as quickly as they came, Jordan and Felicity make their way down the hall, disappearing around the corner.

"So, my friend, when were you planning on telling me that you signed us up for a recruitment event? Didn't you need my school badge number?"

"Yes, I called your mother."

God dammit, Deborah.

"Now, come on, before you fall into more furniture."

—

By the time we make our way to the student center, I'm hungry, bruised, and more than a little annoyed by CeCe and my mother's interference. I'm self-aware enough to know that I would have signed up for recruitment, but it's the deception. By taking away my choice, they planted a seed of rebellion, a kernel of defiance, that makes me not want to participate, even if I maybe, kind of, sort of, want to.

The student center, and the quad surrounding it, hold an interest fair for new and returning students. When we were unloading our cars for move-in, our resident advisor, or RA, handed us a flier for the event. Clubs, academic departments, sports, and Greek life litter the building and lawn, drawing hundreds of lonely young adults in with the promise of belonging to something. While Marymount University isn't one of the Big Ten universities, it does have impressive athletic teams, namely soccer and football, and a huge Greek life.

"Ava, look, there's the English Honor Society. I want to go speak with them about membership."

I squint at the banner pinned to the table CeCe points to. Sigma Tau Delta. STD. You'd think an English honor society would have chosen better letters from the Greek alphabet.

"You go get that STD, you skank. Make sure you tell them you always wrap up... your textbooks."

CeCe gives me her sixth eye roll of the day. "Stop yelling about STDs. You're never going to lose your virginity if guys think you have anal warts."

"CeCe, I find it telling that the first STD you thought of was anal warts." I raise my eyebrow. "Do you have something to share with the class?"

"Ava, seriously, stop talking about STDs; people are staring." She's right. People are staring at us.

I mime zipping my lips and throwing away the key. CeCe accepts my silence with a sigh of relief, grabs my hand, and leads us toward the table of venereal disease. As we approach, the two guys and the lone girl are engaged in what appears to be a heated debate. I catch the tail end of the girl's words, "...incompetent parasites."

Now that is my kind of girl. I take a closer look at her: tousled dark blonde hair falling to her shoulders, petite frame, and golden skin that hints at a Hispanic heritage; she is stunning.

And young. How old is this girl that she is hosting a table at a college event?

The three look over to us, and while both boys offer well-rehearsed smiles, the girl grimaces. "I'm so sorry you heard that. My name is Serena. I'm the secretary of the English Honor Society. I was just explaining to these idiots that I won't give them my old assignments for Poetry II with Dr. Rembach as "reference material." She air quotes for emphasis. "Which translates to plagiarism because these lazy morons won't bother doing the work themselves."

I look over at CeCe, watching her eyes narrow and mouth pucker in evident disgust. "That doesn't seem very literary of you." To CeCe, claiming someone's writing as your own was akin to homicide, genocide, and the puppy commercials with Martina McBride. These guys are definitely bros—egotistical, self-important, and not used to hearing the word no.

"Baby, we're on the lacrosse team. We work on the field, not for professors that think poetry will help us in the real world." Bro One speaks directly to my boobs, not bothering to make eye contact with CeCe when replying. Bro Two holds up his fist, offering a, "That's right, bro."

Like I said, total bros. Though they were both good-looking in the blonde hair, blue-eyed, all-American, apple pie kind of way, I can tell that every word out of their mouths will just piss me off.

"John, you are one concussion away from never playing lacrosse again. You need to take your coursework seriously," Serena chides him. "I won't continue to tutor you if you're just going to waste my time and expect me to do your work."

Clearing her throat, CeCe jumps in. "So my name is Celeste, and this is Ava. We're freshmen and super interested in joining Sigma Tau Delta. What are the membership requirements?"

Smooth transition, CeCe, *super* smooth.

Serena startles. "Oh, well, you have to have at least fourteen credits completed and a GPA of 3.5 or above." Leaning over John, or Bro One, Serena picks up a pamphlet. "This lists some of the events we host this semester. If you're into poetry, we do an event at the local coffee shop and donate all proceeds to the children's center at the local library."

Bro Two snickers. "If you like a group of depressed hipsters crying about climate change and cows, you'll be happy."

Serena huffs. "Please, ignore John and Liam. They're here for extra credit and to make my life a living hell."

I let out a laugh. "Don't apologize, especially not on their behalf. By the way, how old are you?"

"Ava, you can't ask strangers their age!" CeCe growls at me, sounding like a demon is crawling its way out of her.

"I'm sorry, Serena. I don't mean to be rude, but you seem closer to our age rather than an upperclassman."

Serena smiles. "It's okay, I get that a lot. I'm eighteen. I skipped a few grades when I was younger. I'm a junior and an English major."

"Wow, that's amazing. Your parents must be so proud of you," I say.

Serena ducks her head and nods.

I turn toward CeCe, and she looks one step away from beheading me and putting my head on a pyre. "Right so, like CeCe said, very interested in STD."

CeCe and Serena let out groans while the bros laugh. But honestly, who the fuck thought of this name?

"We're having an event on Saturday at the coffee shop I mentioned, Beans & Things. Are you both English majors?"

Celeste smiles. "I am; I'm concentrating on creative writing. Ava is in the culinary arts program."

All three of the STD's eyebrows raise at the mention of my major. Serena looks at me with a warm smile. "That's awesome. What do you plan to do with that?"

I'm used to this question; every time someone learns about my major, they ask one of two things: what am I going to do with a culinary arts degree and when can I cook for them? It surprised my parents when I told them about my culinary dreams, given my hang-ups with food. I may have a love-hate relationship with calories and eating, but watching people eat food that I've prepared is one of the most rewarding experiences that I can indulge in. There's something so incredibly satisfying about cooking a meal and listening to the appreciative moans that accompany the first bite.

When I was eight, the same year that the concession stand became my confessional, my maternal grandmother taught me how to cook Sunday sauce. I spent hours in the kitchen with her every Sunday morning after church, rolling meatballs and lacing twine around thin steaks rolled with breadcrumbs and cheese. I remember squeezing the meatball mixture in my fingers, memorizing the texture and feel of the meat, while my grandmother watched over me. "Ava Maria, the difference between Italians and everyone else is that we live to eat, the others eat to live." She ingrained those words into my soul, cementing food as love, comfort, and survival.

In between cooking for our household, which included both of my mother's parents, my parents, two younger sisters, Seraphina and Bianca, and my younger brother, Rafael, my grandmother would take me out into the garden to forage our ingredients. Basil, parsley, and other herbs grew wild in our little garden, tucked far away from my mother's landscaping because God forbid the neighbors saw our tomato plants from the street.

"Ava Maria," my grandmother would say, always using my first and middle name. "Don't step on my squash flowers, or I'll hit you with my spoon." My grandmother, like all Italian women, had a collection of wooden spoons that were tools for both deliciousness and viciousness. Poor Rafael had permanent welts on his ass from all the swats she gave him for stealing the cigarettes she thought she hid so well.

She was a very loving woman.

That time spent working at our kitchen counters and in our garden became the catalyst for my dream of owning my farm-to-table restaurant. My culinary arts degree was the first step to achieving that dream.

"I'm going to open an Italian farm-to-table restaurant. I'm double majoring in hospitality, so I'll have all my bases covered between front of house and back of house." I even had the name picked out: Maureen's, an homage to the woman that taught me everything I knew about food, and a way to continue her legacy after her death five years ago.

"You have to try her food, it's insane. She makes these rolled chicken things in a lemon butter sauce that tastes like actual heaven." CeCe has always been the best hype woman, especially when it comes to my dreams and food.

"C, they're called spiedini, for the millionth time. I'll make them for you when we visit home on fall break if you can remember their name this time."

"Can you spell it for me? I'm writing this down for posterity."

Rolling my eyes, I take her phone and type the name into her notes section labeled "Food Requests for Ava." For the last three years, CeCe has sent me food and recipe requests at least once a week. Probably because her mother doesn't know how to cook.

Serena clears her throat. "I have an apartment off campus if you'd like to come by and hang out or cook sometime. I'm decent in the kitchen and would love to have someone teach me a few things if you're free?" There's so much uncertainty in her invitation that my heart breaks for this young, smart girl, intellectually mature but so lonely that it's palpable.

"We would love to, Serena." I glance at CeCe, who's nodding her head in agreement. "We just got invited to a sorority mixer tonight. Alpha Nu or something like that, I think. Why don't you come with us? We can get ready together before we head over to the pregame."

"Are you sure? I'd love that. Thank you so much!" The words leave Serena's mouth in a rush, almost like she's worried I'll rescind the offer if she doesn't accept quickly enough.

After exchanging numbers and setting a time for Serena to come to our dorm, CeCe and I make our way to the rest of the tables at the interest fair. Other than the STD table, we stop at the girls' field hockey club table and two other sorority tables, Gamma Phi and Sigma Kappa Epsilon. Linking my arm through CeCe's on our way back to our dorm, I laugh. "C, look at us, making friends and shit."

"I know, Serena seems so sweet. I'm so happy you invited her out with us tonight. Do you think I need to give Felicity or Jordan a heads-up that we're bringing her?"

"There's going to be so many people there. I don't think it'll make a difference."

CeCe hums in agreement. "I can't believe those guys. They all but admitted to cheating in their English class." A visible shudder works its way down CeCe's body. By the time we left their table, both John and Liam had snuck off. It was a testament to their stupidity that even the threat of failure couldn't keep them at their assigned post.

"I know, but forget about them. Let's go figure out what we're wearing tonight. We should probably figure out something for Serena, too. I have a feeling she won't know what to wear."

Ava

Serena had no idea what to wear, evident from the three duffel bags and two garment bags she brought with her to our dorm room.

What eighteen-year-old owned a garment bag?

"I have no idea what to wear, so I brought options."

I raise an eyebrow. "I can see that."

Serena begins unpacking the clothes haphazardly thrown into her bags, and I notice the tags are still on most of them. Picking a sleeveless turtleneck up from the pile, I can't help but question, "Serena, did you just buy all of these clothes?"

Her blush is all the confirmation I need. "I've never been to a party before, well, unless you count the Chuck E. Cheese birthday parties when I was ten." A grimace mars her pretty face. "That rat always terrified me. Why do you think they would choose a rat as their mascot? It seems unsanitary."

"Serena, focus. You brought enough shit for the entire floor. We need to narrow down your options here. Wait until CeCe comes back from her shower. She's going to freak out over all of this." Serena bit her lip, worry creasing her brow.

"I'm so sorry, Ava. I didn't mean to bring this much with me. I can just go. I'm so sorry." Serena begins to stuff the clothes back into her bags just as CeCe opens the door to our room, coming back from her shower in the communal bathroom. Taking a look at the piles of clothes and bags around the room, her eyebrows shoot up in confusion. "What is all this stuff?"

Before Serena can answer and apologize again, I hold up the largest garment bag and place it on my bed. "Serena brought options. We're going

15

to sort it into piles to figure out what she'll wear tonight." I turn to Serena. "And you, stop apologizing. You didn't do anything wrong. I'm sorry if I offended you when I asked why you brought so much, but you have no reason to be sorry." I offer her a smile and take the bag she was packing to my bed, too. "We're so excited that you're coming out with us tonight, and we're going to have an amazing time. Now, show us the goods, and let's get ready."

CeCe grabs two other bags and places them on the remaining space on my bed. Looking over her shoulder at Serena, CeCe teases, "Girl, if there's anything good in here, I might just call dibs." Laughing, Serena works her way over, dropping her shoulders with a sigh. "I'm sorry." She glances at me with a shy smile. "I'm just so nervous for tonight and couldn't help buying out Lucy and Jane's inventory." Lucy and Jane, one of the specialty boutiques in town, sells high-end clothing and caters to the wealthier students at Marymount. Truthfully, I love the store and probably have a lot of her recent purchases hanging in my closet.

"Hmm." I admire an emerald green corseted satin dress. The off-the-shoulder neckline and dropped sleeves would look stunning on Serena's petite, tanned frame, while the corset would highlight her tiny waist. Holding it up, I thrust it into Serena's hands. "This, you beautiful little brainiac, is your dress for tonight."

She sputters. "Uhm, are you sure? I bought this on a whim. I've never really worn something like this before."

"Well, I would hope not since you were, what, fifteen when you started college?" I shudder. "That would have been weird and marginally pedophilic for a lot of guys." I push her to our floor mirror, spinning her around so that she's standing in front of me, looking at her reflection. "Serena, you are beautiful and will break hearts in this dress. If you're not comfortable in it, then fuck the 'dress to impress' theme and we'll wear jeans and make our own rules." I squeeze her shoulders. "But if you want to step out of your comfort zone and experience college, wear the dress and know that everyone will be looking at you, envious that they don't have your brain or your beauty."

A moment passes while Serena stares at the dress in her hands. Lifting her eyes to me, she nods. "You're right, I want to experience college. I'm going to go put this on."

CeCe lets out a loud whoop. "That's right, you hot bitch, and I say bitch in the most loving, empowering sense. The bathroom is three doors down, on the right. Go change and when you come back, Ava and I will help with your hair and makeup, if you want."

Serena smiles at both of us before going to change. CeCe looks at me, pointing. "You, Ava Maria, are the ultimate hype woman. Now, if you could just tell yourself those same words, we'd be in a good place."

I release a sigh. I'm sick of talking about my issues with food, my body, and myself. "Celeste Lauren Downing, if I hear one more word about how I hate myself, I will start hating you. Now shut up and get ready, your wild mane of hair isn't going to dry itself, and we have places to be."

—

Two and a half hours later, the three of us stand in front of the mirror, analyzing our appearances. Just like I thought, Serena looks incredible in the rich green dress, which not only compliments her small waist but makes her honeyed skin glow. Her short blonde hair is tousled and sexy, almost like she just got done with a sex marathon and threw a dress on right after. If she doesn't have every guy drooling over her tonight, then I have no faith in the male population of this university.

Next to me, CeCe is wrapped in a square neck, white knee-length dress with a thigh-high slit. Honestly, if she makes one wrong move, everyone is seeing her vagina. CeCe's defining features, her bright green eyes, are lined with thick, winged eyeliner, making them appear catlike, while her dark auburn hair falls in smooth waves down her back. She looks both angelic and mysterious, a lethal combination.

"Jesus, Ava, your body is unreal. Are your boobs even natural?" I glance over at Serena and laugh before looking at my reflection. My breasts, double-Ds cursed by God, are almost spilling out from my strapless, black faux-leather tube dress. I tug the material up in a failed attempt to cover more of my boobs. It's useless; there's barely any room to breathe in this dress, let alone adjust the basketballs attached to my chest. My dark brown hair is pulled up in a messy bun with my bangs down, framing my face.

"Unfortunately, they're real. Now, let's call an Uber and make our way to the pregame, it's almost ten."

—

It took fifteen minutes for the Uber driver to show up and another ten minutes to get to the address Jordan sent. We wisely spent that time chugging tequila from plastic water bottles. Liquid courage counts for something, right?

By the time we make it to the pregame, the music is pouring out of the house, a heavy techno beat set against Birdie's rendition of "Skinny Love." I can see countless bodies through the front windows of the two-story colonial, dancing and drinking in the middle of the suburbs. The neighborhood looks like a typical family area—black, wrought-iron fences divide the backyards of cookie-cutter homes. Stepping out of the Uber, I look around the street at the near-identical houses surrounding the pregame house. Were these houses all college rental properties, or were these sorority girls living next to, and corrupting, the children of West Helm?

The Uber speeds away as soon as Serena steps out, nearly running over our feet. "Asshole," CeCe mumbles under her breath.

"Was it just me, or did the car smell like beef jerky?" Serena questions.

She's not wrong; the guy smelled like a Slim Jim. I sniff my dress, making sure that the stench of dried meat isn't clinging to me.

Serena holds out her hand with a small tube of perfume. "Here, I brought this just in case. I sprayed myself because there is no way I'm meeting people smelling like jerky."

"Serena, you are a goddess among mortals." I douse myself in her light, floral perfume and then spray CeCe, because let's face it, if one of us smells like meat, all of us do. Serena tucks the bottle back into her clutch and turns to face the house. "I can't believe I'm here. I can't tell you how much it means to me that you invited me tonight."

I throw my arms around Serena and CeCe's shoulders. "Enough with the gratitude, Serena. Now, let's pop our college party cherries, and maybe our actual cherries, tonight."

Serena raises a brow. "Our cherries? You're both virgins?"

CeCe and I both laugh. CeCe shrugs her shoulders and scoffs. "Trust me, it's not for lack of trying on our parts. With Ava's famous lawyer parents and my cousins running interference on every date I've ever been on, there hasn't been much opportunity on that front." I roll my eyes at her explanation of my parents, though she isn't wrong about them being well-known. Both of my parents are prosecutors and partners at Gregori, Schwartz, and Moreno, one of the largest and most selective law firms in the tri-state area. They rose to fame in the early 2000s as part of the prosecution that convicted one the country's most prolific serial killers, The Clown Killer—a lunatic that murdered young women and carved a clown face into their faces postmortem. Their winning prosecution paved the way for book deals, television appearances, and even their true-crime podcast.

To say that my parents intimidate guys I'm interested in would be putting it mildly.

"I'm a virgin, too. Just in case you were wondering."

"Yeah, no shit." Serena pales. Dammit, I said that out loud. "I just meant that you've been in college since you were, like, five and are just turning legal now. I'd imagine that dating anyone would be virtually impossible."

CeCe nods. "Well, as enlightening as this is, we should probably go inside before the cops get called on us for lingering on the front lawn."

CeCe grabs our hands and leads us toward the front door.

Ava

Three things simultaneously happen when we enter the Alpha Nu house:

First, two girls squeal in greeting, asking us for our names, dorm halls, and car keys, if we have them.

The second thing I notice is that the dining room table breaks, most likely because a group of girls is dancing on top of it like *Coyote Ugly*.

And, lastly, Serena hides herself behind my back muttering, "Shit, shit, shit."

I'm trying to figure out where to direct my attention, but it's a lot to take in. The two sorority girls win out, solely because of their proximity.

"Welcome to Alpha Nu's first rush mixer of the semester. We're so happy you're here!" Between these girls and Felicity and Jordan, I can't help but think that Alpha Nu is the extremely energized, peppy sorority on campus. Suffice it to say, not my kind of people. "I'm Lizzie and this is Katie. We're the Membership Recruitment Chairs of Alpha Nu and just need some information before you ladies join the pregame." Lizzie hands each of us clipboards to fill out questionnaires about ourselves. Serena's arm sneaks out from behind my back, grabbing her clipboard, while still hiding from the room. If Lizzie and Katie notice, they don't say anything.

I lean back, whispering to Serena, "Is there a reason you're hiding?"

She sighs. "Do you see the girl in the purple dress by the coffee table in the living room?" I look toward a statuesque blonde in a god-awful purple sequin dress and matching heels. "Well," Serena continues, "that's my stepsister, Marina. She's a freshman this year and hates me. The feeling is mutual."

"I assume you didn't know she'd be here."

Serena scoffs. "We don't talk. I found out she was coming here when my dad asked if I wanted to join his family for lunch after they moved Marina into her dorm."

Ouch. I didn't miss that she said *his* family, not hers.

"If you want, I can find some Visine to put in her drink. She'll be shitting her brains out in, like, fifteen minutes, easy."

Serena looks at me with the first smile since we walked through the door. "Thanks, but I'll just avoid her tonight."

"Suit yourself, poison control is just one call away."

We turn our attention to the clipboards, quickly fill them out and hand them back to the welcoming committee. Lizzie directs us to the dining room, which has dozens of bottles of cheap vodka and tequila along with store-brand soda and juice. I pick up one of the handles of vodka and read, "Lairds. I'm almost positive this is disinfectant, but I can't be certain." Serena laughs while CeCe just rolls her eyes and picks up three red cups and a generic cola from the table. "Listen, Ava, it's free alcohol. Don't be a snob." I pour the vodka into the cups and then hand them off for CeCe to pour in the cola before she distributes the drinks.

I take a sip and nearly choke. It tastes like bad decisions and a hangover.

I open my mouth to tell both of them my feelings when we're interrupted by a shrill voice.

"What the fuck are you doing here, nerd?" Our heads whip around to the nightmare in a purple sequin dress, Marina.

Serena groans and runs a hand through her hair. Before she can respond, CeCe steps forward. "Who the fuck do you think you're talking to, Barney?" I try to contain my laughter, I do. CeCe shoots me a look before continuing, "I know that you did not just come over here, while we were enjoying ourselves and minding our own business, to harass our girl. I suggest you turn your skanky ass around, get a drink, or better yet, a joint to chill out, and fuck right off." CeCe flicks her hand in a dismissive gesture. Serena's jaw is on the floor, but I'm used to CeCe's mama bear display. She may look like a pint-sized model, but she grew up with fifteen male cousins and learned how to hold her own at a young age.

21

Marina eyes my friend with a mixture of disdain and fear. "Whatever, bitch." She then looks at Serena. "Stay out of my way or I'm telling Dad." With that, she flips her hair and walks back to her group of friends in the living room.

"He's not your dad," Serena whispers to her retreating form. CeCe and I look at each other.

"Well," CeCe begins, "I have to say, that was the most anti-climactic confrontation I've ever had. Who was that?"

"My stepsister, Marina. My parents got divorced when I was a kid, and he replaced us with a new wife and daughter pretty quickly."

"You're related to that harpy?"

Serena shrugs. "She wasn't always this terrible, but as we got older, she became more competitive and couldn't handle me being the smarter one."

CeCe scoffs at her response. "So she had to make herself the gaudy one? Seriously, who wears purple sequins after elementary school?"

"Forget her," I urge. "Let's drink these horrid drinks, shake our asses, and meet some cute boys."

We spend the next fifteen minutes sipping our drinks, teasing CeCe about how deceptively angelic she looks, and surveying the party around us. We're drinking our second cup by the time Felicity and Jordan make their way over to us.

"You ladies came!" Felicity exclaims, running over to hug me and CeCe before looking at Serena. "And you brought a friend. Next time, make sure you let us know; it's an exclusive guest list."

Serena's eyes widen and red splotches start creeping up her chest and throat. "Oh, I-I'm so sorry. I can go if it's an issue."

Fuck that. "Sorry, Felicity, we didn't know that we needed to RSVP for a plus one. Our girl, Serena, is with us. If she goes, we go. So just let us know if it's going to be a problem, and we'll be on our way."

Felicity eyes our trio for a moment before plastering a fake smile on her face. "I'm sure it's fine. We're going to be heading over to the main party soon, so line up by the door when you're ready and a sober sister will drive you over. And here, we refer to each other as women, not girls." With that, she turns her back on us and walks away.

"Well," CeCe begins, "it's safe to say that we're not getting into Alpha Nu anytime soon."

"Guys, I'm so sorry. I know how interested you were, and I've done nothing but cause problems since we got here."

"Nope, absolutely not. The actions of your stepsister and the snotty attitude of Felicity are not your fault. If you feel uncomfortable, we're leaving and saying 'fuck you' to these assholes."

I nod my head in agreement. "I'm with CeCe on this. Say the word, and we'll leave to veg out in our dorm and watch re-runs of *Grey's Anatomy*."

Serena takes a deep breath, shaking her head. "No, no. Let's just go to the party. I don't want to be in this house for another minute."

—

We're the first ones at the party, which would be extremely uncomfortable under normal circumstances, but after the attitudes given by both Marina and Felicity, I think the three of us are just focused on getting wasted as quickly as possible. I grab CeCe and Serena's hands and walk to the keg in the corner of the front room. Grabbing three cups next to the keg, I hold the nozzle and begin foamy pours.

"Aves, you're pouring straight foam. It's going to take an hour for this to settle and be drinkable."

"I've never poured beer from a keg before, so just be thankful I'm trying." I give CeCe a sideways glare. "I didn't see you volunteering to pour the drinks."

Serena laughs behind us. "Are you two always like this?"

"Like what?" CeCe and I respond at the same time.

"Like sarcastic jerks while still being extremely protective and supportive. I'm getting whiplash."

I think about that for a moment. While I love to tease CeCe and provoke her, she's my best friend, and I would bury bodies with her, if it ever came to that. "You know, Serena, we are now that I think about it. Sometimes, when I open my mouth, I'm not sure what's going to come out: bitchy comments or positivity. It's fifty-fifty on any given day."

I hold up my cup of foam beer and motion for CeCe and Serena to do the same. "C, if you'll do the honors and toast to our first collegiate night out."

CeCe clears her throat. "Ladies, may the foam of these beers be the only disappointment of the night. May the mean *women* of Alpha Nu kiss our asses. May the good Lord above bless us with a hangover-free morning. May Ava not fall on her face and embarrass herself tonight. In his name, we pray."

I clink my cup to CeCe and Serena's. "Amen."

Serena smirks. "Amen, *women*."

Looking up from my cup—CeCe's right, it's all foam—my eyes wander around the room before settling back on CeCe and Serena. "So, how are we feeling about our first college party? Honestly, I thought there would be more to it, but it's kind of depressing right now." While a few more girls were dropped off, there are still barely any people in this house. It almost feels like we're trespassers and not welcome.

"It's still early, Ava," CeCe responds. "My cousin, Brent, told me that no one shows up until at least eleven thirty, and it's only eleven. Give it thirty minutes."

She's not wrong; I remember her cousin telling us that only freshmen and losers show up before eleven thirty. His words, not mine.

I shrug. "I guess, but it still seems weird since Felicity and Jordan made such a big deal of us getting to the pregame house and party on time."

"They probably just didn't want to be the first ones here." CeCe looks at me and Serena. "Listen, I'm sorry that I was so excited and wanted to come here tonight. From what I heard about Alpha Nu and saw from their social media pages, they looked like really interesting girls—sorry, women—but how Felicity treated us when she met Serena and the fact that they invited girls—shit, women—like Marina, well, it turns me off from their entire organization."

"At least we know who they are before recruitment weekend. There are nine other sororities on campus, so there must be at least one we'll like." And if none of them are a good fit, I'm fine with that, too. While CeCe and Serena look like sorority girls, I do not. At the pregame, there wasn't a single girl above a size four, except me, and they all looked perfectly put together. I am messy. I have good days, days where I put on a full face of makeup, blow out, and style my hair. But then I have bad days, days where I look slightly homeless and entirely disheveled. On those bad days, I rarely leave the house, but they exist, more often than I'd like them to.

I laugh to myself. Felicity would probably have a heart attack if my size eight, occasionally size ten, body ruined the aesthetic of the sorority. I'm self-aware enough to know that my invitation was extended because CeCe looks like Scarlet Johansson and not because I offer any value to this group. It is what it is; I'm used to it.

I'm snapped out of my internal musings when a pair of hands snake around Serena's waist, eliciting a gasp from her.

"Siren, I thought I told you, parties were no place for girls like you. Why are you here?"

I raise a brow at CeCe. Serena is apparently notorious around campus and having a very eventful night.

"Devin, get your hands off me. If Marina sees you, she'll kill me."

"Doll, I was yours before Marina's."

At this point, my eyebrows are to my hairline because what?

Serena lets out a sigh. "The last thing I need is for you to be next to me when she comes in. Please don't make this night worse for me."

"I told you that I didn't want you at parties, especially at my house. You're the one that didn't listen." He leans in closer, speaking right next to her ear. "You deserve to have Marina see me next to you. I wonder how much shit she'd give you if her perfect little stepsister was too close to her property. Does that make you angry, Siren, knowing that you fucked up and I'm hers now?"

Serena's face contorts in anger. "I don't know how many times I have to tell you, but I was never yours and you were never mine. You have no right to speak to me this way. I didn't do anything to you to warrant your taunts and bullying."

"Tsk, tsk, tsk. You know exactly what you did." Serena grits her teeth in response. His fingers flex against her hips before he releases her. "Now, be a good little girl and go home. You're not welcome here." With that, he turns and walks away.

I have questions. So many questions.

CeCe beats me to it. Grabbing Serena's arm, CeCe asks in a worried tone, "Serena, are you okay?"

I think I've heard Serena sigh more in the last fifteen minutes than in the entire twelve hours that I've known her. "That was Devin, Marina's fuck buddy? Boyfriend? I don't know what they are at this point." She huffs, again. "We all grew up together. That's how my dad and Marina's mom met; we were childhood friends. Devin was our neighbor and would come over every day. For a while, I thought he liked me, but he started hooking up with Marina a few years ago." She looks down at her cup, as though it will have the answers she needs. "Between Marina, Felicity, and now Devin, I just want to go home. I'm going to ask one of the sisters to bring me back to my apartment."

"Of course, we'll come with you," CeCe responds. I nod my head in agreement.

"No, I'd rather just be alone right now, and I'd feel guilty if you came home with me, only to go back to your dorm room. Please, stay. I'll text you guys when I get home."

I look at CeCe before returning my focus to our new friend. "Serena, are you sure?"

Her weak smile guts me. "Ava, I'm sure. After the night I've had, the only thing I want to do is crawl into my bed."

We walk Serena to the front door and arrange for one of the sober sisters to drive her back to her apartment on campus. The guilt I feel for letting her leave alone lessens by her insistence that she needs time to think without questions and background noise, and that she'll meet us for brunch on Sunday to explain. By the time we say goodbye to Serena, the party is thick with bodies, sweat, and sexual tension.

Ava

"C, do you think we should have gone back with Serena? I feel so guilty that we sent her home in a car like that." I wring my hands, guilt weighing on my mind as we watch Serena's ride drive away.

"I'm not sure, Aves. She wanted to be alone and seemed adamant that she wanted us to stay. We can text her when we leave and see if she's still up. Maybe we'll swing by her apartment when we leave to check on her."

Glancing behind me, I notice that the crowd has nearly tripled in size, with girls dancing in small groups in the center and guys watching from the perimeter. The scene reads very Animal Planet, as though these girls are performing a mating ritual and the guys are seeing which option is the best for the night. It's performative and slightly nauseating.

"It's like the introduction to low-budget porn, all these people standing around before they whip their clothes off and start pulling dildos out of the couch cushions." I huff. I'm unnecessarily perturbed by this setup.

"Your porn viewing history is questionable, but I agree. I'm getting creeped out by the guy in the corner running his tongue over his teeth." I look toward the far-right corner of the room and spot the guy in question. As though he feels my eyes on him, he turns his attention to me, looks me up and down, and proceeds to wiggle his tongue at me like a snake. The disgust must be evident on my face because his expression morphs into a sneer.

"C, let's get out of the entryway. I feel like we're on display here."

CeCe and I make our way through the crowded living room that doubles as a dance floor, weaving around writhing bodies and trying not to interrupt the bizarre mating ritual around us. As we sidestep a pair of girls aggressively twerking, I realize that many of the people in the room are staring at the front door. Looking around, I see the unmistakable excitement in their eyes, as though they're lions waiting for the perfect moment to spring forward and attack the hopeless gazelle.

Just as I turn my back to the entryway that holds the attention of the room, I feel the hair stand up on the back of my neck, and goosebumps travel down my arms and spine. Turning quickly, whiplash a guarantee, I see three guys walk over the front door's threshold. Like gods assembled on Mount Olympus, they survey the party, while the party surveys them.

All three are impressive; big-dick energy radiates from them. Imposing and intimidating, it's hard to know where to look, until my eyes snag on the blue-eyed monster standing closest to the door. Tall and broad-shouldered, he has to be at least six-foot-three, with thick, corded muscles on display in his simple black T-shirt. A dead ringer for Charlie Hunnam. His blonde hair falls to his shoulders and looks like he just ran his hands through it. Or maybe someone else did?

In front of him stands two other men. One has smooth olive skin, dark hair, and brightly colored tattoos decorating his exposed arms and neck. His features hint at his Mediterranean heritage while his ink makes me think that no sane Italian grandmother would let him date her granddaughter.

Taking my eyes off my grandmother's worst fear, I look to the third person in their group and am rendered speechless by how pretty he is. Tightly buzzed hair highlights the strong jawline, high cheekbones, and full lips of a walking Calvin Klein advertisement. His light eyes, cold and lifeless, contrast with his caramel-colored skin and give a menacing edge to his looks.

What felt like hours, but were probably only seconds, passed before the party adjusts to their presence. The three guys walk deeper into the room. My eyes follow the blonde giant, desperate for a close-up as they walk past me and CeCe. I can't stop staring at him. Unsurprisingly, they don't acknowledge our existence.

"You've got a little drool, right there," CeCe teases, snapping me out of my obsessive ogling.

I turn to her, frazzled. "Did you see that guy? He looked like Charlie

Hunnam from the Jax Teller days. I think my vagina just exploded."

"Aves, considering that I don't see ovaries, a labia, or cervix mixed with the grime of the floor, I'm relatively positive your woman parts are intact." Rolling her eyes at my response to the stranger, she continues, "Come on, let's go find something other than beer to drink."

"Lead the way, fire crotch."

That earns a scowl. Except for CeCe, with her elegant beauty, she just looks like a pissed-off Cabbage Patch Kid. It's kind of funny.

"Asshole. Remember, when you eventually lock yourself out of the dorm room with nothing but your towel and shower caddy, you're staying out there."

"Good, I can't wait to cause emotional scarring and trauma to the waifs on our floor when they see the stretch marks on my thighs. I wonder if they'll bill me for their therapy?"

Bickering back and forth as we walk in the direction of the hard liquor, I almost miss the blonde stranger standing in the left corner of the room.

Leaning against the wall opposite the counter, he seems to watch all the comings and goings in the room. His black shirt stretches, almost indecently, against his chest and biceps, as if one flex would tear the fabric from his body.

Jesus, he is delicious. What I wouldn't do to be the kind of girl that got his attention—the model-like freshmen with tits to their eyeballs and toned, flat stomachs. Instead, I'm just me. Shorter than most, with thick dark hair and an even thicker waist. My best quality is my personality, and that's just depressing. Even my feet have extra weight on them.

"For fuck's sake, Ava. Would you pay attention? I've been talking to you for the last five minutes," CeCe hisses in my ear.

Shit. I need to stop salivating before I offer myself to him like a sacrificial virgin.

"Sorry, sorry. What were you saying?" I could predict that she was about to shove shots down my throat, but I thought humoring her may remove the stick from her ass.

"We're taking shots. Fireball. Don't be a little bitch." Arguably, I was a big bitch.

"Okay, fine. But if I start to throw up in bushes, just leave me to fertilize the mulch beds in peace."

"Deal. Now, drink up," CeCe toasts right before the cinnamon whiskey burns our throats.

"That tastes like a bag of dicks," I groan.

"Ava, you have never tasted one dick, let alone a bag of dicks. Let's do another." CeCe, the devil reincarnate, pours us two more shots, handing one to me with a smirk on her face. "Who knows," She pauses to lick droplets of the whiskey from her shot glass. "Maybe you'll find the lady balls to talk to Adonis over there."

With a roll of my eyes, I grab the shot and throw it back quickly. "He's more likely to go for you than me, C." I let out a sigh.

"Sure, and that's why he's been staring at you for the last ten minutes."

Wait, what?

Looking up, my eyes meet the cool blues of my stranger, and I'm startled to be the apparent center of his attention. Fuck, do I have something on my face?

"CeCe, what the fuck is on my face? Did I spill a fireball? Does it look like cum? Oh my God, does he think I have cum on my face?"

CeCe's incredulous glare should have stopped me, but I continue, "Is my dress see-through? Can you see my areolae? Or is it areolas? Are my fucking tits out?" I start to feel myself up, making sure my nipples aren't in danger of poking anyone's eye out. If I was more sober, I would have realized that this drew more attention to me.

"Ava, babe, I need you to take a deep breath and exorcise the demon that just inhabited your thick skull." CeCe takes my face in her hands and forces me to look at her. "You are a hot, curvy woman with a body people spend thousands of dollars on plastic surgery to achieve. Why you think that anyone wouldn't be looking at you is beyond my comprehension."

She has to say that. I've been her friend since before my mom let me shave my leg hair in fourth grade. She was loyal but biased.

Just as I was about to respond, a throat clears behind us, startling both of us.

Turning around, we come face-to-face with the olive-skinned tattooed guy.

Smirking, he reaches around us for a bottle of Johnny Walker and a red Solo cup. Shaking his head, he announces, "Ladies, if you think the room hasn't noticed the two of you over here looking like you're about to either scream at each other or make out, you're wrong." Finishing his heavy pour, he continues, "I wouldn't mind seeing the two of you make out. The thought of you two getting hot and wet sounds like a good fucking time. Let me know if it's going in that direction, and I'll get us a room."

My face contorts in disgust. Before I can even formulate a response, CeCe starts in on him. "Listen, you dickwad, if we decide to make out, fuck, or pray to the Virgin Mary, we'll do it without you watching like John Wayne Gacy, ready to murder us as soon as the show's over." CeCe's face, turning red from the exertion of her cut-down, is starting to blend in with her hair. I smother a laugh, thinking that now may not be the best time to tell her that she looks like an overripe tomato. "Run along, you pervert. Go find some other girls to bother."

Raising an eyebrow at us, his gaze turns intense while staring at my red-faced friend. "Sweetheart, the only thing I'd do after watching you finish is work you right back up again. Maybe with my fingers, maybe with my tongue, just to get you ready to feel that tight pussy clench around my cock." Okay. I was turning red now, too.

"Remember that as you finger-fuck yourself tonight, Red. Make sure to whisper my name into the dark like the fucking boogie man and maybe, if you're a good girl, I won't torture you too much when I eventually have those legs wrapped around me."

Holy shit. Though the words weren't directed, or intended, for me, I couldn't help the flutters in my stomach or suppress the need to squeeze my thighs together. I look at CeCe, twisting her lips and trying her best to appear unaffected.

I decide to throw her a bone. "Just out of curiosity," I begin, "you do want her to scream your name while she, uhm, 'finger-fucks' herself. What name do I have to look out for?" He gives me an incredulous look as I use my fingers to air quote finger-fuck. The irony is not lost on me.

"It's Dante."

I laugh. "Are you planning on making CeCe your Beatrice? Because I can assure you, she is no angel."

"Ava, I know you did not"—she points at me for emphasis—"just give him my name." She transfers her slender finger to Dante.

"Can you please put your finger away? I don't want to think about what you may use that for, and now I can't get the image out of my head." CeCe continues to glare at me while Dante chuckles, watching her tantrum.

"Red, I would have found out your name regardless. This isn't the last time you'll be seeing me." With that, he gives us one last once-over and walks away, toward my blonde stranger. As soon as he leaves, CeCe starts in about his audacity, his nerve, and his fucking balls.

I watch them for a moment, ignoring CeCe's tirade. Heads leaned in conspiratorially, Dante and the blonde seem to be deep in conversation, engrossed in whatever bullshit college guys must be consumed by. Returning my attention to CeCe, she continues, "And to call me Red like a proper fucking noun? How original, how unlike any nickname I've ever had before." She's not wrong. She's spent most of her life being referred to by her hair, mostly with thinly veiled sexual innuendos about her carpet and drapes.

Suddenly, I feel the weight of eyes on me, a caress down my spine. Looking around, I realize the blue eyes of my stranger are back on me, pinning me in place. His eyes drop to my heeled feet and work their way up my body, surveying my black dress and heavy breasts until his gaze finally returns to mine. Then, he smirks and turns his back to me, as if to say he finds me fundamentally lacking.

I'm not sure why I'm surprised. Ever since I was thirteen, I knew I would never be viewed as conventionally pretty. My hips have always been a little too wide, and my breasts were always too big, too full, for the bras and clothing that were trendy for girls my age. I learned to rely on a passably pretty face and my personality to make me likable. This was probably why I've never had a boyfriend and will likely die a virgin. Maybe I should change my major to theology; I would probably kick ass as a nun.

Lost in my thoughts of the Catholic sisterhood, CeCe shoves another shot of fireball under my nose, breaking me from my musings. She looks at me with an expectant stare as her shot is paused at her lips. Not saying anything, I grab the shot, hold up the glass in a salute, and drink the cinnamon liquor.

If I can't intrigue the blonde stranger, I may as well get drunk.

Greyson

"Did you see those fucking girls? What I wouldn't do to get that redhead on her knees, begging for my cock. And you should see her friend, tits the size of fucking watermelons." Dante shakes his head in reverence. "The redhead is mine, but that curvy brunette is all yours. I know how you like your women with something to grab onto."

He wasn't wrong. I did like women to look like women, not prepubescent boys with knobby elbows, flat chests, and bodies that looked like the wind could blow them over. He also wasn't wrong that the brunette was all mine.

I saw her standing by the stairs as soon as we walked in, wearing that indecent fucking dress that called attention to her large breasts, narrow waist, and flared hips. My walking wet dream, with an innocent face that begged for my cum to paint pretty pictures all over it. The sight of her staring at me across the room, with her big eyes devouring me like a hungry kitten, had my dick hard instantly. I needed to play with her, possess her, own her.

There was no doubt, she was mine. My visceral response to her should have scared me, but I was too fucking hard to care.

"I saw them." I look up. "I still see them." The brunette and the redhead stand by the alcohol, not realizing the stares they're getting from the horny bastards surrounding them. A quick scan of the room confirms that half the guys were staring at the tits spilling out of my brunette's dress and the other half were trying to see through the redhead's dress to see if her pussy was as rosy as the rest of her.

I turn toward Dante and see him glaring around the room.

"I'm telling you, Grey, there's something about that redhead. She told me to fuck off and I think I fell in love."

"That sounds like a fucked-up kink. I don't want to hear about you getting spanked and paddled to get off." Dante and I have been friends since middle school, and I knew too many things about his sex life. Sure, we've shared girls, sometimes at the same time, but it didn't mean that I needed a play-by-play about his fantasies with the ginger. As long as the brunette wasn't in those fantasies, he needed to keep that shit to himself.

"I'm thinking about putting her over my knee for her smart mouth. I wouldn't be mad if she wanted to do a role reversal, though." Dante shrugged and looked back toward the pair at the makeshift bar. "Hell, it could be fun seeing her with a whip and leather."

Here we fucking go.

Dante details every single thing he'd like to do to his redhead's body, going into painfully anatomic detail about the positions he plans to have her in. I zone him out because I don't care about his lick-to-thrust ratio. Three years ago, Dante came up with the "perfect" number of pussy licks to cock thrusts ratio for optimal pleasure, both his and whichever girl he's fucking. He told us about his theory while smoking a joint in the shed behind my dad's house. He spent five months testing his hypothesis before typing it out in the notes section on his phone. Whenever he's asked about it, he pulls it out like a thesis and delivers his rehearsed speech. "You need to lick her cunt eighteen times, blow on her clit, and then thrust for ten to fifteen minutes. If you tilt your hips up while pounding her, you'll get to her G-spot, even if you have a shrimp dick." He sounds like a moron every damn time.

I hear Dante say, "Right in the pussy," and barely resist smacking him on the back of his head. I continue blocking him out and observe the two girls that are unknowingly encouraging his tirade. Objectively, the redhead is pretty and looks like Scarlett Johansson from her *Black Widow* days. She's tiny, both in height and form, and has fire in those eyes that will probably incinerate Dante's dick and his lick-to-thrust theory. The brunette, on the other hand, is every dream I've ever had brought to life.

Taking in her sinful curves and messy dark hair, I watch her turn around, meeting my eyes instantly. Licking my lips, I trail my eyes from the tips of her shoes, over her body, and finally, settle on her face. It's fucking stunning. She is fucking stunning. I smirk and slap Dante on the back. "Come on, introduce me to them," I say, urging him forward.

We reach them just as they lift their shot glasses to their lips. She sputters as the alcohol slides down the back of her throat, letting some of the liquid trail down her chin. We'll have to work on her gag reflex to get her to swallow my cock. I let out a groan, imagining how good she'd look on her knees, deep-throating me like a good girl.

My groan caught their attention, and they turn to us.

"What the hell do you want? I thought we got rid of you fifteen minutes ago." The redhead sounds unimpressed with Dante. That was going to be hell on his ego. It makes me smile just thinking about the hits he was going to take.

"Red, you wound me." Dante covers his chest, placing his hands over his left pec, as if that fucker's black heart is pained. Though he'd deny it until his dying breath, his family, the Camaros, were rumored to have ties to the New York Italian mafia. His uncle, a New Jersey senator, and his mother, a well-known journalist, vehemently deny any affiliation, but unfortunately for them, rumors couldn't disappear with cement shoes.

Growing up, Dante used the fear that accompanied that association to his advantage, scaring the shit out of a lot of guys we grew up with. Ever since his mom entered the national media and his uncle became senator, they placed as much distance as possible from that association, especially after his father died. I wonder how the redhead would feel if she knew Dante could promise her the world and deliver it, thanks to his connections through his mother and uncle. Would she be like every other girl he pursued, eager for the privilege his name afforded?

"My name is Celeste, you asshole. No, you cannot check if the carpet matches the drapes. No, I don't have a soul. And, finally, yes, you can fuck right off." Jesus, she was like a pit bull.

Taking my eyes from the brunette, I look between Dante and his pit bull. She's Dante's type, with pale skin, long red hair, and dark green eyes. I've always found it funny that my Italian friend obsessed over redheads. They

36

weren't fucking unicorns, but Dante treated them like the holy grail of pussy.

The clearing of a throat has us all turning our heads to the curvy little friend at her side. "CeCe, I think they might just want to get to the alcohol."

Looking behind her, Celeste turns red. "Oh."

Dante doesn't miss the opportunity to deepen that blush. "Red, I would love to see those pretty lips of yours. But for now, I'll settle for a shot."

Dante reaches behind Celeste, grabbing a bottle of Jägermeister. He takes Celeste's chin and tips her head up. "Now, pretty girl, will you open that mouth for me?"

A strangled laugh comes out of the brunette. "Does that work?"

Dante's answering scowl makes her laugh even harder. Who the fuck was this girl?

I knew grown men whose spleens fell out of their assholes for looking at Dante the wrong way, yet this girl didn't think twice about making fun of him. I was mesmerized.

Celeste grabs the bottle out of his hand, smirking at his annoyance. "Be careful, I'm not afraid to bite, big guy."

"Red, I'd like that bite."

Rolling her eyes, Celeste holds up the bottle, "Ava, let me give you a haircut. Get a chaser."

So that was my girl's name, Ava.

I watch as she licks her lips, the confusion clear on her face. "CeCe, you're not touching my hair. Are you high? The scissors in this place probably have hepatitis, and I just had my hair dyed."

Celeste rolls her eyes again. "Aves, a haircut is when you tilt your head back, open your mouth, and someone else pours in a shot and then a chaser."

Ava's cheeks flush. "Right, I knew that."

Her innocence was a fucking aphrodisiac; between her porn star body, Bambi eyes, and naivety, I was hard as a goddamn pole. I wanted to fuck that innocence out of her, starting with her mouth.

I take the bottle from Celeste. If anyone was going to give this girl her firsts, it was me.

"What is this, pass the fucking bottle?" Dante snorts. "Can we just drink, or does Ava need to hold it next before I can get a shot?"

I look at Ava, her full lips are tilted at the corners, and she seems to enjoy the back and forth between Dante and her friend. Someone must say something amusing because she throws her head back and laughs a full, throaty laugh that sounds like everything good in the world. Her face transforms from beautiful to breathtaking when animated like this, and I have the overwhelming need to see her laugh every day.

"Come here." I hold out my hand to guide her to me. "Now, vixen, tip your head back. Yes, just like that." I stroke her throat as she tilts her head back, exposing the column of her perfect olive skin. "Good girl," I murmur into her ear. Her quick intake of breath is fucking music.

"Now, open your mouth." Parting her lips slightly, I lift my hand from her throat and bring it to her face, squeezing both cheeks in. "Wider, Ava. Show me how wide your mouth can open."

Ava opens up for me, stretching her lips past her teeth. "Ready, vixen?"

She offers a head nod in confirmation.

I slowly pour the Jägermeister into her mouth, careful not to feed her too much of the liquid. Reaching behind me, I grab a bottle of soda from the table and pour it in after the alcohol. "Swallow." As the dark liquid works its way down her throat, I imagine it's my cum she's swallowing. She would look so pretty on her knees, mouth full of my cock, while spit and cum run down her face. Just the thought nearly has me shooting my load into my jeans.

My thoughts are alternating between fucking her until she can't walk and making her laugh daily. What the fuck am I supposed to do with that?

"Good job, vixen."

Ava brings her chin down and looks at me. "Most people call me Ava or Aves. Why are you calling me vixen?"

I pull her to me, not wanting my words to be broadcast to the entire room. "Sweetheart, if no one's told you what a fucking wet dream you are, then I'll be the first." My hand trails down her arm, encircling her wrist. Her pulse flutters under my fingers. "Come out back with me."

Ava pulls away from my grasp. "Thank you so much for that. I appreciate it, but I don't know you, and Ted Bundy was also super flattering but ended up killing, like, seventy people."

Did she just compare me to Ted Bundy?

"Did you just compare me to Ted Bundy?"

"No, I just made a note that you were flattering but could also be a serial killer." This girl must have a steel pussy if she feels confident enough to compare me to a notorious murderer. Most men cowered in my presence, let alone had the balls to insult me so blatantly.

"Vixen, I'm not planning on killing you. I'm sure your location is shared with your pit bull, so even if I were to take you, we wouldn't get very far. Come outside with me."

"Pit bull?"

I let out a laugh. "Celeste. She looks like she would cut my dick off and feed it to me if I did something to hurt you."

"You're not wrong. She loves watching people eat dick." Her cheeks redden. I raise an eyebrow. "No, no, that's not what I meant. What I mean is that she enjoys putting people in their place, when it's deserved."

"Vixen, I'm not concerned about what she watches." I hold out my hand. "Come with me."

Ava gnaws on her lip, seemingly weighing her options of whether or not I'll kill her once I get her alone.

"Please, pretty girl." I never say please. Fucking never.

"Okay." She takes my hand and I lead her outside.

Greyson

I pull Ava into my body, turning her so that she stands in front of me.

"Walk, pretty girl," I whisper into her ear. I see the goosebumps erupt on her arms, and the shiver that takes over her body.

Placing my hand on her back, I lead her toward the patio door. Looking over my shoulder, I make eye contact with Dante as he verbally spars with the pit bull. He nods his head in acknowledgment that I'm taking my girl away from their little match. I don't need to hear their shit-talking to know that they'll probably fuck by the end of the semester, if not by the end of the night. I look down to where my hand meets Ava's dress-covered back. I slip my hand lower, grazing the upper curve of her plump ass.

"If I were you, I'd move your hand to a more respectable location, such as your side or your own ass."

Fuck, the sass in this girl makes me even harder, if that's possible.

"Vixen, if you knew where my hand wanted to be, you'd be blushing like a fucking virgin." I take in the color blooming on her cheeks. "Now open that sliding door and get outside."

Her hands shake as she opens the sliding glass door. I shouldn't like seeing her so nervous, but I do.

The sliding door opens to a large, fenced-in backyard. People are scattered around the yard, huddled in small groups making conversation or whatever the fuck else these people do. My concern is getting Ava to someplace quiet, secluded, and isolated just for me.

That makes me sound like a predator but fuck if I care.

I navigate her toward the left corner of the yard, where a cluster of large pine trees offers natural privacy. Placed between the pines are Adirondack chairs and small wooden side tables.

"You know, if you didn't want me to compare you to Ted Bundy, you probably shouldn't be leading me to a secluded corner in a random yard while my only lifeline is inside." She lets out a cute little sigh that is probably supposed to sound annoyed.

"I've told you, vixen. I don't plan on killing you. You can drop the tough girl act now."

Though it's dark, I can guess that she's rolling her eyes when she drops into a chair with a loud sigh. My hand twitches. I'm going to spank that obstinance right out of her perky ass. Shit, I sound like Dante now, fantasizing about spankings.

The chair she settles into places her two feet away from the closest chair. Leaning down, I pick her up and sit down in the chair I just removed her from. I position Ava on my lap; her back remains stiff as I crush her side to my chest.

"That's better. You were too far away."

"You don't have to manhandle me. I'd rather sit alone." She moves to get off my lap, but I wrap my hand around the back of her neck, forcing her to stay put. She twists her head, facing me with a fire in her dark eyes.

"What part of me wanting to sit alone did you not understand?"

"Oh, vixen, I understood it just fine. That doesn't mean I'm going to let that happen. Now stop squirming." She stills, obeying me without question. "Now that we're comfortable, tell me about yourself."

Looking out to the yard, she clears her throat. "My name is Ava, and I'm a freshman. My roommate, CeCe—or the 'pit bull' as you referred to her—and I came with our new friend, Serena. Serena left an hour ago, but we stayed."

There's no denying that I'm attracted to her physically, but her personality, the intoxicating mix of sass and innocence, is what's driving my attraction now. I want to keep her talking and ask, "Have you decided on a major yet?"

Her shoulders drop, and she releases a breath I hadn't realized she was holding. For the first time since we came out here, she looks relaxed. She turns toward the fence that runs along the perimeter of the property and smiles. "I'm double majoring in culinary arts and hospitality. I came to Marymount because it was one of the few traditional four-year universities that had such a prestigious culinary program."

"Wow, I'm impressed. Aren't most freshmen undeclared?" I wasn't blowing smoke up her ass; I was impressed. I'm familiar with the demands of the culinary arts program. My third roommate, Lincoln, was in the program and had an insane amount of practicals. For her to enter such a program and combine it with a double major took a lot of commitment and drive.

She shrugs her shoulder at my question. "I don't know. CeCe and I are both pretty set in our majors; she's an English major on the five-year plan. Other than Serena, who's a brainiac junior, and Felicity and Jordan, we haven't met that many people yet."

"Did Felicity and Jordan invite you tonight?" I ask.

She swallows. "Yeah, Felicity and Jordan stopped by our dorm room while we were moving in. I didn't catch their last names." Jordan was all right, but Felicity was a dramatic little princess, incapable of losing anything she perceived as hers. I hooked up with her once last year, and she became obsessive immediately after. I didn't do relationships, and spreading your lips and legs in the men's bathroom at Legend's Sports Bar didn't earn you exclusive access.

"Hmm."

"What, do you know them?" Her hands fold in her lap as she turns to face me, studying my features in the darkness.

"You could say that. Jordan's harmless but stay away from Felicity, she'll stab you without thinking twice about it if you have something she wants."

Ava scoffs as if the idea that Felicity could want anything of hers is ridiculous. It's obvious that Ava is the type of woman that doesn't realize how gorgeous she is.

"I don't think I have anything Felicity wants." She lets out a soft laugh and shrugs her shoulders, the movement settling her deeper into my chest. "And to be honest, after tonight, I doubt these girls will ever speak to us again. It's safe to say that we won't be invited back to an Alpha Nu party."

The way she says that, like their blacklisting is a foregone conclusion, has me wondering what happened to set the harpies on edge. Generally speaking, if the girls were hot and came from money, Alpha Nu wanted them in their ranks. Though I didn't know Ava, I had eyes, and a working dick, and could feel how expensive the material of her dress was from where my hand curled around her waist. She was prime pledge material for them, though I wasn't mad that she showed little interest in joining this nest of vipers; there were other sororities on campus that weren't filled with materialistic snobs.

"Alpha Nu sucks. You wouldn't fit in here anyway."

She stiffens in my lap. "What exactly is that supposed to mean?" Her prissy tone makes me smile.

"Relax, vixen. You seem like a normal person, not a girl willing to sell yourself to the highest bidder." Turning her head, she looks at me, confusion drawing her thick eyebrows together.

"What does that mean, 'Selling yourself to the highest bidder?'"

I let out a breath, thinking about the annual Alpha Nu auction and the shit show that goes down. Every. Single. Time.

"Alpha Nu hosts a date auction every spring to raise money for their charity, whatever the fuck that is." More than likely, they use it as a way to fund these rush parties since they never take a dime from our guys. "The seniors force all of the pledges to plan dates, dress them up, and put them on stage for purchase."

"Okay, so it's like a bachelorette auction. What's the big deal?"

I can't help but laugh. Sweet, naïve vixen.

"That's cute, but not exactly. The sisters organize an inside competition: whichever pledges sell for the highest amounts are automatically initiated, no more bullshit for them. For the girls that either don't sell or don't sell over a grand, they're forced to perform for Kappa Gamma pledges." I don't need to tell her that the performance usually involves fucking, and whichever pledges can't get the Kappa Gamma pledges off within ten minutes are thrown out of the pledge class. The Kappa Gamma guys that can't shoot their load are also kicked out of their class.

I may be morally fucked up, but that's too far, even for me. Needless to say, there's an incentive for pledges to offer more than just a date at the auction.

"So, when I say that you wouldn't fit in here, take it as a compliment. You don't want to be part of this house."

She nods her head, clearing her throat before acknowledging what I just told her. "Yes, well, that seems slightly archaic, with a hint of prostitution."

I let out a bark of laughter. She's not wrong.

"How does the administration not put a stop to it?"

I shrug my shoulders, as though I don't know the answer to that question when I do. The faculty are just as guilty of participating as the student population is.

She shifts in my lap again, and I grab her hips to still her. I wouldn't mind grinding my dick into her hip, but something tells me it's too soon for that just yet. Talking about the pseudo-prostitution ring should probably make my dick flaccid, but my vixen's warmth combats it. The more she moves, though, the more I want to say fuck it.

Patience has never been my strongest quality, but my vixen is worth more than a quick fuck outside where anyone could see us. The thought of anyone watching her writhe on my dick, soaking me with her sweet cum, makes my blood fucking boil. Exhibitionism never bothered me before, but her pussy, her mouth, her body is fucking mine.

Fuck if I know why this girl is causing such a possessive reaction after thirty minutes in her presence.

"Well," she begins, "thanks for letting me know about the Alpha Nu girls—I mean, women." Her scoff tells me that she thinks they're anything but women. "I should get going now. We've been out here a while, and I'm sure CeCe is looking for me." I tighten my hold on her at the same time she moves to get off my lap. My pull and her forward momentum cause her to lose her balance, and she pitches forward, falling face-first toward the ground.

"Oh shit, are you okay?" Ava's face is turned toward the trees while her body is sprawled out, limbs and legs in every direction. Her shoulders shake and the thought of her crying and hurt finally makes my dick deflate really fucking quick. "Ava, answer me. Are you hurt?"

Her laugh breaks the tension in my shoulders, and I let out a sigh of relief.

I've had plenty of girls drop to their knees for me, but I've never had one bust her ass trying to get away from me.

"Twice in one freaking day; thank God CeCe wasn't here to see this. She'd never let me live it down."

Planting her hands on the ground, she pushes her body up and moves to her knees. Her wide smile at her own expense isn't something I've experienced before; in the past, any time a girl did something that made her look less than perfect, they'd cry and try to distract me with their body. Ava doesn't seem to be bothered by her fall, if anything, she seems more relaxed.

"Vixen, as much as I love the sight of you on your knees, are you okay? That was a hard fall." There's no denying that she will be wearing bruises for the next week.

"Trust me, I'm fine. This kind of thing happens all the time, just ask CeCe. During my high school graduation, I took down my entire row like a sleeve of dominoes because I tripped on my gown." The light from the house highlights her facial features, and I can see a frown pulling down her pretty plump lips. She shrugs delicately. "Collateral damage, I guess."

Ava stands to her full height, which can't be more than five feet, and starts to brush the dirt from her body. Her hands roam over her knees, her softly curved stomach, and her large chest. Her body, framed in the dim light from the back porch, is a road map of curves and dips and valleys; her thick thighs are strong yet feminine, a testament to the perfect female form. She looks like a woman, not a girl, and her body reminds me of a goddess, Venus or Aphrodite, and whoever the fuck else stands for sex and lust and desire.

What's more surprising is that I enjoy talking with her. I can't remember the last time I was content to just sit and talk with a woman without the overwhelming need to stuff my cock in their mouth just to shut them up. But Ava, she's special. She's funny, clumsy as fuck, but quirky and different. Watching her, listening to her, has knocked me on my ass, and I don't think I want to get up. I'm not sure what to make of that, but I know that I need more.

Ava interrupts my thoughts with a loud clearing of her throat. "Well, as fun as this was, I'm going to get going. It was great meeting you. Have a good night." Before I can voice my protest, she spins and practically runs for the porch's sliding door, quickly disappearing inside the house.

Not for the first time since I met her, I can't help but wonder, *What the fuck just happened?*

Ava

God, if you can hear me, please strike me dead and deliver this mortification from my body. There is no way, absolutely no way, that I can survive this level of embarrassment and continue functioning at this prostitution ring impersonating a frat party.

There. Is. No. Way.

Not only did I fall on my goddamn face in front of a human Hercules, but I then ran away from him as though he was the serial killer I accused him of being. I can't imagine what's going through his beautiful head right now.

I pause as soon as I enter the house, reliving my fall and remembering how my body pancaked the cool grass. Oh, sweet baby Jesus in the manger, please tell me that he didn't see the control top underwear I have under this dress. That's just what I need, not only to die of embarrassment from busting my ass while sitting on the most attractive man—because he is no boy—but to also be labeled as the fat girl that needs a girdle just to wear a dress.

God, if you're still there, please open the earth and swallow me whole.

I shake my head and continue the trek through the house, looking for CeCe and working on my excuse for the grass stain I currently have on my left knee. I had no idea that one could get a grass stain on their actual skin, but here we are. I wonder if she'll believe that I was attacked by garden gnomes on my way to go smoke. I don't smoke, but it seems safer than telling her the truth. For some reason, telling her that I was scrambling off the blonde Viking's lap before I dry-humped him doesn't sound great. We'll see which excuse I'll use in the heat of the moment.

I walk through the kitchen, living room, and dining room but still can't find my ginger friend. I start to turn to retrace my path when I hear her voice yell over the music pouring out of the speakers. "So help me, I will knee you in your dick and make sure that you will never be able to procreate."

Oh, good, an altercation is sure to draw more attention to us.

I follow CeCe's voice and stop short at the scene in front of me. CeCe sits on the couch with Dante, gaming controllers in both of their hands, while they play what looks like an intense game of Mario Kart. I laugh because the poor guy doesn't stand a chance—in fifth grade, we spent every day of summer break playing Nintendo, Xbox, and PlayStation. According to all tween movies, boys loved girls that played video games, so we made sure that we dominated every game we could get our hands on before we entered middle school.

We were both still virgins, so those movies lied.

CeCe's talent was getting inside her opponents' heads. I've watched as she made adults cry with her taunts and insults; telling a grown man that his mother never loved him and that he should just give up, while playing Mortal Kombat at the boardwalk arcade, was a scene I'll never forget.

"Jesus, Red, I didn't realize you were so ruthless. It's fucking hot." Dante stares at CeCe, practically drooling at the mouth, sending his character over the track's bounds.

"Eat a bag of dicks, pretty boy. Get your head in the game. You're making it too easy to beat your ass." CeCe doesn't look away from the TV as she trash-talks him. He shifts on the couch, not so subtly adjusting himself. I should probably intervene before he has an orgasm from her degradation.

"Wow, C, I leave you alone for an hour and you've become a video game dominatrix. That escalated quickly."

Dante moans, "Fuck. Red, are you a domme? Will you be my mistress?"

That finally has her looking his way. "Ew. No." She glances over to me and then looks back at her character's position before whipping her head back to me. I groan; she noticed the fucking knee.

"Ava, what the fuck is on your face? Is that dirt?"

Oh, so it's more than just my knee? I touch my face and examine my dirt-covered hand. Great.

"A house plant attacked me."

Dante stifles a laugh while CeCe raises one perfectly waxed red eyebrow. "I haven't seen any houseplants here."

"Oh, they were hidden in a corner where no one goes, very secluded. Great for oxygen circulation, you know." I should probably stop talking about houseplants now. "Anyway, are you ready to head out? I think I have a piece of twig, from the house plant, stuck in my hair. I'll let one of the sisters know we're leaving. Okay, great, see you at the front door in five minutes. Bye!" I race out before she has the opportunity to deny me.

I make it to the front door without any more mishaps, grateful for small miracles. The sister manning the front door must realize that I am in fucking shambles because she looks at me with a pitying smile and tells me that a sober driver will be pulling up in a few minutes to take me back to the dorms. I count down the seconds until I'm back in my room, reliving the greatest and worst moments of my night, both witnessed by the blonde Viking, Greyson. God, even his name is hot.

"Come on, CeCe," I mutter under my breath. Willing her to materialize so that I can get the hell out of this house as soon as possible.

"Chill out, I'm right here." I turn around and thank God my incantation worked.

"Good, you're here. A driver will be here in a few." We wait in silence, CeCe studying me while I look everywhere but at her. I do not doubt that she'll interrogate me the moment she has the chance, but I can't do that here, where anyone can overhear my embarrassment. I'd rather it stay between me, Thor, and the hard ground where I made my landing, but I know I owe CeCe an explanation for the dirt covering most of my body. Where the hell is this driver?

The sister manning the door signals to us that our ride is here, and I breathe a sigh of relief.

—

I barely close our dorm's door before CeCe turns on me.

She approaches me like an injured animal, cautious and watching for signs of my escape. "Aves, you are covered in dirt, you have a leaf in your hair,

49

and you have mud caked on your very, very expensive shoes." She eyes me carefully. "Are you okay? What happened?"

The leaf is a new development. I truly thought it was a twig. I'm not sure which I'd prefer.

"I'm assuming that a garden gnome attack wouldn't be any more believable than a house plant catching me off guard?"

She shakes her head and waits me out.

I chew on my bottom lip, a nervous habit I developed while dieting in the sixth grade and trying to abstain from chocolate chip cookies. CeCe's eyes zero in on it, and I know that anything less than the truth won't be believable. An annoying side effect of being friends for so long.

"Promise you won't make fun of me? I'm serious, I do not want to hear any of your bullshit about me falling or making a fool of myself, because trust me, I know. I freaking know."

"Okay, I promise. Now will you just tell me what happened?"

I take a deep breath and recount the time I spent with Greyson, nestled against his chest. I tell her everything he said, about Felicity, Alpha Nu, and the hazing, but I don't tell her how he touched me like he would die if he couldn't put his hands on me. I tell her about my fall and the way I ran off, embarrassed and mortified, but I don't tell her how he made me feel like my heart was beating too fast in my chest. I don't tell her how his touch made me squirm, desperate for relief, and I don't tell her that I wanted nothing more than for him to walk his hand from my hip to the heat between my thighs and show me just how experienced with women he was.

Normally, I'd have no issue telling my best friend all about my interactions with a guy, but for some reason, the minutes I spent with Greyson seemed sacred and private. To him, I was probably just a mess of a girl, one of many, and would have been easily forgettable if I hadn't launched myself to the ground in such a spectacular display. Maybe even that isn't unique. By tomorrow, I'll be just another girl he met at a party, and my face will fade into the deepest recesses of his mind.

Short of falling on my fat ass, I wonder if there was anything else I could have done to remain in the forefront of his mind. He is, without a doubt, the most breathtaking man I have ever seen. When he asked me to go outside with him, it was almost like my brain was short-circuited, and I couldn't perform basic functions, like talking without sounding like an idiot. A vague memory comes back to me when I compared him to Ted Bundy. Twice.

God, help me. He definitely thought I was insane.

"Well, Aves, you have had quite a night. You may want to shower all that"—she waves her hand in my direction—"off yourself. You kind of smell like dirt."

I sniff my dress and grimace at the smell. "Yes, Princess Peach. However, while we're on the subject of tonight's party, let's talk about your little race with a large Italian man. Care to share?"

She huffs, looking like an annoyed Cabbage Patch kid again. "He was following me around the party when you disappeared with your Viking. By the time we made it into the front room, there was a Mario Kart tournament happening, and you know how I get when it comes to a challenge. I couldn't just stand there and not participate, so I told him we were up next, and that I was going to kick his ass." She shrugs as if it's no big deal, but I know her too well. She's leaving details out, but so am I, so I don't press.

"Well, it sounded like he wanted you to step on his balls and spank him with a riding crop. Did I hear him correctly when he asked if you'd be his mistress?"

CeCe laughs and shakes her head. "Trust me, there is nothing submissive about him, and he knows it. He just wanted to see how I'd respond." She pauses and looks at me closely. "Wait, why do you know so much about kinky sex and sex toys?"

"Uh, I watch porn."

"The kind that has riding crops and mistresses?"

I laugh. I may have never participated in the sex part of sex, but I was well-versed in all kinds of intercourse. Lovemaking, hate fucking, revenge sex, BDSM. No one could claim I was naive. She takes my laughter for what it is: the only answer I'll provide to her question.

"Wow, okay, you little freak."

"Whatever you say, Princess Peach. In more important news, what are we going to do about Alpha Nu?"

"What are we going to do? We're going to avoid them like the bubonic plague, that's what we're going to do." She shudders dramatically. "I can't believe girls are so desperate to join them that they'd willingly prostitute themselves out. How does the administration not put a stop to it?"

I shake my head in disgust. "I'm not sure, but they have to know. I mean, Greyson made it seem like their dating auction was one of the most popular Greek life events."

"Well, we aren't going to that shit show, that's for sure. Let's make sure to tell Serena when we meet her for brunch on Sunday." CeCe moves around the room, getting ready for bed and throwing her dress, shoes, and bra in different directions. I pick up her discarded clothes and place them neatly on her dresser.

"C, stop throwing your clothes around this room like a stripper. I don't have any singles to tip you with." I barely finish my sentence before a pair of folded socks are thrown at my head. "Rude."

"Speaking of strippers, I am dying to hear about Serena's sprint out of that party. That Devin guy was hot but also an asshole. I don't like how he treated Serena like she was his to command before she ran home."

I'm not sure how strippers made her think of Serena, but I'm used to the inner workings of CeCe's mind and don't question it. I think back to how abrupt he was, demanding she leave the party, and making her question why she was there in the first place. My heart hurt for Serena, between her dad replacing her and her mom with a new family and then entering college freakishly young, her loneliness is suffocating. She seemed to brush off Marina, but with Devin, it was like she crawled into a shell and snuffed out her inner light. It was tough to see someone that kind, that beautiful, fold in on themselves.

I pull my pajamas out from my drawer and grab my shower caddy, towel, and shower shoes. Making my way to the door, I say over my shoulder, "I'm not sure who he is, but he seems like a douche canoe, and I hope she stabs him with her Louboutin. I'm going to take a shower and wash this grime off of me. I'll try to be quiet when I get back in."

—

The communal bathroom at the end of our hall hosts four private water closets and five showers for the thirteen girls that live on this side of the dorm; all of us nestled into six two-bedroom dorm rooms and one single for our RA, Bethany. How they factored in the number of toilets and showers doesn't sit right with me. What if we all get a massive case of food poisoning and have a mini pandemic in our wing? Will we have to puke in buckets like maidens in the sixteen hundreds?

I check my phone on the way to the bathroom, noting the late hour, and pray that no one is in the bathroom, or if they are, that they aren't looking for a conversation. Between the leaves in my hair and dirt covering my body, I look like I came back from a stakeout in the bushes. Greyson's face races through my mind; he looked mortified on my behalf when I fell off his lap and ate shit.

There's no use wondering over it. Odds are, our meeting will fade into the ether for him, and neither my name nor my face will be recognized if we ever cross paths again. He knew all about girls—sorry, women—like Jordan and Felicity. When he spoke about Felicity, it was obvious he knew her, intimately. I can't say I'm surprised; her perky chest and beautiful face are hard to miss. She may not have been the... nicest person at the pregame, but she was gorgeous and thin. If that's his type, then why was he pulling me closer during our entire conversation?

Ugh. I hate that I'm spending this much energy thinking about a guy that probably thought the chubby girl of the party was the easy lay and hungry for affection. His pursuit was nothing more than trying to get a blow job out of the easiest target, and I can't lose sight of that. This isn't the first time a hot guy came onto me with the sole purpose of sex; when I was a sophomore in high school, the star linebacker of our football team relentlessly pursued me. When I finally said yes to a date, he made it clear that he expected "at least a hand job" for his trouble, and when I refused to touch his dick, he called me a fat cunt and kicked me out of his car in the movie theater parking lot. I had to Uber home and refused to tell my parents why a different car dropped me off.

The next day, I told everyone in school that he had a tiny dick and smelled like moldy jock straps. Needless to say, he had a difficult time finding a prom date. I don't think Greyson is like that fuckhead, but I still don't trust his motives for getting me alone and pulling me onto his lap. Whatever. I need to stop this line of thought and focus on getting the leaves out of my hair.

I push open the bathroom door and peek around, making sure there's no one here. Setting my shower supplies on the small wooden bench outside of the stall, I turn the water temperature to scalding and close the heavy curtains around me, blocking out the rest of the bathroom in case someone does come in this late. The shower quickly heats up and I step inside, reveling in the feel of the hot water cleansing my body of dirt and embarrassment.

My hands follow the path of my lemon verbena body wash. Running my hands over my chest, my fingers trail the suds over my nipples. Jesus, I can't help but picture that it's Greyson's hands caressing my body. I moan, pinching my nipples and twisting them into peaks, imagining his mouth and teeth and warm breath on my skin.

Moving one hand lower, I pass over my soft stomach and work my hand between my thighs, caressing my fingers over my pussy lips. I'm already soaked, and not from the shower. I may be a virgin, but touching myself, grinding the heel of my palm into my clit until I come, is one of my favorite nighttime activities. My knees nearly give out when I circle my clit, pleasure forming in the base of my spine and radiating out. My fingers work into my opening, tight and hot and so fucking wet from the images I'm conjuring up in my head: Greyson on his knees in front of me, feasting on my lips. Greyson's big hands grabbing my ass, spanking me for being a bad girl and running away tonight. Greyson above me, shoving himself down my throat, fucking my face with wild need. I move my hand faster, chasing my orgasm until, finally, I come with Greyson's name on my lips.

He may forget about me easily, but he'll be the star of every fantasy I have.

Greyson

It's been three days since I saw my little vixen, and I can't get her out of my fucking mind. I replay how she left me, a beautiful mess on her knees before jumping up and running faster than an Olympic runner. I didn't even get her number before she booked it out of the party, something that is pissing me the fuck off. Women don't run away from me, ever. Her little stunt had cum shooting out of my cock as soon as I grabbed it in the shower that night. Yesterday, the day before, and today, I've come thinking about her each time, but I'm not satisfied. No, the only thing that will satisfy me is her under me, above me, or on her knees. Preferably all three positions.

So far, all I know about her is that her name is Ava, her roommate, Celeste, wanted to cut Dante's balls off and keep them as a souvenir, and she falls a lot. I shouldn't find her lack of balance attractive, but it stirs every protective instinct I have. She also compared me to a serial killer more than once, so she must be one of those people that get off on Netflix documentaries about murder. I tried to find her on social media, but without a last name, hunting through private profiles made me feel like the psychopath she compared me to.

Not being able to find her on social media hasn't lessened my need to find her, I just need to change my tactics. I palm my phone, weighing the consequences of sending the text that I know will get me what I want when Dante storms into my room like a bull. The house Dante, Lincoln, or Linc, and I share is fifteen minutes from campus and looks like a fucking McMansion. I laughed when my dad bought it and handed me the keys after he retired from the pros. "Son," he said. "This is your first investment property. Don't fuck it up."

Because of him, Dante and Linc pay shit for rent, and we have a sick, state-of-the-art movie theater and game room. I know I'm privileged; it's hard not to be aware of it when your dad was one of the most famous baseball players in the country before his retirement. After he retired, he signed on with ESPN and started hosting a few baseball segments. For as long as I can remember, baseball has been part of my life, and all I wanted to do was follow in my dad's footsteps. Those dreams went to shit when I blew my knee out in high school, but Dad always encouraged me to look at a situation and pivot. Not like my egg donor, who walked away because having a kid didn't work for her coke habits.

"Bro, just text Felicity and ask her for your little girl's number." He shakes his head while looking at the phone in my hand. "While you're at it, could you ask for Red's number, too? I'm pretty sure I'm going to marry her." One thing about Dante, he falls in love quickly and loses interest even faster. The last thing I need is for him to fuck over Ava's roommate and mess my shit up.

"I don't know if I'm texting Felicity yet. You know how she is; she'll see Ava as competition and try to either kill her or me. I can't deal with her bullshit drama this year." I won't deal with it. Last year, Felicity put "dibs" on my dick and tried to ruin the lives of every other girl I fucked. Felicity sucked me off in the bathroom one time and turned it into an exclusive relationship in her warped mind. When she first started her shit, I spoke to her and reminded her that I never promised commitment, let alone monogamy, but she twisted my words and became relentless. Texting her about my vixen is the last fucking thing I want to do. "And I'm also not helping you with Celeste. You'll fuck up my shit."

"That's fucked up, man. She's my future wife. I won't hurt her." Dante's face transforms into a grimace and tells me that he remembers all the shit Felicity put me through last year. "But that's fucked, man. What about Jordan? She's not bad."

He's not wrong. Jordan's relatively chill, but she lives in the Alpha Nu house with Felicity and tends to hang close to her. How those two became friends is beyond me since she's normal and Felicity is delusional.

"Maybe Linc can ask Jordan? Their families are close. He has Christmas dinner with her, for fuck's sake." That's not a bad idea. Before I can respond, Dante opens his mouth and calls out for Linc.

"LINCOLN!" Dante calls out.

"Dude, what the fuck? I could have just texted him to come up here." More than likely, Linc was in the kitchen cooking. We may be kings of this school, but we take our shit seriously; our parents would kick our asses if we didn't. Dante and I are business majors and plan to start our own investment company someday, but Linc is artistic and always creating something, be it food, poetry, or art. He is a culinary arts major and had an internship in Paris last summer at a Michelin-star restaurant. Like I told Ava that night, the culinary arts major was tough, and he would spend hours in the kitchen preparing for his practicals. Dante and I always benefited from his trials, since we were able to eat them every time, but I know it weighed on Linc, especially when he couldn't get a recipe correct. While Dante and I are on the analytical side, and our large, in-your-face bodies can be intimidating for some girls, Linc is expressive and looks like a model. His pretty-boy good looks, tattoos, and skills in the kitchen mean that he has no problem getting a lot of pussy. Compared to him, I was a choir boy.

Quick footsteps sound on the hardwood floor just before Linc comes into the room. "I just pulled my soufflés out of the oven, and if you broke them, I'll fucking kill you." Normal college kids didn't say shit like this, but Linc was in a league of his own.

"Calm down, Gordon Ramsey. Grey needs a favor." Linc raises his eyebrow in question, and I roll my eyes at the theatrics of the two of them.

"Fucking Christ, D. I told you I didn't know what I wanted to do yet."

"What, are you two trading secrets and braiding each other's hair up here? What the fuck is going on?"

"Do you remember the girls we saw at the Theta Phi house? The redhead and the curvy brunette in the black dress? I'm trying to get the brunette's number."

Linc's face drops into a frown. "What do you mean? You didn't ask for it there?"

"I would have if she didn't run away," I mumble under my breath.

"I'm sorry, I didn't hear you right. It sounded like you said she ran away?"

My jaw tightens and I look away, running my tongue over my teeth in pure fucking frustration. Like I said, women didn't run away from me.

"Oh shit, she fucking ran away from you." Dante and Linc laugh their asses off like it's the funniest shit they've ever heard. I'm putting crushed laxatives in Linc's fucking baking flour if he keeps this up. And Dante? Good fucking luck getting in Celeste's pants by the time I tell her about all the shit he's done with the female population of this school.

"Stop laughing, you fucks. Do you want to help me or not?"

Linc sobers. "What can I do?"

Dante rubs his hands together. "Okay, so you're going to text Jordan—"

"Hell fucking no I am not." Dante and I look at each other before turning back to Linc.

"Why the fuck not?"

"She followed me to Paris. Paris, as in fucking Europe."

Dante scoffs. "She probably just had a trip planned at the same time. That doesn't seem like Jordan."

"When she tells you, 'I came to Paris for you,' it means she fucking followed you to Paris. I was elbow deep in a goddamn chicken for dinner prep when she walked through the kitchen door in a trench coat and beret. She ripped that shit open like we were in a hotel room and not in the middle of a five-star restaurant. The sous chef almost had a heart attack." He takes a deep breath. "So, I will not be texting her. I will be staying far, far away from her. I already told my mom to stop trying to set us up. I'm done."

Damn, Christmas was going to be awkward as fuck at his house this year.

"Grey, I hate to break it to you," Dante began, "but if you want Ava's number, you need to text Felicity."

Fuck.

—

Grey: Hey.

Felicity: OMG hey handsome. Long time, no talk. How are you? How was your summer? Do you want to get together soon? I can come over. I'm sure you've missed my... assets ;) ;*

Christ. I could smell the desperation coming off the text; it was palpable. If she wasn't such an asshole, I would feel bad for her. That empathy goes out the fucking window when you threaten to run a girl over with your car if she looks at me. Last spring wasn't a good time for all because of Felicity.

I need to keep this text exchange brief and as short as possible.

Grey: There was a girl at your party the other night, Ava. Freshman, short, brown hair. I think her roommate is a girl named Celeste. I need her number. Do you have it?

Three dots quickly appear and I hold my breath, waiting to see how she's going to respond.

Felicity: Um, why do you need that fat bitch's number? She's a fucking embarrassment and looked disgusting in that dress. You better not be hooking up with her. WTF Grey, I thought we had something???

My blood is boiling and I flex my fist, trying to control my anger and not tell her what I think about sweet Ava's body. I think about her dress that night, tight, black, and just barely decent; it showed every dip and valley, her curved waist and perky ass. She's fucking perfect.

What the fuck do I say to get her to give me the number and leave me the fuck alone? I'm not above lying to her at this point to keep Ava away from Felicity.

Grey: Felicity, we talked about this last semester, there's no "us." You're too good for me. And about Ava, nah, nothing like that. We have a bet going on with the guys.

I think I just threw up in my mouth from that entire text.

Felicity: OMG, Grey Grey, you're so sweet <3 I'm so not too good for you. You know I will always wait for you, baby. And ohhhhh, I love a bet. What are we betting??

Grey: Just guy stuff. I'll let you know when I win ;). Now, can you help me out with that number?

Now I know I just threw up in my mouth with this "Grey Grey" bullshit. Why can't she be like other girls and take the hint? I've never lied to a girl or been an outright dick to them, but they always know where we stand before and after the hookup. Felicity may not be following me to other countries, but she's a fucking menace. Though I'm annoyed I have to pretend Ava is less to me than what she is, and what she will be. The worst thing in this situation would be to make Felicity aware that Ava was special. Putting a target on her back and subjecting her to possible harm is the last thing I want to do.

After a few more text messages, she finally gives me Ava's number with instructions to call her later if I'm bored. I immediately block her number. I save my vixen's number and smile to myself. Catching this little fox is going to be so fucking sweet, and I can't wait for my reward.

Ava

After Thursday night, the weekend flew by in a rush of getting ready for the first day of classes. Between waiting in line in the school's sole bookstore three times and following the routes to my classes to ensure I wouldn't walk into the wrong room during the first week, I was pretty sure CeCe was sick of my shit.

"I am sick of your shit, Aves. Settle down before you give me secondhand anxiety." As I suspected, she was sick of my shit. I tried to explain to her that I had these recurring nightmares of walking into the wrong class, like mortuary sciences, and having to explain to a full lecture hall that I was in the wrong place. Then I would have to transfer schools because I'd be too mortified that I'd be recognized as the idiot that went into a lecture hall for embalmers.

I didn't say it was a rational nightmare, okay?

Aside from my nightmare, I was also anxious about starting classes and taking the first steps toward fulfilling my dreams of owning my little restaurant. Maybe I was a loser for being excited about my ridiculous class load, but it meant that I was exactly where I needed to be.

"Sorry, C. I'm just anxious to get this semester started. Anyway, we have to meet Serena in fifteen at JJ's. Are you almost ready to go?" We haven't seen or spoken much to our new friend since Thursday night's mess of a party, and we were both dying of curiosity.

CeCe looks at me through the makeup mirror on her wooden desk. "Yeah, just give me a minute. I need to cover this pimple on my forehead so that people don't think I have a third eye."

"Okay, cyclops."

"I said third eye, dumbass, not one eye."

I laugh to myself. It's easy to rile her up, especially about anything dealing with Greek mythology. She went through a phase three summers ago where she read every piece of Greek literature she could get her hands on and tried to change her first name to Penelope in honor of Homer. Her parents put a stop to that real quick.

"Okay, all done. Let's go eat. I'm starving." CeCe stands from her desk chair and pulls a sweatshirt over her head. Even with a pimple on her forehead and an oversize sweatshirt, she looks beautiful. Meanwhile, I look like a soccer mom in my compression leggings and lululemon zip-up. We grab our student IDs and make our way outside to begin the short walk to the campus diner, JJ's. When they designed Marymount, they did it with the intent that students wouldn't need to venture off campus much and could access all of life's necessities within walking distance. With three restaurants, a pharmacy, a bodega, and a coffee shop, it was like an insular little town, all within a ten-minute walk from the heart of campus.

I turn to CeCe as we walk. "So, do you think Serena will show up, or do you think she's too embarrassed to come eat with us?"

She worries her lip before answering me. "Honestly, I'm not sure. Like you saw in the group message, I tried to text her about needing to skip out on the poetry reading last night but she didn't say much." She shrugs. "I guess we'll find out in a few minutes."

In between my first day nightmares and thoughts of Grey, Serena's been on my mind. She was so excited when we asked her to join us, only to have that excitement snuffed out by Marina, Felicity, and Devin. The poor girl looked like she was starving for friendships and connections outside of the academic confines she was imprisoned in, and she faced unnecessary hostility for most of her night out. It was sad and it pissed me off.

I sigh. "I hope she shows up. I want to induct her into our little group." My sisters, Seraphina and Bianca, were also part of our pack. Growing up, CeCe was as much a sister to me as Sera and B, and I know they feel the same way about her as I do. It was weird being here without them, but Sera was a senior in high school, along with her twin, Rafael, and Bee was a junior. I know that the short drive home wasn't an obstacle, but I still missed having them close.

"How is Sera doing with that asshat boyfriend of hers?" Sera's boyfriend, Mitchell, was a grade-A asshole. Sure, he came from a wealthy family, was generically good-looking, and played football—he was mediocre, at best—but his personality was the epitome of Jekyll and Hyde. When Sera first brought him home, he was okay enough and seemed to worship the ground her little feet walked on. In recent months, however, she was crying more often than not. Despite my best efforts, she still didn't want to break up with his lame ass.

"Eh, same as it was all summer. I texted her last night, and she said she found naked pictures of some girl on his phone." CeCe matches my scowl. "He claims they were sent to him by one of his friends, but if that were the case, why would he save them to his camera roll? At best, he's a creep for keeping photos of her; at worst, he's a liar and a cheat."

"My money is on the lying and cheating, unfortunately. Why won't she just break up with him? Is his dick made of gold?"

I can't help but laugh. He came from so much money that he probably did have a gold replica of his penis as a bookend in his bedroom.

"I have no idea what his appeal is. As far as I know, they still haven't had sex, and I keep asking but Sera tells me to stay out of it and that I don't know everything about their relationship." I'm so worried about driving an irreparable wedge between us that I tread as lightly as possible when it comes to them. What I do know is that he gave her a purity ring and told her he wanted a virgin bride. I thought my dad was going to call his brothers and get the baseball bats to break Mitchell's kneecaps when he found out. Instead, Sera was told that she wasn't allowed to wear the ring and that she wasn't going to be a teenage bride.

Can't say that I disagree with my parents.

We're still lost in conversation about Sera and Mitchell by the time we make it to JJ's. Unsurprisingly, it's packed and there doesn't seem to be a single table available. I make my way to the hostess stand to put my name on a list but stop short when I see Serena sitting in a booth by herself with three mugs and a carafe in front of her. I breathe out my relief—she showed up.

"C, Serena got us a table. Come on."

We smile at Serena as we slide across from her. "Hey, stranger, good job on getting a table. How are you doing?" I pick up the carafe and pour coffee into our mugs, handing the cream over to Celeste after I use a generous helping.

Serena offers a weak, close-lipped smile. "I'm okay. I wasn't sure if I should come today. I'm so embarrassed from Thursday night and need to apologize to you both. I don't have many friends, and I was hoping we'd hit it off. I'm so sorry if my drama ruined that."

I snort. Does this poor girl think their behavior is her fault? "Serena, as we were walking over here, I told Celeste that my sister's boyfriend is trying to convince her that anal sex is okay because her 'hymen will be intact.' That's a direct quote." I shake my head at her and reach out to grab her hands. "Trust me, your drama is no bigger or smaller than anyone else's. You deserve to have friends you can rely on when the drama gets to be too much, and we'd love to be there for you."

Tears well up in her eyes. Pulling her hands back onto her lap, she looks down, twisting her mouth before taking in a large breath. Squaring her shoulders, she begins, "So, you guys met Marina, my dad's stepdaughter. Marina's mom, Brandi—with an 'I,' mind you—was my mom's best friend from college. That's how our parents all met. When I was eight, Marina's family moved down the street from my house." She looks up at us, smiling ruefully and shaking her head. "I remember being so excited," she continues. "When we were little, Marina was my best friend, and her mom was like another mother to me. Devin, you met him last night, was my next-door neighbor, and I think I loved him most of my life. He's an asshole now, but when we were younger, I used to imagine him as my knight in shining armor, a Prince Charming."

This story is not starting at all like I thought it would.

She clears her throat and continues, "Anyway, when we were eleven, Marina's parents split up. I don't remember much of it, but she would leave every weekend to spend time with her dad. Her mom would come over to my house while she was away, drinking with my parents and shopping with my mom. Being a rich, bored ex-housewife. Eventually, my dad found his way into her bed."

"Damn, Serena. That sucks. But that's not your fault," CeCe states as she blows on her steaming cup of coffee. "Why was she so rude to you last night? Does she always act like that?"

Serena scoffs. "Well, after my mom found out that my dad wasn't going over to 'fix the plumbing issues' in their house, she filed for divorce. Around the same time, Marina's dad moved back to Italy, where he's originally from, to be closer to his parents. From what I know, he stopped paying alimony and child support as soon as he moved and hasn't seen her since. I guess, to her, my dad is her dad now. She's territorial over him, especially because she lived with him full-time in the house I grew up in, in my old bedroom, no less. Mom and I moved to a different school district so that I wouldn't have to see her every day before they transferred me up to the high school."

"Wait, wait, wait. She took your old bedroom?" CeCe looks at me in horror. "Did she want to be you?"

Serena's quiet, sad laugh succeeds in breaking my heart just a little bit more. "I think she wanted to erase me. I was a daddy's girl before the divorce and so was she." She shrugs as if that explains it. "One of us couldn't be the center of his attention anymore, and I was too angry at him to fight her for it. Besides, when I moved, they began testing my IQ pretty rigorously, and I didn't have time for family, friends, or distractions. My mom tried to get me involved socially, but the coursework was just too heavy, and I was too depressed to interact with kids my age after school."

Holy shit. What kind of parent not only cheats on his wife with her college friend but then moves her daughter into his daughter's old room? It's like a soap opera, and not the good kind. If I ever needed evidence that men think with their dicks first and brains later, this is it.

I look at Serena, taking stock of her kind eyes and sad smile. This eighteen-year-old girl has been through so much heartache and has done so friendless and alone. I don't know her dad, but I hate him for what he did to her and her mom. Maybe that was overly dramatic, but when I envision myself in her position, my dad leaving for another woman and replacing us overnight, I feel physically ill.

"So, how does Devin factor into this?" I question. That night, he mentioned that he was connected to both Serena and Marina before pressuring her to leave.

"Hmm," she hums softly. "That's the worst part of this entire thing. Not that I lost my dad, because I think I've hated him since he cheated on my mom. That resentment was abrupt and all-encompassing. Devin? That was different." Serena's head tilts back, her eyes searching the ceiling for answers. "Just like Marina, I had to go to my dad's each weekend—it was an order of the court. There's an old, solid oak tree on my dad's property that borders Devin's house. When I was little, my dad had a tree house built for me. I used to sneak out there, read, and just escape from all the turmoil in my life. Devin used to check up on me." She smiles fondly, seemingly at a memory. "He used to bring me English tea biscuits because he knew they were my favorite. He'd bring me his mom's old Nancy Drew books because he knew how much I wanted an adventure of my own." A laugh escapes her before her face transforms into a scowl. Leaning forward, she puts her elbows on the table, lowering her voice to a near-whisper. "Like I said, I always loved Devin, and it's no secret, he's well aware of my past infatuation. He's a couple of years older than me, but he would tell me all of his secrets, and confide in me. He was... sweet. I fell in love with him quickly, like lightning hitting sand during a summer storm. He was—"

"What are you ladies having?" We all startle, looking toward the waitress at the end of our table. Serena places her order: French toast with bananas and strawberries. CeCe immediately shouts for the same while I settle for an egg white veggie omelet with a fruit cup on the side. The waitress takes our menus and flits to her next table. The waitress—whose name tag reads Fiona—had impeccable timing in the sense that she interrupted just as it was getting good. I look back to Serena, waiting for her to continue. From my peripheral, I see that CeCe is doing the same.

"As I was saying..." Serena pauses to sip her coffee. "He was just everything to me. The older we got though, the less I came over to my dad's house.

I was busy with high school by the time I was twelve and shuffled from one academic after-school program to another. Soon, my weekly visits transitioned to monthly visits and then it became sporadic. Sometimes, I would go six weeks without going over there. As my visits became more infrequent, Marina and Devin got closer. They started dating a year or so ago."

"Okay," I hedge. "But that still doesn't explain why he was so pissed you were there on Thursday." He was aggressive in his words and movements, intent on hurting Serena as much as possible. It was obvious that there was a deeper issue than the one she laid out to us moments ago.

"I made a promise a long time ago and couldn't deliver on it when he came to me."

I roll my eyes. "Promises made as a child can't always be honored."

"Serena," CeCe says her name softly, as though she's afraid of scaring her off, unlike me, who wants to pound her father, stepmother, stepsister, and former neighbor with my dad's golf clubs. "Whatever promise you broke, you need to remember you went through something traumatic at the same time. From what you said, it doesn't seem like he was there for you all the time, either."

I nod in agreement but keep my mouth shut. Telling her that I'll get my dad's Callaway five iron and drive to their house in a rental car probably won't do much good. If she gives me a sign that retribution is on the table, I'll be sure to speak up.

"Allow yourself to move on from this. Don't listen to him if he tries to pressure you into leaving again. You have every right to a happy life; he doesn't get to control that." CeCe may be dramatic, but it's times like this when I'm grateful for her compassion. Where I'm a swing first, think later type of person, CeCe empathizes and looks at a situation from every available angle, even if her first response is aggression. Her support of Serena mimics my thoughts, but her way of expressing herself is more mature and well-thought-out.

"Yeah, what she said," I echo.

We fall into comfortable conversation. Serena tells us about STD's poetry reading event the previous night while I recount how our parents drove up and forced us to dinner because they already miss us at home. When our food arrives, CeCe is in the middle of telling Serena about the mud and leaves caked to my body by the end of the party. Serena's snort of laughter convinces me that her spirits are lifted from the black cloud that encapsulated them since Thursday night.

"Oh my God, you fell off of Greyson Jansen? That is the most amazing thing I've ever heard."

His last name is Jansen? Jesus, my grandmother would be so disappointed that I'm this interested in a non-Italian. Maybe he's Italian on his mother's side?

"I didn't know his last name, but if Greyson Jansen is a cross between a Viking and a motorcycle outlaw, then yes, I fell off his lap, into the mud, and then ran away after calling him a serial killer."

CeCe continues eating her breakfast; she's heard this before, but Serena stares at me with a slack jaw and wide eyes. In the few times I've interacted with Serena, she didn't seem easily shocked. Based on her expression, I assume this is a big deal.

"Serena, why are you looking at me like that?" It's unnerving, like her face is frozen in place. I have the overwhelming urge to close her mouth but keep my hands on my fork and knife. After minutes of silently staring at me, she finally snaps out of her trance.

"I'm sorry, but Greyson doesn't show interest in anyone. He's never lacked admirers and doesn't have to make any effort in getting a girl into bed. If anything, he must push them out."

I bristle; it sounds like she knows him well, or maybe his reputation precedes him. I can't help but ask how she knows this about him.

"Well, he is pretty well-known on campus. His dad is Greg Jansen, the baseball player turned sportscaster. His whole family is loaded and famous. We also have a mutual friend." A blush forms on her face. I raise my brow, surprised to hear about a shared friend, but even more shocked that Greyson is related to one of the most famous sports figures of our generation. I glance at CeCe. From her facial expression, it seems like she's just as surprised. "No shit?" I begin. "Wait, who's your mutual friend? Was it one of the guys he came with last night?"

Serena shrugs. "I'm not sure who he came with. His name is Dylan. We grew up together, too. He's Devin's less douchey friend. I didn't see Dyl there, but I'll text him later to see if he showed up." She looks away in consideration. "I think Greyson probably came with his roommates, Dante and Lincoln. They tend to travel together like a pack of wolves."

"Fucking Dante," CeCe mutters into her French toast.

I'm not surprised that Greyson attracts women without much effort; not only is he the most gorgeous man I've ever seen, but he's wealthy, well-connected, and has a famous family. I remember watching a documentary on Netflix about Greg Jansen's baseball career. His father, Greyson's grandfather, was a sought-out hedge fund manager that made billions for his clients while his brother, Greyson's uncle, is a prominent movie director. I vaguely remember the reference to a wife and son, but it didn't show their pictures or mention their names.

If I thought Greyson was out of my league before, now it's confirmed. There's no way in hell he's interested in me when he has access to models, movie stars, and beautiful women from all around the world. My self-loathing sinks in just a little bit deeper, grasping my heart and squeezing painfully. I may have interacted with him only briefly, but the fantasy of what could have been, in a world where girls like me dated guys like him, filtered into my thoughts frequently.

He'll just continue being the fictional giver of my stolen, self-induced orgasms. Under the covers, where no one can see me touch myself, I'll pretend it's his hand until someone more realistic can erase those dreams.

Ava

Though the start of brunch was filled with gossip and family drama, by the end of breakfast, Serena, CeCe, and I were laughing over the "bros" from the interest fair where we initially met Serena. It was refreshing to meet another girl that was genuinely nice but also had a wry sense of humor.

After saying goodbye to Serena, who had to go back to her apartment to FaceTime her mom, CeCe and I made the short trek across campus back to our dorm in silence. A key part of our friendship was our ability to recognize when the other needed a moment to themselves. We updated each other on almost all aspects of our lives, but we also respected each other's need to be left alone. Serena dropped several bombs on us today; between her home life, its tentacles on her student life, and the infamy of Greyson's family, my mind was reeling. I suspected CeCe's was too.

Making it back to our dorm, I threw myself on my bed and absentmindedly scrolled through my social media accounts. Swiping through pictures of our high school classmates and their documented "first night of college" photos, I zoned out to the world around me until CeCe threw a pillow at my head, diverting my attention. I look over at her, annoyed. "You could have just called my name. No need to get violent."

She rolls her eyes. "I said your name twice and you didn't hear me." She bends over to tighten her running sneakers. Sometime between getting back to the dorm and her pillow assault, she changed into her running clothes. "I'm going on a run. My location is on, so if I'm not back in an hour, I'm probably dead. Send police out for me."

"Got it. If you die, can I have your shoe collection?"

"Yes, it's in the will. Anyway, I'll be back soon. Maybe we'll catch up on *Shelter's Point* when I get back. I think there was a new episode on Wednesday."

I give her a thumbs up and go back to my phone. Most people would balk at the exchange CeCe and I just had, but when your parents are famous for the Clown Killer's conviction and travel the country doing true crime docuseries and podcasts, it's second nature. Couple that with CeCe's dad who is a medical examiner, and well, we were no strangers to death. It was just as common to ask about the toxicology reports as it was to pass the gravy at our dinner tables. It's probably why we've grown so close over the years.

A few minutes after CeCe leaves for her run, my phone starts ringing with an incoming FaceTime call. Blindly answering my phone, I smile when my sisters' faces pop up on the screen. Before I can say hello, they start in. "You were holding back at dinner last night. Tell us everything about college. Don't be a little bitch; we need all the details."

"Uh, hello to you guys, too."

"Cut the shit, Ava Maria. We are on house arrest right now and need to live vicariously through you. Are you partying every night? Have you had sex yet? Are you pregnant? Mom told us about your frog. Why are you so weird?"

Like rapid fire, my sisters throw questions at me, not necessarily expecting answers, but needing to hurl everything they can at me so that I can answer at least one of their inquiries.

"Okay, I'm going to need both of you to take a deep breath and calm your tits. First and foremost, why are you on house arrest? I didn't speak with Mom yet today."

Sera and Bee look at each other before turning their faces back to the screen. Bianca bites her lip before answering. "Well, we went to the top of Penn last night. I guess the cops got wind of it and ended up busting the party." In our hometown, Monroeville, there wasn't much in the way of after-hours entertainment. A few years ago, a group of seniors designated the woods behind Pennsylvania Street as the place to party whenever there wasn't a house party. For the most part, the cops avoided the area since it was tucked away on the near outskirts of town, but every so often, they would get a tip-off and would raid the woods at the height of the party.

"Oh? And what happened?"

Sera scoffs and jabs her thumb toward Bianca. "This idiot fell while trying to jump over a cooler of beer. I couldn't leave her, so I tried to pull her up, but she twisted her ankle during her fall." Shaking her head, she sneers. "We had to wait for the cops to come get us so that they could pick her up and bring her home. I couldn't carry her to the car because on top of twisting her ankle, she was drunk and was as floppy as overcooked tagliatelle."

I tuck my lips under my teeth, containing my laughter as she continues documenting their ordeal. "Mom and Dad nearly had a heart attack when the police cars rolled up, sirens on because the cops in this town are a bunch of dildos. Anyway, we're grounded for a month and are going to a convent upon our graduation."

"I truly have no words," I laugh. For as refined and accomplished as my parents are, all of their daughters are messes. They got lucky with Rafael, who rarely parties and is in an intimate relationship with soccer. But their daughters? Disasters, every one of us.

"Okay, so we told you about my mishap," Bianca complains. "Now tell us about your life so far. You were so cagey at dinner, and we know you held back because of Daddy."

"There's not much to tell. C and I went to one party so far and made a new friend, Serena. You'd love her. She's like a prodigy and is an eighteen-year-old junior because she's so brilliant." I tell them about the prostitution ring that is Alpha Nu and all about Serena's family drama, trying to divert them from asking any more questions.

"Did you meet any guys?" My mind immediately conjures up visions of Greyson in his tight black shirt. "Uh, you could say that," I reply, looking away from my phone screen.

After a moment of silence, I look back to my sisters and expectant looks adorn their faces. I sigh. "CeCe and I met these guys at the party. They were both good-looking, but I doubt we'll ever see them again. They didn't ask for our numbers."

"Damn, that sucks. What are the guys like there?"

"They're men." It's true. Except for the guys from the STD table, every guy I've met so far is more man than a boy: mature, confident, and self-assured. It's unnerving. Both of my sisters groan, commenting on how jealous they are that I get to meet guys outside of the little town where we grew up. I look at Sera and raise an eyebrow.

"How's that dickhole, Mitchell, doing?"

Sera mumbles something that sounds suspiciously like they broke up. "I'm sorry, what? I can't hear you."

She clears her throat and sits up straighter. "We broke up."

"It's about fucking time. Thank God," I nearly shout. "Is it for now or for good?" Behind my back, I cross my fingers, praying that it's for good.

"Oh, it better be for good," Bianca scoffs. "Sera, tell Aves why you broke up with that fuck boy. Go on, I'm dying to see her reaction."

She sighs, rolling her eyes before explaining, "I refused to have anal sex with him. Which isn't a new conversation since he asks me at least once a week to do it." She turns to glare at Bianca. "The reason why we broke up this time is that someone—she tilts her head at our youngest sister, clearly talking about her—"overheard the conversation, called him an anal invader, and proceeded to tell the entire school that he got denied from, and I quote, 'fucking me up the ass.'"

Damn. "For what it's worth, I always thought it was weird that he was desperate for anal sex but refused to have actual sex. The purity ring he gave you was creepy and should be thrown into a fire pit." It never sat well with me that he wanted Sera to be both the virgin and the whore, the Madonna and the Jezebel. His obsession with Sera's body was uncomfortable, and though he swore to her that he wouldn't have sex with her until their wedding night, he was constantly pressuring her to conform to his rules.

He couldn't go down on her because he would risk "popping her cherry" with his stubby little tongue, but blow jobs for him were fair game. Fingering her was absolutely off the table, but he could fuck her boobs as often as he liked. He claimed he did this in the name of "religion," but it became obvious early on that he wanted to control Sera as much as possible, especially since he wasn't a virgin. Did I want to know this information about my sister's weird sex life? No, but she frequently vented her frustrations to me, Bianca, and CeCe.

At seventeen, almost eighteen years old, Sera had experienced doing everything for a guy but had never experienced reciprocation. He'd used her, time and time again, as a vehicle for his pleasure, a vessel for his selfish use. I'm relieved that they're done, and I don't blame Bianca for embarrassing Sera. This rumor ensures that Mitchell will leave my baby sister alone, once and for fucking all.

"I gave him back that disgusting piece of jewelry. I hate jewelry to begin with, so wearing that diamond that was surrounded by the thorns of Jesus's crown was just too much." I forgot that he had that ring custom-made to resemble the crown of thorns Jesus wore to his crucifixion. I'm still not entirely sure which religion he is, but he's aggressively pious for a seventeen-year-old guy that's obsessed with fucking someone up the ass.

"I suggested that we throw all the shit he gave her over the steps of his parents' mansion, but she vetoed that," Bianca complains. "Pussy," she adds helpfully.

"B, I told you to just drop it. I'm going to put everything in a box and give it to him after school. I just want to be done with this relationship and move on. I spent far too long being his little housewife-in-training."

We spend the next fifteen minutes talking about their visit to West Helm for my nineteenth birthday and Sera and Rafe's eighteenth birthday. My parents didn't believe in contraception in the early years of their marriage so all of us were born one year apart. Though my parents won't allow Bianca to stay unsupervised, probably because she's the wildest of the Gregori children, Sera and Rafe are spending a weekend here after our family dinner to celebrate.

"It's an injustice that I'm not allowed to stay up. First and foremost, I don't look like I'm sixteen. Additionally, I will be seventeen in three months, and in summation, this is a load of ageist bullshit." It's no surprise that Bianca is planning on being a lawyer. She studied my parents' behavior from the time she could distinguish between colors and emulated it from a young age. Her poor teachers must hate having her argumentative ass in their classes.

74

"God, I miss you guys. I can't wait to see you in a couple of weeks."

"We miss you, too. Mom's calling us to set the table for dinner, so we need to go. Have an amazing first day of classes tomorrow. We love you, asshole Ava." I laugh at their nickname for me, say goodbye, and leave them with instructions to hug and kiss Mom and Dad for me. A wave of homesickness envelops me; reminders of Sunday dinner, my little side garden, and the comforts of home make it hard to breathe for a moment. I'm excited about school, about finding myself and having the freedom of an adult, but at this moment, I yearn for the simplicity of home.

Caught up in my memories of home, I startle when my phone starts vibrating in my hand, signaling a text message. I glance down at the unknown number that pops up on my screen and quickly swipe to open the message.

Unknown: Hey, vixen, how are you?

Holy fucking shit. I nearly drop my phone in shock. The only person that has ever called me a vixen is the Viking god from three nights ago. Do I tell him that I know it's him? Do I play it cool and pretend that I have no idea who is texting me? Also, how the hell did he get my number because I don't remember giving it to him? Fucking of course when something this monumental happens, I'm by myself with no one to help me.

After writing and rewriting a message more than ten times, I settle on playing dumb.

Ava: Who is this?

Unknown: Come on, vixen, don't tell me you don't remember me.

Ava: Greyson?

Greyson: That's right, beautiful. How are you?

I think I'm having a heart attack, judging by the rapid beat of my pulse. Sure,

I've been called beautiful before, but there's something about this man that makes me almost light-headed.

Ava: I'm well. How are you? How did you get my number?

Greyson: I have my ways, vixen. And I'm good, just thinking about you. How is your knee? You fell pretty hard on Thursday.

I'm not sure if I should be mortified that he wants to recap one of the most embarrassing nights of my life or pleased that he remembers me well enough to hunt for my number and ask about me post-fall.

Ava: I'm good, thanks for checking in on me. You can check off that you did your civic duty for the week now.

Greyson: Good. I won't comment on your civic duty bullshit. When can I see you again?

My heart stills. He wants to see me again?

Ava: You want to see me again? I figured that you'd be running in the opposite direction after I called you Ted Bundy and fell on my ass.

Greyson: If I remember correctly, you compared me to Ted Bundy, you didn't call me Ted Bundy. Are you free later? My roommates and I are having a barbecue with some of our friends tonight. Bring your pit bull.

I laugh out loud. I forgot to tell CeCe that he called her a pit bull. I bite my lip, contemplating a response. I'm in the middle of freaking out over what to respond when CeCe finally comes back to our dorm, sweaty and red-faced from her run.

"Aves, do you want to try that Thai place off Main Street for dinner tonight? I ran by it and it looked good—"

"C, he fucking texted me," I interrupt. She stares back at me in confusion. "Who texted you?"

I groan. "Greyson, from the party. The Viking Adonis god. He invited us to his house later for a barbecue." Her eyes widen in response.

"Oh shit. What did you say?"

"I haven't responded yet. I've been freaking out in silence for the last fifteen minutes. He probably thinks I'm ghosting him, like that would ever happen. Ugh," I groan. "C, what if he's inviting us because he thinks that I'm an easy conquest? I don't think I could handle that kind of embarrassment."

"Aves, why would he think that about you? You're a virgin; you don't exactly scream 'experience' when looking at you."

"Ugh. I don't know! Why would he text me? Why would he invite us?"

"Well, you're beautiful and fun, especially when you're not being neurotic by overthinking everything. A guy can text you because he's interested in getting to know you better and seeing if you have a connection."

I start to open my mouth to question her when she cuts me off and points a finger in my direction. "If you give me any of that self-deprecating humor right now, I'll shave your eyebrows off in your sleep. Do you want to go to his house tonight?"

"Dante will be there. Would you be okay with that?"

I get an eye roll in response. "Aves, answer my question."

I hesitate before replying. "I-I want to see him again."

"Okay, we're going. Text him back and ask for the details."

—

Grey:

Ava: I spoke with Celeste, we're in. Would you mind if we brought our friend, Serena? What time should we be there? And do you need us to pick up anything?

My hand tightens around my phone; pleasure from Ava's easy acceptance of my invitation courses through my veins. On Thursday night, it was easy to tell that she was stubborn by nature, so her agreement comes as a surprise.

I quickly shoot off our address and the time they should be here. Though I tell her not to bring anything, I have the feeling that Ava is a good girl, the kind of girl that brings something with her when she's invited to someone's house and helps clean before leaving for the night. She's sweet, too sweet for a guy like me, but I want a taste.

I already know that a taste won't be enough for me; I'll want to consume her, devour her until she's part of me.

I walk out of my room, calling the guys to meet me in the kitchen to discuss the additions to our guest list. I hear my roommates before I see them, stomping like a herd of rhinos before appearing in the kitchen. Talking about some bullshit drama happening at the fraternity house over a girl and two of the brothers, I have to wait nearly five minutes before they turn their attention to me.

"And here I was, Dante, thinking that you'd want to know that your little redhead is coming to the barbecue later." I shrug my shoulders, being an asshole just for the hell of it. "I'll just let Ava know that she shouldn't bring the pit bull tonight."

"Don't you fucking dare, bro." Dante turns to face me fully, his prior conversation forgotten about at the mention of Celeste. "She's coming, for real?" I nod in response, and you'd think he just won the fucking lottery. His face breaks into a huge grin and he pumps his fist into the air. "Fuck yeah. She was so fucking hot playing Mario Kart. I need to make sure the console is set up for her. I swear to God, I popped a chub when she started to shit-talk like a guy."

"Spare me the details. I don't need to hear about your weird-ass kink again."

"Did you invite any girls for me, or are you two going to be selfish pricks?" Linc complains like a little bitch.

"She's bringing another girl, Serena." If it's who I think it is, I'm pretty sure she has some weird shit going on with Devin or Dylan. Or maybe it's Devin and Dylan? I've met her a few times over the last two years, but she was an underage genius and I'm not a creep.

"Fuck, that's the girl Devin and Dyl have been fighting about. I'm not touching that shit with a ten-foot pole, doesn't matter how smart or hot she is." Lincoln glares at both of us. "Just so you know, fuck you both for not hooking me up. If I'm no longer needed here, I'm going to the store to grab the buns, because someone"—he points at Dante—"is a fucking moron and grabbed moldy bread because it was half-priced."

"What? We're college students and I was trying to save money."

I look at him in disbelief. "You don't pay rent and your family is rich as fuck. Get the fuck out of here with that shit." More than likely, he couldn't find the bread aisle and picked up the discounted buns because they were right in front of him. Lazy, lying shit.

"Whatever. Linc, can you pick up a box of rubbers? I need to stock up for Red."

Linc and I look at each other before barking out our laughter. "D, she told you to suck your dick. There's no way you're getting into her pants."

He flips us both off. "You didn't see how she reacted to me when you went outside with her curvy friend. She's fucking into me, I know it."

"Want to bet on that?" Linc throws out. I groan. Linc has an obsession with winning, more so than any other person I've ever met. He tosses out bets like they're candy, just for the small high he gets from winning. They're normally harmless, but they're typically annoying as fuck.

"Absolutely not."

"What are the stakes?" Dante responds at the same time.

I look at Dante. Is he stupid? I barely know the girl, but it seems as though she'd cut his balls off if she found out she was the center of a bet. "D, are you dumb?"

He looks at me and smirks. "No, but I'm fucking marrying that girl one day, so there's no way in hell I'm losing this bet. What are we betting for?"

Linc raises his eyebrow. "You just met her. You're acting like that guy from the Netflix show that kills everyone and is obsessed with that baker chick."

"When you know, you know. She'll be mine one day, with a ring on her finger and my baby in her stomach. Don't doubt that. Now, what's the bet?"

Linc pauses, seemingly weighing the seriousness of Dante's conviction over a girl he met once. His face suddenly lights up, and if I were Dante, I'd be scared by the look in his eyes. "Okay, you ugly fuck. If you fuck her this semester, I'll give you my Camaro." Oh shit, he has no faith in Dante that he'll succeed with Celeste. Linc's prized possession, his restored 1969 Chevy Camaro ZL-1, is worth over half a million dollars. Linc's modeled since he was a kid and bought that car on his eighteenth birthday. It's his baby, and there's no fucking way he'd bet it if he thought Dante would win this dumb ass bet.

"And, if you lose," Linc continues, pausing for dramatic effect. "You give me Francesca's number and tell her to give me a shot."

Dante looks at him in confusion. "You know my sister is a lesbian, right? And happily married. Why would she want to date you?"

"You're dense. I want her to hire me in her restaurant."

Dante shakes his head and looks at him in pity. "Never going to happen, doesn't matter if I win or lose. You know how she is, only the best can step foot in her kitchens." Dante's sister, Francesca, or Franki, owns some of the most exclusive restaurants in New York, Aspen, and Los Angeles. Linc's been trying to get a job in her kitchen since he turned eighteen. She's turned him down every single time.

"If I win this bet, you're going to make it fucking happen. You'll babysit her cats for the next six years if that's what it takes. Do we have a deal?" He holds out his hand to shake on it. Dante laughs at him, grabbing his hand and shaking it twice.

"Deal, pretty boy. I can't wait to take my new car for a spin with my girl."

Ava

The women of my family always told me to never show up empty-handed. I use that as my excuse for making over one hundred homemade cannoli for a college barbecue. It was like the ghost of my dead grandmother possessed me, forcing me to make the most stereotypical Italian dessert for the most attractive man I have ever seen.

Hyperbole? Maybe, but that didn't make it any less true. I'm just lucky Serena has a full-service kitchen and had no problem letting me use it.

CeCe, Serena, and I step out of the Uber we ordered at Serena's apartment, and my hands sweat holding the tray of dessert. I bite my bottom lip, contemplating whether or not I should toss this tray into the bushes. God, why couldn't I have a fake ID like a normal eighteen-year-old and just bring a bottle of cheap vodka? I had to go full-blown "nonna." I'm going to scare him off with this gesture, it's too intense.

Fucking, fuck, fuck.

"Guys, I think I should just leave these cannoli out here. Is it weird that I brought them?"

"Are you nuts?" "No, bring them," CeCe and Serena say at the same time, somewhat calming my nerves.

"Aves." CeCe steps in front of me, blocking my view of the house. "If he can't appreciate that you just spent three hours making something for him to enjoy, then he's not worth your time." She grabs my shoulders, squeezing them in support. "Calm down, don't create scenarios in your head. We haven't even walked inside yet."

"Agreed," Serena chimes in. "Most girls our age have no idea how to navigate a kitchen, let alone do what you did in such a short amount of time. Don't be embarrassed, you're badass."

I offer a smile to my friends, grateful for their encouragement before walking into the unknown. "Thanks, guys. I'm sorry I'm so neurotic. I've never been invited to something like this, and I don't want to come across as too intense." From what I saw on Thursday, Greyson was close to perfect and the last thing I want to do is call attention to my quirks. But CeCe and Serena are right, I need to calm down. I let out a breath I didn't know I was holding and walk around CeCe, heading to the front door.

"Come on, let's get this over with." I raise my hand and knock on the front door. Almost instantly, it opens with the tall model of their group on the other side.

"Ladies, welcome. Grey told us you were coming. We're all out back." He ushers us inside, closing the door behind us. "I'm Lincoln," he says and turns toward Serena. "Dylan just got here." My friend offers a blush and a small smile in response.

"You"—Lincoln points to CeCe—"must be Celeste. Dante won't shut the fuck up about you." He smirks, turning his finger to me. "And you must be Ava. Grey won't shut the fuck up about you either." I raise my eyebrows, surprised that we've been the topic of conversation.

"Didn't your mama teach you not to point? It's rude," C starts in on him, living up to Greyson's nickname for her. "But I'm just happy he told you my real name and not Red. And if you even think about calling me Red, I'll cut your dick off. Got it?"

"Easy, killer." Lincoln lets out a laugh. "God, it's going to be so much fun watching D get his balls handed to him. Promise that you'll film it?"

I clear my throat, eager to move the conversation away from Dante's dick and balls. It seems as though every time he's brought up, CeCe brings up his male anatomy. If she thinks she's fooling me with the tough girl act, she's sorely mistaken. She confirmed she was interested in him when she didn't balk about coming here today, knowing that he lives here and would surely be present.

"Uhm, I brought cannoli." I thrust the tray to Lincoln, interrupting his laughter. "They need to be refrigerated if you have space."

He eyes me closer, a critical gleam entering his eye. "Where did you buy these? Vita Bella?"

"No. I made them." His brows raise. I continue, "My grandma always said, 'Never show up empty handed,' so I made a few batches at Serena's after Greyson invited us. I probably should have waited to fill the shells before they were ready to be eaten, but I thought it would be weird if I came with my pastry bag to a virtual stranger's house."

Lincoln keeps staring at me, and I wonder if I need to fill the silence with more ramblings. Just as I'm about to offer more unnecessary information, he removes the tinfoil covering the tray, grabs a cannolo, and bites into it. The moan he lets out makes me smile. "Good?" I ask.

"Fuck, these are amazing." He shoves the rest of the pastry into his mouth. "How did you make these? Did you strain the ricotta before adding in the sugar?"

I'm surprised by the question; not many people know the nuances of baking without looking them up online or in a recipe book. "I did. The secret is the pastry shell, though. I use lard instead of butter in the mixture. But don't tell anyone; my mother would disown me if she knew I shared her little hack."

"No shit?"

"You should try her lemon drop cookies. Insane," CeCe adds.

"Thanks, C. Anyway, I'm glad you like them."

"They're fucking good. I'm keeping half of these to myself. Fuck those guys." Serena, CeCe, and I laugh and follow Lincoln further into the house. From the outside of this house, you'd think an established family would live here, not a group of college guys. Inside, the decor is masculine but inviting, almost like a Restoration Hardware catalog. This is not a typical bachelor pad, but a home away from home for the guys living in this house.

We walk into the kitchen and my mouth drops. "Wow," I can't help but comment. Lincoln looks over his shoulder, nodding in understanding.

"I know. When Grey's dad bought this place, he renovated the kitchen into this masterpiece." I take in the solid natural wood cabinets wrapping around the perimeter of the kitchen, the gleaming white marble countertops, and the modern finishes. In the left corner, a glass barn door hides, what I assume, is a killer pantry. The sleek, stainless-steel appliances are so shiny that they look like they're rarely, if ever, used.

The true star of this kitchen, though, is the double islands in the center of the space—one for cooking and preparation, the other for dining and entertaining. My fingers flex, dying to touch every visible surface and create magic in this beautiful space.

"Are you sure you guys live here? This looks like my dream kitchen." The words barely leave my mouth when a loud crash is heard from outside followed by yelling.

"Goddamn morons," Lincoln mutters under his breath. "I need to get out there before they kill themselves."

Lincoln excuses himself, walking out the back door with instructions for us to make our way outside when we're ready.

"So," I start. "He seemed weirdly nice. I thought he'd be a dick since he's so pretty." Pretty didn't accurately describe him; he looked like a walking underwear advertisement, photoshop and all.

Serena shrugs. "He's always been nice when I've interacted with him. Let's get outside. I need to speak with Dylan."

"Lead the way, bitch."

—

The nerves that dissipated while speaking with Lincoln about pastries return in full force when we step outside. The crowd isn't large, and it's easy to see that everyone here is comfortable with each other based on the casual vibes. Spread out throughout the yard, a foursome plays corn hole while a group of six seems deeply invested in a game of flip-cup. I catch sight of Greyson by the grill, looking like a sexy pit master, and my stomach flutters in anticipation. Though he's in the middle of a conversation with a statuesque blonde, the moment he catches sight of me, he starts in my direction.

His longer blonde hair is loose around his shoulders, looking every bit the Viking I imagine him being. He looks like barely contained movement, a tornado in pause. He quickly eats up the space between us with his long, quick strides.

"Vixen, you made it." He grabs me, pulling me into a brief hug. I'm too stunned to react and leave my arms hanging at my sides. He releases me from his embrace and turns to greet CeCe and Serena. "Hey, ladies." Refocusing his attention on me, he asks, "What can I get you to drink? We have cans of hard seltzer and beer. If you want something harder, we have vodka and tequila inside."

"Hard seltzer works, thanks. We can grab them; just point us in the right direction," CeCe responds for us. We drank hard seltzers at Serena's, so sticking with the same drink is probably for the best, though I wouldn't mind a cold beer right now. Greyson nods, walks to a cooler, and returns with three cans.

"Here, I'm not sure what flavors we have, but they're all sweet as fuck." I reach out, my fingers skimming Greyson's as I take the offered drinks. I suck in a breath at the contact, warmth and tingles spread through me, like a zap of electricity. I hesitate, savoring the feel of his skin, remembering how his hands caressed my thighs just a few days ago. I look up to find Greyson's gaze on me. His blue eyes are cloudy and boring into me, communicating so many things without words. I pull my hand back, cradling the cold can in my still-tingling hand.

"Make sure you don't accept drinks from anyone except me, Dante, or Lincoln." I startle, surprised by the warning.

"Okay, but aren't these people your friends? Why would we have anything to worry about?"

He steps closer to me, leaning down to whisper in my ear. "Humor me, vixen. I won't allow anything to happen to you, but I need to make sure you're safe. Now, be a good girl and say, 'Yes, Grey.'"

"Y-yes, Grey," I stammer.

"Fuck," he groans into my ear. "I like how my name sounds in your sweet voice." His breath is hot on my neck, causing goosebumps to break out on my skin. I breathe in, inhaling the scent of pine and leather that surrounds him, and shiver on my exhale. I'm close to orgasm just from his smell; part of me is mortified while the other part wants to keep sniffing him. I take a sip of my drink, looking toward my friends as I swallow. CeCe and Serena eye us, and I do not doubt that I'm going to be interrogated as soon as Greyson—Grey—walks away.

"Celeste, Dante set up a gaming console for you inside. I'm pretty sure he's had fantasies of you beating his ass, so steer clear if that's not your thing."

"Do you mean beating his ass in Mario Kart?" I question.

He smirks. "Same thing."

Oh, wow. Okay, then.

I look toward CeCe and find her staring at the group playing flip cup, where Dante holds court in the center of the table. Her face is blank, and for once, I can't read her emotion. Dante must feel our eyes on him because he looks up and his face splits into the goofiest grin I've ever seen. For being well over six feet and covered in tattoos, he looks like a boy on Christmas morning who just got the toy he's wanted all year. He runs over to us, nearly sprinting across the yard.

"Red, you're here. Fuck, you look good," Dante pants, though I'm not sure if it's from his run or proximity to CeCe.

"Stop calling me Red." CeCe scowls and then mutters a quiet, "Thanks." She says it so low, I'm not sure we were supposed to hear it. Unfortunately for her, Dante did hear her gratitude and responds, "Anytime, beautiful. You're an English major, right? There are a few people I want you to meet. Come with me?" He says the last part as a question, clearly uncertain if she'll accept his offer. After a tense silence, where Grey, Serena, and I stare between the two of them, CeCe nods her head before looking in my direction.

"If I'm not back in thirty minutes, tell my parents I've been kidnapped by a psycho from New Jersey."

I roll my eyes in response. "I'm sure you'll be fine."

Dante tugs on her arm, sliding his hand down until he captures her fingers with his own. His move is possessive, and I see quite a few pairs of eyes on them, mainly of the female variety, and none look happy. He tugs her hand, giving her no choice but to follow him toward the patio where a group has gathered.

"I see Dyl over there." Serena points to the table Dante came from, where six guys continue playing flip cup. "I'm going to go talk to him. I'll see you in a bit." Serena strides over confidently, approaching a tall guy in the center of the group. He wraps his arms around her, holding her to his chest while his head dips down to kiss her head. I look at Grey, who's been silent since Dante approached. His eyes are on me.

"Well," I begin, "this has been an eventful ten minutes. It seems I've been abandoned."

Grey smirks. "Vixen, I'm still here, and I'm not going anywhere." He brings his bottle of beer to his lips, taking a deep pull, all the while his eyes remain on me. His eyes darken, desire swimming through the blue depths. His tongue runs along his bottom lip, licking up droplets from his beer, and I imagine his tongue on me, in me. I've never had anyone lick me before, and truthfully, I've never really thought I'd want someone to lick my body; it would give them uncensored access to every dip and crevice and mark on my skin. But something about Grey is different. His attraction to me is tangible, a heavy fog that descends when he's next to me. Though I don't know him well, and I still doubt his motives, I can't deny that he's interested in me physically. I felt his dick harden when I sat on his lap at the party, and the comments he's made have been charged with so much sexual frustration. I feel my nipples harden against my thin bra, and I inwardly groan, almost positive that Grey can see the evidence of my own attraction. I move my gaze from his mouth back to his eyes; that need is still there, even more prominent if that's possible.

He wraps his hand around my hard seltzer, removing it from my grasp, and places it, along with his beer, on a table close by.

"You looking at me like that is dangerous, vixen."

"How am I looking at you?" Heat swarms my face and I look away. I'm almost positive that I'm as red as CeCe's hair right now.

Hands ghost over my waist, trailing upward until his hands capture my neck and tilt my head back. He leans forward, grazing his lips over the shell of my ear before whispering, "Like you want me to worship you on my knees." I suck in a breath; his pine and leather cologne fills my lungs as a throbbing between my legs consumes my focus. His teeth clamp down on my earlobe, stinging before he soothes me with gentle flicks of his tongue.

"I-I—what are you doing?" I stutter, closing my eyes as he continues playing with my ear. He sucks me into his mouth, nibbling on me like I'm a treat he can't wait to eat.

"Come with me," he whispers into my ear, lifting his head to look me in the eyes. I feel like the only answer is "yes."

—

It's not lost on me that this is my second interaction with Grey and the second time he's successfully gotten me alone. If I were in a horror movie, there's no doubt I would be the first one dead—or the girl that runs into the attic when the killer is in the basement.

I follow Grey into the house, where we bypass the hellos that assault him as we make our way inside. I take in the kitchen again, sighing in appreciation as I trail my hand over the counter when we cut through it. "This kitchen is stunning," I tell him. Because three college guys should not have this kitchen in their home, even if Lincoln seems to know his way around food. It's like an oxymoron; it just shouldn't be a thing.

"You can use it anytime you'd like. Lincoln is the only one that uses it and he's territorial," he offers. "Something tells me that he wouldn't mind sharing the space with you, though. He sent us a text about your pastries. Told us they were fucking delicious."

I blush, absorbing his offer and his compliment. "Thank you, Grey." His eyes narrow at my use of his shortened name, and he increases our pace, leading me down a wide hallway off the kitchen. He opens the door at the end of the hallway, pulls me inside, and closes the door behind me.

"Is this your—" I'm cut off when his hands push me against the door, his arms on either side of my head, caging me in.

"Vixen, I need to taste that sweet mouth. It's all I can fucking think about." I swallow, my audible gulp lost in the heavy breaths coming from Grey's mouth.

He shifts his face forward, his lips inches from mine. His breath smells tart from the beer and minty, a mixture that shouldn't be potent but is. I look from his eyes to his lips, unsure where my attention should rest. His arms flex beside my head, hinting at the control he's exerting at this moment. He's not touching me, but I feel him everywhere.

"Tell me, vixen." He's so close that, when he speaks, I feel his lips move against mine. Teasing me before he retreats, waiting for me to tell him something, but I'm not entirely sure what. He reads the confusion in my gaze. "Tell me I can kiss you. Tell me I can touch you," he growls, sending shivers down my spine. "Say, 'Yes, Grey.'"

"Yes, Grey," I respond. There's no hesitation. I need him as much as I want him; my body feels like an inferno that only he can extinguish.

"Good fucking girl," he rasps before launching himself at me. His lips take mine in a desperate kiss like I'm water and he's a man parched. His lips are firm and confident as they mold against mine before coaxing my lips open to massage my tongue. I gasp, and he takes advantage of the widening of my mouth, licking his tongue in and possessing me with this kiss. I submit to him fully, letting him lead me wherever he wants to go, like I'm a disciple and he's my God. His teeth pull on my bottom lip, nipping me and making me moan from the erotic mix of pleasure and pain. He sucks on the bite, lathering it with attention before diving back into my mouth.

His hands move from the door, one to the back of my head and the other to my waist. He starts to pull back, but I follow his lips, refusing to let his mouth go. He nips my bottom lip and pulls my hair, forcing me to break the kiss and look into his eyes. The hand at my waist flexes, pulling my body into his. He's hard everywhere, from the muscles of his arms to the fingers biting at my waist. He presses his hips forward, and my breath hitches at the hardness pressing against my stomach.

"My greedy, sweet Ava," he murmurs against my lips, pulling my head back to give him access to my neck. He licks me, tasting my skin with deceptive gentleness. "Do you feel how fucking hard you make me?" He grinds his hips against me, emphasizing how turned on he is right now. "I'm about to come in my boxers like a goddamn kid, vixen." His lips descend, latching onto my pulse and sucking until I'm panting beneath him. His tongue and hands are everywhere, burning into me and branding me as his. The hand at my waist moves to my ass and he squeezes; our moans mix in the silence of the room.

"Grey, please. I need more." He stops the ministrations at my throat, straightening to his full height. Maybe I should hide how needy I feel, play coy or aloof, and not like I'm in heat. But I can't.

"Tell me what you need, baby."

"I-I don't know. I just need more. I need you."

"Tell me, vixen. Has anyone ever touched your pretty pussy before?" I open my mouth, wondering if I should lie to him and claim experience that I don't have. I'm not sure how he'll feel about me if he realizes that the most I have ever done was make out. He does not need to know that I had to Google "How to Make Out" when I was sixteen because I still couldn't understand the logistics.

Fuck it. If he doesn't want me after learning I'm an inexperienced virgin, then it's his loss.

"No, just me." I blush, ducking my head in embarrassment.

"Fuck," he breathes out, tilting my chin back up to look me in the eyes. If possible, his dick grows harder against my stomach from my admission.

"Vixen, do you have any idea how hot it is that you're my untouched little good girl?" His fingers pinch my chin, popping my mouth open. "My wet dream, brought to life. I can't wait to dirty you up, just for me." I'm a panting mess, between his words, his mouth, and the hands that alternate between squeezing and caressing, I'm ready to hump his jean-clad leg just to feel release from the pressure building inside me.

"When you touch yourself, how many fingers do you put in your pussy? How many until you're dripping down your hand?"

"Just one. I l-like playing with my clit." He picks me up, turns to his king-sized bed, and deposits me in the center.

"Fuck," he groans, dipping his head into the crook of my neck. He steps away from the bed, leaving me a panting mess.

"W-what?" I stammer.

"Fucking hell, vixen. We need to stop." His voice comes out strained, like it's taking Herculean effort to mutter those words. "If I get my hands on you, I'm going to fuck you and you're not ready for that."

I raise my eyebrows. "I-I," I pause, collecting my thoughts. Clearing my throat, I continue, "So you're going to work me up just to leave me on the edge?"

"I don't fucking trust myself to touch you right now. But," he gives me a lingering look, "you could show me."

I let out a nervous laugh, positive that I imagined he just asked me to masturbate in front of him.

"I said, 'Show me.'" He quirks an eyebrow, begging me to challenge him.

"Why do you want to see that?" I ask. His expression turns fierce, and he takes a seat in the armchair across the room.

"Why do I want to see you play with your wet, tight pussy? Because, vixen, I need to know what you like and how you like it. I need to know that I'm the only man that will see you this way, the only man that you can pleasure yourself in front of." He leans forward, running a hand down his face. "I need to see you fuck yourself because it's all I've thought about since Thursday night, and I need the memory of your hands spreading your cunt wide open for me like I need to fucking breathe." He takes a deep breath and leans back in the chair. "Now, are you going to be a good girl and do as I ask, or are we going to end this fantasy here?"

My mouth hangs open as I stare at him, wide-eyed and a little breathless. His words, so deliciously dirty, spur me into action. I thank God that I'm not wearing any shapewear today, not that I could have predicted this moment. I should probably take off my pants slowly, seductively, but I'm too turned on to drag this moment out. I rush through undressing the lower half and pause, looking at Grey for guidance.

"Take your shirt off, too."

I hesitate; the room is bright and every large inch of me will be on display. "I'd rather leave it on."

"And I'd rather see all of your perfect skin, vixen. I'm dying to see all of you. Please." I weigh his words. From his angle on the chair, he'll see everything I have to offer. Playing with the hem of my shirt, I consider his words and actions; he's been forthcoming in how much he likes my body in my clothes, but would it disgust him to see every curve and mark outside of the confines of my clothes? If he is disgusted, wouldn't it be better for me to learn that now before we become intimate, and I become emotionally invested? I nod my head, my resolve firm.

I pull my shirt over my head and lean forward to unhook the back clasp of my bra before dragging the straps down my arms.

He wants to see me? Well, here I am.

I draw in a breath, stealing myself for the possibility of Grey's disappointment. When I look at Grey, disappointment and disgust seem to be the very last things on his mind. Gripping the arms of his chair, it's like he's physically restraining himself from coming to me. Another rush of desire runs through me, and for the first time, I feel like the vixen he claims I am.

"Do you have any idea how fucking sexy you are?" he grits out. "Fucking Jesus, your body should be illegal."

I smile, and I don't even try to hide it from him. "Grey, tell me what to do. Tell me what you like."

"No, vixen. Show me what *you* like."

Greyson

She sucks in a breath, not expecting my demand to show me what she likes. Even if tonight ends with her putting her clothes back on and telling me to fuck off, this was still the most intense sexual experience I've ever had. Yes, my dick may be uncomfortably hard, and I'll need to jack off when she leaves, but her scent hangs in the room. Her long, curly brown hair is splayed on my pillow while her body lays on my sheets. Her scent is going to linger long after she's gone. I'm not even sorry to admit that I won't be washing my sheets any time soon; her lemony scent makes my dick hard and sleeping on those sheets each night, her scent wrapped around me?

That sounds like fucking heaven.

"...tell me what you like." I catch the tail end of her statement, too busy admiring her curvy body on full display.

My sweet, naive vixen. Doesn't she understand that her naked and on display for me is the height of my desire? She could ask to play goddamn Scrabble right now, and I would gladly comply with a raging hard-on.

"No, vixen. Show me what *you* like."

Her eyes widen, caught by surprise again. She sucks her bottom lip into her mouth; the same lip I bit raw against my door. Her delicate hand moves between her thighs, lightly stroking her pussy in timid little passes. She can do better than that.

"Vixen, did you fuck yourself the night we met?"

She hesitates before offering a whispered, "Yes."

That's fucking right she did. "Tell me, what did you think about?"

"You," she offers immediately. I grow harder in my jeans at the knowledge that she played with her pussy with me in mind.

"And what did you imagine me doing to you?"

"I imagined you on your knees, licking me, playing with me. I—," she pauses, swallowing audibly. "I imagined riding your face until I came all over it." She doesn't realize it, but her hand moves against her cunt faster, the intent clear: a messy orgasm.

"After I licked you clean, what would I do?" She slips a finger inside her swollen pussy, pushing it in and out at a slow, measured pace.

"You'd stand up, demanding I returned the favor." I groan. Her on her knees, sucking my cock, was the scenario I used to jerk off last night. I'm beyond pleased that her mind had the same thought.

"Vixen, eating your tight cunt is my reward. I wouldn't expect you to suck my dick."

"I–I wanted to." Fuck me. I palm my cock through my jeans, nearly positive I'm going to come in my jeans from her fantasy.

"How would you take my cock?" She slips another finger inside, moving her fingers in and out faster, the heel of her palm grinding against her clit on each pass. Her eyes close as she chases her pleasure.

"I've never given a blow job before, but I'd let you tell me what you like. I just want to please you." That's fucking enough. She can't look like this and say these things and expect me not to devour her. I have no patience when it comes to this woman.

"Fucking Christ, Ava." I get up from my chair and quickly cross the room to her. She's even more stunning up close. My eyes feast on her, and my mouth waters as her tits lay heavy on her chest. Her large nipples are so pale, they're almost the same color as her skin. Her body is flushed from her arousal, making her hair seem darker and richer against my pillow. Her pussy is bare and on full display, dripping on my comforter. I'm not washing that.

She's lost in the moment, unaware that I'm next to her until I lay my hand on top of hers, guiding her movements. She startles, whipping her head to stare at me. Fuck not touching her. I need a taste, otherwise, I'm going to go fucking insane. "Let me help you, vixen." I lean down, capturing her plump bottom lip in my mouth. I bite into her mouth, tasting her need with the warring of her tongue against mine. I pull back, waiting for her response.

"God, yes. Please, Grey." I move my hand against the one in her pussy, increasing the speed of her fingers pushing in and out of her wet heat. She starts to struggle against me, and I remove my hand, looking at her for her consent. "Grey, I need more. My fingers aren't enough. I need you."

"That's right, baby. You need me." I push her hand aside and use my middle finger to circle her clit, coating her cunt in her wetness. "Fuck, you're soaked. Is this for me?"

Ava lets out a moan, pushing her hips into my hand, trying to find release. "You're such a greedy girl." I lean down, sucking a nipple into my mouth. Her body arches, twisting into me. I suck harder, alternating between biting her and soothing the pain with my tongue. I wait until she's thrusting her hips up, and then I slide one thick finger through her slit, spearing her to my third knuckle. My fingers are bigger than hers and the walls of her pussy are tight, fluttering around me as she adjusts to the size.

I shift my attention to her other breast, worshiping her as I finger her.

"You're so tight, baby. I can't wait to feel you around my cock." Her breathing grows heavier, her body more restless as I pay equal homage to her tits and her pussy. "Baby, I'm going to add another finger. It's going to sting, but I need you to breathe for me."

I slip another finger in, the snug fit of her forcing me to insert it slowly. She cries out, cursing at the fullness. "That's right, baby. You're doing so good, taking my fingers like a fucking champ." I sink my fingers in deeper, grinding the heel of my hand against her to heighten the pressure. "Good girl, fuck my fingers."

"Holy fucking fuck. Shit, goddammit. Greyson, it's too much, it's—" She cuts herself off on a scream, her body freezing as an orgasm washes through her, the aftershock causing her body to spasm in relief. Once the spasms subside, I remove my fingers, lick her sweet juices off, and wrap her in my arms as her labored breathing slows.

We're quiet for a long moment, absorbing everything from the last forty-five minutes. I didn't expect to have her naked and in my bed, but I'm not mad about it. I knew from my first conversation with Ava that she wasn't the type of girl to be impressed by fame or money, not like a lot of other women I've met. No, she was the kind of girl that you needed to work to impress; she'd expect nothing but respect, loyalty, and love out of her partner. I've never loved a woman before, but there was something about Ava that made me think I could easily make her the most important part of my life.

"Grey." She licks her dry lips. "I've never come that hard before."

I pull her in tighter, pressing her head against the rapid beat of my heart. "Vixen, you are so fucking sexy. This body, your response to my touch…" I let out a groan. "You're fucking perfect."

She lets out an awkward laugh, pulling away from me. "Grey, I need to get dressed. My friends are probably looking for me."

I'm reluctant to let her go, content keeping her in this room and all to myself. I loosen my hold and fall on my back, my dick standing up in my pants. Her silence has me looking her way, smirking at her blatant interest in my boner.

"Do you need me to, uh, take care of that, or something?" Jesus, what kind of guys did she know if she thought I'd force her to take care of me now? I knew she was a virgin based on her admission that no one's ever touched her pussy before, but was she so inexperienced, or so conditioned, that she'd think I'd make her return the favor?

"Let's get one thing straight, vixen," I say as I adjust myself and sit up. "Taking care of you, and your needs, is going to fuel every jerk-off session I have for the next three months. I will never expect you to 'return the favor' because that's not what this is." I run a hand through my hair, grabbing it in both hands before twisting it into a bun. "Ava, if a man ever expects you to give something you're not ready or willing to give, you run in the opposite fucking direction." I scowl at the thought of Ava with another man, not liking the idea one fucking bit. "Come here, I need my hands on you when I say this." I swing my legs over the side of the bed and cage her in between them when she's close enough.

"I can't wait to take care of you again and help you explore this side of yourself, if that's what you want. I pray that one day you'll be ready to explore me, but I don't need or expect it. I'd gladly have a case of endless blue balls if it means I can worship your curvy, sexy as fuck body."

She clears her throat. "I—thank you. I don't know what to say."

I cup her jaw, unwilling to take my hands off her at this moment. "Vixen, just say you'll answer my texts. We can see how everything else plays out, but don't ice me out."

She offers me a small smile. "Okay, I promise."

I kiss her again, savoring the connection. She's so short that, with me sitting on the bed and Ava between my legs, we're nearly at eye level.

"Good girl. Now, as much as I hate seeing this gorgeous body covered up, get dressed. We'll go find your girls." I pause, considering her friends. "We should probably check in on Dante and Celeste to make sure she hasn't killed him yet."

—

It takes us less than ten minutes to put ourselves back together and head out to the backyard. I glance at Ava, aside from the flush in her cheeks, she looks just as perfect as she did when she arrived. Her legs are covered in jeans that mold to her body, her ass plump and perky in the denim. She's wearing a simple white tank top. On anyone else, it would look plain, but on Ava, it accentuates her large, round tits and the indents of her waist. This girl, with her sarcastic humor and endless curves, has no fucking idea how beautiful she is. I grab her arm as we walk past a group of girls I didn't fucking invite. I stop her, turning her to face me. "Vixen, you look fucking beautiful."

She gives me a confused look like she can't understand why I'd throw out a compliment. Before she can respond, a high-pitched—and whiny—voice calls out my name. We turn toward the voice, though I know without looking that the owner of the voice needs to fuck right off.

"Grey Grey, there you are. I've been looking everywhere for you." Felicity charges toward us with the grace of a bull. "Oh, what is she doing here?" Ava begins to step away from me, putting distance between my body and Felicity's nasty tone. Hell fucking no. I wrap an arm around her, pulling her closer.

"Felicity, what are *you* doing here?" There's no way in hell Linc or Dante invited her, and this is an invite-only type of event.

Her eyes narrow at my hand on Ava's waist, her mouth twisting in annoyance. "You're so funny, Grey Grey. You knew I'd be here, I'm sure of it. Now, let's go talk somewhere private. You know, just the two of us." I don't miss that she didn't answer my question, but I let it go; I have no desire to talk to her longer than I must.

"I'm busy."

She pouts, pushing her overly-filled lips out in what I think is supposed to be a sexy look. Ava leans into me, whispering, "Is it me, or does she look constipated?"

I bark out a laugh. She's not wrong. To my amusement, Felicity's face transforms into a scowl. "Avery, what the fuck are you doing here? Don't you know it's invite-only? I highly doubt Greyson would invite a freshman that looked like you." What the fuck did she just say? I'm about to lay into her when Ava opens her mouth.

"Felicity, it was great seeing you, too. I'm going to go find my friends. Thanks for the uhm, the thing, Greyson." She offers me a fake smile before walking out of my arms and into the crowded yard to find her friends. Motherfucker. I turn to Felicity, growling at the smirk on her face. I probably sound feral, but I don't give two fucks.

"What the fuck was that?"

She shrugs her shoulders, walking closer to me, trying to take the space where Ava was just standing. "What the fuck are you doing?"

"Grey Grey," she whines, "don't be like that."

"So help me God, if you call me Grey Grey one more time, I'm going to lose my fucking shit." I have never, and would never, strike a woman, but Felicity makes me want to spoon my own eyes out.

"Baby, don't be like that. I'm sorry I ruined your little bet, but she's a big girl; you don't want to get crushed under her." She giggles, fucking giggles. But fuck, I forgot I told her I needed Ava's number because of a bet.

"Don't you ever fucking talk about her like that again."

"Oh, so noble of you now, Grey Grey. You know as well as I do that you need a woman like me, not that fat ass, to stand by your side." She flips her hair over her shoulder, as though she made her point, and she's just waiting for me to agree.

"Felicity, I don't know what shit you're smoking, but you and I are never going to be a thing. Fucking never. I told you last year, I told you over the summer, and I'll fucking tell you again right now. We are nothing, we will never be something, and I need you to leave me and my girl the fuck alone." I breathe out a heavy breath; my anger rising the longer I'm in her presence.

"Your girl?" she screeches. "You've known her for, like, two fucking minutes. And now she, that overweight freshman, is your girl?"

I step into her space, daring her to continue with her bullshit tirade. "That beautiful, curvy fucking goddess is my girl. She has more fucking brains, more class in her goddamn pinky, than you have in your entire fucking body." I seethe, gritting my teeth to keep from screaming at her like I want. "And if I ever, fucking ever, hear you speak about her like that again, I will fucking bury you. You will be blackballed from every fraternity house, every fucking sports house, if I hear so much as a fucking whisper against Ava. Do I make myself clear?" She glares at me, refusing to respond. "I said, do I make myself fucking clear?"

"Fuck you, Greyson. You're going to regret this."

"Stay the fuck away from me. Stay away from her." Done with this conversation, I follow the path Ava took, desperate to have her next to me and help me forget about this fucking conversation.

Fucking Felicity.

—

Ava:
Seeing Felicity and being at the receiving end of her condescending tone, has me in a tailspin of self-loathing. I need to be alone; I need to get out of here, now.

I see CeCe and Serena in the far corner of the yard, talking to Dante and a few guys I don't recognize. I love CeCe, and Serena seems like a great person from our fast friendship, but the last thing I need is to stand next to their near-flawless, size two bodies and compare every single thing about my own body. Felicity's bitchy comment, "a girl like me," hit its mark.

It's been years since I felt this debilitating need to rid myself of everything I've eaten, and fucking Felicity sent me into a dark hole with an offhanded, shitty comment. I'm ashamed that I'm this weak, that a mean girl who never left high school can reduce me to the fifteen-year-old that took laxatives like candy and would try every diet pill to lose ten pounds.

I send a text to our group chat, letting them know I'm not feeling well, and that I'm getting an Uber home. I don't even wait for their response before I break into a near-run toward the backyard gate. A single glance back tells me that no one's watching me amid my mini breakdown, but when my eyes snag on Greyson stepping closer to Felicity, my heart drops.

The triumphant look on her face transforms into an ugly scowl, emphasizing her black heart. Grey turns away from her, walking toward CeCe and Serena and the group they've amassed. I should be relieved that he's seemingly chasing after me, but the only thing I can think about is how he can't see me right now, not when I feel like everything I am is not enough. I continue toward the exit, breathing easier as soon as I'm on the opposite side of the fence.

My phone vibrates and I look down, expecting a text from our group chat, but an unknown sender mars my screen. I open the text and my blood freezes.

Unknown: You're pathetic if you think Greyson wants a slob like you. Ask him about his bet.

Ava

By the time I get home from Greyson's house, I'm flustered, tired, and more than a little confused. Earlier tonight, I gave Greyson an intimate, private part of myself; I shared my body, and my inexperience, and put my stretch marks on display. His hands touched me in places that even my gynecologist hasn't seen, and, my God, it felt so good. I rub my thighs together at the memory of him over me, spreading my folds with his thick fingers as he brought me to the highest point of pleasure. The warmth inside of me evaporates once I remember why I left his house alone. Between Felicity's shitty comments, insinuating that I was less than her, and the text message I received hinting that Greyson paid attention to me because of a bet, my post-orgasmic bliss is nonexistent.

I'm trying not to be one of those girls that believe every rumor without a conversation, but that text seemed to confirm my deepest fear: that I was nothing more than a sure thing. I know that I need to confront Greyson about it. I owe it to myself, and to him, to talk to him about the alleged bet before writing him off entirely. I may be inexperienced, but I'm not a moron. Greyson made me feel safe, wanted, and respected throughout every conversation and interaction we've had. I would never have spread my legs solely because the guy was good-looking. Right?

The Uber ride home helped cool my anger and self-hatred. Can I say that I'm unaffected by Felicity and her obvious reference to my weight? No. But the urge to make myself sick to conform to her idea of beauty has subsided, as has the need to compare my physical attributes to those of my friends. Though I'm relieved the dark thoughts retreated, I'm terrified that they'll come back, more present and insistent each time. It's like I have these long stretches of being comfortable with myself and who I am, and then a setback hits me and I'm a young girl again, sneaking Hershey kisses in the bathroom at school because I don't want the other kids to see the chubby girl eating chocolate. It's a vicious cycle, one I thought I moved past.

Taking a deep breath, I force myself to push Felicity, my weight, and my hookup with Greyson out of my head. Letting these things consume me will drive me crazy, and I can't allow anything to derail me or my dreams. I grab my Tumi backpack off the back of my desk chair, empty the contents on my bed, and begin to repack for my first day of classes tomorrow. Though most of my classes are general education courses, I was able to sneak one elective into my schedule: Fundamentals of Baking and Pastry. Baking wasn't necessarily my passion, but I appreciate the precision and attention to detail that it requires. Though our practical won't happen at the start of class tomorrow, I am eager to make a good impression on the professor teaching the course.

I double-check that I have everything I'll need for my classes tomorrow: a pair of notebooks, pens, highlighters, a calculator for my Algebra I course, and my recipe binder. Realistically, I won't need my binder, but I can't help but be over-prepared. The mundane tasks of packing my bag, picking out my clothes for tomorrow, and taking a long, hot shower, helped to keep my mind off of the events of the day, especially Greyson. That went to shit as soon as I got back to my dorm room.

Taking off my robe and hanging it on the hook by my closet, I reach into my dresser to grab my sleep set only to stop short at the marks all over my skin.

"What the fuck?" I whisper into the room, turning fully toward my mirror. Looking from my neck to my chest, I have hickeys everywhere. Surrounding my nipples, I look like I got into a fight with a fucking wildebeest. How did I miss these marks in the shower? They are, quite literally, everywhere. I groan, hanging my head. I'm going to sit in my classes tomorrow, meeting my professors and all these new people, with goddamn hickeys covering the upper half of my body. I am going to murder Greyson, fucking kill him. I take a picture of my neck, careful not to show any unnecessary skin, attach it to a text message and start to type out my annoyance with that Viking-looking asshole.

Ava: Greyson, I am going to fucking kill you. Look at my neck. <attachment 1>

I throw my phone on my bed, not caring what he replies. Instead of the sleep set I initially planned, I grab a sweatshirt and sleep shorts, determined to sweat my annoyance out and hide these hickeys at the same time. The very last thing I need right now is for CeCe to look at me like a leper and start romanticizing whatever happened today.

My phone goes off on my bed, but instead of reaching for it and devouring his words, I push it aside, climbing into my bed and pulling the covers over my head.

It's eighty degrees out and here I am in a damn parka, avoiding my roommate, my feelings, and the text message that just came through my phone. Thank God this dorm is air-conditioned.

—

CeCe wakes me when she comes in around eight. She eyes me, suspicion cast over her pretty features as she takes in my sweatshirt. After making sure I was okay and recovered from the mysterious illness that struck me—Felicity's bullshit, though I won't tell her about that interaction—she grabs her shower caddy and leaves for the communal bathroom down the hall.

I steel myself, get my mental shit together, and look at my phone. I have over ten missed calls and a collection of text messages from Greyson, CeCe, and my mom. Tapping on my mom's contact information, I pray to God she's already in bed for the night and left her phone downstairs. I don't have the mental capacity to deal with her questions, excitement, or gossip tonight. I love my mother and my entire family, but they are... a lot. All the time. Loud, boisterous, and obnoxious. They're amazing but have a penchant for producing migraines. Luckily, the phone goes to voicemail; I do not doubt that she and my father are already in bed, snoring while pretending to watch the latest true-crime documentary, probably based on a case they worked on.

I click on my text messages and select Greyson's text thread.

Greyson: Fuck, that's so fucking hot. Are you going to show off that pretty neck around campus tomorrow, let everyone know you're off-limits?

I raise my eyebrows. His possessiveness sends a flare of heat through my body, and there's an intense ache between my thighs. I shift my legs, pressing them together, and try to alleviate the pressure without snaking my hand below my shorts. I'm desperate to repeat the ministrations Greyson showed my body, but also hesitant to slide my hands inside myself. CeCe will be back soon, and I don't want to risk stopping close to orgasm because my best friend came into the room while I was being a horny wench. We're close, but not that close. I look at his next two texts.

Greyson: Vixen, I need you to know that whatever Felicity said, she was wrong.

Greyson: Vixen, are you going to answer me?

I chew on my lip, both grateful and annoyed that he presented the opening to question why he's interested in me. My fingers hover over my phone, contemplating what to say in response. Do I ask him straight out why he's pursuing me? Do I pretend that I don't care and ghost him for a week, see if he reaches out to me? Do I do nothing and keep going as I am? A knot forms in the pit of my stomach; either I hide from him, or I hide from my worries. Either way, it's a mess. What a clusterfuck.

Ava: Tell me about the bet.

Shit, I didn't mean to send that. I see the text bubbles appear and disappear, almost like he's typed out and then deleted his response. Is he thinking of a lie to feed me to cover his tracks? Or is he trying to let me down gently? More than ten minutes pass without a response; I should take that as my answer. I throw my phone back down on my bed just as CeCe comes back into the room.

"Aves, you okay?"

"Yeah, I'm fine. I'm just anxious about tomorrow." It's not exactly a lie. I am anxious about my classes tomorrow, especially with my neck covered in vampire bites. I omit that Greyson is also a part of that anxiety. I don't want to see a pitying look on her face, so I keep his contribution to my nerves to myself. My phone starts vibrating in a pulsing rhythm, alerting me that a call is coming through. I grab my phone, fully expecting to see my mom's contact picture on my screen, despite the late hour, but suck in a breath when I see Greyson's name pop up. I press the ignore button on my phone.

CeCe is like a shark, smelling the blood in the water. "Who was that?" My phone starts vibrating again, and just like seconds ago, I press ignore on his call.

"Just my mom," I lie. "She wanted to talk about my first day. I'll call her tomorrow on my way to my class." I look over at CeCe, a disbelieving look on her face. "I'll just send her a text and let her know I'll speak to her in the morning." I unlock my phone and begin typing a text to Greyson when one comes through from him.

Greyson: Answer your goddamn phone.

Definitely no.

Ava: CeCe's here, I can't talk. Your lack of response said it all though. Don't worry, I won't lose sleep over you. Thanks for the orgasm. Have a nice life, Greyson.

This time, his response is immediate.

Greyson: Vixen, you promised that you wouldn't ice me out. I'm not done with you. We're just getting started. There's no fucking bet. Let me explain.

I mull it over, annoyed that there's any explanation needed. Shouldn't it be a simple, "Yes, there's a bet," or "No, there's no bet?" If there's more to it than that, I'm not sure I want to hear it. I'm here, in college and away from home for the first time, to discover who I am outside of my family. I'm not prepared for Greyson, not physically or mentally, and I'm not prepared for the obvious drama that being with him provokes. Being in his orbit has already threatened my mental state, and I won't be able to look at myself if I allow myself to succumb to the demons I fought so hard against. I refuse to allow myself to be reduced to the shell of a person I was at fifteen.

Ava: Bye, Greyson.

—

My phone's alarm goes off at six-thirty, waking me from a deep, dreamless sleep. I turned my phone on do not disturb last night after sending my final text to Greyson. My dismissal of him hurt, especially after the intensity of our hookup, but I know I made the right decision. After a quick check of my phone, I realize that he didn't respond to my last text. That's good.

Great. Super.

CeCe's first class is at one this afternoon, so I grab my clothes, toiletries, and makeup and head into the bathroom to get ready for my eight o'clock class. Why I signed up for an algebra class at the ass crack of dawn on Monday mornings is anyone's guess. I pay careful attention to my makeup before running my concealer over my neck in an attempt to hide the bites and bruises that Greyson gave me. I scowl in disgust as I try blending the concealer with bronzer and my contour stick, making my neck look even worse than it did without the makeup. I look like I have a skin disease; there's no covering this. Thank God I have a sleeveless turtleneck because if I show up to my classes like this, there's no doubt everyone would question my sanity.

I run a makeup wipe over my neck, remove everything I just applied, and then pull the black sleeveless turtleneck over my head. Paired with my relaxed-fit jeans, white platform sneakers, and layered gold chains, I look like every other college girl on campus. I slide my oversize black frame glasses on my face and fluff my dark hair around my shoulders. It's hot as balls outside, but my thick hair provides extra coverage of my neck.

Looking at myself critically in the mirror, I take in my appearance and accept the reflection there. I swipe on lip gloss before gathering my bags and walking back to my dorm room. I deposit my things on my desk—I'll worry about putting them away when I get back—grab my backpack and make my way to the dining hall on the opposite side of campus. There's no way in hell that I'm going to this ungodly math class with no caffeine in my veins.

It takes me ten minutes to get to the dining hall, and I'm surprised by the number of people I see through the windows. After swiping my student ID at the entrance, I make my way to the grill station, where fresh omelets dosed in butter are made to order. At least six people are waiting in line and judging by the pace of the omelet maker, it's going to take way too long. Looks like yogurt and fruit are all I'm getting this morning. The yogurt selection is sparse while the fruit options are apples, apples, and more apples.

You know what? Coffee sounds great.

I stop in front of the coffee station which has two large vats of coffee with a selection of creamers and milk. At least they got this right; if they fucked up the coffee, I would cause a damn ruckus. With my to-go mug in hand, I pull the handle of the coffee dispenser, and then, hell breaks loose. Either I have Hulk-like strength or God hates me because as soon as I pull the lever to fill my mug, the handle breaks off and gallons of coffee start pouring out of the machine.

Fucking gallons.

I'm too shocked to do anything as the coffee runs with the force of the freaking rapids, spilling all over the floor and counter.

"Fucking shit." My shock finally wears off and I spring into action, grabbing napkins from a nearby dispenser to try and soak up the mess. The flimsy, climate-friendly paper does nothing to clean the insane quantities of coffee coming out, and I start panicking. "How much coffee is in this shit?" I mutter to myself, burning my hand in the napkin-soaking business. "And why the hell is no one coming over to help me?" I look around, noticing that all eyes are, of course, right on me. Fucking hell, Celeste is going to find out about this and never let me live this down.

"Fuck your goddamn sister's ass. Would you stop going, you fucking asshole?" I've lost all semblance of sanity. I am cursing at an inanimate object, and I don't even care.

"Uh, Ava?" a voice behind me calls.

I whip around, in no mood for anyone's shit. "What?" I screech. I sound insane, I know I do. But the coffee will not fucking stop.

Dante stands there, trying to suppress a smile, based on the twitching of his weirdly perfect lips.

"You need a little help over there? You seem to be having a moment with the coffee machine." He tilts his head, and his eyes flick to the ravine of caffeine running along the grout in the tile floor. "That was an interesting string of curse words. I'm not sure I've ever heard someone say, 'Fuck your sister's ass.' It's kind of disturbing as fuck."

"Well, I wouldn't have to say it if this coffee machine would just stop dispensing fucking coffee." I gesture wildly to the offending vat. "It's like a volcano erupted."

Dante walks past me, reaching to the side of the coffee machine, and suddenly, the coffee stops flowing like lava from the pits of hell. "Wait... what? How...?" I look at him in accusation. "How the hell did you know that button was there?"

Dante sucks his lips under his teeth and points to a sign above the machine. In large, bold, red letters, the sign reads, "In the event of lever malfunction, press the button on the right side of the machine to stop the flow of coffee." There's even a series of diagrams showing where and how to press the button. Huh, I guess I missed that.

"Right, I uh, guess I missed that." I look around at the mess all over the floor and the counter. I estimate that I'll need to boycott the dining hall for three weeks to work through the embarrassment I feel right now. Coffee splatters line my arms, but somehow, praise Jesus and the powers that be, my clothes remain coffee-free. I grab one of the biodegradable napkins and begin cleaning up the droplets on my arms and hands. "Well, thank you. No one else seemed inclined to help."

"In their defense, they probably thought you could read the sign." Dante starts laughing and I scowl. "This isn't the first time it's happened; that's why there's a sign. They need to replace the machines, but I guess all of our tuition goes to lawn care and recruitment commercials." He shrugs.

"Whatever," I start. "While you're here, can you fill up my mug from the other coffee machine? I am traumatized and will be hiding my face for the next twenty-one days to recover from this." He laughs and takes my mug, filling it with coffee from the other dispenser. It works perfectly, exactly like it was made to.

Asshole.

"Milk? Sugar?"

"Just some half and half, if you don't mind." He pours a splash in, looking at me to make sure it's enough before capping the container and handing my mug back to me.

"Thanks. I don't think I would have made it through my algebra class without this, and I was tempted to run out of here once the rivers of hell opened on me." As it stands, there's coffee everywhere. Shit, I need to get a janitor. I must have said that out loud because Dante shakes his head. "I already told them that the machine broke again. They should be coming over with a mop and some caution signs."

"You're a lifesaver."

"Right, right. So, since I helped you, you think that maybe you can put in a good word with Red?" I laugh. I was wondering how long it would take for him to bring CeCe up.

"If you grab my arm and make sure I don't fall on my ass in coffee, I will tell her to buy a wedding dress and to pick her bridesmaids colors, if that's what you want."

"Oh, fuck yeah. Here, give me your arm." Dante reaches for my arm, pulling me to him and guiding me past the coffee spillage. I was kidding about the wedding, but apparently, he's not.

"So, if you could also tell Red to text me, that would be solid. That hellion has my number but refused to give me hers." His eyes suddenly light up. Oh no, I know what he's about to ask and the answer is no. "Ava, Ava, Ava. Why don't you repay the favor and give me Red's number? I'm sure she won't mind."

"We're talking about the same CeCe, right? Celeste Lauren Downing? You realize that she has a black belt in karate and, like, fifteen male cousins that taught her how to fight. Not to mention, her dad's a medical examiner, and I'm pretty sure she knows how to kill without leaving evidence." I pat his hand in apology. "Thanks for helping with the coffee, but there is no way in hell that I'm going to be on the receiving end of C's retribution." I shiver just thinking about it.

"Fuck, that's so hot." He must have a torture fetish because, what?

"Uh, sure, yeah." I walk out of the dining hall, Dante still on my heels. I figured that after I accepted his help and agreed to put in a good word with Celeste that he'd leave me alone. Apparently, I was wrong. "Okay, so thanks again. Bye." I pick up the pace, walking toward Howard Hall, where my class is being held.

"Ava, wait." I sigh and turn around, raising a brow in response.

"I know someone mentioned a bet, and I just want you to know, there's no bet about you or Grey. Fuck, he really likes you, Ava. He needed your number and didn't want to put his interest on display, so he told Felicity there was a bet so that she wouldn't question it or try to make your life hell." He runs a hand through his hair, drawing in a breath before continuing, "Felicity, she's batshit crazy, and the last thing Grey wanted was to have her target you out of some misplaced jealousy. Believe me, nothing is going on and he's into you. I've never seen my boy so hung up over a girl before. Just give him a chance to explain."

I had suspicions that Felicity was the sender of the text, and now it's all but confirmed. What a miserable, angry person she is to send catty messages under a blocked number. I don't love confrontation, but my God, grow a pair of ovaries and either talk to me face-to-face or leave me alone.

"Dante, you're a good friend. I'll make sure Celeste knows that."

"Does that mean you'll give Grey a chance to explain?"

I chew on my lip, remembering Greyson's face when he asked me not to ignore him. "I don't know. I guess we'll see. Bye, Dante. I need to get to class."

I leave Dante and make my way to algebra, lost in thoughts of Greyson throughout the entire introduction to the class. The professor, a kind, elderly man that reminds me of a movie grandpa, lets us out fifteen minutes before the end of class, and I nearly cry in relief. Thoughts of Greyson, our afternoon together, Felicity, the text message, and the fucking coffee explosion of 2023 run through my head, and all I want to do is go back to my dorm and hide until my next class. I'm one of the last to exit the classroom, my head down and dreaming about my bed and invisibility cloaks. There's a small crowd gathered in front of the door, and I work to weave my way through, trying to put as much distance as I can between me and this morning.

I'm almost out of the building when I hear my name called out.

"Ava," a deep voice bellows across the hallway. I turn, my stomach erupting into a flurry of hungry little butterflies. Greyson stands at the opposite end of the hall. Once we make eye contact, he begins to stride down the hall in purposeful steps. His legs are so damn long that he reaches me in seconds.

"Vixen, we need to talk."

Greyson

Dante: Just with Ava. Some shit went down in the dining hall. Spoke to her about you, call her, I think she'll listen.

Dante's text came through a little before eight, just as I finished my morning run at the track on campus. As soon as I read it, I booked it for home, probably breaking every traffic law in this shitty college town. Fuck it. I plug my phone into the docking station in my car and find Dante's contact information at a red light to call him.

"Come on, you fuck, Answer your phone."

After three rings, Dante answers. "Hey."

"What did she say? Where is she?" I ask once he's on the line.

"I'm doing good, thanks for asking, you asshole."

"Dante," I growl. "I don't have time for this shit. Tell me what happened."

"She broke the coffee machine, and I helped her turn it off. I walked with her to her building after and put in a good word for you while asking her to put in a good word for me with Red," he responds. "I think she'll talk to you. I told her there was no bet, at least none involving her." He pauses, probably thinking about his bet with Linc and how fucked he'd be if Celeste ever found out. "You better not say shit about my bet with Linc."

"I'm not going to say anything. What building is she in?"

"Howard Hall. She said she had algebra."

I look at my dash, it reads eight-thirty. The morning gen eds are typically an hour, so I don't have much time to shower, get dressed, and get my ass back to campus to wait her out.

"I owe you, D."

"Remember that, bro. I need to get to class. Later." Dante hangs up and I push my Jeep faster.

She's going to fucking talk to me and hear me out. There's no way we're done before we even got the chance to start.

—

I make it back to campus by nine-fifteen, ready to drag this girl back to my house if that's the only way she'll listen to me. The sounds she made in my bed yesterday run through my mind like a fucking playlist, the image of her sweet body tangled in my sheets lives rent-free in my head, and I don't care that we just met. This girl is different, made specifically for me, and I'm not going to let her slip through my fingers when I just found her. The only person that would tell her about the bet is Felicity or one of her minions, and she's next on my list; you don't fuck with my shit and expect to get away with it.

If Ava doesn't give me a chance after this, Felicity is going to need to transfer because I will make her life a living fucking hell. Bet on that.

Walking through the doors of Howard Hall, I start looking into classrooms and lecture halls, desperate to find the one containing my vixen. There's a room at the end of the hall with no window in the door. I crack it open, not giving a shit that I could be interrupting a class. There's no one inside, and I see that there's a crack in the smart board on the wall, indicating that there are no classes held in this room. Perfect.

I walk out of the abandoned class just as a door down the hall opens and people spill out. Instinctually, I know she's part of that crowd. Holding my breath, I stand there, waiting to see if her pretty face emerges from the classroom, ready to fucking sprint down the hall if she tries to ignore me. I release my breath when I spot her; she's the last one out of the room and gets caught in the mob outside the door. She bobs and weaves, clumsily hitting at least three people with her bag. She's almost at the exit when I get my head out of my ass and call her name.

"Ava," I yell, getting more than a few stares. Fuck them.

She whips her head around, surprise written all over her features. She takes me in, her every emotion is displayed in her eyes: confusion, residual anger, desire. She looks insane today in her tight black shirt and a pair of jeans that hug her ass. I'm not happy that her shirt hides the marks I gave her yesterday, but I appreciate that the high neck calls attention to her perky tits.

I walk over to her quickly, not giving her the opportunity to leave. I'm near her in seconds and reach out to her, wrapping my hand around the back of her head to pull her close.

"Vixen, we need to talk." She's staring into my eyes, looking straight into my soul. She licks her lips and I follow the movement, stifling a groan. I'm watching her mouth so closely that I almost miss the nod she gives me. Dropping my hand from the back of her head, I reach out and grab her bag, slinging it over my shoulder before taking her hand and tugging her toward the empty room.

I pull her into the room, not giving a shit who sees us, and close the door behind us. I reach for the switch, dimming the fluorescent lights to create a warm glow in the room. She's staring at me, waiting for me to say something, maybe about the bullshit bet or maybe about dragging her into this room.

"There's no bet, vixen. I swear to you."

"I know. Dante told me."

"I would never demean you that way. The things Felicity said, fuck. She and I, we—"

"Greyson, it's okay. You don't need to explain it to me."

I stare at her and try to make eye contact, but she's looking down, almost like she's afraid to look at me. Something isn't right. "Ava, look at me."

She raises her eyes, briefly meeting mine before dropping them back down to the floor. I take a closer look at her, seeing beyond the clothes that show off her figure, and realize that she's huddled as close to the door as she can get without leaning against it. Her body language is so closed off that I doubt anything I say will make much of a difference. It seems I need to show her what I'm thinking and how I feel.

"Ava, vixen, why are you standing all the way over there?"

"I-I just feel more comfortable over here," she responds. "Besides, we had fun, but I'm sure you're used to the kind of fun we had yesterday, hm?"

"You look like you'd rather be anywhere but here." I advance on her, approaching her like an injured animal. "Yes, I've fucked other women, I've made them come on my fingers, my tongue, and my cock, but you are the only one that I can't get out of my fucking head. You're the only one who's so fucking sweet that you bring handmade pastries to a college barbecue and refuse to take credit. You're the only one that's you, my little vixen. You promised me that you wouldn't ice me out or ignore me after I made that pretty pink pussy come. Does it need a reminder of who it belongs to?" Finally, she looks at me with wide eyes. About fucking time.

"Greyson," she groans, as though the walls can hear her speak. "We are on campus. We cannot hook up here." She raises her chin in indignation, a fire warming her eyes and defrosting the chill I received from her initial reception. "Besides," she continues, "we just met. I am your nothing. I'm just another girl that warmed your bed, an easy freshman that let you take a small piece of her innocence. It's no big deal."

"No big deal?" I chuckle, rubbing my thumb over my lip. Her eyes track the movement; she's such a little liar. "Vixen, it was a big fucking deal. You got under my skin the moment I laid eyes on you in that indecent black dress last Thursday. We"—I gesture between us—"are fucking combustible. You can't tell me that you don't feel it too. And stop putting yourself down. You're fucking amazing."

"I-I don't feel the same way," she stammers out. She doesn't acknowledge how she puts herself down or promise that she'll stop. I caught on to her self-deprecating humor at the party on Thursday night and in my room yesterday. I don't like that she doesn't see herself as she is: a goddess.

I back her into the door, not giving her a chance to retreat. "You're a fucking liar, Ava." I run one hand over her cheek, tracing the line of her jaw, her plump lips, and the tiny mole above her full cupid's bow before moving my hand lower to lightly circle her throat. "Tell me, sweet Ava, if I were to lower my hand, would I find your pussy soaking wet in these jeans?"

"Grey," she exhales. I lean in, running my nose over her cheek. She smells like lemons and coffee, and I can get drunk on her scent.

115

"You smell like coffee, baby. I wonder, if I lick you, will you taste like it, too?" Without waiting for her reply, I trace her jawline with my tongue, savoring the feel and the saltiness of her skin. Her sharp gasp fills the room, and I retrace the path my tongue just took. "Mmm, you taste like heaven. Do you think you taste this good everywhere?" I lick my way down her neck, shifting my hand to cover every inch of skin above the high neckline. Her body is pressed firmly against mine, and I catalog every breath she takes and moan she makes. Her pulse beats rapidly against my hand, and I know she's in this with me, feeling just as turned on as I am. I get my confirmation when her hips start to move against me, trying to find friction against my thighs.

I move my free hand to grip her ass, placing my leg between her thighs and pull her close. "That's right, baby, rub that pussy over me. Use me to get off."

"Grey," she pants, increasing her movements. "Grey, I need, I need more."

I feel a grin spread over my face, loving how responsive she is to my touch. When I had her spread out for me yesterday, she detonated, gifting me with the sweetest cries I've ever heard. I didn't doubt her virginity; her pussy nearly strangled my fingers, but she was not innocent. I did not doubt that she spent her time fucking her hand while watching porn or reading romance novels. Her body sought its pleasure, rode my hand to a rhythm only we could feel, and she took her orgasm. She reached out and grasped it, she didn't wait for me to just give it to her.

"Ava, tell me what you need."

"Kiss me." I dive in, capturing her lips. They're soft beneath mine and taste faintly of cherries, like she rubbed ChapStick over her lips right before I dragged her in here. Her tongue sneaks out, pushing into my mouth and tangling with mine. I flatten her against the door before grabbing her legs and lifting her to straddle me. I let her lead the kiss, allowing her to set the pace as we eat at each other's lips.

I pull back, breathing heavily as she stares up at me with swollen lips. She wiggles and starts to unwrap herself from my hold. Fuck that. I tighten my grip on her, not willing to put her down and sever the connection between our bodies.

"Vixen, are you still going to bullshit me and tell me there's nothing there between us? That you feel nothing?"

"Greyson, I—," she sighs, looking away from me. "It's not that I feel nothing. It's that I don't know how you can feel so much."

"Ava, look at me." Her eyes slowly lift to mine, betraying every fear and anxiety rolling through her. I move my hand from her throat, tipping her chin up to prevent her from looking away. "I've been through shit, Ava. My parents split up when I was a kid, and when my mom was around, well, she wasn't the kind of parent any child should have. I've been in therapy since I was eight years old; all I know is talking about shit. I don't hold back. I don't play games. I don't fuck around. When I say I want you, it's because I want you. I told you yesterday, you have consumed my thoughts for the last four days."

From the moment that my mother left us, my dad did everything he could to make sure I didn't have a toxic view of women, abandonment issues, or baggage. My mother never loved me, or if she did, she loved her drugs more. Luckily, my dad wasn't an asshole and loved me enough for both of them. My weekly sessions with Dr. Eckle, my therapist, keep me clear and focused. I wasn't lying when I told Ava that I don't play games. The minute I meet a woman, I make sure they know that I don't fuck without a condom and that I don't want a relationship. It wasn't until meeting Ava that I reconsidered, and I've got big enough balls to admit it. Dr. Eckle was always on my case to explore my vulnerability more and to open my heart up to being hurt. She was going to have a fucking field day with this.

"Wow, such a long time," she mutters under her breath.

"Smartass." I nip at her lips. Hers part in a smile, tempting me to resume our kiss before I finish what I need to say. I resist. How? No fucking clue. "You're right, it hasn't been a long time, but Dante is convinced he's marrying your little pit bull, so I'm not alone."

"Oh, Celeste is going to love that for herself," she laughs. "I'm pretty sure she's waiting for her Heathcliff or Darcy, and I'm not sure Dante fits that bill."

"Let them figure that out for themselves. I know it's quick, and I'll take it as slow as you want to go, but Ava, I want to get to know you."

She looks at me with her large onyx eyes. Seconds stretch into minutes while she stares at me, and I hold her between a door and my dick. It's starting to get uncomfortable how hard I am.

"I need words, Ava. Are we exploring this? Or am I putting you down, adjusting my dick, and walking out of this room? If you tell me to leave, I won't be happy about it, but I'll fucking do it and leave you alone. So tell me, what's it going to be?"

"Okay."

Internally, I breathe a sigh of relief. Externally, I smirk and can't wait to fuck with her a little. "Okay to which part, sweet Ava? I raised two different scenarios. Tell me which one you want."

"The first, Grey. I want the first."

"I need to hear you say it. Tell me exactly what you want."

She scowls at me, annoyance written all over her face at my request. "Fine. I want to explore this. I want to explore you." Her eyes widen at her slip up and I chuckle. "With you. I meant with you."

"Sure you did, vixen."

Kissing her in this dimly lit room, with a smashed smart board and musty stench, has been one of the greatest decisions of my life, and in this moment, I promise myself that I won't do anything to make her regret this.

"When's your next class?" I ask, trying to figure out how much longer I can steal her away.

"Not until later this afternoon. Why?"

I shift her lower, letting her center brush against my erection, and her gasp fills the room.

"Can we make it to another base?"

"Did you just reference baseball regarding sex?"

"You're not going to lose your virginity in a dirty classroom, don't worry." With her glasses, she does look like a sexy teacher, so we'll need to revisit that, just not for her first time. "But I'd be lying if I said I didn't want to taste you right now."

Her cheeks flush. "Wow. So, you want to load bases at third?"

"Only if you tell me yes."

"I think, yes." She shakes her head. "I mean, yes."

"Are you sure? Once I have my mouth on you, there's no way I'm walking away."

"Yes."

I back us away from the door, setting her on the large desk at the front of the room. "Vixen," I whisper, hovering just above her ear and using my tongue to trace her earlobe. She fucking loved when I did that to her yesterday, and I'm more than happy to remind her. "The walls are thick, but if you yell, you're going to have some nosy fucks running in here real quick. I'm going to need you to be quiet for me this time." She sucks in a breath when I bite her and then suckle my mark to remove the sting. "I promise, next time, we're going to be alone, in an empty fucking house, where I can hear every moan, whimper, and cry you make."

I feel her hands in my hair, pulling me away from the worship I've devoted to her neck and ear. I look at her, panting and flushed from just my mouth, and feel pride swell in my chest that I'm the only man to ever see her like this. I capture her mouth, parting her lips with my tongue, and sink into the kiss. Her kisses, which started as timid and unsure yesterday, are confident and knowing today. Like a switch flipped within her, she bites at my lower lip, sucking it into her mouth like the temptress I knew she was.

I work my hands down her body, cupping her full tits before squeezing. Breaking from the kiss, I murmur, "I can't wait to see these tits again," against her mouth, before diving back in. Her mouth parts wide beneath mine, a strangled gasp tearing through the room as I alternate between caresses and gentle kneading. Her breasts are a work of art, and if we were anywhere other than an abandoned classroom on campus during the first day of classes, I wouldn't hesitate to rip her shirt and bra off. I'd take my time, sucking and nipping at each breast, pinching and blowing on her nipples until they stood out hard against her chest. But despite the heat burning between us and the need I can taste, I'm not going to strip her naked in the middle of a classroom.

Our mouths break apart and our heavy breathing fills the silence of the room. My hands drift lower, resting at the top of her jeans. Playing with the button, I look at her, trying to decipher the look in her dark eyes. "Tell me to stop," I grind out, giving her the chance to end this. My words hang heavy, resting between us before Ava shakes her head.

"No."

Her button opens easily. Parting her jeans, black silk greets me with the sweetest fucking bow on the waistband. I run my thumb over the useless ribbon. "Fuck, it's like you're a present wrapped just for me." I look at her face again. "Tell me to stop."

"No."

I pull on her jeans. She follows my wordless command, leaning back on her hands and lifting her hips upward. "This is your last chance, vixen. Tell me to stop."

There's a pause before her voice fills the space.

"No, Grey. Don't stop."

—

Ava:

I think I'm hallucinating. Or maybe I'm dying. Am I hallucinating while dying? I'm not entirely sure, but my current reality is a blonde Viking god kneeling between my legs while I recline like a Roman noblewoman on this desk.

I'm not complaining about it, but I cannot believe that this is happening. When I experienced the wrath of the coffee machine from hell this morning, I didn't think that my coffee-covered body would become a personal ice pop for the hottest man I have ever seen.

It's an interesting turn of events, to say the least.

There's a tug on my jeans and I lift my hips, watching his face as he takes in the skin slowly becoming visible. His thumb rubs right over my pubic bone, sending chills down my spine and a rush of wetness between my thighs. He seems mesmerized by the stupid bow on my panties. They're one of my favorite pairs, even though they offer no coverage and no one besides me has ever seen them before. I put them on this morning in the hopes that they would bring me good luck and confidence for my first day of college. My lingerie manifested this without my knowledge.

With my pants strangling my thighs, Grey looks back up at me, telling me to stop him again. I appreciate that he's checking in on me, making sure he has one hundred percent consent before he continues, but I know what I want, and it's to feel his mouth against me. I return his gaze, feeling myself get wetter at the sight of this larger-than-life man on his knees for me. "No, Grey. Don't stop," I plead. It almost sounds like I'm whining. Tomorrow, or later today, I'm sure I'll care, but right now I can't be bothered to. His answering smirk lets me know that he knows exactly what he's doing to me, drawing this out as long as he can to make sure that I'm out of my mind for him. Such an asshole.

Finally, he shoves my pants down to my ankles and lifts my legs, hooking them over his head so that my thighs rest near his ears but my feet are bound by my jeans. In this position, I can't move, not that I want to, but I am completely at his disposal. He's looking at me with hunger, his eyes set on the strip of black satin between us. I shift my hips, pressing my pelvis closer to him, urging him to do something, anything, while I'm on display like this for him.

"Fuck," he groans, lifting one hand to trace the seam of my panties before running his finger down one side of my lips. "You're so wet for me, vixen." His other hand comes up, tracing the other side slowly. He's doing nothing more than petting the edges of my sex, teasing my folds before pulling back. Every time I've touched myself, I've done so with a detached efficiency, intent on the orgasm that I knew awaited me at the end of my ministrations. I've never trailed my fingers through my folds with butterfly touches, not like what Grey's doing to me now.

His fingers part me, pulling my thong to one side and exposing me to his view. He's seen me before, hell, his fingers were inside of me last night, but his closeup of the most intimate part of myself is almost unnerving. Warm air blows on me before I feel the press of his tongue against my slit. Flattening his tongue against me, he laps at me, tasting me like I'm the most delicious thing he's ever had. His movements are slow, unhurried, but expert; he spears his tongue into my opening, pushing in and out just like our fingers did last night. My head falls back, absorbing how good each new sensation feels.

His hands snake around my thighs, pulling my legs wider apart while pressing his face deeper into my wetness. His mouth finds my clit, sucks it between his lips, and all coherent thoughts go out of my brain. "Holy fucking shit, Grey." I bow off the desk, grabbing his head and keeping it exactly where it is. Grey chuckles against my sex, lifting his head to smirk at me.

"You taste fucking delicious, baby. Do you like how I eat this pussy?"

"God, yes."

Rubbing lazy circles over my clit with his thick fingers, Grey demands, "Whose pussy is this, vixen?"

"Mine." Grey growls, sounding feral, and offers a sharp slap between my thighs.

"Try again."

"You're the only man to touch me between my thighs, and you know it."

He returns his attention to my clit, parting my lips and circling the bundle of nerves. "Say pussy, baby." Since we met, he's interchanged vixen, baby, and my name. I'm not sure which endearment I like more. He puts his mouth back on me, sucking my clit back into his mouth, raking his teeth over it before releasing me. "Say it, baby. Say pussy for me."

"Pussy," I whisper.

"Good girl." His deep voice and the praise he gives me sends goosebumps down my exposed arms. If he notices, he doesn't say, instead diving back into my pussy like he's starving for it. He alternates hard, punishing bites with gentle suction and slow licks, sending every nerve ending fucking wild. I tighten my grip on his hair, grinding into his mouth as he eats at me like a five-course meal.

"That's right, baby, ride my face." Thick fingers push into me, hooking at an angle that has me seeing double. I feel the sweat dripping down my brow, hear the pants and moans and slurping between our bodies, and do not doubt that I'll need another shower before my afternoon class. But at this moment, with Greyson worshiping at the altar between my thighs, I welcome the sweat, the messiness.

"Are you going to come for me, baby?"

"Yes, I'm so close, Greyson."

"Good, come all over my fucking face." Grey increases the speed of his fingers, moving them quickly, as though this orgasm is for both of us, and he couldn't wait to get there. His mouth latches onto my clit, sucking in rhythm to his fingers. He's fucking me and sucking me at the same time, and I can't hold back my release any longer. Like a live wire, I go off, arching and writhing all over the desk while keeping Grey's head in my hands. He holds me through my orgasm, licking me as I come back down and relax against the desk.

I'm so high on dopamine from the intense orgasm that I almost miss the click of the door. Grey and I whip our heads toward the classroom's door, relieved to find it closed and the room empty, save for us.

Grey rights my panties, placing a chaste kiss over the bow. I laugh, humored at his interest in such a frivolous adornment.

"Something funny, vixen?"

I shake my head. "No, I'm just making note that you like bows. I'll make sure to remember that in the future."

The Viking between my legs rolls his eyes. "I don't have a thing for bows. I just like you wrapped up like a gift for me." He lifts my legs from his shoulders and places them on the floor. Grabbing my hands, he pulls me to stand in front of him before working my pants up my legs, over my ass, until once again they're buttoned at my waist. Standing in front of me, the outline of Grey's dick is pressed against his jeans. "That looks painful," I comment.

Grey laughs without humor. "I'll survive. Did you eat yet? There's a diner close by, JJ's."

"Well, other than the coffee that assaulted me, I haven't had anything. I should probably go back to my dorm, though." I look down at my rumpled clothes. "I look like I just had sex. I probably smell like it, too."

"You look perfect, but if you want to go back to your dorm, I'll drive you before we grab breakfast."

I raise a brow at his assuredness. "You seem pretty sure that I'll agree to eat with you."

"Ava, you had a coffee shower this morning and just got mouth-fucked on a desk. You need food, otherwise, you'll pass the fuck out before your afternoon class."

When he says it like that, I can't do anything but agree with him.

"Fine, but you don't have to be so graphic about it. Besides, the coffee attacked me. I was a victim."

As we leave the classroom that holds our moans and my pleasure, I start telling Grey about the incident this morning, how rivers of steaming coffee surrounded me while people just stared at me. We're almost out of the building when my phone starts vibrating, alerting me that a text just came through. I'm distracted, talking to Greyson and reveling in his laugh, while I pull out my phone. Checking the screen, my blood runs cold at the unknown number on the screen. My change of mood must be obvious because Grey looks at me and pauses in his laughter. "Vixen, is everything okay? You're pale."

I look down at my phone, deciding that I need to tell Grey about how I found out about the bet in the first place. Holding my phone up to him, I explain, "I never told you why or how I knew about the bet. When I was leaving your house yesterday, I got a text from an unknown number or blocked sender, or whatever, telling me that you'd never be interested in me and to ask you about the bet. At first, I thought it was Felicity since she was such an asshole at your house, but I'm not sure." I swallow, glancing at the storm brewing in his blue eyes and the heavy set to his jaw. "Anyway, another text just came through from an unknown number."

"Open the text." His voice is so low, so deep, that it almost sounds like a growl.

"What?"

"Ava, open the fucking text. I already want to kill whoever is trying to fuck with you. I'm trying to not lose my shit right now, but I'm close, real fucking close. So, please, open that fucking text and let me see what the fucker has to say."

Unlocking my phone, I go to my messages and click on the new message from the unknown number. Grey's hovering over my shoulder and we read the message at the same time.

Unknown Number: Do your parents know what a little whore you are?

"What the fuck?" Grey nearly yells as my heart plummets. Below the message is a picture of me, lying back with Grey between my legs. With my legs and ass exposed, it's obvious what's going on, while the desks in the background make it clear that we're in a classroom. Grey's face is obscured by my legs, making him unidentifiable, but there's no denying who I am. My head is thrown back, but my distinct nose and mole on my upper lip are evident in the photo.

I feel my chest start to compress, my breaths becoming shallow and short while I try to catch my breath. This person took a private moment, a moment that felt special, and made it sordid and dirty and intruded on my body. I pull on the neck of my shirt. Fuck, it's hard to breathe.

"Vixen, baby, look at me." Grey's voice breaks through the fog clouding my brain. "Ava, look at me and breathe. Take a deep breath. Good girl. You're doing good, baby." Grey stands there with me, breathing through my freak-out. His hands cup my face, and he continues tracking my breaths. "I'm going to find whoever sent this and fucking eviscerate them."

"Nice word choice," I mumble.

"There's my girl." Grey smiles.

The panic that seized my chest loosens just in time for another text to come through.

Unknown Number: I can't wait to tell everyone what a fucking whore you are. End things or I'll be sure everyone you know gets a full view of your fat ass.

Ava

The minutes between receiving the last text and arriving back at my dorm are a blur. Vaguely, I remember Grey hustling me to his car, buckling me in, and driving in silence to the lot closest to my dorm room. I must be in shock right now because everything seems to just slow down and go mute. It's like I'm aware that things are happening around me, but I can't quite comprehend what's going on. My stomach is twisting, knots form and loosen like a boy scout trying to earn their merit badge. Nausea rolls through me, and I need to get the fuck out of this car before my stomach acid melts the window.

Grey parks close to the woods, furthest away from the entrance and the people scattered along the lawn in front of the building. I'm out of the car and bent over, dry heaving, before the car comes to a full stop. I feel a hand wrap around my hair, pulling it back from my face, while another hand strokes my back, offering comfort as I try not to vomit on my shoes. With nothing besides coffee in my system, I don't have much to lose, but the nausea is never-ending. Gagging while Grey tries to console me, I could probably die at this moment if I tried hard enough.

"It's okay, baby. You're okay."

"Everything hurts and I'm dying," I grunt between dry heaves, not caring to hear Grey's attempts at calming me down. Greyson isn't the one whose face is perfectly visible while getting fucked in the middle of a classroom. God, if that picture circulates, my parents will kill me. My stomach clenches. My dad's eyes will probably burn from shame if he sees me in that position. "My parents are going to murder me. I'm going to end up on one of their podcasts because it will be considered justified filicide," I wheeze. "They won't even have to do time. They'll get off with a warning."

"Ava, let's go inside. You'll breathe easier when you're in your own space."

"Shut up, Greyson. My father is going to see my bare ass, and then I'll need to drop out and join a convent." I drop my head between my legs. To a casual observer, I probably look like I'm about to do a forward roll on the lawn. "The closest I'll get to a kitchen is in the convent's cafeteria."

"Okay, that's enough. Let's go." Strong arms swoop me up and carry me bridal style across the parking lot and into my building. My head is buried in his neck, and though I can't see the stares we're getting, I can feel them. If I weren't having such a fantastic meltdown right now, I would soak up the feel of Grey's arms around me. As it stands, I just want to disappear.

"Vixen, which floor are you on?" I mumble my floor and room number into his neck, surprised when he heads toward the stairs instead of the elevator. Lifting my head to make sure I'm not imagining it, Grey strides up the stairs like I weigh nothing more than a backpack.

"What are you doing?" I question. "We have an elevator." I should ask him to put me down, but I'm too emotional and doubt that I'll be motivated to move once he sets me down.

"This is quicker. I wasn't waiting for a fucking elevator when I can walk."

"Okay, but you're also carrying me, and I'm not exactly light."

He squeezes me closer to him. "Ava, I told you twice already, stop talking about yourself as though you're anything less than perfect. It pisses me off and makes me want to show you just how flawless you are."

My eyes roll heavenward. "I'm not shit-talking myself. I'd say that about any grown-ass adult being carried up three flights of stairs." We reach my floor, and Grey walks us out of the stairwell and into the common room.

"Yeah, well don't. Which way?" I point him in the direction of my hall. Luckily, the common room and my hallway are empty, saving me from one tiny slice of mortification today. With Grey's long legs, we're in front of my room and pushing our way inside in seconds. CeCe bolts upright on her bed and gasps at the intrusion. Even in her sleep-addled state, she takes one look at me and knows something is very, very wrong.

Granted, Greyson carrying me into my dorm room at ten in the morning is a giveaway.

"Aves, what's wrong? Are you hurt?" Her eyes narrow on Greyson's hold. "You slimy motherfucker. What did you do to her?"

"Put me down, Grey," I whisper. His arms don't budge. "Grey, please."

A grunt is the only response I receive before my feet are back on the ground. "C," I start, my voice breaking almost instantly. "S-someone saw us, saw me."

CeCe climbs off her bed and runs over to me. Her hands grip my shoulders, as though she can physically hold me together. "Aves, what do you mean someone saw you? What happened?"

I take a breath and recount how Grey and I were together in a classroom and someone, somehow, snuck a picture of us in a compromising position. I don't give her particulars on what we did in that room because there's only so much chaos I can experience in one day. And, if I know anything about CeCe, a revelation like that would send us into complete mayhem for the rest of the morning.

"Wait a goddamn minute, Ava Maria," CeCe fumes, dropping my shoulders and pacing the room. "Are you telling me some cretin took a picture of you without your knowledge and then accused you of being a whore?"

She knows the answer to the question and doesn't wait for my response before she continues, "I will kill them, snuff the life out of them with my bare freaking hands. If they think I don't know my way around a ten-inch scalpel just because I'm an English major, they have another thing coming."

Grey steps closer to me, reminding me of his presence. With Cece's ranting, I nearly forgot he was in the room with us. "She's kind of terrifying," Grey whispers loud enough so that I can hear, but quiet enough that CeCe doesn't notice. I smile at his observation. It's times like this when I thank God I have her on my side.

"You have no idea." She once put bleach in Mikayla Johnson's shampoo during a sleepover because she told me I couldn't eat a donut for breakfast since I was too fat. Where she found bleach, she never said.

"Okay, so, here's what we're going to do—"

"No," I cut her off. "We're not going to do anything. I am going to lay low and pray to God that this just goes away."

"And how exactly do you plan to lay low?" CeCe questions me, not buying into my plan based on her tone.

"I'm going to go to class, hang out with my best friend and new friend, and come back to my dorm and sleep."

"And what about me, vixen?" Grey's voice fills the space. Stealing my shoulders, I turn to face him. Before I can respond, he continues, "We talked about this. You're not icing me out or pretending I'm not there. I don't give a fuck what this pussy behind the phone says. It's not fucking happening."

"But I care, Greyson," I rasp, trying everything I can to keep the tears from spilling over. "They've threatened me, taken pictures of me, and called me a whore, all because I've been in your orbit. What if—" I stop, a sob breaking free. "What if they send it to my parents? Greyson, I can't have my parents see me like that."

He stares at me, taking in the tears freely running down my face. "Is this what you want, vixen? To be done with me?"

I shake my head. "It's not that I want it, Grey, but what choice do we have? I need to think about what's best for me. I can't risk having my naked body advertised around campus."

Grey steps close to me, bringing his hand to my face before capturing my lips with his. The kiss is brief but possessive, as though he's marking me as his and taunting me to challenge him. "I'm going to figure out who this asshole is and fucking end this. Answer my texts."

"Grey, I just told you—"

"Oh, I'll leave you alone, physically. But, like I told you, I want to know you, and I'm going to get to fucking know you, vixen. We're not over, not by a long shot." He places a quick kiss on my lips before turning toward the door and walking out of our room.

"Holy shit," CeCe breathes out.

"I know."

I threw myself on my bed after Grey left, blocking out reality, and CeCe's constant stream of threats to my blackmailer, as she calls them, by napping the morning away. I don't feel better when I wake up hours later; I don't look better either. Truthfully, I don't smell too good. The musk of sex lingers on my skin and permeates the air, reminding me of how good Grey made me feel before everything came crumbling down. I huff and roll to my side, what a shit show. While most college freshmen are free to explore their newfound freedom and sexuality, I acquired a fucked-up peeping Tom, determined to have me star in the next Marymount porn. It's not lost on me that this would only happen to me.

Picking up my phone from the docking station on the table beside my bed, I check the time, noting that I have two hours before my next class. I have missed calls and texts from my mom and Sera and a voice message from Grey. I know he's determined to find the person responsible for the texts and picture, but I can't deal with him right now. Whether it's Felicity or one of her followers, I just want them to leave me alone. Even though it sucks, it seems like avoiding Greyson for the foreseeable future is the solution to this problem.

Unlocking my phone, I bring up my mom's contact information and call her. It's just before noon, so she should be on her lunch break. The phone rings twice before she answers, nearly shouting my name into the receiver.

"Ava! Baby, we miss you so much. How is everything? How are your classes? Are you making friends? Any boys?"

I laugh, rolling my eyes at the rapid-fire questions so typical of my attorney mother. "Calm down, Deborah. One question at a time before you give me a headache."

"You're so difficult, Ava. Let's start simple, how are classes?"

"I've only had one class so far; I have another one in about two hours." I shrug as though she can see me. "My class this morning was algebra, so it sucked."

"Well, it's a requirement, so you'll just need to get through it."

"No shit, Mom."

"Ava, do not give me an attitude. You called me, remember?"

"Only because you called me, like, six times, Deborah." I love giving her shit and this felt like a much-needed dose of normalcy to the mess I found myself in.

"Well, you have a phone, so answer the damn thing." She sighs into the phone. "What about friends? Have you and Celeste met any nice people?" My mother knows that CeCe and I are a package deal, and if one of us forms a friendship, it's inevitable that the other will follow suit. Some may say we're codependent, but she's my best friend and brings out the side of myself that I often keep hidden, while I ground her and make sure she doesn't end up on a show like *Snapped*. It's a give-and-take relationship.

"We met this genius, Serena. She's our age but started college when she was, like, fifteen." She offers a surprised sound. "She has an apartment on campus," I continue. "She said I can come over and cook whenever I need or want to, as long as I feed her."

My mom laughs, knowing how excited I am to have free reign over a kitchen. "Just make sure you don't spend every second cooking, Ava. You're there to learn and figure out what you want to do with your life, but don't forget you need to explore yourself. College is a time to explore who you are apart from the Gregori family name or as 'CeCe and Ava.'" She pauses and I hear talking in the background. "Aves, listen, a client just walked into the office. I'll call you later with Daddy, okay? And don't think I forgot that you didn't answer my question about boys. Expect a cross-examination tonight."

My stomach tightens at the mention of boys, bringing my mind right back to Greyson. I say a quick goodbye and make a promise that I'll speak to them later, though I know I won't answer the call. My mother will hear right through my lies if I tell her I haven't met any guys and telling her that I got eaten out in a classroom seems like too much information.

Ignoring my sister's text—I'll read it later—I open Grey's voice message. His voice fills the space.

"Hey, vixen, I can't stop thinking about you, the way you taste, the way you look when you come. I know you don't want to be seen with me, but baby, I don't want to stay away. As soon as I find out who's behind this shit, I'll do everything I can to make their lives a living fucking hell. No one hurts you and gets away with it, remember that, vixen." I pause the message, breathing in deeply before I continue his recording. "Linc is in your class this afternoon; he'll look out for you and make sure no one bothers you. I

131

have class until seven tonight, but I'll call you after. Answer your phone, baby; don't leave me hanging."

His possessive tone was hot, and though I knew that I should avoid all contact, even through the phone, there was something about his authoritative command that just did it for me. Unlike my parents' call tonight, I won't ignore Grey.

I don't bother responding; part of me knows that he isn't expecting a response. Another part of me, the one that's just a little cruel, wants him to sweat and wonder where I stand. He has bulldozed into every part of my life within days of meeting him, and I won't let him think that he can tell me to jump at any given minute.

Tossing my phone aside, I get out of bed, ready to wash the remnants of sex, desire, and shame from my body.

—

By the time I make it to my next class in the kitchen lab, I'm breathing easier and have rationalized the events of the morning. I'm not sure if my improved disposition is thanks to my nap or the stainless steel appliances surrounding me. There's something calming about the gleaming silver countertops combined with the sterile smell of bleach; it doesn't remind me of home exactly, but it does ease the storm in my mind.

Most of the lab tables are filled with students, significantly more than I had anticipated. Surveying the room, my eyes catch on Lincoln, waving wildly in the front of the room, right next to the demonstration table. Next to him is an empty stool that, apparently, is meant for me. I notice the glares aimed at me as I walk toward Lincoln, some are curious but most, especially the women's, are downright hostile.

"If Grey thought you would be doing me favors by having me sit with you in this class, he underestimated the female population in this program," I whisper to Lincoln as I take a seat.

Lincoln looks back toward the class and scowls. "They're just pissed that you'll be my partner for the practical."

"Oh?" I question.

"I'm the best one in this class and they know it. Fucking losers. The doe-eyed twins over there..." Lincoln gestures with his chin toward two brunettes with the longest eyelashes I've ever seen. They must be twins, or cousins, or something because there is no way God produced that in two separate families. Taking a closer look, I realize that they're probably false lashes. Lincoln continues, "They tried to fight each other for your seat."

"The one on the right looks like her eyelashes are about to fall off," I observe, horrified by the thought.

"They probably are. Her extensions fell into her cassoulet last year and she failed the French practical. I would rather eat maggots on a deer carcass than work with her."

Laughter bubbles out of me, both from his disgusting visual and the thought of a floating extension in a classic French soup. "That is unfortunate."

"It was a fucking disaster. Besides, Grey would have my balls if I left you over there with the vipers. We're partners from here on, buttercup. You're lucky you make banging cannoli, otherwise, I'd leave you to the wolves."

"Uh, thank you?" We fall into a comfortable silence as the professor walks in, distributing our syllabus as she makes her way to the demonstration table. My hands sweat and excitement shoots up my spine, the texts and taunts from this morning momentarily forgotten in my excitement. The class moves quickly after introductions and icebreakers wrap up. After going over the syllabus and the expectations for each class, the professor dismisses us.

Lincoln walks at a leisurely pace, allowing my short legs to match the strides of his long ones. "I'm driving you back to your dorm," he says once we're out of the building.

"Uh, thank you, but it's a short walk."

"No," he chuckles, shaking his head. "It's not a request. Grey will cut my balls off and wear them like a goddamn necklace if I don't make sure you get home safely."

I scowl, annoyed that Grey is trying to dictate my life. "Lincoln, seriously, I'm okay."

"Nope, no. Not up for discussion." His hand grabs my shoulder and steers me toward the parking lot. "Do you realize that Grey's default personality is overbearing asshole? It's not just you; he's like this with everyone."

Lincoln looks over at me, seemingly contemplating if he should offer further explanation. His face scrunches, and he looks slightly constipated trying to get his thoughts in order. "Listen, I won't gossip like a little bitch behind his back, but... Grey is complicated. He's a good guy, but he likes to be in control at all times. Don't make this harder on us, just fucking comply and let me take you to your dorm so that I can keep my balls this week."

I look Lincoln over as we stop in front of an expensive cherry-red car. "Nice car," I comment.

He runs his hand over it like he's making love to his car. "Thank you. She's beautiful, isn't she?"

Honestly? It feels a little weird and like I'm intruding on a private moment. "Yes, very pretty."

He offers the car another lingering look before turning to me with a frown. "Get in the damn car before I have to call Grey and tell him you're making shit difficult."

"Fine, but I'm not happy about this." I pause, looking at him over the hood of his car. "And your obvious obsession with your car is weird."

Greyson

My blood is pounding in my ears, drowning out all sound as I sit through my business ethics class. It's one of my most challenging classes this semester, but I couldn't give two shits about what Professor Rawlins is saying because Ava's tears and disappointment play on my mind like a video loop. Seeing her so disgusted with herself because of the decision I made to bring her into that abandoned room makes me want to smash skulls.

My phone vibrates in my pocket, letting me know a text just came through. I grab my phone as discreetly as I can, not trying to completely piss off this professor, and see Linc's name flash across my screen.

Linc: Just dropped Ava off at her dorm. She wanted to kill me and insulted my car. You fucking owe me.

Lincoln and his fucking car, it's like he was pussy whipped by metal.

Grey: Thanks bro

I originally planned to call Ava as soon as I left this class, but based on Linc's brief overview of their encounter, I'm going to need to calm her sass down. I don't doubt that I need to wait until I'm back home, alone in my room, before I call her and coax her into relaxing.

Rawlins dismisses the class, but before I stand up from my seat in the back of the lecture hall, he calls, "Greyson Jansen, can I see you for a moment?" I make my way to his podium at the front of the room, waiting for him to look up from the stack of papers in front of him.

"You asked to see me, sir?" His eyes lift to mine and his lips thin, as though I'm disturbing him.

"Yes." He clears his throat. "You seemed distracted, son. This is an important class for you; don't make a habit of checking your phone during my lecture."

Fuck. "Yes, sorry, sir." I don't offer excuses because he doesn't want to hear them. I fucked up and made it obvious I wasn't paying attention to him, not that I regret checking in with Linc.

"Good." He nods his head, as though the conversation is settled. "Now, tell your father to talk to his former GM. I'm expecting big things from the Rockies this year, and they can't seem to get their heads out of their asses." My shoulders tense. It always goes back to my family, every single fucking time. If it's not my dad and his baseball career, it's my grandfather's company or my uncle's Oscars. I may have grown up amongst wealth and fame, but my dad never allowed me to act like a spoiled little bitch. And after everything that went down between him and his former GM, Dane Slater, he'd probably rather lose his left nut than associate with him.

"My dad stays on the reporting sidelines now, sir. He doesn't get involved with the teams." My eyes narrow on Rawlins. "Integrity and concise reporting mean something to him, you know?" I can't help but add.

Instead of tensing or bristling as I expect, he just laughs, a full, booming sound that makes it seem like I said something funny. "Mr. Jansen, there's no such thing as integrity. It's all about who you know and how much you're willing to do to get ahead." Still chuckling to himself, he makes his way to the front of the room, walking out without sparing me a backward glance. Fucking tool.

Exiting the room moments after Rawlins, I make quick work of getting to my Jeep. I could call Ava now, but between Linc's description of her mood and the sour taste in my mouth from Rawlins, I know I need to calm down. I grab my phone, dialing the one person I know that will help me put shit into perspective.

"Grey, I was just thinking about you," my dad's voice fills the car, flowing through the Bluetooth connection. I lean back into my seat, breathing easier already.

"Hey, Dad." Since my mom left, it's just been my dad and me. I'm close to my paternal grandparents, uncle, and cousins, but it's nothing like the support from my dad. Despite my dad's age and his divorce, he hasn't been with anyone seriously since my mom's bullshit went down. Even with all the therapy he put us through and my urging him to stop being a pussy and date, he refuses to tie himself down to anyone. I don't blame him; he's been through some shit. My parents were in high school when they found out they were pregnant with me. Before she left, my mom let me know every chance she got that she wanted to abort me but that my dad wouldn't let her. Even as a seventeen-year-old kid, my dad protected me. My grandparents stepped in, making sure that I had everything I'd ever need, and helped take care of me while my dad was in college.

Statistically, teen parents struggle and scrape by. My dad became a professional baseball player by twenty-two, carrying along a five-year-old kid and a coke addict of a wife the entire way. The day my mom left, on my eighth birthday, was the best day of my fucking life, though I didn't know it at the time. As a kid, I was desperate for her love; as an adult, with years of therapy embedded under my skin, I'm grateful she left and never came back.

"How was your first day of class? How are the guys doing?" My hand clenches around the steering wheel at the reminder of Rawlins.

"It's all good," I respond. I'm not the kind of rich prick that runs to my dad, complaining about trivial shit in the hopes he'll fix it. "Listen, I called you because I need your advice." I'm also not the kind of moron that won't ask for help or advice if it means that Ava's naked body will remain viewable to my eyes only. I'm a possessive asshole, and there's no way in hell I'm letting her body be the image guys jerk off to. The text claimed that they'd leave her alone if she left me alone, but that's not fucking happening.

"Of course, what do you need?"

I take a deep breath, knowing my dad will have sound advice but also give me shit for putting myself and Ava into this situation. "I met someone. Her name is Ava." I work my jaw, bringing her pretty face to the front of my

137

mind. "She's...fuck, Dad, she's pretty amazing."

"That's great, Grey. When did you meet her?"

"Last Thursday."

Laughter greets my response. "Well, that's quick. Tell me about her."

I tell him about her wit, the sarcasm that's been evident in every interaction we've had. I detail her gorgeous face, her deep, expressive eyes, and the dreams of opening her own restaurant that she shared with me. "She's in one of Linc's classes and the asshole agreed to be her partner."

My dad lets out a low whistle, understanding the volumes it speaks for Linc to pair with her. "He's more of a Type A personality than you, so she must be pretty talented to warrant that."

"She is."

"Grey, she seems like a special young lady. What else is going on? You said you needed my advice?" I laugh at my dad's use of "young lady." He's thirty-eight but tries to act like an old man with this shit.

"Listen, I need you to promise that you're not going to shit yourself when I tell you what's going on."

"Grey, what's going on?" My dad's voice is tense. To most people, they'd think he was over my shit, but I know it's his concern bleeding through.

"We hooked up in a place we probably shouldn't have, and some asshole took a picture and sent it to her." My blood starts boiling again at the mention of those texts. "They're threatening her with releasing it unless she stays away from me."

"Fuck, Greyson. Is she okay? Jesus Christ, what were you thinking, hooking up in a public place? Haven't you learned anything from my mistakes?" My dad doesn't do relationships, but he dates... a lot. When I was in middle school, pictures of him and models would consume magazines. His bare ass has been on TMZ more times than I can count, and there are social media accounts dedicated to his dick. A twelve-year-old shouldn't have to see his old man's balls when he Googles him.

"Not really. She's using this bullshit to push me away, but I'm trying to fix it without that happening. And it just happened. She left the house yesterday after this girl tried to lay claim to me. She wouldn't answer my calls or texts, so I got her in a private room. Things... escalated." That's putting it fucking mildly.

"Do you know who is sending the text messages and the picture?"

"I have an idea, yeah."

"You need to respect her wants and give her space. Son, I know you're hurting right now, but if a picture gets out with your dick flapping in the wind, you'll look like a hero. For a woman, she'll be reduced to a commodity and will have to fight tooth and nail to recover from that kind of violation. I'm not saying either of you should be okay with your privacy being compromised, but you need to understand that she will take the brunt of the attack."

"Fuck." I grip the steering wheel tighter, all the color draining from my fingers. "I fucking know, okay. But how do I make this better? I can't explain it but this girl, Jesus, Dad, she's different. She's special, and I don't want her getting hurt because I pissed off the wrong person."

"You think this has to do with you?"

"I know it does." I tell him about Felicity, her near-obsession, and the shit she spewed at Ava yesterday.

My dad sighs into the phone, sounding much older than his thirty-eight years. "You're going to give me gray hairs, Grey. Let me speak to some people I know and see what they say. I have a buddy in the NYPD that handles computer crimes. I'll see what he thinks."

"Thanks, Dad."

"Thank me by keeping it in your goddamn pants, Grey."

I hang up on my dad, not bothering to respond to his last comment. I get where he's coming from; Ava stands to lose more than me if that picture gets out there. Running my fingers through my hair, I lock my emotions down before reversing and hauling ass home. My fingers grip the steering wheel like a vice during the drive, imagining that I could strangle the shit out of Felicity and whoever else is working with her on this. My speculation doesn't do shit to help Ava, but the fantasy of ruining Felicity's life helps my drive home pass quickly.

After parking my Jeep in front of the house, I grab my shit and make my way inside, heading right to the primary on the first floor. My phone is to my ear, and I wait for Ava to answer her phone. I warned her that I was calling, so she shouldn't be surprised. The line continues ringing and my frustration grows. Clenching my fist, I drop to my bed, still listening to the ringing on the other end of the line.

"Hello?" Ava's voice is a balm to the storm brewing inside me.

"Hey, vixen." I rub a hand over my face, trying to wipe away the last eight hours. "I didn't think you'd answer."

"I almost didn't." I can't help but laugh; at least she's honest.

"So why did you?"

There's a moment of silence before she clears her throat. "Because I know it's not your fault, even though this person is obsessed with you." Her voice rises at the end of her sentence, as though she's annoyed that someone would be interested in me. I smirk at her jealousy, relieved that she's feeling something besides disgust at me, the situation, and this asshole. "And," she continues, "I enjoyed our morning before, you know, everything happened." I lean forward, more than willing to follow her lead on this.

"Tell me what you enjoyed, pretty girl."

"You know what I liked, Greyson. Don't make me say it."

I can picture her eye roll. Craving more of her sass, I tease, "Tell me, vixen, did you like it when I put my mouth on your sweet cunt?"

"Greyson," she groans.

"Or maybe you liked when my fingers were fucking your tight little hole," I continue, remembering how her body responded to me. "Do you want to know my favorite part?" I question, wanting to see if she rises to my bait. "Come on, vixen, ask me."

A minute of silence ticks by before Ava's low voice asks, "What was your favorite part?"

"How sweet you tasted when you came on my mouth. Fuck, Ava," I groan, palming my growing dick through my jeans. "Do you have any idea of how sexy you are, how delicious your little pussy is?"

"Greyson, please," Ava whispers.

"Yeah, baby, tell me what you need."

Ava draws in a ragged breath before releasing a sigh. "Greyson, stop. This is moving at lightning speed. Let's just, I don't know..." She pauses. "Let's just talk. Get to know each other."

Fuck, she's right, I need to rein it in. She's a virgin for fuck's sake and I'm here, picturing how tight her walls will squeeze my cock when I finally have her under me. I fall back on my bed, letting out a loud sigh before responding, "You're right, I'm sorry. There's something about you, something about us together, that makes me lose my goddamn mind."

"It's okay, it's just a little bizarre. I mean, you know what my vagina tastes like, but you don't know my favorite color or how I like my coffee."

"What's your favorite color, vixen?"

"Well..." she begins, and I can hear her smile through the phone. "It depends on my mood. When I'm happy or feeling optimistic about life, I love red. Not a cherry red or an apple red, but a deep blood red. Like when you get a paper cut and drops of blood fall on paper." Well, that's weird as fuck, but I can't say that I'm not intrigued. "If I'm feeling moody, angsty, or like I need to listen to 2010's emo music, my favorite color is black or a dark gray, like charcoal or gunmetal."

"What's your favorite color today?"

She pauses before answering. "It's a solid black tonight, dark as midnight without stars to illuminate the sky."

"Ava, fuck," I rasp out, her omission and her haunted voice causing an ache in my chest. She's fucking gutting me without even realizing it. "I'm sorry, I shouldn't have brought you into that room this morning. I just, fucking..." I pause, running a hand over my face. "I'm just fucking sorry."

A heavy silence greets me, and I have to look at my screen to make sure she didn't hang up on me. I wouldn't be surprised if she did; I've taken a critical piece of her innocence, not only by savoring her body but by leaving it vulnerable for someone else to see, scrutinize, and covet. Moments become minutes and I'm losing my goddamn mind trying to figure out if she's going to respond to me.

"Vixen, please, say something."

"What's your favorite color?"

—

It's been three weeks since I've seen Ava, and even though my right hand is practically raw from the amount of attention it's been paying to my dick, I can't lie and say that getting to know Ava isn't worth it. Without the option of fucking, or hell, even looking at her in person, we've gotten to know each other pretty fucking well.

We spent hours the first night talking about our favorite colors, our majors, our dreams, and our families. She nearly made me piss my pants when she recounted how she snuck up behind a grown-ass man and hopped on his back because she thought it was her brother. Turns out, he was a middle-aged man with zero interest in piggyback rides.

From that night on, we spoke every day, multiple times a day. She tried to keep things casual through text messages at first, but it didn't take long until she was spending hours on the phone or FaceTime with me.

I told her about my family, the unwavering support of my father, and the abandonment of my mother. I didn't shy away from talking about how the fame of my family follows me like an albatross, a constant reminder that I'm not a normal college student but come from a family that's had multiple documentaries made about their lives. It surprised the hell out of me when she admitted to watching the Netflix documentary about my dad's career, especially since she does not know shit about baseball.

She detailed her family dynamic and how her lawyer parents make her life just as public. I didn't admit it, but I've listened to her parents' podcast a few times; it freaked me the fuck out. They use phrases like "bludgeoned to death" and "decapitated by a machete" with such cool detachment that I can't stomach listening to it.

Ava's opened up to me in a way I didn't expect, a way that's not fueled by her desire to own me or my dick. She's refused to talk about our bedroom or classroom encounters, and I've been careful not to bring them up after she told me to stop, but I'd be lying if I said I didn't think of her naked and beneath me, or on top of me, every hour of every fucking day. You don't get a woman like Ava naked and pliant in your arms just to forget how they look in that position.

During our daily FaceTime, calls, and texts, Ava spoke about her siblings a lot. As the oldest in her family, it's clear that she's protective of her sisters and brother and that she'd throw down for them if it ever came to it. She can't be more than five feet and one hundred-forty pounds, so there's no way she's beating anyone's ass, especially with her lack of coordination. It kills me to hear her talk like she's a seven-foot linebacker with a black belt in jujitsu. I'd intervene in any fight she found herself in, but she talks and acts like a little killer. I fucking love it.

She hasn't gotten another text or picture message since our morning in the classroom. I'm trying to convince her that the threat has passed, but she's stubborn as fuck and refuses to be seen with me in public, or even sneak me over to her dorm. I won't pressure her, but my hand is fucking tired of gripping my dick to the memory of her taste. I'm sick of seeing her over the screen of the phone and listening to her voice through a fiber optic network and underground cables. The three weeks I've kept my physical distance have sucked balls, but Ava's finally gotten to the point where she's calling me, texting me first, and not waiting on me every time. Her smiles, her laugh, are addictive, and I crave her in a way I've never craved a woman before. It's not just the physical with her— it's everything.

She's everything.

On our call last night, she couldn't hold back her excitement that her family is visiting this weekend. I helped her map out where she would take them for dinner and then where she'd go out with her brother and sister out after. She didn't mention that it was her birthday, but Dante's pit bull offered up that information. I'm not sure what's going on between them, but Celeste has Dante's balls in a fucking jar. He doesn't make a move without considering what Celeste would think about it. Dante has one hand glued to his phone, constantly waiting for a message from Celeste that rarely comes.

I'd give him shit about it, but I'm not much better.

My little vixen withheld important information, information that I shouldn't have heard through a fucked-up grapevine. I can't decide if I want to call her out on it or surprise her with my knowledge. Throughout these last three weeks, I've realized she has a short temper and gets worked up quickly. I've threatened to spank her perky ass for that mouth of hers, but she thinks I'm joking. I'll never tell her that the fantasy of her ass turning pink from my hands is one of the sexiest images. When I finally have my hands on her, she'll realize that I'm not fucking around.

This weekend can't come fast enough.

Ava

When I was younger, I always imagined that my birthday would be greeted with confetti, my grandmother's icebox cake, and video montages of me on social media from my many, many friends. At nineteen, I've realized that I hate confetti, dairy makes my skin break out, and I have two friends outside of my family. Well, three friends if I count Greyson as a friend, though I'm not sure he would be pleased with that designation.

As a preteen, I would get so upset that I didn't have a larger circle of friends, or that I wasn't part of the popular group like my younger siblings. Now, however, I'm relieved I don't need to field endless messages from people that pretend to give a shit about me.

Speaking of messages, my sisters will kill me if I don't return their FaceTime call. I've been a shitty communicator lately, mainly because I'm terrified that every time my phone goes off there will be another message from the asshole that decided to violate my privacy. Thankfully, there hasn't been a single text since the first day of classes. I'm not sure if that's because I've avoided Grey or because they've lost interest in my life.

I bite my lip at the thought of Grey. When he answered my FaceTime last night, he was shirtless and in the middle of his workout. My jaw was damn near unhinged at the sight of his endless rows of defined abs and a chest that had the perfect amount of hair. I never thought I'd be into chest hair, but something about seeing Grey glistening from his workout, with sweat gleaming off his tattooed arm and chest, made me salivate. Even Grey's knowing, cocky smirk didn't stop my ogling.

Without knowing it, Grey gave me one hell of a birthday present. In the dark, under the covers and away from the risk of cameras and judgment, I touched myself to thoughts of Grey's delicious body, the tattoos decorating his pale skin, and the memory of his lips. Though no orgasm can compare to the two he's given me, I imagined that it was his fingers inside me and rubbing against my clit. When I came, it was his name on my lips and his face in my head. Even now, sitting here in broad daylight with my dorm's door wide open, I'm getting hot remembering how freaking good he looked.

I'd never tell him, because the cocky asshole would never let me live it down, but he's ruined every other sexual fantasy I have ever had. Probably all future fantasies, too, if I'm being honest. A twenty-one-year-old guy should not have as much sex appeal as he does, yet he defies the odds. Despite the picture taken without our consent, I don't regret giving Greyson my body and letting him command and contort it to his will. Now, three weeks later, I can admit that there was something so hot about hooking up in public, the threat of discovery only made the orgasm that much more explosive. Grey's hinted more than once that he's done with the unknown number's bullshit, especially since it's been radio silence for over three weeks.

Maybe it's my paranoia, or maybe I fear that once Grey has me at his mercy again, he'll quickly lose interest, but I'm hesitant to see him in person. I couldn't resist him when I barely knew him, but now that I know his innermost wants, fears, and trauma, I am a fucking goner. I'm trying to push our next in-person encounter as far out as possible because I know I will act like a dog in heat as soon as I see him. There is a one hundred percent chance that I will physically maul him the next time we're together, and I am terrified of what that means.

He doesn't realize how far gone I am, and that's the whole reason I didn't mention my birthday or how badly I want him. If he knew, he wouldn't take my resistance seriously and would march his perfect Viking ass to my dorm room immediately.

Lost in my thoughts, I nearly miss my vibrating phone laying on my desk. Picking it up, I see Sera's name flash across the screen, alerting me to a FaceTime call. Propping the pillows up behind me on the bed, I accept the call.

"About time, you jerk." Sera's beautiful face fills the screen, a scowl marring her delicate features. "I've been calling you for like three days and you keep sending 'I'm busy' text messages. I am not happy, Ava Maria. Not happy at all."

I laugh at her, unable to take her seriously. "I'm sorry, Sera, but I have been busy. College isn't like high school; I have classes throughout the day and my breaks are filled with studying and homework. I promise I'm not ignoring you intentionally." I never thought I'd be able to lie to my sister so easily, but here we are, avoiding all conversations of Grey, the anonymous text messages, and the shit show that is my life.

"Fine," she huffs, blowing her bangs off her face. "Happy birthday, Aves. I'm excited to see you this weekend. Where are we going again?"

"The soccer house. There's no theme or anything."

"Theme?"

I grimace. "Yeah, for some reason, all the Greek parties have a theme. Last week, C and I went to an anything but clothes party, or ABC, and had to leave the dorm in artfully draped curtains and hot glued leaves."

Sera's jaw drops. "What? Why would you do that? What were you even trying to be?"

"Well..." I begin, pursing my lips in memory of the cheap, scratchy fabric against my skin. "We were trying to be Lilith and Eve after being cast out of Paradise, but all of our leaves fell off on the walk to the pregame house, so we just looked like we were wearing cheap curtains." Weirdly enough, both CeCe and I received a lot of male attention, and I even had a few guys ask for my number. The entire time, my phone was burning a hole in my bag, the incoming texts from Greyson taunting me. I didn't tell him we were there, but he saw my Instagram stories of me and CeCe in our outfits and wouldn't leave me alone until he knew I was back in my dorm, safe and tucked in.

I wish I could have been into the two Sigma Kappas that showed interest in me, but neither of them was a Viking god. Grey has ruined everything.

"Ava, that is the most bizarre thing I have ever heard." She pauses, tilting her head in consideration. Lowering her voice, she whispers, "Don't you dare tell Bianca. You know she's part exhibitionist and will hitchhike to you

147

if she finds out about parties like that." I cringe. Bianca is insane enough that she would do that.

"How pissed is she that Mom and Dad aren't letting her stay for the weekend?"

"She put together a PowerPoint explaining why she should be allowed to stay up there. So, there's that."

"Insanity. I'm so excited you and Rafe are staying up here though."

"Yeah, so about Rafe," Sera says hesitantly. "He's coming to dinner but he, uh, isn't staying. But, before you freak out, he has a good reason. He met a girl from Crescent Hills and they have a date on Sunday, so he wants to be home to prepare." She shakes her head, as though that explains everything. When I'm not being a self-centered jerk, I'll be able to admit that it does. Rafe is a planner and hates feeling unprepared. After his shit show of a relationship with his ex-girlfriend, I know that his need to prepare is driven by fear and uncertainty. But, since I'm being a self-centered bitch and he's not coming out for our birthdays, I'm not going to be understanding. At least, not initially.

"Are you kidding me? I've been looking forward to having both of you up here for so long."

"I know, I know. To our credit, if you would have answered your damn phone two days ago, we could have talked this out. You have to accept some of the blame, big sister. And, anyway, I'm bringing Hyacinth up with me."

I suppress a shudder. My sister's best friend, Hyacinth Montgomery, is the youngest of four sisters and they all have floral names: Rose, Lilac, and Juniper being her elder sisters. I went to school with Juniper, and let's just say, she's a raging monster and hates the ground I walk on. Hyacinth isn't much better, she may even be worse, but for some reason, Sera keeps her close.

"Oh, how... lovely?" I supply.

Sera rolls her eyes. "Don't be a brat. It's my birthday, too. Cin is harmless, she's just a little high-strung and misunderstood."

"Mhm. Sure, she is."

"If this is how you're going to act when we speak, I'm not sure why I even bother calling."

I smirk, enjoying the feeling of annoying my younger sister. "You call because Bianca is batshit crazy, and you miss me."

"True."

I look at the time on my phone and offer an apologetic smile. "Sorry, Sera, but I need to get ready to meet C and Serena before class. I'll see you on Saturday, and don't forget to bring stuff to go out with."

"Fine. Bye." My sister hangs up before I have the chance to say goodbye or ask her to relay a message to my parents. I try not to be too annoyed with her, especially since she's pissed at me for ignoring her for the last few weeks. Between my constant conversations with Grey, class, and otherwise avoiding my phone, I haven't made a lot of time for my family. I should feel guilty, except I can't apologize for taking care of myself and what's important to me right now. While, yes, I should probably avoid all interactions with Grey, I can't deny that he makes me feel seen for the first time in my life.

Gathering my things in my bag and draping my double-breasted chef's jacket over my arm, I turn the lights off in the room. I have my second practical for my Fundamentals of Baking and Pastry class. Though I was thoroughly annoyed with Grey for forcing Lincoln to partner with me on my first day of class, I can't deny that he's a knowledgeable partner. In our first practical, our professor had us work together to create pâte à choux, a staple in French patisserie. The choux, which is used to make desserts like eclairs, churros, and beignets, needs to be light and airy, rich but light. Lincoln, with his model looks and surly attitude, is like a wizard in the kitchen and led us through a successful bake. We were one of the only pairs to present something edible to our professor, Chef Adrian. The poor doe-eyed twins presented the equivalent of a Lego. I smile to myself as I walk across campus, remembering the look of utter disbelief and revulsion on chef's face.

Normally, I wouldn't find joy in someone else's failure, but the doe-eyed twins were dickheads. From the moment Lincoln made it clear he and I were partners, they decided I was enemy number one. Between their comments about the way I look and their nasty looks in my direction, they acted like I killed their dog. Whatever I thought college would be, it didn't include making enemies in every group I came across.

Luckily, the maintenance technician in the dining hall forgave me for the coffee attack of 2023. Granted, I had to bring him the leftover pastry from my first practical, but he was no longer eyeing me warily every time I walked up to the coffee dispensers.

My trip across campus to the local coffee shop, Beans & Things, takes less than ten minutes. I inhale deeply as I open the door to the shop, appreciating the fragrant smell of coffee and buttery baked goods. If I could, I would bottle this scent up and douse myself with it every day instead of perfume.

Glancing at the tables, I see CeCe and Serena huddled in a corner booth with three drinks in front of them.

"One of those better be for me," I joke, sliding into the seat across from them.

CeCe rolls her eyes, pushing the mug toward me.

"You look great, Ava," Serena rushes out.

I look down at my black long-sleeved T-shirt and leggings before looking back up at her.

"Uh, thanks?" I'm in the plainest clothes I own, not willing to risk staining my beloved clothes while baking. She seems unusually peppy, but I won't question the compliment.

"Of course. You're glowing. Your hair looks great. Did you do something to it?"

"Okay, I was willing to accept the first compliment, but you're rambling." I eye her, then CeCe. Raising an eyebrow, I question, "Okay, what's going on?"

"Nothing." They respond at the same time. Not suspicious at all.

"Cut the shit."

They share a look, one that immediately sets me on edge. "Okay, so we were going to wait to tell you," Serena begins. "I spoke to Dyl, and the guys are going to the soccer house this weekend."

I look at her, confused. "Okay, will that be an issue for you with Devin and Marina?"

CeCe shakes her head. "No, Aves, like all the guys. Meaning Dante, Lincoln, and... Grey."

"Oh."

"Yeah. And before you even suggest going to a different party, no."

"Wait, but it's my birthday." I drop my voice, leaning in closer. "You know why we can't go to the same party as them." In addition to telling CeCe everything about the text messages and picture, I confided in Serena, too.

"It is, my little birthday honey. With that said, the soccer party is the only one that's open. We don't have invitations to any of the other houses," CeCe responds. Dammit. Because of the limited number of sports and fraternities, most parties were invite-only to control the size. Now, a month later, it was easy to understand why Felicity was such a bitch about Serena joining us at the rush event. Invitations and RSVPs were sacred here.

"Maybe we should try Redford College?"

"Ava, we are not going to a different campus to go out." Serena sounds scandalized by the thought.

I sigh, resigning myself to a potential run-in. Fuck, who was I kidding? Knowing Grey, he would make a spectacle. My skin started to feel tight, like cellophane was shrinking around me, making it hard to breathe.

"Guys, but what happens if I get another text? W-what if they post that picture?" Beads of sweat form on my brow, and any levity I had from talking to my sister and memories of Grey's tattooed chest, vanish.

"Aves, it's been three weeks. There hasn't been a single message in all that time. I know you're freaked out. I understand you're scared, but you cannot live your life shrouded in fear over a potential calamity." CeCe reaches across the table and grabs my hand, pushing my mug of coffee away from me. Squeezing my hand, she continues, "You know that I would never willingly encourage you to jump into danger, but you like him. He's borderline, creepily obsessed with you. Are you going to let some faceless, nameless, dickface dictate your life?"

"Yes, I was planning to do that."

Her eyes roll with such force, I wouldn't be surprised if they got stuck like that. "The worst that could happen is your hot, sensual body is distributed to the masses. So what? Kim Kardashian made an entire career after her sex tape. Her dad was a lawyer, too."

Serena places a hand on CeCe's arm, pulling her away from me. "CeCe, I don't think that's helping here."

"I'm going to pretend that you didn't just say that. And it's not just that my parents will kill me, but my privacy was violated, Celeste. I can't just wipe it under the rug and say, 'Well, I look good in the picture, so it's okay.'" I shake my head, my annoyance growing. "It's not enough that they called me horrible things, that they made me doubt Grey's interest, but then they had to take a picture of my naked body while getting eaten out." My voice breaks and I swallow back the lump forming in my throat. "They fucking took that from me, from us, and made it a joke. I can't get over that and don't you fucking ask me to." My emotions are all over the place, and I want to vomit, punch something, and cry all at the same time.

Grabbing my coffee with shaking hands, I bring it to my mouth, inhaling deeply before swallowing a lukewarm sip.

"Aves, I'm sorry. I'm just trying to lighten the mood. But if you're serious about not being with Greyson in public, then this is an opportunity to show you're not together."

"I've been talking to that man every day, multiple times a day, for the last three weeks. He is possessive as fuck and the most alpha asshole I know, in a good way, but still. Do you honestly think he'll leave me alone if we're in the same space?" The question may as well be rhetorical because I know with absolute certainty that he will not.

"Ava, he's not a werewolf that recognized you as his fated mate, as hot as that is." This time, it's me rolling my eyes at CeCe's comment.

"Hey!" She smacks the table to get my attention. "I'm being serious. He's not feral, just speak to him before and let him know to stay away, even if he doesn't want to."

"Can we stop talking about this? My anxiety has anxiety at this point."

Serena offers me a small smile. "Of course, Ava."

We sit in silence for a few minutes, absorbing the shit show that will be this weekend. I sip my cooled coffee, wishing that it would settle my nerves.

"Oh, you have to be fucking kidding me," CeCe spits out, eyes on the door.

Turning in the booth, I see Felicity and Jordan walk in like they're in the middle of a photoshoot in Antarctica.

The weather is unseasonably warm, almost seventy degrees at the end of September. Looking at Felicity and Jordan, however, you would think they're snow bunnies in a lingerie campaign in the Alps. In mini slip dresses with faux fur puffer jackets on top, both have furry boots, plain baseball caps, and monogrammed designer bags. While Jordan is in black, literally from head to toe, Felicity is in a beige so light, it looks like she's not wearing anything under the fur jacket.

"I would never want someone to judge me, truly and honestly, and I say this with all the respect in the world, but what are they wearing?" Serena whispers, her face a cross between horror and awe.

"Fuck them. They don't deserve our respect. They're fucking blackmailers," CeCe seethes.

"C, we don't know that it's them for sure."

"Yes, we fucking do. Who else could it possibly be?"

"A million other people, C. I won't go on a witch hunt just because I suspect them to be behind it."

"Your passivity is pissing me off. You're content to just lie on your back and take this bullshit, yet you're mad at the prospect of seeing Grey. You just told us you would rather try to party at another college over an hour from here because of this shit. Grow a set of tits and face this." CeCe gets up and crosses the room until she's standing directly in front of the Bobbsey twins.

Celeste Lauren Downing has bigger balls than most of the men I know.

"Are you aware that it's seventy-five degrees outside? You look like idiots."

Felicity's sneer twists the features of her pretty face, reflecting the ugly personality she keeps hidden. "Listen, freshman, I don't know what hole you crawled out of, but we came in here for our iced lattes and didn't do shit to you. If you ever want to join a sorority on this campus, I suggest you turn around and walk your skinny ass far, far away from us."

"I could give two shits about joining a sorority if the other girls—sorry, women—are anything like you."

Felicity gasps like she's been hit. Her hand flies up to her chest like her heart is about to burst from the insult.

"How dare you."

"No, how dare you. You made enemies out of the wrong people, little girl. You see, I know people, and more importantly, I know how to dispose of a body. Leave me and mine alone, and we won't have any problems. Is that understood?"

Felicity's face contorts, continuing to morph into such a pinched expression, I wouldn't recognize her if I didn't witness the change. The entire coffee shop is staring at them, enjoying the show CeCe freely put on display. Suddenly, Felicity's face smooths, and her perfect, porcelain mask returns.

"Casey, I'm not sure that I know what you're talking about."

"Don't play stupid, you know my name. Stay away from us." She gestures toward our table, calling attention to me and Serena, like an idiot. I try to duck down, sliding deeper into the booth until I'm sure I'm no longer visible.

But you know what they say about trying? It's an omission of failure.

Felicity's laugh rings loud in the shop, making me groan because I know that she saw me.

"Trust me, Casey, I want nothing to do with you, your fat friend, or the brain. You're all fucking pathetic. I mean, really? Coming up to me in a coffee shop while I was minding my own business? If I didn't know better, I'd say you were stalking me. Hm, maybe I should take a picture of this and send it around to show everyone how pathetic you are?"

"Go ahead. But just know, my father is a medical examiner, and I know how to kill a person and make it look like natural causes." Oh fuck, CeCe's crazy is showing. Felicity must realize it too because she pales and backs away quickly, nearly sending Jordan to the floor.

"Stay away from me, you fucking psycho," Felicity nearly screams but CeCe just smiles, looking like the picture of an innocent angel.

"Now, Felicia, I'm sure I don't know what you're talking about." With that, CeCe turns her back on Felicity and saunters back to the table with the regal grace of a queen.

"I feel like I just watched a deleted scene from *The Godfather*. I am equal parts impressed and horrified," Serena whispers as she slides deeper into the booth to make room for CeCe.

"She needed to know that she cannot fuck with you, with us, and get away with it." CeCe shrugs. "Besides, she all but admitted it was her."

"No, she did not," I argue. "She said that she'd take a picture of you acting like a mob boss from 1952. She never once mentioned or alluded to anything about me or Grey."

"Ava, you don't think that it was a little too coincidental that she threatened to take a picture of me for retaliation? You don't think, in that big brain of yours, that she all but confessed that she was behind the texts and picture with that one statement?"

"No, Celeste, I do not."

"Well, you're an idiot then."

"Okay, ladies," Serena chimes in. "Let's agree to disagree about that. Plus, Felicity is toxic, and we don't want her in our lives anyway, right?"

"Right," I grumble. CeCe follows suit.

"Great, we can agree on that. So, let's finish our coffees. Talk about our outfits for Saturday night." She pauses, pointing at me. "We're going to the soccer house, Ava. Talk to Greyson and let him know to avoid you. Hopefully, by next semester, your unknown sender will forget about you and Greyson and be onto their next victim so that you can live your life."

I fucking hope so.

Greyson

"Hell fucking no, Ava."

"Greyson, please. You know that if you come up to me tomorrow night, you'll unleash a shit storm."

"No, Ava, I don't know that. It's been three weeks. You haven't gotten a single fucking message, picture, threat, or goddamn letter through a carrier pigeon in that time. The threat, the fucking risk. It's over. They forgot about us. They don't give a shit anymore, we're old news." I inhale, trying to calm how pissed off I am. "God dammit, vixen. I told you, you're mine, and I'm fucking sick of hiding it. You won't even let me fucking see you."

During our regular evening call, after our classes are finished and we're holed up in our rooms, Ava dropped the bomb that Serena and the pit bull told her I'd be at the soccer house tomorrow night. I'm fucking livid. If there's anything I've learned in the month that we've been talking, Ava overthinks every fucking thing. Her clothes, her assignments, her words, and her actions. I knew that if she had advance notice that I'd be there, she'd freak the fuck out and pull this shit. I told Dylan and Dante to lock this shit down and not to tell their women, but they fucked me over.

Her request to act like we don't know each other, like I don't know the sound she makes when she comes all over my face, is fucking comical.

"Vixen, can you honestly tell me that you can handle seeing me and not acknowledge me?"

She lets out a breath. "It's not what I want, Greyson, but what are we supposed to do?"

"Come over."

156

"W-what?" she startles, not expecting my demand.

"If you want to act like we don't know each other, come over tonight, now, and talk to me face to face."

"Greyson," she hisses, lowering her voice like there were listening devices planted in her room. "You know I can't do that."

"Who the fuck is going to see you come over? We need to talk, and I'm sick of talking over the phone every single night. I need to see you in person, I need to make sure you're okay." It's not sexual, I just crave her presence.

"I-I," she sighs again. "Greyson, it's a risk."

"Take the fucking risk, vixen. I will protect you. I will always fucking protect you." I knew it was a promise that I couldn't make, not with some asshole out there with a picture of her on their phone.

"Greyson, you know that's not true." I clench my fists, knowing that she's right but pissed about it anyway.

"Please, vixen. I need you. I need to see you, need to make sure you're okay. I know you're scared, but, baby, please."

A heavy silence filled the space between us, so goddamn tense.

"Okay."

"Don't lie to me, vixen."

"Grey, I said okay. I'm not a liar." There was that sass that I loved. This entire phone call has been one piece of shit after another, and I didn't get any of my girl's sass until now.

"Come whenever you're ready. Did you eat?"

"Why, are you expecting me to cook for you?" I'm going to bend her over my knee for that comment.

"No, I can cook, smartass. Just stop being difficult and let me take care of you."

"Fine. No, I didn't eat."

"Good. Let me know when you leave. The door will be open, just come in."

"Absolutely not. I can't just walk into your house, that's incredibly rude." Her ass was going to be red by the time I was done with her.

"Vixen, get your sexy ass over here."

—

157

Half an hour after we hung up, a knock sounds on the front door. Even though I told Ava to walk in, I knew that she'd be stubborn and would refuse to make herself at home here. With both Dante and Lincoln out at Legend's, Ava and I have the house to ourselves.

I'm not lying when I say that I am not expecting anything sexual tonight. I just need to fucking see her and breathe the same air as her. It's been too long since I was able to look into her deep brown eyes and read the emotions on her pretty face.

Making my way to the front door, I open it to Ava, and my dick immediately stirs. Ava is stunning normally, her thick hair, full mouth, and perky tits bring me to my knees every goddamn time. But tonight, she's dressed casually in leggings and an oversize hoodie, with not a trace of makeup on her face. I'm standing here, speechless by the natural beauty she doesn't even realize that she has.

"Are you going to invite me in, or are we going to stand on your front steps all night?"

I step aside, opening the door wider to let her in.

Ava

I'm not sure why I agreed to come to Greyson's house, but if I had to guess, it probably had to do with the prospect of an orgasm and the probability of touching him after nearly a month of tech-based interactions. I should have put more effort into my appearance, but at seven at night, after a full day of classes, the only thing I wanted to do was shower off the stress of the day and throw on sweatpants. After I agreed to come over, I upgraded to leggings because gray sweats look good on men... and that's pretty much it.

In terms of attractiveness, I am undoubtedly looking as appealing as a pair of used tube socks, but it doesn't seem to deter the hunger from Grey's eyes. When he opened the door, looking better than he had any right to in a black tracksuit, his eyes zeroed in on my makeup-free face and heated to a sinful degree. He licked his lips, a seemingly unconscious movement, and my ovaries exploded, essentially.

I can't keep the snark from my voice when I ask if he wants us to stand on his steps all night; his stare is unnerving. As soon as he steps back, I push my way into the house, not expecting the smell that hits me in the face. Breathing in deeply, I can identify the scent of onions and... fried potatoes? Without waiting for Greyson to close the door, I make my way into the kitchen and see a perfectly golden Spanish tortilla on the stovetop.

Whirling around, Greyson chuckles at the disbelief on my face. "Did you make that?"

He rolls his eyes. "Vixen, I told you that I could cook."

"Yes, but I figured you meant a frozen pizza or boiled pasta with a jar of sauce, which, by the way, never serve either of those things to me."

"It's eggs, Ava, it's not that difficult."

"Okay, but how many college guys do you know that just whip up an omelet? I can tell you, none." I pause, considering his roommates. "Okay, I lied. Lincoln would probably do this shit too, but brag about it the whole time and then tell his date that she's lucky to taste his 'divine culinary abilities.'" The last part is a direct quote from the arrogant ass. He's a talented chef in the making, but my God, is he full of himself?

Grey advances toward me, backing me into the pristine island. His arms shoot out, caging me against the cool marble. "First off, vixen, don't talk about other men, it makes me fucking crazy." He leans down, bending his knees to compensate for the twelve-inch difference between our frames. He continues, "And, second, fuck right this is a date."

I stare at him confused until I play back my words, mentally smacking myself in the face over my word choice. "That's not what I meant, and you know it."

"Nah, vixen. You said it, no takebacks."

I resist the urge to stick my tongue out, but just barely. "Whatever, now, tell me where you learned to make this, because honestly? I expected a delivery order from a pizzeria."

Grey stares at me for a beat, his face relaxing into a small smile, almost like he's bringing a distant memory to the forefront of his mind. "My dad traveled a lot during the season; baseball isn't exactly a child-friendly profession. When I was young, I would go with him to each game, sit in the dugout while the team played, and operate as an unofficial mascot." He shakes his head, his smile growing wider, and my breath leaves my body. I've never seen this kind of smile on Greyson's face. It's almost reverent, like he's lost in a memory that brings him so much happiness that he can't hold it in.

If I thought my ovaries were fucked before, they're destroyed now.

"When I got older, I couldn't travel with the team because of school. I told you that my mom left when I was a kid, so my grandparents, uncle, and aunt stepped in while my dad traveled. I love my grandparents, but I always wanted to go to my uncle and aunt's house, partly because my cousins were close in age and two of my best friends, but more because my aunt is an amazing cook. Her rule in their household is that everyone needs to know how to cook, and since I was there so often during the season, I was tangled up in that."

I lean forward, enthralled by this glimpse into his personal life. "My aunt taught me and my cousins, Mateo and Leonel, or Mat and Leo, and we ended up being decent. She's from Madrid, so she taught us mostly Spanish cuisine, but I can make a few other things." He looks at me and smirks. "I'm sure you'd run circles around me in the kitchen."

I scoff, trying to hide how turned on I am that he knows how to use a spatula. I picture him in an apron, holding a frying pan in front of the stove, with nothing on beneath it. I feel my cheeks turn red, the heat traveling from my chest up to my face.

"Well, I'm impressed. Is there anything you can't do?"

"Yeah, convince you to be seen with me in public." And we're back to that now.

"Grey, you know why we can't."

"Vixen, you cannot let this asshole dictate your life. I want to protect you, I need to protect you, so let me do it. Are you ashamed to be with me?" he asks with a serious expression, and I can't help but laugh. He stares at me, jaw ticking like he's dead serious.

"Are you fucking with me?" I give him an incredulous look once my laughter subsides. "Grey, who could be embarrassed by you? You're perfect." I shake my head, gathering my thoughts before I launch into my explanation, for what feels like the eighty-sixth time. "This person has a picture of me, Grey. I told you; I can't have my parents see that. I can't have everyone see me like that." I cast my eyes downward, refusing to make eye contact.

"Ava, you act like we did something wrong. Baby, look at me." He grabs my chin, tugging my face upwards until my gaze meets his. "So, your parents see it, what happens? Will they disown you? Will they love you any less? Will they shame you?" I shake my head at each of his questions, knowing that my parents would be more worried about me than anything else. My shame is internal; the fact that I allowed myself to be so vulnerable in such a public setting—and enjoyed it—will live with me forever.

161

"No," I sigh, giving him the response I know he expects.

"Then if the dick decides to release that photo where I'm worshiping your body, we go after them and go to the fucking police. It's a crime to take a picture like that without consent in New Jersey, and I will rip this motherfucker a new asshole if he comes after you, legally and physically. I know you're worried about it, and trust me, vixen, I don't want the douches on this campus to see that picture, but what are we supposed to do? Hide our relationship forever. Hell fucking no."

I gnaw on my bottom lip, weighing his words. My heart stutters when he refers to our "relationship." During all of our conversations, we've never defined what we are, and I did not expect that Grey would remain invested in only me. Honestly, I'm not entirely sure what we're doing, but I don't want it to stop. I may not want that picture to circulate, just the thought of it makes me want to vomit everything in my body. But, at the same time, I want to explore Grey like a normal college student. How is it fair that they've taken this away from me?

I'm so lost in thought that I don't realize Grey's hand is on my face until his thumb pulls down on my lip, releasing it from my ministrations.

"Every time you bite this goddamn lip, I want to spank your ass, I swear to fucking God."

"W-what?"

He steps closer, crowding around me and taking all the oxygen in the room with him. "These lips are fucking mine." Somehow, he shifts closer, his mouth hovering just above mine. "Ava, vixen. You have three fucking seconds."

I look at him, quietly begging him to explain in the charged silence that follows his decree.

"You have three seconds before I taste your lips. So, figure out what you want, vixen, because I already know."

My throat is suddenly thick with want and a foreign emotion that I can't quite place. I'd say that I'm turned on—and I am, there is absolutely no denying that—but it's more than that. I feel like there's a riot in my stomach, chills race down my spine and I feel the goosebumps covering my arms and legs. I either have swine flu or my body is about to ignite.

I look from his eyes to his lips. There's no question of what I want; I've been fantasizing about Greyson Jansen since I met him.

"Greyson," I murmur. "Kiss me."

"Fuck," Grey growls, grabbing the back of my head and pulling me forward until he captures my lips with his. I was prepared for an onslaught, but his lips are gentle against mine, almost worshiping. He pulls back and places playful kisses just above my cupid's bow and on the cleft in my chin. Returning to my lips, he coaxes my mouth open, nipping my bottom lip when I finally open to him. God, it's been too long since I felt his mouth on mine.

"Goddamn, vixen. It's been too fucking long since I tasted you," he growls. Grey catches my bottom lip, biting harshly before soothing the spot. I gasp at the contact, the dichotomy between pleasure and pain surprising me.

He chuckles, finding humor in my response. "You must have forgotten how you like it, vixen." His hand snakes down, cupping my sex through my leggings. "You're already so fucking wet for me that I can feel it through your tights. Does my girl need a reminder of how I eat her pussy?" Grey's fingers begin moving, rubbing lazy circles, and driving me fucking crazy.

Every time I've taken care of myself in my dorm, it's been the memory of Grey's touch that finally brings my orgasm. But honestly, I didn't give him enough credit. His movements are so controlled, but I can feel the tension radiating off him, as though he's doing everything he possibly can to hold back. His fingers continue exploring me, alternating between slow strokes and even lazier circles around my fabric-covered clit. I start to move my hips, doing anything I can to increase the pace Grey set. I start to grind against him, arching my back as soon as I feel the climax start to come, but he pulls back, sliding his hand up and over my hip to grab my ass.

He stills my hips and kisses my lips softly. He knows exactly what he's doing to me, working me up just to bring me back down with no relief. Dickhead.

He spends long minutes kissing me, teasing my lips and tongue, before finally gliding his hand back to the heat between my thighs.

"Grey," I plead. His name is a benediction on my lips, and I'm praying to every deity that has ever existed to not smite me for idolatry before he can get me off. "Greyson, please, I need more," I plead, ready to drop to my knees if that will increase the pressure of his hand.

"Tell me that you're mine, Ava. Tell me that we'll deal with this together," Grey whispers into my ear, feathering his fingers over my soaked leggings.

"Greyson," I growl. I don't even recognize my voice. "Don't you fucking dare pull back."

Grey leans over me, placing his mouth beside my ear. "Then give me what I fucking want, Ava."

Fuck it. At this point, my body can be in the campus newspaper, and I won't give a shit as long as I can come. "Fine, but we're talking about this afterward."

His hand leaves me entirely and I groan. "Greyson, what the fuck?"

"Vixen, we're talking about this now. Tell me that you're mine; use the words I know you have built up in that brain of yours." He would make this difficult, not accepting my half-assed agreement. Again, such a dickhead.

"Greyson, the apple of my eye, star of my evening sky, commander of my universe." I pause for dramatic effect. CeCe would be proud of me; I'm using her for inspiration right now. "Oh, handsome one. I declare that I am yours." I look him in the eye, daring him to complain about my second delivery.

"Such a smartass. You forgot, 'Defiler of your virgin pussy.'" With that, he grabs my ass with both hands before lifting me over his shoulder like a sack of potatoes.

"Grey, what the fuck? Put me down."

There's a sharp sting on my ass. It takes me a moment to comprehend that he just smacked my ass.

"Did you just hit me? Greyson!" He starts to move faster, not deterred at all by my extra weight. He refuses to answer me, just chuckling to himself like a fucking lunatic as we make our way down the hallway and toward his bedroom.

"Greyson, I swear to all that is holy. I will knee you in your testicles if you don't put me down this goddamn second." We reach the door, walking through it before he locks us in.

One minute, I'm upside down over his shoulder, screaming at him to let me down, and the next I'm tossed on the bed.

"Jesus, Grey. You could warn a girl first. What if I got motion sickness, or didn't want you to manhandle me?"

He stands at the foot of the bed, shaking his head at me with a small smirk on his face. "But you didn't, and you did. Now, stop talking and listen to me." He leans back, crossing his arms over his chest. His tracksuit should make him look like a dad bringing his kids to soccer practice, but somehow, he looks sexier than normal. I consider that train of thought; Grey as a dad is also hot. Freaking hot.

"Okay," I start. "But one question before you bulldoze the entire conversation."

He sighs, probably trying to figure out why he's interested in me. "What about dinner? Please tell me that you don't have anything in the oven. I know there's the omelet, but you're not going to burn the house down in your lust haze, right?"

"No, Ava, the house will not burn down."

I nod, knowing that he probably will spank me again if I ask another question right now. Not that I'm entirely opposed to that, but time and place.

"Now, you agreed to be mine, so I need you to understand what that means. This body? Mine. Your kisses? Mine. Your fucking thoughts and feelings and insecurities? Mine to listen to, mine to evoke, mine to expel. Do you get that, vixen?"

My mouth is dry, all the moisture traveling south from his little display of possession. I nod my head in agreement.

"Fucking good. Do you know what else is mine?" he asks, walking toward the bed. "Your sweet little cunt, all of your goddamn orgasms, and every single drop of cum in your body. Do you want to get off? You do it with me, for me, or because of me. There's no one else that touches this besides me and you." He drops to his knees, pulling my legs forward until my ass is perched on the edge of the bed.

"Ava, tell me you understand. I'm a possessive asshole and I don't share. I will not share you; that's why I'm not worried about the goddamn picture because I will destroy anyone that sees it and anyone that shares it." His hands trail up my calves, his thumbs pressing against every pressure point as he advances up my leg. I hold my breath, anticipating the feel of his fingers on my inner thighs. With anyone else, in any other situation, I would feel self-conscious knowing that a man was about to have an intimate viewing of the stretch marks decorating my body, but Greyson is different. He's seen me naked, twice now, and seems more desperate than ever to see my body again.

"Ava, do you understand?" His hands still on my knees, refusing to go further until I agree to every single thing he's laid out for me.

"Yes, I understand." I don't hesitate. He starts to move again, reaching just below my sex before I place my hands on top of his, pausing his exploration. "But I have one condition." He raises an eyebrow, waiting for me to continue.

"I want to wait until after this weekend, after my birthday, when there's less attention."

I watch his jaw clench, the muscles hardening in annoyance. "Why would you want to wait until after your birthday? Why wouldn't you want to be free to go to a party together instead of going to those fuckwit frat parties?"

"Aren't you in a frat?"

"Ava, that's not the point."

"I'm not hiding this, but you need to understand this from my perspective. Everything has moved so fast, at this insane breakneck speed. One minute, I'm almost naked on a desk, the next I have a very real threat against me. For my birthday, I want one last weekend where I don't have to worry if someone has seen my ass. Please, just, give me that, okay?"

He works his jaw, shifting from side to side while he weighs my words. His hands squeeze my upper thighs before he nods his head, agreeing to my concession.

"Do you have any other demands, vixen?"

I nod my head and bite my lower lip. "Just one more, Grey?"

His eyes narrow on my mouth, not missing my taunt. "What is it, baby?"

"Well, what I'd like for my birthday is for you to give me something no one else ever has."

"And what's that?"

I tilt my head, enjoying the tease but also eager to end it. "Your cock, Greyson." I don't think I've ever been so bold in my entire life. I most definitely have never asked a guy for his cock. If Grey is surprised, he doesn't show it.

Leaving me lying on the bed, he stands up and begins to lower the zipper on his jacket, revealing a white T-shirt. There's no reason why I should find this erotic, he's dressed like a rapper or a dad in his fifties, for fuck's sake, but he looks indecent peeling the fabric from his body. Tossing the jacket toward his desk, Grey does that ridiculously hot one-armed grab and rips his shirt from his body. I shift my legs, trying to find some relief from the need pooling between my thighs at his little strip show.

If his investment dream doesn't work out, he'd make a killing as a stripper. His body is a testament to how hard he works out and maintains his physique. In contrast to my soft stomach and curves, Grey is hard lines, corded muscle, and a planned chaos of tattoos and piercings. Wait, piercings? I take a closer look and see barbells protruding from each nipple.

"Well"—I gesture toward his chest—"those are new."

He smirks, shrugging at my obvious appraisal. "Lost a bet with Lincoln. The fucker made me get pierced."

"Did it hurt?"

His smirk transforms into a full grin. "Vixen, I have tattoos and piercings in places you haven't seen yet. This fucking tickled." I stare at him unconvinced, raising a brow in disbelief. Finally, he laughs and shakes his head. "Well, it didn't feel fucking pleasant, but I've had worse."

I immediately look at his chest and arms. The artwork framing his body is extensive, but also not in the most sensitive areas, at least from what I've heard. CeCe's cousin is a tattoo artist; he's covered in ink, head-to-toe decorated, and he always said the hands, kneecaps, and ribs are the most painful.

"Ava, look at me." Grey's voice forces my gaze from his chest, and I make eye contact. "Do you still want this?"

I nod, my throat suddenly thick with nerves and an overwhelming amount of desire.

"Good." Grey grabs the waistband of his track pants and pauses, looking me over with a critical eye before working the fabric over his hips and thighs until he's left in just his boxer briefs. I've seen him shirtless before, albeit over FaceTime, but seeing Greyson stripped down to just his underwear, barefoot and aroused, is a transcendent experience. The hard outline of his cock strains against the remaining barrier between us, and my hands flex with the need to touch him. To my surprise, his legs are covered in dark tattoos.

Unlike Dante, whose tattoos are obvious and shout for attention, Grey's are always hidden, with the exception of his left sleeve. Under each article of clothing is a message, a secret that reveals itself the more exposed his body becomes.

Grey stands at the foot of the bed, staring at me with a shuttered expression, almost like he's afraid I'm judging him and finding him lacking. Not freaking likely.

"What do your tattoos mean?" I ask, because how can a person go through that much pain and not have the final product mean something?

Greyson points to his left arm and the three-headed dog that travels from his wrist to his chest. "This is Cerberus. In Greek mythology, he guarded the gates of the underworld." He looks down at the dog's three protracted jaws; they're so realistic that they seem ready to strike his skin. "He kept the living from seeking death and kept the dead from haunting the living. And then these"—he gestures to the symbols on the right side of his chest—"are things to remind me of what I value, who I am. This one"—he lays his hand below an image that looks like an intricate evil eye—"is the evil eye or Eye of Horace. This one is the Key of Hades; it symbolizes the control I have over who is in my life." My eyes trace the antique key design of the tattoo.

"And what about the art on your legs?" I question, more than a little intrigued by the graphic imagery decorating most of his legs. On his right leg, there's a stunning depiction of warriors in battle from his calf to his knee. The artistry is so impressive that it looks like a picture, the capture

AVA

of a moment printed directly on his skin. Above the warriors is a stunning woman, her body is shown above the scene as if she's watching from the heavens. Interspersed throughout the scene are flames and intricate details that solidify the awe of the piece.

On his left leg is a wolf so intricately created that every single inch of the tattoo is a braided design of knots and lines and shadows. It's almost mechanical in its composition.

The muscles on each of his legs flex when he looks down at his wearable art. "These are more mythology designs." He looks up, smirking. "My dad's family is Scandinavian, but my grandmother loves Greek mythology." He gestures to his body. "Anyway, this one is Aphrodite watching over the Trojan War, and this guy is one of Apollo's wolves."

"What does he symbolize?"

"Knowledge, complete domination, and power."

"Wow."

"Scared yet, vixen?"

"Not scared, exactly. Just intrigued, I guess." I'm not lying. I don't think there's anything about Greyson that's scary. Intimidating? Yes. Intense? One hundred percent. But scary? No. There is nothing he has done to evoke fear in me, despite the situation we've found ourselves in.

"Good. Now, are you ready to see the real reason why Lincoln's dare did fuck-all to me?" I swear to God, if he makes a joke about how his dick is so hard that it hurts worse than a piercing, I am walking out. Grey raises an eyebrow, waiting for my response.

"Yes, please, show me why nipple piercings didn't faze you, freak." With a swift tug, Greyson's briefs fall to the floor and his extremely hard, extremely thick, and extremely pierced penis is on display.

"Is that fucking pierced?" I blurt out, nearly screaming from shock.

Grey's soft laugh penetrates through the fog surrounding my brain. I'm sitting on his bed, fully clothed, while he stands at the foot of his bed dressed in nothing but nipple rings and dick jewelry.

What the fuck?

"It's called a Jacob's ladder." He lifts his erection, showing the five rows

169

of piercings on the underside of his dick like it's show and tell. "It hurt like a motherfucker, which is why these nipple piercings didn't bother me."

I stare at him, my mouth hanging open, and I'm not sure what to say. He looks like a tattooed and pierced rocker god, and I'm trying hard to compute how I ended up in his bed. I open and shut my mouth, trying to figure out the right words. I probably look like a fish gasping for water right now, but instead of going limp, Greyson's dick seems to get harder the longer I stare.

"Vixen," he begins, "say something."

"You're fucking pierced, Greyson," I say directly to his penis.

He tugs on his erection. "I am, Ava." Taking slow steps forward, Grey reaches the bed and bends over me. "Are you scared now, baby?"

I look into his eyes, shifting back and forth, trying to find any reason to be scared, other than of his dick and the overall practice of sex. I still can't find it in me to be scared.

"Your pierced monster cock surprised me; I won't lie about that. But no, I'm still not scared."

He cages me with his arms and leans down until his mouth is at my ear. "Good," he repeats before sucking my earlobe into his mouth. Pleasure shoots down my spine and I arch up, desperate to feel Grey's body against mine. Grey's tongue sneaks out, flicking my earlobe the same way he did my nipples, and I feel my body heat rise like a flame quickly growing from embers.

"Grey," I moan, lifting my hands until they're tangled in his long hair, keeping his mouth tethered to my skin. Releasing my flesh, wet, open-mouthed kisses trail from behind my ear to the base of my neck. He latches on to my pulse, the same spot where he marked me almost one month ago, and sucks. His mouth pulls at my neck and it's like I can feel the bruise forming, the blood vessels popping in rhythm to my heartbeat. Grey's mouth lifts from my pulse before descending on another spot, sucking, and biting, and marking like a beast. Part of me, a small, minuscule, nearly invisible part, worries about looking like a leper tomorrow. A larger part of me, however, aches for his mouth to continue marking my skin with the evidence of his desire for me. That part takes over and I tug on his hair, directing his mouth up to mine.

Our lips fuse, a mess of tongues and teeth, and we fight for dominance. It's not like our other kisses; the politely passionate thrill has morphed into a chaotic desire, and I need him right this fucking moment.

He pulls back, panting against my lips. "Fuck, vixen. You have too many goddamn clothes on."

Grey rolls off my body and I start to protest.

"Grey—" His hands pull my sweatshirt up and over my head. Understanding his intent, I pull my leggings off, discarding my panties and socks seconds later. I'm left naked in front of him, a sacrificial virgin laid out to a Nordic warrior. His eyes devour me, taking in every exposed inch, and I shiver under his gaze.

At this moment, like every other intimate moment with Grey, I don't feel self-conscious or the overwhelming need to cover the parts of me that are anything but flawless. One of Grey's hands drifts to my stomach, clutching at my waist, while his other grabs my hip. His fingers graze my ass and I suck in a ragged breath.

The hand on my waist travels upward, ghosting over my skin until it reaches my nipple. I don't need to look down to know that my nipples are hard, all but demanding his attention. His thumb strokes over a hardened tip, teasing it like he has all the time in the damn world. I'm so lost in the feeling of him surrounding me that I almost forget Grey is completely naked until the hair on his leg tickles my smooth skin.

Refusing to lay pliant while he controls my body, I lift my hands, gliding them over his biceps and then down his back. He groans, the hand on my ass squeezing firmly. "Don't touch me unless you want me coming all over these pretty tits before I've gotten my mouth on you," he bites out. Grey releases me and grabs my arms, pinning them above my head. "Keep your arms here, vixen."

"But—"

"No," he interrupts. "I'm not going to come on your stomach like a little fuckboy and leave you disappointed beneath me." He squeezes my wrists for emphasis. "Now, leave these fucking hands here until I tell you that you can move them. I'll turn your pretty ass pink, vixen. Don't test me."

"Asshole," I mumble under my breath, making sure my voice is loud enough that he can hear me.

"I heard that. That's one, vixen." His mouth finds my collarbone and his tongue traces the bone.

"You were supposed to hear that," I respond. "Oh, God," I gasp as his tongue lashes my skin. He moves down, placing warm kisses from my collarbone to my nipple before finally sucking it into his mouth.

"Fuck, Greyson." On instinct, I move my hands, grasping his hair and pulling him closer. He lifts his head and grabs my arms, placing them above my head again.

"That's two, vixen. Let's not make it three." He captures my other nipple and bites down, nipping the sensitive skin before soothing the ache away.

He worships my chest, alternating between biting, sucking, and soothing. Grey spends long minutes outlining the curve of my boobs, dragging his tongue from my sternum to the heaviness just above my ribs. I'm covered in bite marks and bruises, and I'm not lying when I say that I think I can come from nipple stimulation alone. My hands grip his sheets, and I am ninety-nine percent positive that I've ripped his comforter trying to keep my hands off of him.

"God dammit, Greyson. If you don't let me touch you, I'm—I'm going to—oh shit, fucking hell," I grind out. I look down, trying to figure out the new sensation that has me fumbling with my words. Grey's mouth is latched onto my nipple, sucking in hard, greedy pulls while his hand cups my sex, applying just enough pressure to send a jolt through my body.

All it takes is one pass over my clit and one more tug on my nipple and I'm detonating. Not caring about the threat Grey proposed, my hands bury in his hair and pull his lips to mine, attacking his mouth as I buck and thrust and die against his hand.

"Fuck," I breathe into his mouth, still thrusting my hips into his hand as I ride out my climax.

Grey smiles against my lips, and I'm sure he's looking smug as fuck. "That's three, vixen. Turn that pretty ass over."

Greyson

"Oh, hell no. Absolutely not," Ava complains against my lips. "Right now?"

I don't bother responding, knowing she'll give me shit anyway, and fuck it, I warned her what would happen if she touched me. I climb off my little vixen and stand at the foot of the bed. Not giving her a minute to figure out what's going on, I pull her legs down until they're set on the floor and then flip her over, hiking her ass in the air.

Fuck, her heart-shaped ass looks good like this. I'm not going to fuck her for the first time like a dirty little slut, bent over and ready for my cock. But we will be adding that to the goddamn rotation. I slide my hands up her ass, squeezing her cheeks together. Fuck, that's hot too.

My dick is leaking on the fucking hardwood. I need to make this quick because there's no way in hell I'm going to last much longer without her tight pussy wrapped around me.

"Greyson, what the fuck are you doing?" she screeches, and if it weren't for how hard I am right now, I'd probably find it more amusing.

"Quiet, vixen. Or do you want to make it four?" My girl doesn't respond and instead grips my sheets while seething silently. She's probably trying to figure out how to kill me in my sleep and get away with it. I'd be worried if her little pit bull was here because she's scary as fuck. Ava's soft and warm and sweet; she doesn't seem like the black widow type.

But, then again, what the fuck do I know?

"Good girl," I praise, trailing a hand over the hip. She preens under the compliment, thrusting her ass out even farther. I fucking love how responsive she is to my touch and my words.

173

I run a hand over her ass, gently petting the plump curves before rearing back and delivering three sharp smacks against her right cheek. Red blooms on her skin, and I have to rein it the fuck in before I slam my pierced dick, or "monster cock," as she called it, into her tight heat. I'm reciting basic accounting principles, trying to tame my dick, when Ava looks over her shoulder, wide-eyed and pink-cheeked.

"Fuck, vixen, you should see yourself right now." She ducks her head, burying it into my bed.

Ava mumbles against the comforter, her words barely discernible. "What?" I ask.

"Grey, I need you. That was…" She pauses, considering her words. "I just need you." She turns over and moves to the center of the bed. I watch her, cataloging every inch of her skin, every expression on her beautiful face.

"Are you sure?" She nods. "Words, Ava. I need words."

"Yes, I'm sure. Please."

"Are you on birth control? I'm clean. I haven't been with anyone since, fuck, a while." I have my test results on my nightstand, ready to show her and put to rest any doubts about my commitment.

"Yes. And I trust you, Grey." I've tasted her, fingered her, and sucked on her nipples until they were raw, but nothing turns me on as much as her trust. Warmth spreads in my chest, and I know it's not just my dick that loves the idea of Ava's faith in me.

Crawling onto the bed, I move my body over hers until I'm bracing my forearms against her head. I brush my lips against hers, gradually deepening the kiss from playful brushes to fucking with our mouths. I work my hand down Ava's body, not stopping until I reach her pussy.

"Fuck, vixen. Did taking my punishment like a good little girl turn you on? You're fucking soaked." I sink a single finger inside, circling her tight opening before adding a second finger, preparing her as much as possible. "Are you going to take my cock like a good girl?" I scissor my fingers inside and rub her clit with my thumb; she's trembling beneath me, and I feel her pelvis push forward, trying to take me in deeper. She's wet as fuck and taking my fingers well, but I'm not small and my piercings are going to rub against her inner walls, making her feel things she probably never thought she would.

"Come for me, vixen. Let me feel you come against my fingers, baby." Like my words are a command, Ava's body responds. I swallow her gasps and feel her walls contract against my fingers, milking me until my entire hand is covered with her juices. Pulling my fingers out, I position myself at her entrance and pause. Looking up at her, I ask, "Ava, are you ready, baby?"

She nods her head and grabs my shoulders, pulling me closer. "Please, Grey."

"I'm going to go slowly, baby. Tell me if it hurts, if it's too much, and I'll stop." It'll fucking kill me, but I'd rather die with blue balls than hurt her. Staring at her face, I push the head of my cock through her folds, getting her used to the intrusion. "Okay, vixen, I'm going to the first rung." I push forward, feeding her my cock until the first piercing disappears into her pussy.

I grit my teeth, steeling myself against the feel of her wet heat surrounding the few inches she's taken. "Good girl. Are you okay?"

"Yes, just keep going slow." I lean down to kiss her, needing the feel of her lips on mine.

"Next rung, baby." She stiffens as I slide in another inch, breaking her barrier. "Fuck, Ava, I'm sorry. Do you want me to stop?" I've never been this fucking paranoid before and all I can think about is how she's feeling.

"Just give me a minute," she breathes out.

We continue like that, slipping in further, stretching her wider, pausing for full minutes while my cock grows harder inside her until, finally, she's taken every last piercing and is filled with me.

"Fuck, baby. You're such a fucking good girl, taking my entire cock. How do you feel?"

"Jesus, Grey. I feel so full." Her hips press upward, and my vision blackens. "But so good."

Stilling her hips, I warn, "I don't want to hurt you, give me a minute before I fuck you into this mattress."

"Greyson, if you do not start moving your hips, I will throw you off of me and find a goddamn cucumber in your refrigerator to get me off."

I raise an eyebrow, smirking at her challenge. "I thought virgins were supposed to be shy?"

"I have never been shy, and I thought Vikings were supposed to know how to fuck."

Challenge fucking accepted. I pull back, nearly taking my dick out before pushing back in slowly, making sure she feels every piercing as they rub along her inner walls. "How's that feel, vixen? Does it feel like you're being fucked by a Viking, baby?" I repeat the movement, grabbing her hips to pull her closer, fully impaling her on each forward thrust.

"Oh my God, oh my God, oh my God," she chants. I'm fucking relieved my roommates aren't home to hear her. These screams are mine.

"Not God, baby. Say my fucking name." I lean forward, changing the angle and hitting deeper with each pass. I slow even further, twisting my pelvis and grinding against her clit each time I surge forward.

"Fuck, baby, you're so tight. So fucking wet." I reach my hand between us, rubbing on her clit. "Goddamn, you're taking my cock like such a good girl." She's fucking dripping at my words. Her cries grow louder and her movements get more frantic, like she's desperate to find her release.

"That's right, fucking chase it, vixen. Fuck my cock." She's meeting each thrust with her own, our hips moving in a chaotic rhythm. "Fucking knew you'd be like this, vixen, perfect for me. Fucking shit, these tits." I bend over her, grabbing a nipple between my teeth. I bite the hard peak before releasing it. "Come on my fucking cock, let me feel that pussy squeeze me. Show me how much you fucking want it."

"Oh my God, Greyson. Grey, Grey—" Ava breaks off, throwing her head back in a silent scream. Her pussy squeezes me, and I fucking lose it.

"Fuck, vixen. I'm going to come in this tight little cunt, fucking paint your walls white." I piston my hips forward, stilling when I'm buried balls deep inside her. "Fuck," I growl, gripping her hips tighter as I find my release. We stay joined for long minutes, our cum mixing and seeping further into her.

Pulling out, I look down at where our bodies were joined and stare at the blood from her virginity and my thick white cum leaking out. Tracing her lips with my fingers, I push my cum back into her, refusing to let a single fucking drop go to waste.

Ava

If I thought that losing my virginity and sleeping with Grey would make him lose interest in me, then I was wrong. Most definitely, unequivocally wrong.

After showering together, which led to Grey rubbing my body down with his body wash and teasing me until I begged him to use his mouth, fingers, or dick to ease the ache between my legs, we ate the reheated tortilla and binge-watched Netflix. He refused to relieve the tension he built during the shower, probably because he's a masochist, but mostly because he worried that I would be too sore for a second round. When I tried to leave his bed at one in the morning to drive home, he grabbed me around my waist and pinned me down, threatening another spanking if I left his house before morning. He held me tightly against him all night and ran his fingers lightly over my body, a whisper of what he had already done to me.

By the time he finally let me out of bed, just before nine in the morning, I was throbbing with the need for another orgasm and more than a little annoyed with Grey's self-control. I could feel the hardness of his dick through the briefs he wore to bed, so I know he was affected. Annoyingly, every time I pressed my ass against his erection, he would just chuckle and say, "My sweet little vixen," or "Are you hungry for my cock, baby?" before pulling back and pinning my hips in place.

So freaking annoying.

I disappear into his en suite bathroom to clean up before driving back to the dorms. Not finding an extra toothbrush in his vanity or medicine cabinet, I steal Grey's. At this point, traces of his cum are still inside me, so does it matter if we share oral hygiene products? The answer is probably, "Yes it does matter," but I'm not going to give it too much thought.

Grey's sitting on his bed waiting for me when I exit the bathroom, staring at me with a hard expression on his face. My stomach immediately drops; no positive conversation has proceeded a face like that.

"Vixen, let's talk before you drive home." Grey holds his hand out to me, and like a fool, I take it. He pulls me onto his lap, wrapping his arms around me and anchoring me to his body. Silence engulfs us, and I can't help but squirm, both uncomfortable by the silence and the conversation I can't help but dread, but also from the arousal I feel from being nestled against him. Grey's arms squeeze me, stilling my movements. "Dammit, vixen, you'll make me lose my damn mind if you don't stop grinding that sweet ass against me."

"You better start talking then because nothing good comes from 'let's talk,'" I comment.

Grey lets out a small laugh, and I feel his warm breath against my neck. "Relax, vixen. You're not getting rid of me that easily. I want to talk about the party tonight."

"What about it?"

"Your sister and her friend will be there, right?"

"Yes?" I question, unsure of where he's going with this.

"I'm not going to lie and say that I'm happy you won't acknowledge that we're together until Monday, especially since you and your little crew draw attention everywhere you go." He pauses. I shake my head, about to interrupt when he slices me a look. "No, don't try to deny it. If there's anything I've learned about your stubborn ass this past month, it's that you don't understand how fucking gorgeous you are. I'm not going to argue with you about it, but you are a fucking wet dream, and I have to hold myself back from breaking skulls and letting all these little bitch boys know that you're mine every time you leave your damn room."

"That's a little dramatic," I mumble under my breath.

"No, it's not. You don't see it, but I fucking do. I see the Snapchats on Campus Hotties; you, the pit bull, and Serena have been pictured multiple fucking times. Did you think I wouldn't notice?" Grey's referring to a

Snapchat channel some losers set up for Marymount where guys send in pictures of women to be featured as their "Hottie of the Day" or in their stories. How it hasn't been shut down yet is anyone's guess.

"It's not my fault we ended up on there," I argue.

"Ava, baby, I'm not saying it is, but I wouldn't worry as much if these assholes knew and understood that you're off-limits and fucking mine." He takes a deep breath before continuing. "I'm going to be there tonight, and I'm not letting you out of my sight. I'll stay back and won't come up to you unless I need to."

"Grey," I sigh. "Nothing is going to happen."

"And I hope you're right, but there's no way in hell I'm going to leave it to chance and not look after you."

"You're being very paternal right now."

"Vixen, there's nothing paternal about how I feel." Grey's hand lowers, dropping to the curve of my hip. "If you haven't figured it out after last night, I'm all in." His voice drops as he pulls me closer.

I swallow, my body warming at the mention of last night. "Well, you've been a cockblock for the last twelve hours, so I wasn't sure what was going on there."

His answering chuckle is low and ominous as if to tell me I just fucked myself over. "Are you feeling neglected, vixen? You were a virgin twelve hours ago, don't forget." As he speaks, he shifts my body so that I'm straddling him. Taking advantage of our new position, I wrap my legs around him, crossing my ankles to bring our bodies flush against each other.

"You kept pushing me away last night."

"You're going to be sore today. If it hasn't hit you yet, it will. I don't want to push you over your limits."

I scoff at that. "I'll worry about what I can and cannot handle, Greyson." I shift against him to emphasize what I want. Just like last night when I asked for his cock, I feel uncharacteristically bold and in charge. Grey's eyes darken as I rub against him and they narrow into slits.

"You little fucking tease," he grinds out before pressing his lips against my throat, kissing lightly over my pulse. "I told you, you're going to be sore.

You're riding out a wave of adrenaline right now, but as soon as you get back to your little dorm, your pussy is going to be aching from my dick and my piercings. Besides..." Grey pauses, nuzzling the underside of my jaw. "I'm not fucking you again until we go public with our relationship."

I pull back, not bothering to hide the scowl on my face. "So, you're going to hold out on me until I capitulate and give in to your demands? That's like blackmail."

"I'm not the one being dramatic and refusing to acknowledge each other in public. That's on you, vixen."

"You said you understood why I wanted to wait until Monday." I feel like we're talking in circles, going around and around, revisiting the same conversation in the hopes of arriving at a different conclusion. The definition of crazy doesn't even begin to cut it.

Grey nips my jaw before soothing it with a kiss. "I understand, Ava. But just because I understand where you're coming from and will go along with it, does not mean I agree."

—

By the time I make it back to my dorm, I'm thinking of every possible way of tormenting Grey tonight at the party. I know he won't go back on his word, but I am delighting in how much he'll suffer.

I think of every part of my body he's paid close attention to, every place he's left his mark, and I know that I need to highlight each area so that he's salivating from afar. Is it petty that I want him to froth at the mouth as soon as he sees me because he denied me an orgasm this morning? Yes. Do I care? No.

Rifling through my closet, I don't bother being quiet for CeCe's sake, even though she's still sleeping at well after ten in the morning. She sleeps like the dead, and judging by the drool pooling on her sheets, it seems like she'll be out cold for a while. Pulling out the more conservative outfit I'm wearing for dinner with my family, I set it on my bed to steam later. The white button-down dress is reminiscent of a men's dress shirt and is both flattering and comfortable; however, it wrinkles easily and needs to be steamed within an inch of its life to make it through dinner intact. Pairing it with chocolate suede thigh-high boots gives the masculine shirt a feminine edge, and I can't wait to send a picture to Grey.

Though I love the outfit, and truly cannot wait to wear the boots that cost a disgusting amount of money, there is no way that I'm wearing it to the party tonight. No exaggeration, if any sort of fluid got on the boots, I would throw myself against a wall in commiseration.

Sifting through the hangers, I stop on a white corset. Though parts of the lining are see-through, the bone-in corset doesn't reveal more than a tank top. Originally, I planned to wear a halter dress, but fingering the corset, I can't help but imagine the look on Grey's face when he realizes I'm in little more than lingerie. This, paired with tight jeans and heels, will undoubtedly test his resistance. It's freaking perfect.

"Can you think a little quieter? I can hear your scheming from over here, bitch." CeCe's voice startles me, and I whip around.

"You were drooling all over your sheets ten minutes ago. How the hell did I wake you up?"

"You think out loud, you freak. You were talking to a corset for five minutes. Either I'm hallucinating or you are losing your shit and talking to inanimate objects at an ungodly hour."

I hold up my phone, showing her the time. "It's ten thirty, C. Don't be a brat. Get your ass up and let's go to Serena's for breakfast."

A loud groan sounds from CeCe's side of the room, and I look over in time to see her burrow deeper under her covers. "You're the Antichrist," she mumbles through the fabric.

"And you're lazy. Now let's go." I walk to her bed and pull the covers off her. Her screech fills the room.

"Fucking fine, but your ass better fill us in on your night. Don't think I didn't notice that you spent the entire night out, only to return in the same clothes you left in," she grumbles. "I just bet you got laid." CeCe climbs off her bed and makes her way to her closet. Grabbing her leggings, a Marymount University sweatshirt, and a plain black baseball cap, she grabs her shower caddy and towel and heads toward the door.

Before she leaves for the shower, she turns. "And you better make your stuffed French toast for breakfast because I am sick of your waking up early shit. We're finally away from home, stop waking up so goddamn early. It's fucking weird." With that parting shot, she leaves the room and slams the door behind her.

So dramatic.

—

After spending the morning and early afternoon at Serena's apartment, gossiping and gorging on fruit compote-stuffed French toast, I'm relieved to be back at the dorm to get ready for dinner. I barely made it out of Serena's apartment alive with the inquisition they put me through. While I couldn't lie about where I was last night, I refused to give specifics. For some reason, the night we shared, the things we did, feel too important, and I don't want to cheapen it. CeCe was relentless and would not shut up, so I finally gave in and told her we slept together but somehow avoided going into detail. If I told them that he has five dick piercings, CeCe would demand photographic evidence and possibly even a demonstration.

I know she's not interested in Grey, nor would she betray my trust like that, but she is the most curious person I know and would never let it go if she found out. My stomach clenches in... jealousy? Anger? At the thought of CeCe seeing Grey in a position only I'm allowed to see him in.

Shit, that sounds just as possessive as Grey. I stare into my makeup mirror, noting the slashes of concealer outlining my cheekbones, jaw, and nose. CeCe doesn't need to do shit like this; she can slather on mascara and look like a supermodel. But me? If I don't have at least six coats of mascara on and a face full of makeup, I look like my brother with a wig. I cringe, remembering Grey's reaction when he opened the door last night. Grey saw me naturally, and while I'd like to not give a shit about it, I can't figure out how I was so unconcerned about my appearance last night and this morning. He didn't seem bothered by my unenhanced look.

Would he prefer someone like CeCe? Someone more confident in themselves, in their appearance, who they are, and who they want to be? I shake my head, willing the self-loathing away while I spread cosmetics over my face, creating a perfect veneer.

After curling my hair and brushing the curls out to create soft waves, I douse myself in hairspray and perfume and exchange my robe for my dress.

Zipping up my boots, I stand and survey my appearance in our floor-length mirror. While I may have more self-esteem issues than I care to admit, I can't deny that I look good in this outfit. The dress flatters my shape, emphasizing my chest while laying loosely over my stomach and hips. The boots paired with the dress's length, short enough to be flirty without showing my vagina, give the illusion of long legs, which I definitely do not have.

Dropping to my knees to pull a clutch from the storage container under my bed, I wince at the soreness between my legs. Though I'd deny it like Rose denied Jack a spot on the door in *Titanic*, Grey wasn't wrong when he said I'd be sore today. I tried to massage myself in the shower, but all it did was make me ache for Grey in a way that wouldn't be relieved tonight.

I'm only slightly ashamed to admit that I contemplated grabbing an ice pack to put on top of my labia. The only reason I stopped was because I read about ice play in a romance novel, and honestly... it didn't sound terrible. I was worried that the ache would grow into a stabbing need and that I'd be like a dog in heat around Grey tonight.

I couldn't risk it. Hell, I wouldn't risk it. So, here I am, wincing at the slightest bend, just like Greyson-freaking-Jansen predicted.

The door opens while I'm on my knees, picking through the few bags I brought from home. Looking over my shoulder, I see CeCe walk in, beautiful and ready for dinner with my family. Dressed in a simple hunter green sweater dress and matching boots, she looks stunning.

"Damn, C. Are you trying to give the male population a heart attack?"

She raises an eyebrow and rolls her eyes at my comment. "The whole population? That seems unlikely. Dante, on the other hand? Yes."

Well, that's new. I've asked about Dante a few times since the barbecue, and she's been consistently tight-lipped. "Dante?" I question. "Is there something you haven't told me, Celeste Lauren Downing?"

"Don't middle name me, Mom. We've been texting and he's annoying, like a gnat that won't go away. He likes the color green, and I just so happened to need two oat milk lattes for us before dinner." She lifts a to-go tray that I didn't realize she held. "Let's just say, I wanted to give him something to think about before tonight." She shrugs, sipping on one of the lattes. "He liked how I looked."

"Jesus, Celeste. You made that boy grab us coffee just to torture him with that dress? That's fucking devious." I stand up and reach for the other coffee, lifting it to my lips. I pause. "But I thank you for considering me in this plot."

"Please, he's no boy. Dante is a man. Besides, he gets off on shit like this. Last week, he showed up at my class with a burger and fries because he saw I shared a reel of Tap House on my Instagram. I gave him shit for stalking me, but the food was greatly appreciated."

My eyes widen, and I nearly spit the sip of coffee I just took. I swallow, questioning, "Why the fuck am I just hearing about this now?"

"Because, Ava Maria, you've been so consumed with Greyson that I didn't want to intrude on your little love bubble."

"We are not in a 'love bubble.'" I use air quotes to emphasize my point.

"You spent three hours on the phone with him last week and slept at his house last night. You, my friend"—she points at me—"are in a love bubble. I'm happy for you, but you have tunnel vision. It's like all you see is Greyson lately, even if you refused to literally see him."

Shit, was I being a bad friend this last month? Was I more concerned with myself than what was going on around me, what was going on in CeCe's life? "I'm so sorry if I've been a bad friend recently," I say, feeling chastised, though I don't think that was her intent.

She rolls her eyes again, her trademark reaction to pretty much everything. "You're not a bad friend, and I'm not mad at you. This is the first guy that isn't a douchebag that you've been interested in. Plus, you trusted him enough to give him the most sacred thing you own: yourself. I'm happy for you, but I just don't want you to project and then try to pair me and Dante up."

It's my turn to roll my eyes. "C, I'm pretty sure you're already paired up with Dante. He's delivering food to you regularly, and you don't seem to be saying no."

"Whatever, we're not talking about this." She pauses, looking me up and down. "Also, good God, your tits look amazing. Greyson is going to shit himself when he sees you."

"Thanks, but I'm not wearing this to the party tonight."

"Oh, I know." CeCe smirks and holds up her phone. "Smile," she says, before a flash goes off.

"C, what are you doing?"

"Damn, you look hot in this. Only you could look like a Victoria's Secret model in a candid, bitch," she mumbles under her breath. Looking up, she eyes me with a mischievous grin. "I'm making sure Greyson knows how hot his woman is. Check your social media. I'm tagging you and you better repost it. Let's get one more in the mirror before we leave."

"You're ridiculous," I laugh, grateful for CeCe's guileless compliment, especially after my freakout earlier. "Come on, we need to get to the restaurant before my parents freak out that we're late."

—

Grey:

"Jesus fucking Christ," I mutter to myself, clutching my phone so hard that I'm surprised it doesn't shatter in my hand. If this shit broke, it would be Ava's fault, considering the picture she just reposted on her social media has my blood pressure skyrocketing.

The little fucking tease. When she left my house this morning, rumbled and annoyed that I wouldn't give into her sweet demands for round two, she looked like a woman well-rested and well-fucked by her man. Now? She looks like a damn goddess.

Pressing on the picture, I see that she reposted it from Celeste's account; the pit bull has Dante's balls in her purse and seems to be helping Ava with mine. There's no denying that Ava already has my balls firmly in her grasp, but I'm not a pathetic sap like Dante.

So what if I spend hours texting her, talking to her on the phone, and thinking about her? I'm committed and invested, not pathetic. I run a hand through my hair, thinking about the hours I spent cooking and cleaning yesterday to prepare for her coming over.

Fucking shit, I'm pathetic.

"Fucking hell, woman," I hear Dante shouting from upstairs, where Dante and Linc's bedrooms are. Pounding footsteps echo through the house like a stampede of goddamn elephants right before my door swings open. "Did you see this shit?" He throws his phone at me.

I look down and see his phone is opened to the Campus Hotties channel on Snapchat and tap on the "Hotties of the Day" icon. Immediately, a picture of Celeste and Ava fills my screen with a caption that forces a deadly silence to come over me. Positioned below the frame, my future murder victim wrote: "Two freshman sluts looking to spread their legs. Follow their handles for exclusive content." Their phone numbers and social media handles are imposed on top of their bodies, letting everyone know exactly who they are and how to contact them.

"What the fuck is this?" I throw the phone back at him and get up from my desk chair, ready to kill whoever stole that photo from their profiles and posted that shit.

"I'm going to fucking kill someone. I already reported the picture, but it's still fucking there, and fuck knows how many ass wipes saw it." Dante's seething, his anger tangible. Though his is louder and more evident, my fury is no less intense and no less murderous. Dante's phone goes off with a notification. "Oh fuck, it just got deleted. How long do you think it was up there?"

I check back on Ava's story; the original picture was posted ten minutes ago. "It could have only been up for a few minutes. But, fuck." I run a hand through my hair, pulling at the ends. "Someone's watching their shit. This wasn't random." Every account they have was listed, even their goddamn Reddits.

"Jesus, Grey. Does this shit have to do with the fucker bothering Ava?"

My hands clench, because it probably does. "I don't know, but if it is, they just escalated. Did you take a screenshot of the post?"

"Yeah, I have it."

"Send it to me." Ava's not going to be happy with me, but if this is related to our peeping Tom, they just declared war. I told Ava I would never let anyone hurt her, but what I should have said is that I'll never let anyone hurt her and get away with it. I won't ruin her dinner; I'll give her a few more hours until she has to face the fact that the fucker is back. But tonight? Everyone will know that I'm hers. And that she's mine.

My little vixen isn't going to be happy.

Ava

"Not to be rude, but Ava, you could have put a bit more effort into your appearance. Like, white? God, we all know you're a virgin, but way to call attention to it," my sister's friend Hyacinth whines. Normally I'd block her out, but right now I'm contemplating stabbing her with a butter knife before turning it on myself.

"Cin, stop being catty just because you're jealous Aves has boobs and you don't," my sister responds. "She could ban you from her room tonight and you'd have to Uber home, so don't be rude." Under her breath, Sera mumbles, "Please kick her out. I'm going to lose it."

Throughout dinner, Hyacinth complained about the service, the food, the weather; nothing was good enough for her. It took everything in me to hold back my comments, but I can't say the same for Celeste and Bianca. For every complaint Hyacinth had, B and CeCe would volley back a retort, striking her down as soon as she started to rise.

And now, here we are, sitting in an Uber as Hyacinth makes false assumptions about my hymen. Overall, the last forty-eight hours have been interesting.

"Hyacinth, go eat a bag of dildos, you jealous plebeian," CeCe's voice rings out.

"What did you just call me, bitch?"

"A peasant. Now, shut up. Your screeching is giving me a migraine." CeCe turns to look at Sera. "You need better friends. I can call my cousins to pick up the stray if you want."

"CeCe, be nice," I murmur, not in the mood to referee. "Oh, thank God, we're here." I bolt out of the Uber as soon as it stops in front of the soccer house. Though I'm not extremely familiar with the town around Marymount, we came to a party at this house two weeks ago. I grab CeCe and Sera's hands and drag them behind me, not caring to wait for my sister's friend. "Serena texted us. She's inside with Dylan already."

Unlike the first party we went to, I don't bother knocking and walk into the house. Already brimming with sweaty, writhing bodies, I thank my foresight for wearing minimal clothing, despite how revealing it is. The only thing worse than having my tits out on display is boob sweat.

I chose the lesser of two evils.

Squeezing through the crowd, I look for Serena. From the text she sent five minutes ago, she's by the pool table with Dylan and his fraternity brothers. It doesn't take a psychic to predict that Grey, Dante, and Lincoln are probably amongst the group with Serena, but at this point, I don't care if we're seen in public together if it takes me away from Hyacinth's grating voice.

Not paying attention to what's in front of me, I round the corner and slam into a body, nearly falling back from the force of the collision. "Shit, I'm sorry," I apologize before looking up into a pair of faces that are openly hostile. Felicity and Jordan glare at me, as though I intentionally attacked them.

"Watch where you're going, loser." Loser? What are we, in elementary school?

"Sorry, I didn't see you." I try stepping around them, my hands still pulling CeCe and Sera behind me, when Felicity strikes out and grabs my arm, ripping me away from my sister and best friend and into her personal space.

"Listen, you fucking cunt," her voice is low and menacing, not the peppy sorority girl I met at move-in. "You think you're hot shit because you were featured on Campus Hotties, but you're a little whore and we all see it. Grey doesn't want you; I've asked around and no one has seen you together since the barbecue. None of the sororities will touch you. Your social life will be ruined as soon as I say so. So," she leans in closer, whispering directly into my ear. "Do yourself a favor and transfer schools, move back home, and get fucking lost. No one wants you; no one likes you. You fucking cow." With that, she shoves me back and walks away, Jordan trailing closely behind her.

Stunned by the harshness of her words, I can barely process CeCe's yelling or my sister's soft hands rubbing my back in comfort. If I ever had any doubt as to what Felicity's opinion of me was, she just solidified it. It's not that I care that she doesn't like me—to be honest, I think she's an asshole—it's that she is so aggressive in her distaste solely because I gained the favor of the man she wanted.

I'm compartmentalizing the words, and her insults, and breaking them down into a way that I can understand them without allowing self-deprecation to creep in.

She said Grey and I haven't been seen together and that he doesn't want me. But *he* begged *me* to be exclusive and go public; it's me that refused. She claims no sororities will touch me, but I have more rush party requests than I know what to do with. Does her sorority want me? No, probably not. But do I want to belong to them? Immediately no. She called me a cow, which is better than the insults I've said to myself when I look in the mirror on my darker days. So that doesn't faze me.

"I hope you get explosive diarrhea, you small-minded, egotistical kumquat," CeCe yells into the crowd, garnering her more than a few looks.

I can't help the laugh that bubbles up. "What an insult," I giggle. "C, I'm fine. I was shocked for, like, two minutes that she was so cruel, but I'm over it." I tilt my head, remembering the Campus Hotties comment. "C, have you checked the Campus Hotties channel today? Felicity said something about me being on there."

CeCe grabs her phone out of her back pocket and opens the app. "No, there's nothing there. At least, not anymore." I shrug. Weird. "Come on, I see Serena." She grabs my hand before shooting a look over her shoulder. "And you"—she points at Hyacinth—"if I hear one more nasty comment come out of your mouth, I will stab you with my shoe and then call my cousins to clean up the mess." Hyacinth shoots her a disgruntled look but remains silent.

Thank God.

—

It takes ten minutes to make it through the crowd and to the room where Serena is. When we finally meet her in the center of the room, CeCe is red-faced from yelling at the people that were in our path, putting her residual aggression from the interaction with Felicity to "good use," as she puts it.

Arms are thrown around me from behind and a feminine squeal sounds in my ear. "Finally, I was worried you wouldn't be able to get through the oppressive crowd and stench of Axe body spray."

I laugh. Turning around and embracing Serena, I reply, "Now that you mention it, there is a cloud of cheap cologne in this house." Pulling back, I take in her petite form. In an outfit that is more revealing than I've ever seen her wear, Serena is wrapped in a black shirt that is completely see-through with a bikini-like bra underneath. With black leather pants and black boots, she looks like a cross between Buffy the Vampire Slayer and a dominatrix. "Holy shit, you look incredible."

"Me? Your boobs look fake, that's how impressive they are."

She pokes one of the swells over the corset cups to test the give. I swat her hand away and turn toward Sera. "This is my sister, Seraphina. Her friend, Hyacinth, is here too, but don't blame her. Childhood friends and all that, even though she's a monster now." I look at Sera pointedly, who just gives me an eye roll. "I see CeCe has already approached her mark for the night."

Just like I expected, CeCe found Dante as soon as we came into the room. Though they're not touching, their heads are bent conspiratorially, and Dante's fists are clenched by his side, like he's waiting for permission to touch her. For all of her talk, it's obvious that CeCe is into him, not just physically, but mentally as well. I've seen her chew up and spit out more guys than I can count, never bothering to play this cat-and-mouse game like what she's doing with Dante.

Goosebumps erupt on my neck, and the heavy feeling of eyes on me has me turning away from Dante and CeCe. My gaze lands on Grey, standing tall and imposing against the pocket door separating the room from a hallway. Flames engulf my skin as his eyes trail from my face to my chest, to my waist, and back up again. Lifting a hand, he runs his thumb along his bottom lip.

"Aves, care to explain why that Adonis is eye-fucking you?" Sera asks.

I open my mouth to respond, but Serena beats me to it. "That is Greyson Jansen, your sister's number one fan." I glare at her but that just seems to encourage her to keep talking. "Ask our dear Ava what's going on between her and the 'Adonis,' as you put it." My sister looks at me, curiosity written all over her face.

"He's more Thor than Adonis, okay?" I start before looking back at him. His eyes are still on me. "We're... a thing." They both remain silent, begging me to continue. "We're together, okay? A thing. It's complicated," I grind out. I turn around, putting space between us and this conversation when I feel myself collide with a body. A-fucking-gain. This time, though, the collision causes a cool liquid to spill down my body, drenching my corset and jeans in... beer? Disgusting.

"Watch where you're going, you fucking slut," the guy I collided with barks out. What the fuck is it with everyone calling me a slut? I lost my virginity twenty-four hours ago. Between Hyacinth talking about my inexperience, and now Felicity and this random man referring to me as a slut, it's like I'm the living personification of the Madonna and the Jezebel.

"Excuse me? You walked into me and now I'm drenched." I'm soaking wet, fed up with being called a slut, and annoyed that this guy just ruined my outfit.

"I bet you are wet, little whore. I heard you give it to guys real fucking easy. I bet you and that fire crotch sent that Campus Hotties post in. Fucking desperate."

A growl comes from behind me. "What the fuck did you just say to her?" Grey's voice is cool and menacing, and if I weren't intimately acquainted with him, I'd be petrified of that tone.

"Grey, man. How are you? I was just telling this bitch to watch where the fuck she's going. You feel me?" The obliviousness of this guy is nearly comical. Nearly, because according to him, I'm a bitch, slut, and a whore.

Grey's arm wraps around me, guiding me back against him. I could fight him right now, fight against him and demand that he listen to my rule about waiting until Monday to publicize our relationship. But at this moment, with my top see-through and insults coating me like the cheap beer on my clothes and skin, I don't have the will or inclination to struggle. Instead, I sink into his body and grab his arm, pulling him closer to me. If he's surprised, he doesn't show it, just flexes his arm at my contact.

"If you ever talk to my girlfriend like that again, I will beat the fucking shit out of you." Grey's voice is so cold and detached, completely at odds with the heat of him against my back. "And make sure all your soccer buddies know that if anyone speaks to her the wrong way, looks at her with anything less than the utmost fucking respect, I'll make sure everyone knows about the little coke problem their beloved captain has."

"Greyson, my man. I didn't know it was like that. You'd snitch for a piece of ass?" This guy is a damn moron.

"Say one more word, one more fucking word, and I'll have the cops here so fucking quick. I'll make sure they know exactly which rooms to search. Do you feel me? Now get the fuck out of my face before I do something my girl won't like." The threat of police must have been enough to put sense into his thick skull because he all but runs out of there.

Tilting my head to the side, I ask, "Girlfriend, huh?"

"Damn right, you are."

I step out of his embrace and turn on him. "What happened to waiting until Mon—?" My words are cut off as Grey whips off his Henley shirt and tugs it over my head. "What the hell are you doing?" I mumble through the fabric.

"Vixen, you're pretty pink nipples are on full display. I told you that no one is allowed to see that but me." Working my arms through the sleeves, I'm swimming in his shirt, and suddenly, the comments, the ruined outfit, and the pressure to keep us hidden become too heavy, and I feel tears well in my eyes.

Grey, who thankfully wore an undershirt, sees my tears and pulls me back into his arms. "Baby, you didn't think I'd stand by and let someone speak to you like that, did you? He walked into you, purposely tilted his beer on your tits for a free show, and then spewed that shit. You're my girl; there's no fucking way I'd let that shit fly." I nestle my face into his chest, not caring if my bronzer gets all over him. "Let's get out of here, go back to my house, yeah?"

"My sister is here," I say against his chest. "I can't leave her and her horrible friend here alone."

A soft chuckle leaves his lips. "Vixen, she's not alone. Linc's looking at her like she's his next meal." I jerk back and follow Grey's line of sight. Just like he said, Lincoln is looking at her with a hunger in his eyes that I do not like at all. Though she's talking to CeCe and Serena and gesturing wildly toward me, Sera's profile is in clear view of Lincoln, and he's observing her with an intensity that does not bode well.

"Greyson, she is eighteen and too fucking young for him. She's still in high school. My mother will kill me."

"Relax, vixen. He knows better than to get involved with someone in high school. But he'll make sure they get back safe, either to the house or to your dorm."

"Fine, but I need to speak with her." I turn from Grey but pause when his hand intertwines with mine. I look up at him, frowning.

"Vixen, I just claimed you as mine to every person in this room. Soon, every damn person at this school will know that I belong to you. Hold my damn hand, woman." I roll my eyes but don't pull away. He's not wrong, as annoying as that is to admit. Ignoring the shit-eating grin on his face, I tug him toward my sister and friends.

Interrupting the gesticulating arms and hand motions of Sera, and shooting a scowl at Lincoln's watchful presence, I offer a chagrined smile.

"You have been holding out on me and B, you little liar."

"I have no idea what you mean."

"Really?" She raises an eyebrow at me. "First, we get here and a sorority girl on speed verbally attacked you, prompting Celeste to declare nuclear war on her and her house in retaliation. Then, your Nordic god over here"—she waves her hand toward Grey—"undresses you with his eyes from across the room. And *then* some douche throws a beer at you and the Nordic god rushes over and declares that you're his girlfriend. So, tell me again that you have no idea what I mean."

"Oh, that."

"You have some explaining to do."

"And she'll tell you about it over breakfast at the house tomorrow morning, right, Linc?" Grey responds for me.

"Yeah, we'll make breakfast for our girls," he adds eagerly. Did he just say, "Our girls?" What is with the damn possession in this group? I shoot him another look and mumble, "She's eighteen, asshole," under my breath.

Grey continues, "Serena, have Dylan bring you by, too."

"Oh, that's okay. CeCe is spending the night so that Sera and her friend can have her bed." I look toward Dante at Serena's comment, noting he looks like a puppy that just had his favorite treat taken away.

"Sera, do you want to come back with me? And where the hell is Hyacinth?" I look around, realizing that she hasn't been part of this conversation and isn't even in the room with us.

"She texted me and told me that she was sick of CeCe giving her shit, so she texted her cousin that goes here and got an Uber back to her dorm." She shrugs her shoulders as if it's no big deal that her friend just freaking left her. "But it's fine, I shouldn't have brought her anyway. Safe to say that it's the last time we'll ever hang out."

"Thank fuck for that," CeCe calls out.

Ignoring CeCe's outburst, I tell her, "I can come back with you. I just need to leave; my shirt is ruined, and I have more beer on my body than I'd like to think about. Let me just call a car and we'll head out." Sera grabs my arm and shakes her head, glancing up at Lincoln before settling her gaze on me again.

"I want to stay. It's my first college party, after all. I'm sure Lincoln will keep me safe, right?" She offers a shy smile, and he eats it right up. Nodding his head in enthusiasm, he readily agrees. I narrow my eyes, telepathically communicating that I will sabotage our next practical if he lets a single thing happen to her.

"Fine, but you," I turn to Lincoln. "I will kill you if something happens to her, then resurrect you to do it again, and again, and again."

Grey, Lincoln, and Dante just laugh, thinking that my declaration is a joke.

Grey pulls me against his body again and bends down to whisper in my ear,

"Let's go home, vixen."

I follow him out, letting everyone know, without words, that I am his and he is mine.

—

Luckily, Grey was the designated driver and drove to the party, allowing us to avoid waiting for an Uber in front of throngs of people that had plenty to say about our linked hands. As we walked, I heard the nasty comments from women and the wolf whistles from the guys; it was as though Grey being well-known on campus permitted them to have an opinion on our relationship.

To be honest, it scares the shit out of me, and I feel the anxiety clawing at my chest. Before the picture, I would have relished being on Grey's arm and been excited to proclaim him as mine. Now? I have visions of my parents opening an email with a link to my half-naked body. Part of me feels terrible that the joy that should surround me, and my first relationship, is overshadowed by the very real threat of the explicit photo. The other part of me, a very small, minuscule, truly microscopic part, feels the excitement and jitters that should be overpowering.

I glance at Grey, who's leading us down a surprisingly deserted side street to his car. He seems so self-confident and aware like we weren't just the center of attention at a party of over two hundred. He smirks as he continues walking.

"I can feel you thinking, vixen."

"What the hell? CeCe said the same thing earlier."

"It's probably because you mumble to yourself when you're deep in thought." He shrugs as if it's no big deal. "It's cute, a little weird, but cute as fuck."

"Well, that's embarrassing and now I need to stop thinking so hard," I mutter as we reach Grey's Jeep. I'm opening the passenger side door when Grey's large, calloused hand shoots out to hold it closed, crowding me in from behind.

Leaning down, Grey's hot breath coasts along my neck. "Vixen," he whispers into my ear, sending goosebumps down my spine. "Those thoughts

that just ran through your mind earn you a spanking. We're starting at four."
His free hand moves from his side to my hip, pulling me back so that his hard
length presses against my back.

"W-what?" I sputter. "I didn't say anything."

"No, but every thought you had is written across your face, and I won't
accept that shit. You thinking that you're anything less than perfect doesn't
sit right with me. I won't let anyone talk shit about you, not even you. So,
for those nasty little thoughts, your cheeks are going to turn red tonight."

"Greyson, I am not a child, and you cannot just spank me because you
don't like what I'm thinking." His hand glides lower, dipping to the front
of my jeans and then back up until he's cupping my sex and squeezing me
through the fabric. My breathing goes shallow, as though there's not enough
oxygen in this entire world to regulate my lungs. His thick fingers glide along
the seam of my jeans, rubbing a delicious pressure right where I need him
most, especially after his dismissal earlier today.

"Vixen, I can feel how warm and wet your pretty cunt is through your jeans.
Lying to me, pretending you don't like being spanked, and being reminded
that you're my fucking good girl, earned you two more. Keep going, baby,
we can be at it all fucking night." He bends down and nuzzles into my neck
as he says it, his affectionate touches completely at odds with his words.

"Grey," I moan, the friction set off by his fingers building and spreading
like wildfire throughout my body. "If you keep doing that, I'm going to
come." Secretly, I pray that he doesn't stop because it feels so damn good.

I'm not disappointed.

Grey quickens his movements, rubbing the sensitive spot between my
thighs with more pressure. I feel the tension mount, starting at my spine
before traveling up and exploding, throwing me into the fastest orgasm I
have ever experienced. I should be ashamed that it took less than five minutes
for Grey to bring me to climax, but I'm too impressed to care. And so freaking
turned on.

Spinning around, I grab his neck and pull him down, crashing my lips to
his in a kiss that is all tongue and zero finesse. Grey doesn't seem to care;
if anything, he grows harder against my stomach. He takes over the kiss,

pushing my back into the car door while his hands go to my face, cradling me like I'm something precious while fucking my mouth like I'm his whore.

The dichotomy is heady.

I break from the kiss, panting as I stare up at him. "I want to taste you," I say into the night, speaking a collection of words that I have never uttered together before.

"Fuck." Grey pulls me back in, claiming my mouth before reaching out and opening his back door. "Get in, vixen." I slide in until I rest against the opposite door and then he's on me, ravaging me while concealing us in the heavy tints of his Jeep, the sporadic streetlamps the only witnesses.

Tugging at his Henley, we part long enough to remove our shirts before diving back in. Long fingers ghost up my corset-clad torso until they pull my cups down, acting as a shelf for my breasts. He squeezes my nipples, plucking them until they're firm points begging for his attention.

I shift while Grey plays with my nipples and devours my mouth. He's so lost in the worship he's paying to my chest that he startles when I grip him over his jeans, squeezing slightly to show what I want.

Breaking away from the kiss, he says, "Fuck, vixen. You want my cock?"

"Yes," I moan in response. My voice sounds so horse, so turned on, that it doesn't even sound like me.

"Take it out, baby. It's yours." I swallow, gripping the button on his jeans to pop it open before I slowly unzip him. I revel in the power I have over him in this moment, above him with his dick literally at my mercy. I tug on the waistband of his jeans, dragging them, along with his boxers, down to his ankles. His piercings shimmer in the darkness, the light from the streetlamps bouncing off them.

I take a moment to stare at him, absorbing how massive he looks squeezed into the back of a Jeep while his pants are pooled at his ankles. If a cop drives by and happens to look inside the tinted window, they'll get an eyeful of pierced dick and tattoos. We, undoubtedly, would end up in handcuffs, and not the sexy kind.

My train of thought has my laughter filling the space of the car, something that Grey does not seem to find too funny at all.

"Vixen, if you're laughing at my cock, I'm going to need to add a few more to your spank count. Now," he grabs the back of my neck, pulling me down toward his fully erect penis. "Fucking suck it like a good girl." My laughter drains away as my face lowers to his pierced dick. Opening my mouth, I lick from the base of his shaft up to the mushroom tip, swirling my tongue around the head before sucking it into my mouth. Hollowing my cheeks to take him deeper, I glance up at him, gauging his reaction.

Grey's eyes are on me, watching me fuck him with my mouth, with a look of reverence on his face. His hand flexes in my hair, guiding me further down his length, encouraging me to take all of him.

"Fuck, Ava, you're sucking my dick like a champ. How the fuck is this your first time?" Now, I'm not saying that CeCe and I googled "How to Give a Blow Job" and "Tips for Deep-throating like a Porn Star," but I'm also not saying we didn't. It appears our research has paid off.

I slow my pace, taking him deeper and scraping my teeth along his piercings. His low hiss is the only warning before Grey flexes his hips and thrusts until he hits the back of my throat. I can feel the tears running down my face and the drool pooling around my mouth.

"You're fucking beautiful when you cry for my cock, baby." Grey releases the back of my head, letting me come back up for air. Almost immediately, he shoves me back down. He continues the unrelenting pace until I feel him pulse inside my mouth. "I'm going to come down that pretty throat, vixen, and you're going to hold in every last fucking drop until I say swallow." His words precede the thick cum that coats my throat and fills my mouth.

My cheeks balloon out, and I probably look like a chipmunk with the amount of sperm that's filling my mouth. It's salty and thick and kind of disgusting, but in the context of this moment, it's hot as hell.

"Open that pretty mouth, Ava," Grey growls, pinching my chin until I open for him, showing him the load he just shot into my mouth. "Fuck, you listen like such a good girl." He shuts my mouth like a marionette before moving his fingers around my throat. "Now swallow." I gulp him down, his fingers flexing at the muscles in my throat.

"Get that pretty mouth up here." Grey grabs me, lifting me to straddle his lap, and rubs his lips along mine. It's a gentle caress, if not a little dirty, and has me clenching at my core. "Goddamn, Ava. You're a fucking goddess." I duck my head, preening under his praise like the good girl he claimed me to be. I never considered myself kinky; the porn I watch mostly consists of for-women, by-women videos that start under the sheets and end in cuddles.

Who knew I'd nearly combust from dick rings, deep-throating, and a praise kink?

Greyson

I shove my dick back into my jeans so fast before hauling Ava into the front seat and breaking every speed limit on the way to my place.

I didn't bother with a fucking shirt, didn't give two shits that my jeans were unbuttoned or that my hair looked like a damn nest from having her fingers run through it. All I care about is getting my girl back to my bed and showing her just how much I appreciated her mouth.

Fuck. Her goddamn mouth. For an innocent little virgin—ex-virgin, thanks to me—she has the skill of a seasoned veteran. My God, it took everything in me to not bust a nut in her warm mouth the second she inhaled the head of my cock like it was her favorite meal. I'm growing hard again just thinking about it.

In minutes, we're pulling into my driveway and then I'm out of my car, rounding the hood, and scooping Ava into my arms to carry her inside. She walks slow as shit and there's no way I'm waiting longer than I have to to get her naked.

"Woah, what the hell are you doing, Grey?" Ava asks, surprise clear in her voice.

"Baby, you're damn near perfect, but you walk like a fucking tortoise. I'm expediting the process."

If she responds, I don't hear it because of the blood rushing to my dick. I'm focused on getting us to my room, to my bed, and putting the shit show of a party out of my vixen's mind. It's not okay what that fucker did, and I'm going to kick his ass when my woman is fully satisfied, but Ava takes precedence. It was easy to read the disappointment, anger, and embarrassment all over her pretty face when the douche nozzle doused her in beer. She may not be happy that I pushed up our timeline, but no way in fuck would I let that shit slide and let my woman be spoken to that way.

Fuck that prick.

Walking through my bedroom door, I slam it closed behind us and rush to the bed, setting Ava down gently. I may want to spank her sassy ass, but I don't want to hurt her.

"Naked, now," I growl, sounding like a caveman but not giving a fuck. I make quick work of my jeans and boxers, while Ava remains motionless and smirking on the bed.

Ava raises an eyebrow. "How are you hard already?"

"Ava, vixen, for every minute you make me wait, I'm adding another smack to that peach of an ass. Now, get fucking naked." She eyes me for a minute before unbuttoning her jeans and sliding them down her legs. Left in her stained white top, she looks like a disheveled angel. "Keep going," I command, watching her slide the zipper down the side of the mesh contraption holding her in.

Within seconds, Ava has her shirt off and is laying in my bed naked.

About fucking time.

Standing at the foot of the bed, I watch her, taking in the flush traveling from her cheeks to her chest. She's as delicious as the food she makes, and I can't wait to devour the shit out of her.

"Vixen, are you sore?" I ask. It's difficult to remember that just twenty-four hours ago, she was a virgin. I told her I wouldn't fuck her again until her soreness ebbed, but that was a shit promise.

She shakes her head. "No."

—

Ava:

Grey pounces on me. Literally launches himself across the bed and lands on top of me, catching himself on his forearms so that he doesn't suffocate me. Before I can offer any comment on his Olympic jumping, Grey's mouth descends, aiming straight for the pulse at my neck.

"Oh my God," I gasp at the onslaught of his mouth.

"Not God, say my fucking name." Grey's lips travel from my neck to my shoulder, sucking and biting on skin that I never considered erogenous before. I moan, the sound echoing in the room. Grey's mouth continues downward, stopping at the swell of my breast. He suctions his mouth to my nipple, drawing it in before opening wider and taking as much of my boob as he can.

It feels so good that I whimper when he releases me from his mouth.

"I told you to say my fucking name, vixen. Who makes you come?" He punctuates his question by reaching down to spread my legs, giving him access to my most sensitive area. He pushes the tip of his cock inside of me, stopping once the head disappears.

"Vixen, don't make me ask again. Whose fucking pussy is this?" Grey pushes inside an inch more, his first piercing rubbing against the perimeter of my opening. I moan at the feel of the cool metal against my heated skin. "Who makes you come?" Another inch disappears, gifting me with one more piercing. I squirm, trying to gain more friction, seeking the pleasure I know he can give me.

He holds my hips down, stopping my movements. The control he's exerting right now is as intoxicating as it is frustrating. His smirk makes me want to punch him in the face and then fuck the shit out of him. The order of that may vary.

"Fucking tell me, Ava." He surges forward, burying himself to the hilt, his balls slapping against my ass with the move.

"Grey!" I scream, overwhelmed by the piercings and size of him inside of me. I lied to him when I told him I wasn't sore. I am, but my need for him overrides rational thought.

"Fucking right, vixen. It's me; I make you come. This pussy is mine." He rises to his knees, grabbing my hips and lifting them off the bed to change the angle. "This tight fucking cunt is going to squeeze every last drop of cum out of me, and you're going to take it like a good girl." He moves me on his cock, making sure each pass rubs against my clit. He's so attuned to my body and the friction that I crave, the pressure that I need to come.

Just like earlier this evening, I feel the tingles start to spread from my spine.

Grey must feel me clenching because he pulls out and throws his body on the bed. Grabbing me, he lifts me on top of him, my center aligned with his pierced cock. "Ride me, baby. Let me see those tits bounce while you ride my cock."

I've never taken control before; with Grey being my only partner, and his dominant personality in all things, the only experiences I've had are with him guiding my body toward pleasure. I can't say that I'm not excited.

Shifting my hips, I sink down on him slowly, allowing both of us to feel every inch of him until he's buried inside of me. Rocking forward, I move at a languid pace, exacting payback for his display moments earlier, despite Grey's hands on my hips trying to move me faster. His answering groan ignites a fire inside of me. I get caught in the rhythm, the fullness of his cock, and the rub of his piercings setting off a frantic need.

I increase my speed and bend down to capture his mouth in a messy kiss. Fighting against his tongue, I change my motion, lifting off him just to drop back down. Over and over again, I repeat the movement, losing myself to the drag of his ladder against my inner walls.

"Fuck, Ava, just like that. Goddamn, bounce on that cock," Grey grinds out. His filthy words set me off, throwing me into another intense orgasm. I clench around him and convulse as I pull every last ounce of pleasure.

"Your cunt feels so fucking good, vixen. I'm going to fill this pussy up, baby." Grey lifts his hips and surges upwards, burying himself even deeper inside me. I feel him twitch with his release, the warmth spreading throughout my core. I shudder, overcome with our shared release and the sparks consuming my body.

"Fuck, Ava." Grey thrusts twice more before dropping his hips back down and pulling me into his arms. He's still inside me, large and thick even when soft, almost like he's making sure none of his cum drops from my womb. I know we're young, and nowhere near the babies and children talk, but his obsession with coming inside me and making sure I keep every drop of him feels a hell of a lot like a breeding kink.

Like most things with him, I shouldn't find it hot, but I do.

It's Grey who breaks the silence. "Happy birthday, vixen. I fucking love you."

"I—what?" Did I just hear him correctly? Or did he fuck me so well that I'm hallucinating?

—

Grey:

Fuck. I didn't mean to announce that shit tonight, not because it isn't true, but because Ava isn't ready to hear it. One look at her face and I can tell that she's freaking out behind those big eyes.

"Shit, I didn't mean to say that." That's got to be the worst thing I could have said at this moment, second only to "I love you."

"Fuck."

She recoils like she's been slapped. "So, you don't mean it?" Ava questions, misreading the entire situation. She starts pulling away, but I tighten my hold on her and shift, pinning her beneath me and forcing her to stay put.

"No, vixen. It's true, of course it's fucking true. You should know by now that I don't lie." I kiss her lips lightly in an attempt to calm the pulse that's pounding against my chest. "I love you, vixen. Jesus, I'm borderline obsessed with you and kidnapped your hot ass tonight. Isn't that enough of a confirmation that I'm not lying?" She rolls her eyes in response, but I don't miss the smile she's trying to hide by biting her lower lip. My little tease.

"No, I meant that you'll think it's too soon because you panic about everything." She stiffens beneath me, and I know that she's dying to correct me. "Don't start, Ava. You sent me a minute-long voice memo detailing how nervous you were to use the coffee machine in the student center."

"Yeah, because I was freaking attacked by that cauldron of death in the student center!" she spits out.

Raising a brow, I question, "Yeah? And what about the voicemail you left because you didn't want anyone to make small talk when you were early for your algebra class, so you pretended to be in a conversation with my voicemail?"

"Well, that..." She pauses, furrowing her brow and looking fucking adorable. "You know I hate small talk, and everyone always talks about mundane things like the weather or their grade on the last test. It makes me panic because I don't know what to say." She scowls as soon as she realizes what she said.

"See, you panic, baby." I smirk, enjoying her annoyance. "It doesn't change the fact that it's real, that it's fucking true. I love the shit out of you, whether you're ready to hear it or not."

"You're lucky I love you, and your dick, otherwise I would knee you in the balls so hard that you would be searching for your damn testicles for weeks."

I stare at her, dismissing all of the shit she said about my dick and focusing on the three words she uttered in her sassy comeback. I grab her throat, just below her chin, and use my thumb to tilt her head up. Looking her in the eyes, I growl, "Say that again, vixen."

"That I want to knee you in the balls?" I squeeze her throat, applying just enough pressure. I'm fucking lucky to find this curvy woman that likes it as rough as I do, despite her inexperience. I'm not above using that shit against her to get what I want.

"You know what I want to hear, brat."

"Fine, I love you. But don't make a big deal out of it." She releases a sigh, almost like this conversation is boring her. The hand at her throat itches to spank her ass for that response.

"Oh, I'm making it a big fucking thing, vixen. And for that little response, I'm turning your ass red before I sink back into that hot little cunt. But that can wait." I release my grip on her neck and slide off the bed. Reaching down, I grab Ava bridal style and walk into the bathroom. "First, we're going to shower the cheap beer off this beautiful body, then I'm going to eat this sweet pussy until you're screaming my name again. After, I'm going to spank your ass raw before I fuck you from behind and come on that pink asshole. Sound good, vixen?"

She nods her head, eyes wide and hungry as she stares up at me. "Good. And vixen," I pause, leaning down to bite her jawline. "I know your cunt is sore, so if it's too much, fucking tell me. I'm trusting you to know your limits.

I don't give her a chance to respond before I turn the water to hot and step inside the two-person shower.

Ava

Three things hit me the moment that I wake up:

One, my vagina physically hurts from the number of times Grey and I had sex last night. Like, on a scale of one to "I need ibuprofen and a massage," I fall on the end of the spectrum.

Two, my back is sticky and adheres to the sheets thanks to our final round. After spanking me until I nearly came from the licks of pain, Grey took me from behind and drove me into the mattress. He pulled out and came all over my back, marking me like property. I tried to get up and wash it off in the bathroom, but he growled that he liked how his cum looked on me and convinced me to sleep with it soaking into my skin. I regret that choice now because I'm human Scotch tape; the sheet is quite literally stuck to my back by sperm and sweat.

And finally, three, Grey's side of the bed is empty except for a single calla lily. A few weeks ago, Grey and I played twenty questions and asked each other a string of random questions. I asked him everything from his shoe size to how he drinks his coffee. One of the first questions Grey asked me was about my favorite flower: white calla lilies.

I pick up the stem, close my eyes, and inhale, smiling to myself that he remembered something so innocuous. Soft footsteps sound to the side of the bed and I open my eyes, meeting Grey's dark blue ones. "Good morning, vixen," Grey mumbles and leans down to kiss me, morning breath a nonconcern.

"Good morning, handsome. What's this?" I hold up the stem.

"Something for your birthday. Now, come eat, I made breakfast." He pulls the top sheet and comforter back, exposing my bare, semen-drenched skin. "Damn, that's a nice fucking sight to wake up to in the morning. We need to do that more often."

"What, come on me like a dog marking its territory?"

"No, waking up together, you brat. Though, I can't say I mind the look of my jizz all over your curvy body."

I roll my eyes. "Whatever. I need to get dressed, but I need a shower first because I'm sticky."

Moving quickly, he pins me down, holding his front against my back to prevent any movement. "Keep it on, vixen. I like knowing that I'm still on you and still in you. Your sister is on her way over with Linc for breakfast. Put on one of my shirts and get that sweet ass out of bed before they get here."

Grumbling to myself, I slip on an oversize Rockies T-shirt with "Jansen 09" on the back. If it's weird that I'm wearing his father's baseball shirt with his cum on my back, I'm trying to ignore it. Even though I'm on the curvier side and can fill a T-shirt out indecently, the size and length of this one is so enormous that it comes just above my knees and hangs loosely from my shoulders. Slipping into the bathroom to brush my teeth and relieve my bladder, I do my business and then pull my hair into a messy bun on top of my head.

Looking at myself in the mirror, I can't help but think that I look like I've been thoroughly fucked.

I find Grey in the kitchen, leaning over a skillet and flipping pancakes like a short-order cook in a diner. His aunt must have taught him well because my brother can barely pour a bowl of cereal without messing it up.

"Impressive spread here, chef. Do you need help with anything?" I take stock of the cut fruit, a pitcher of orange juice, and scrambled eggs already plated family-style on the island. If I didn't confess that I loved him last night, I would probably be unable to hold it in after this treatment.

Without taking his eyes from the griddle, he responds, "No, take a seat on one of the stools and get comfortable. I'm almost done." Flicking off the burner, he scoops the pancakes onto the stacks plated next to him and brings them to the island. Holding the plate out to me, he gestures for me to take one.

"Oh, no. They look delicious, but I'll stick to eggs and fruit. Thank you for making all of this."

He raises a quizzical brow at me. "Ava, you love pancakes; they're your favorite breakfast food." Damn him and damn twenty questions.

"They are, but I'm just more interested in the eggs." I move to grab the eggs, but he pushes them out of my reach. "Hey—" I start, but he cuts me off.

"Nope, you're going to tell me why you're not eating one of your favorite foods and instead settling on eggs. Don't bullshit me, vixen. I'll know if you're lying."

I scrunch up my face, my annoyance stamped all over my features. He wants to get into this now? Fine. "I'm not eating the pancakes because as good as they smell, and as delicious as I'm sure they are, one bite will have me reeling and obsessing over the calorie intake all day. A full pancake will have me starving myself until dinner, just so that I can eat a salad and promise myself that I'll do better tomorrow. If I look at a piece of bread sideways, I get bitch-slapped with ten pounds on my ass." I take a breath, slowly releasing it before I continue, "I have a shit metabolism, and I need to watch every single piece of food that goes into my mouth. I'm already feeling guilty for the bowl of pasta I ate last night and the french toast yesterday morning; I cannot afford to compound that with a pancake."

Grey drops the plate and grabs my face, tilting it up to meet his eyes. Wiping the tears that I don't realize are falling from my eyes, he has a gutted look on his face. "Baby, if I knew the pancakes would trigger you, I wouldn't have made them. Fuck." God, I'm such an asshole for making him feel bad for making me breakfast.

"No, Grey, I appreciate it so much. You have no idea. God, you have no idea what you mean to me. But it's just part of who I am. I'm better now; I get help and talk to a therapist when I need to, but I need to control it because when I don't, I spiral, and it overtakes every aspect of my life. The 'good' foods, the 'bad' foods, I'm learning how to break down and dispel the thoughts I've had for most of my life around food, but I'll never wake up and be one hundred percent comfortable with food or with my body."

"How long have you been dealing with this? Vixen, Ava, shit you're fucking perfect, but not because of your body, because of you."

"Since I was a little girl. I've always been different from my sisters, always bigger and heavier; I take up more space. My body isn't slender or petite. I'm this bullshit in-between, a designation that, up until a few years ago, was unaccounted for in most stores and fashion brands. I would either squeeze into clothes that didn't flatter my shape or swim in clothes that were too overpowering for my height. It's all-consuming," I let out my final words with a ragged breath. "I just... I don't want the pancake, but thank you."

Grey doesn't say anything, just wraps me in his arms and holds me together while I break apart over pancakes in his pristine kitchen.

"Shh, vixen. It's okay, I've got you, baby." He rubs my back, offering comfort for wounds that he had no idea existed. "I know my words won't fix your perception of yourself, and it fucking guts me to hear you speak so damn poorly about your body, but baby? When I look at you, the first thing I see isn't your ass and stomach, it's your smile that brings me to my knees, your sass that keeps me humble, and how fucking devoted you are to everything and everyone you care about. Yeah, I love how you look, but I love *you* even more. Even if I was a fucking blind man, I'd be stunned by your beauty. Your worth isn't physical, it's in what you do, who you are, and what you believe in." He kisses my head and I burrow closer, letting his words wash over me.

"I want to stand beside you as you work on this; I want to help you love yourself and this gorgeous body for what it can do. One day, one fucking day, I'm going to watch this body grow my children and be even more in awe of it than I already am. So, we need to take care of it, and I need you to take care of yourself. You need to speak with your therapist, vixen."

I pull away from him, puzzling through the bombs he just dropped. "Children?"

"This? Us? We're forever. You're not getting rid of me unless you kill me, which you'll probably want to do on occasion but remember that I can eat your pussy better than anyone else can."

"I'm not even touching that. But yeah, you're right. I need to call my therapist." He's not wrong, I've been feeling the need to speak with someone more frequently, ever since the texts and photo started. We pull apart just as the front door opens and heavy footsteps pound on the hardwood.

"Are they running or is there a stampede of elephants?" I question.

"I—"

"Holy shit, you're official," Celeste yells as she runs into the kitchen.

"What?" I look at Grey, who is conveniently looking away from me and piling eggs onto his plate. "Greyson, what the fuck did you do?"

Greyson

I wince at the shrill note of Ava's voice. It's normally deep and husky, not high-pitched. I busy myself with the eggs, trying to prolong the shit she's about to give me, but that just makes me think about the conversation we had moments earlier. I'm fucking wrecked to learn what she thinks about her body, and how she could view herself as anything less than the goddess that she is. I've spent enough years in therapy to know that nothing I do or say will fix her perception, but I'm damn well going to help her shift her mindset.

Yeah, the first thing I saw when I looked at her was the indents of her waist and how it led to the flare of her thick hips. Her tits are works of fucking art, and I would gladly die between her thighs. But now, I see everything that she is: the aspiring chef, the sassy little brat, the clumsy mess that freaks out over coffee urns. I love all the parts of her, all her weirdness. The best fucking thing I ever did was lock her down, and I'm making it my mission to show her just how perfect she is.

"What did he do? He posted this to all his social media." Celeste hands Ava the phone, showing her the picture I posted earlier this morning. In my defense, she looked like a fallen angel wrapped in my sheets with the flower I left for her on the pillow. Laying on her stomach with her face angled toward the flower, her face is void of makeup and glowing from the number of times she came last night. She's covered up to her shoulders by a sheet, but it doesn't take a genius to figure out she's in my bed and that we probably fucked.

Beneath the picture is the only caption worth writing: "Mine."

Probably one of my best posts, if I'm being honest. I feel Ava's eyes on me, and I guess my time at avoidance has officially ended. I look over at her, taking measure of the furrowed brow as she stares at Celeste's phone. Her cupid's bow lips are drawn down, giving her mouth a pouty look, and now I'm envisioning those lips around my dick. Shifting, I adjust my semi; Celeste is a little pit bull and can probably smell how turned on I'm getting for her best friend.

Reaching out, I smooth the creases on Ava's forehead and tug the phone out of her hand. Throwing it on the island, I tug her to me until she's perched on my lap. "Vixen, tell me what's on your mind."

"You posted a picture of me."

I roll my eyes at her statement of the obvious. "Fuck yeah, I did. I need everyone to know that you're fucking mine."

"But, Grey, what about the texts?" She pulls the corner of her bottom lip between her teeth, nibbling in worry.

"Vixen, it's been over a month. There's nothing there, they lost interest. And if they didn't? I told you, I'll fucking end their shit and make them wish they never fucked with us."

Celeste huffs, stealing my attention from Ava. "What, pit bull? You sound like you have something to say, so fucking out with it."

"Well, now that you mention it," Celeste begins, drawing out the moment. Fucking lit major, so damn dramatic. It's no surprise Dante is obsessed with her. "You're both being imbeciles and acting like it's not Felicity and Jordan. Are you not putting together the timeline of events and drawing a reasonable conclusion? My God, it's like I'm speaking to freaking children." She throws her hands in the air, flapping like a damn bird in the kitchen.

"Fuck, Red, I love when you get worked up." Dante silently enters the room, a contrast to Celeste's heavy steps. "Let's go to my room and take that energy out."

She whirls on him like a fucking banshee and holds out one finger. "First off, Mr. Italia, that was a two-time event. I hope you have a photographic memory because that shit is not happening again." Raising a second finger, she continues, "And second, you overgrown ogre, I will take my energy out by killing you and dragging you out into the woods for the bears."

Dante looks at me with a glint in his eyes. "God, this is the best fucking foreplay." Sick fucks.

Celeste is about to explode, but Ava raises her voice, cutting through the impending tirade. "C, logically, it's probably Felicity, but I can't say that with absolute fact. There's no evidence, hell, there hasn't even been a text message or another picture since the first one. So, honestly, we don't know anything for certain."

"Okay," Celeste responds. "But what was that shit with the Campus Hotties last night?"

Fuck, I forgot about that. Shifting Ava off me, I grab my phone and pull up the screenshot from last night. Holding it up, I show both of them the picture posted on the site last night. "Whoever runs this account took a picture of your Instagram story and posted it, along with your contact information last night. D reported it and got that shit pulled."

"Fuck, is that why I woke up to texts asking if I was down to fuck?" Celeste questions.

"Who the fuck sent you those?" Dante bellows, wrapping a hand around his pit bull's wrist and pulling her phone out of her hand. "I'll fucking tear their dicks off."

"Did you get any texts, vixen?"

"I-I don't know. I didn't charge my phone last night and it's in my bag." She looks up at me with wide, watery eyes. "Why would someone do this, Grey? What have I done that's so terrible to warrant the continual invasions of my privacy."

Fuck. I rub a hand down my face, trying to wipe the self-loathing off. The only reason she's going through this shit is because of me. A better man would let her go, tell her to be with a guy that doesn't bring problems to her fucking doorstep. But fuck that. I'll slay the fucking dragons and bring her their heads as a goddamn trophy.

"Fuck, vixen, you haven't done shit. They're coming at you because of me. Your pit bull over there"—I nod my head toward Celeste—"is just being dragged into the crossfire. Fuck, baby, I'm so fucking sorry." I wrap my arms around her waist, pulling her into me.

A notification goes off on my phone, silencing the room. I look down at the blocked number and my blood runs cold. This motherfucker resurrected like a damn zombie. Swiping the message, I see the picture I posted this morning along with a video attached with a text below:

Unknown: Hope your slut is ready for her debut. Didn't know I had a video of the live event, huh? Will she still be interested when she realizes you fucked her over? It's live BTW ;)

"Fuck! Fucking shit!" I throw my phone against the cabinets, standing quickly and knocking my stool back in the aftermath. Ava looks at me with wide eyes, trembling from the outburst. "Fucking goddamn cock sucker." I lean over the counter, gripping the edge while I figure out what the fuck I'm going to do.

"Grey, you're scaring me. Who just texted you?" Ava's voice breaks through my fury.

I turn to her, gripping her face in my hands. "I'll fix this, vixen. I fucking swear."

"Fix what?" Before I can respond, Celeste's phone goes off and dread pools in the pit of my stomach. I close my eyes, breathing in deeply.

"Oh, my God." Celeste's voice is low, a whisper that echoes like a scream throughout the kitchen. "Ava, they posted."

"W-What? What do you mean they posted?" Ava turns to me. "Greyson, what does she mean? Are there—" She pauses, trying to speak through the sobs wracking her body. "Is there a photo of us out there? Are m-my parents going to see this? Oh my God." She grabs the phone and looks horrified at the screen.

I grab her shoulders and pull her in, cocooning her in my strength. "Baby, I'm going to get the best fucking lawyers involved, hell, we'll call our fucking parents and blow this shit up. But right now, we need to screen record this and start reporting it as soon as fucking possible."

"Greyson, my body is on display with the caption, 'A whale gets sperm,' along with all of my fucking contact information." She shakes, seemingly unable to control the movement of her body. "Oh my fucking God, I think I'm dying. I'm in shock. I need a paramedic."

"Ava, baby, you are not dying. We need to report this and call our parents."

"Oh my God, my parents. They're going to kill me." She continues chanting, "Oh my God," unable to comprehend or say anything else. I'm about to shake her when Celeste walks up to her, a cup of water in hand, and throws the water in her face.

"Snap the fuck out of it, Aves. We need to deal with this shit," CeCe shouts. I've never been more grateful for how fucking feral Dante's woman is.

Ava

My parents are going to see a video of Greyson fucking me with his mouth.

That sentence is on repeat in my head. God, how can this happen to me? They're going to murder me and be pardoned for justifiable filicide.

Water assaults me, startling me out of my near-catatonic state. "Snap the fuck out of it, Aves. We need to deal with this shit," CeCe snaps.

"Dammit, C. I'm soaking wet."

"Better that than paralyzed. Now come on. You need to go get your phone, and we need to do damage control before we go to the police."

CeCe moves to lead me into Grey's room, but he holds out his hand, stopping her. "I've got her. You two, eat and wait for Seraphina and Linc. Ava, I will call our parents." He grabs my hand and leads me down the hall into his bedroom. Reaching for my bag, I pull out my phone, noting that it has a 13% charge, and am immediately bombarded by missed calls and text messages from my parents and siblings. I click on Sera's name, opening up her text chain.

Sera (10:21 pm): I'm staying in your room with Lincoln. Don't be mad.

Sera (10:54 pm): Why do you have a dick beer funnel?

Sera (8:13 am): Ava!!! What the fuck is this? < screenshot of Grey's post attached> I'm telling Mom.

Sera (8:37 am): Aves, I was just tagged in a video on all of my social media of you and Greyson. What is this?

Shit, they tagged my sister, too? I feel the tears roll down my face as I select Bianca's thread.

B (8:30 am): Call me right this damn minute, you hot bitch. I cannot believe you had sex and got a boyfriend as soon as you went to college. My freaking hero! But, also, I'll kill the motherfucker that fucked with this family. Celeste taught me everything she knows.

I roll my eyes and leave it to B to be impressed and bloodthirsty all at the same time. I look back at my notifications and see fifteen missed calls from my mother, as well as a text.

Mom (7:51 am): Ava Maria, answer your phone. The firm received an emailed video of you in a compromising position with a man.

"Shit," I whisper, running my hands over my face. My parents are going to kill me.

"Hey." Grey grabs my shoulder, squeezing in reassurance. I look up at him, taking in every feature on his damn face. I should be annoyed with him that he pushed me to publicly acknowledge him, but it's not his fault that he leads women—and possibly men—to obsession. I think back to last night and this morning, how he confessed that he loved me, and how I confided in him my body struggles.

No, I can't be annoyed with him because why should we have to hide that we want to be together?

"We need to call your parents, vixen. The sooner we do it, the better. Let's plug your phone in and call them on speaker." He grabs the phone and plugs it into the charger.

"We?" I question. "I need to call them alone."

"No, vixen. We're a team now. We face this shitstorm together and lean on each other to get through this fucking mess. We're not letting this fucking divide us." The gentle caress of his fingers on my jaw contradicts the aggression of his words. "Okay, baby?"

I stare at him, taking in the man that ignited both my downfall and my passion.

"Yeah, okay. Fine," I respond.

He rolls his eyes, picking me up before sitting on his bed and depositing me on his lap. "We're facing this together. It's you and me, vixen. Now"—he grabs the phone from his nightstand, still connected to the charger—"call your mom back."

I tap on my contacts and scroll to my mother's contact information. Saying a silent prayer to the Virgin Mary and Mary Magdalene, I hit the icon to call her and hold my breath while the line rings.

I don't have to hold my breath long; she answers on the second ring.

"Ava Maria Gregori," my mother growls. Shit, she used my full name, adding the last name to drive home the disappointment. Grey squeezes me, lending me strength.

"Hi, Mom."

"Ava! What the fuck is going on up there?" "I will drive up and sue so many fucking people, they'll lose their assholes in the settlement process," my dad shouts from the background. I stifle a laugh at the imagery that evokes.

Taking a deep breath, I begin, "Before you start on your questions and assumptions, just let me explain, okay?"

They both fall silent, and I can hear the ticking of the antique grandfather clock in their office. My sisters and I found it at a garage sale and bought it for our parents so that they'd always be on time since they're habitually late. The ticking gives me comfort.

"I have Grey—Greyson Jansen—with me. He's my"—I pause to look at him—"boyfriend. We met on move-in day and hit it off. The video you saw was not consensual." Grey stiffens beside me, and I realize what I said. "I mean, the action on the camera was, he had my consent, of course." Kill me now, please. "But the filming was not consented to. We found out shortly afterward that someone had taken a picture, but we just found out they filmed us in a... vulnerable position and planned to use that to keep Grey and me apart."

"How do you know this Greyson isn't behind this?" my father asks. I'm not surprised by this line of questioning; he's one of the best lawyers because he's shrewd and trusts no one.

Grey clears his throat, signaling that he wants to answer my dad's question. "Sir, I love your daughter, and I would never do something to put her well-being, both physical and mental, in jeopardy." My dad grunts in response, which for him is a glowing review.

"Ava," my mom begins, "why would you have sex in a public place, in a school of all places? Do realize that the school could expel you for misconduct and public indecency? You both put your futures in jeopardy when you could have waited fifteen minutes for a damn bed!" My mom's voice rises at the end, and I shrink, absorbing the disappointment and chastising through the phone.

"Mom, I'm sorry," I hiccup, failing to hold in the sobs that consume me. "I'm s-so sorry for disappointing you."

"Ava," she sighs. "I'm worried for you; I'm enraged on your behalf. I could kill this prick that violated your privacy. Am I happy that you had sex in a public space, leaving yourselves vulnerable for something like this? No, I damn well am not. But you are my daughter and I know you. I know that you wouldn't be with someone unless you cared for them. You love him, don't you?"

Jesus, way to blow up my damn spot, Deborah. "Yes, Mrs. Gregori, Ava and I love each other." I elbow Grey in the gut, and he laughs under his breath, almost like I tickled him instead of attacking him with my bony elbow.

"Good. When did this all start?" I detail the timeline and tell my parents about the initial texts and threats, followed by over a month of silence. My mother made me read, verbatim, the text messages that the unknown number sent to both me and Grey, and I sent them screenshots of everything to build a case.

"God, Ava Maria, I could wring your neck for not telling us about this sooner." My dad sounds exhausted. When he woke up this morning, I doubt he anticipated watching a sex video of his eldest child. He's probably traumatized.

Same, Dad. Same.

"Greyson, you need to call your parents or guardians immediately and have them give a call to our office. Because you're a legal adult, you don't need their consent to have us represent you, but we would feel better to be in contact with them. If you have a family attorney, please give me their contact information, and we will work with them on drawing up all the documents," my dad says.

He continues, "Now, it's important that after you call Greyson's family, you go directly to the police station with all the evidence you have. We need to build a criminal case against this asshole to make sure that their lives are ruined. This will help us present evidence to the school to ensure that there are no ramifications for your little morning delight." I cringe at his description and just barely prevent myself from gagging. "We will meet you both there."

"Ava?" my mom's voice rings through the line. "Don't forget, we love you and will move mountains to bring this asshole to justice. Just, don't ever have sex in public again, please."

We trade a few more words with my parents before we hang up, promising to let them know as soon as we leave for the West Helm precinct. Based on the situation, that call could have gone significantly worse.

"That wasn't too bad," I mutter, turning to Grey and holding out my phone for him. There's no way that his phone survived his attack against the cabinets, so he'll need to call his dad from my cell. "Here, call your dad. Do you want me to give you a minute?" He grasps my hand, shaking his head.

"No, we'll do this together. Just don't expect my dad to be as calm as your parents."

"You think my parents were calm?" I nearly laugh. They may have been in lawyer mode during the call, but I know that their blood is raging through their veins.

"Just, trust me. I need to text him first to let him know it's me so that he'll answer." Grey types out a text, putting an emoji of an orange at the end of his text.

"Did you just text your dad an orange?"

He offers a half smile. "A lot of people try to get my dad's number; some have even claimed to be me for an exclusive." He rolls his eyes. "When I was fifteen and tried to call him from a friend's phone when mine died, he didn't answer because he figured it was a reporter. We realized that I needed a way to signal it's me so that he won't ignore it."

Well, that's extremely freaking paranoid, but I can't deny that it makes sense based on his dad's level of fame within the sports community. I don't even like sports, and I've seen his documentary and know who he is by sight.

"Okay, but why an orange?"

"I'm allergic to oranges, so we figured no one would guess that shit."

I open my mouth to question him further—are we talking about itchy throat allergic or death allergic?—when my phone rings. Grey must recognize the number because he picks it up immediately and puts it on speaker.

"Greyson, what the fuck is going on?" His dad's voice booms through my speaker, and I wince at the volume and tone of voice.

Grey looks at me and mouths, "Told you."

"Greyson, are you fucking there? Why the fuck did I get a video of you and a young woman this morning?"

My eyes widen and I feel my cheeks flush. My boyfriend's dad has seen me naked with his son's head between my thighs. Will there be an end to this mortification, or will I die first? I feel Grey's hand cover mine, loosening my grip on his comforter until he cradles my palm in his hand.

"Dad, that's Ava, my girlfriend. The woman I told you about." He looks over at me and I already know where he's headed. I shake my head, trying to silence the words I know are about to tumble out of his mouth. "She's here with me now." I shoot him my dirtiest look, but he ignores me.

"Hello, Ava," his dad responds, his voice losing a bit of its gruffness at his acknowledgment of my presence.

"Hello, Mr. Jansen. I'd say it's nice to meet you but, um, under the circumstances, not so much."

"I'd say you're right, young lady. But please, call me Greg. Now, Greyson, tell me what the hell is going on and whose head needs to roll."

"Jesus, Dad, chill with the 'young lady' shit, you're not even forty." Grey launches into the same explanation that I gave my parents, detailing the threatening texts and the hostility Felicity showed me at every encounter. He spends ten minutes outlining how we got to this fucked up situation before he finally stops for breath.

We're met with silence on the line before Greg replies in a cold, menacing voice, "I will fucking end them." Goosebumps erupt down my spine at the open hostility and foreboding in his words; it's easy to see where Grey got his intense personality.

"You and me both," Grey replies. "We're at the house now, but Ava's parents want her down at the precinct to file a report."

"You're filing, too. I don't give a shit that your face isn't visible; it's obvious to anyone that knows you that it's you in that video." After confirming the time with Grey's dad to meet at the police station, I text my parents to confirm and send them Greg's number. I fall back on his bed, drained from the back-to-back phone calls we just had.

Grey drops down next to me, grabbing my chin and turning my face toward his. "You okay, vixen?" he whispers.

"Not really, no," I reply honestly.

"What can I do to fix that, vixen?" He leans in, nipping my bottom lip before trailing kisses up my jawline. "It fucking guts me to see you upset," he says against my skin. Sinking deeper into the mattress, I close my eyes, letting his lips consume the emotions festering inside me. Grey opens his mouth, sucking the flesh of my earlobe into his mouth before biting down.

Shifting my body, I raise my hands until they're tangled in his hair, holding him firm against me. Releasing my ear on a pop, he murmurs, "Are you going to be a good girl and be quiet while I eat your pussy? Or do I need to stuff that pretty mouth of yours with my cock to keep you quiet?" I nod my head, saying yes to both options he just presented to me.

"Which one, vixen? Do you want this cock, or do you want to ride my face?"

I'm about to respond when someone bangs on Grey's bedroom door. "You two better not be fucking in there," Dante calls out.

"Fuck off, D," Grey calls out, rolling off and pulling me to my feet. He lowers his voice, "Let's go, vixen. We need to meet our parents and get this fucking shit taken care of."

"I know," I sigh. "I would rather crawl under a rock and hide. Is that an option?" I step around him and walk toward the door, ready to face the firing squad that awaits.

"Vixen." Grey's arm shoots out, stopping my progress. "It's you and me, together. Remember that." He links our hands, and we walk out as a united front.

—

Entering the kitchen, we're met with five concerned pairs of eyes. Sera, Lincoln, and Serena having joined while we were in Grey's room. It doesn't take a genius like Serena to deduce a few hard truths about not only our situation but that of our friends, too.

First, the video of me and Grey is all over the school. I've received so many messages in the last few hours to realize that the saying, "It lives forever on the internet," is unfortunately true.

The second, based on Sera's oversize T-shirt and the hickey on her neck, is that she and Lincoln spent the night together. The amount of concern I have for that is overshadowed only by my third, and final, observation: something happened to Serena. I take a closer look at her face and see the bloodshot, watery eyes that seem even huge against the abnormal pallor of her usually honey skin. She looks away as soon as she meets my eyes, and I can't help but ask, "Serena, are you okay? What happened?"

Her soft laugh is twinged with sadness. "Shouldn't I be the one asking you if you're okay? Jesus, Ava, I called Celeste as soon as I saw the video on my socials this morning. It was taken down a little while ago, but it was up long enough for a large population to see it." She winces, as though she's experiencing the same amount of pain I am over the situation, and maybe she is. It doesn't go unnoticed by me that she deflected my question, but I have more pressing issues right now than interrogating Serena.

"Yeah," I start, swallowing the lump in my throat at the mention of how many people had access to that video. "Can't say we're doing too great but…" I pause, turning to look at my hand enclosed in Grey's before glancing up at his face. "We'll be okay. I think." He lifts our clasped hands, kissing the back of my hand before dropping them to his side.

Grey clears his throat, commanding the attention of the room. "We're heading over to the precinct to meet our parents and file a police report." He glances over at Dante, sharing a look that I can't quite decipher, before looking at Lincoln. "D, Linc, take care of the girls. We'll be back later."

"C, I'll meet you back at the dorms later—"

"The hell you will. You're staying here, vixen," Grey cuts me off.

"No, I'm going back to our dorm." I roll my eyes, not surprised by the caveman behavior, but annoyed all the same.

"Ava, just humor me for tonight? If you're still being a stubborn little pain in my ass, I'll bring you back tomorrow. But I need you in my bed tonight, okay?"

"Is that supposed to be an endearment?" Sera whisper-yells from across the room.

"Yes." "No." Greyson and I say at the same time.

I huff, holding back the sharp retort at the overprotectiveness wafting off him like cologne. "Fine, but you're bringing me back tomorrow. I need to prepare for my pastry class and review my notes before the bake."

"Fine. Now, get your tight ass moving; I want to get this over with." He drags me toward the front door, grumbling about "stubborn vixen" and "spanking her ass" under his breath as we approach the threshold.

I wave goodbye over my shoulder before tugging my hand out of his grasp. "Stop being such a dick, Grey."

"I wouldn't have to be a dick if you'd just let me take care of you. And you like my dick."

"Dammit, Grey. I'm serious. You can't just throw out an order and expect me to obey." He comes to an abrupt halt, and I crash into his back. I take a step back, giving him space, but that just seems to piss him off. Grabbing my shoulders, he spins us until my back is flat against the door and he's caging me in. Capturing my lips, he marks me in a blistering kiss before pulling back. It's not so much sexual as it is a claim.

"You've told me all of the ways us being together has affected your life, how you feel about this fucking stalker, but let me tell you how I feel. My girl, the girl I fucking love, is pulling away and being stubborn instead of letting me take care of her. I get it, okay? I fucking get it. You're scared, you're hurting, and you're retreating from me, but I'm not letting you go fucking far. So, vixen, you may not like how protective I'm being, but suck it the fuck up, because I'm not going anywhere. If anything happens to you," he pauses, pulling in a ragged breath before continuing. "Goddamn, if anything happens to you, I won't be able to fucking live with myself. So, just fucking let me take care of you, okay?"

"Okay," I respond, because really, what else could I say?

—

Because of my natural inclination to fall on my face and embarrass myself, there aren't many moments in my life that I wish I could erase from existence, aside from the picture and video distribution. However, Grey meeting my parents in a police station while discussing a video of him eating me out in a classroom is one of those rare moments that I wish I could erase from existence.

Meeting Grey's dad under the same situation also qualifies, as does my dad referring to our actions as "cunnilingus." I am sufficiently traumatized and any past trauma that I've held on to from my childhood is no longer significant.

After four hours spent detailing—and reexplaining—the series of events that led to our current predicament, I am exhausted and mentally drained. My parents were enraged, alternating between silent terror and high-pitched screams. They had to be reminded three times by the detective taking our statement to calm down or get out. Grey's father wasn't much better, except he had well-known fame on his side while my parents had the adoration of the receptionist that was addicted to true-crime podcasts and knew who they were immediately.

Now back home, laying on Grey's bed, I want the world to swallow me whole and absorb all of the mortifications from the last twenty-four hours into its core. As soon as we got back, Grey went in search of Dante and Lincoln while I made a cocoon in his bed out of his comforter and texted CeCe. Though mine and Grey's outing at the station took center stage this morning, there's no forgetting the state of my friends and sister when they showed up for breakfast. Needing answers—and a distraction—I question CeCe after exchanging GIFs about the longest day ever.

Ava: Are we going to pretend that you didn't spend the night with Dante, or are you going to tell me what's going on?

CeCe: Did you know that a shrimp's heart is in its head?

Ava: Celeste

CeCe: Did you also know that tigers have striped skin?

Ava: Celeste

CeCe: Fine. We spent the night together. Don't get fucking excited about it.

Ava: Holy shit, C. Did you sleep with him?

CeCe: We slept, that's it. Seriously, don't make it freaking weird.

Ava: You looked tousled this morning *Bridget Jones GIF*

CeCe: Fuck right off. Bridget Jones is a cinematic masterpiece; have some respect. We made out. Leave me alone, Porn Queen.

Ava: *dancing banana GIF*

Ten minutes pass while CeCe and I trade obscenities back and forth. My shit show of a day is nearly expunged from my conscience when my phone vibrates with a social media notification. Opening my Instagram app, I click on my notifications and am shocked to see Grey's handle tagging me in a video. After the fallout from this morning and the endless calls and texts about the video, I avoided all of my social media like it had a combination of swine flu and smallpox.

I raise the volume on my phone and select the video. Grey pops up on my screen, dressed in a black sweatshirt and backward baseball cap; he looks like most women's fantasy. He's sitting at his kitchen island and based on the angle of the phone, it's propped up on something and set to self-record. I hit play and Grey's voice fills the room.

"By now, you've all seen the video of me and my girlfriend in a private moment. For those sick bastards that have saved, liked, or redistributed the video, stop immediately. My girlfriend and I are not a public spectacle and value our privacy above all else. The violation of our privacy and safety is unacceptable, and the authorities are working to identify the sick fuck that stole that moment from us." Grey pauses, rubbing a hand over his face. "There have been posts, response videos, and disgusting shit spewed that paint my girlfriend, Ava, inaccurately. She is everything and she's fucking perfect, so if you think for a second that the opinions of random, faceless people on the internet have any bearing on my love for her, you're wrong. And to the coward that posted that video and violated every aspect of my girl's privacy and agency, I will find out who you are and you're going to jail for a long fucking time."

The video ends and fades to black. I replay it six times, absorbing every single word he said for the world to hear. I'm unnerved that he addressed it without talking to me about it first, but also speechless that he just proclaimed his feelings to thousands of his followers. The one point that stuck out to me is the mention of the response videos that have been posted. Clicking on my "for your pleasure" page, I'm assaulted by blurred videos and stills of me and Grey. Opening the first one, I read the caption and my blood runs cold.

Beneath the pixilated images, a keyboard warrior captioned: "Curvy slob gets railed #slutsofMarymount." Scrolling through the related content, I see so many variations of the same thing; I'm an overweight slut that opened her legs for the first guy that showed interest in me. It's bullshit. Dispersed throughout the comments of my body are congratulatory messages for

Greyson, as though his part in this is commendable instead of equally mortifying.

It's amazing that in 2023, we still treat women like shit but hold men up on pillars for getting their dick wet. Knowing Grey, and the fiercely protective instinct he has, puts his response video into perspective, though I still wish he would have spoken to me about it first.

I'm still fully immersed in the reaction posts that I'm startled when a large, warm hand coasts down my calf. Looking up, I find Grey staring at me, his expression hooded and surprisingly sheepish. I've never seen Grey contrite, but based on the look on his face, he's preparing for an argument that he assumes he won't win.

I sigh, moving from the center of the bed to make room for him. "Come here," I beckon, patting the mattress. As soon as Grey sits, I climb onto his lap, straddling him. Adjusting my position, my center rubs against Grey's groin and I groan, the hardness momentarily distracting me from the words bouncing around my head. Shifting forward, I grind my pelvis against him, seeking friction. Grey's hands grip my waist, stilling my movements and holding me tight against his growing erection.

"If you don't stop grinding your pussy against me, I'm going to tear your clothes off and fuck you until you forget what you wanted to say to me when I came into this room." He thrusts up, letting me feel how hard he is.

Dammit, Ava. Focus.

I clear my throat and shake my head, getting my thoughts together. "I saw your video. It was... intense, to say the least." Grey doesn't answer, just raises an eyebrow. "I wish you would have spoken to me before posting it," I continue. He opens his mouth to speak, but I raise my hand to his lips, silencing the words that were about to pour from him. "I'm not saying that I don't understand why you posted that recording, but a heads-up would have been appreciated. I-I," I stutter. I draw in a breath, finding strength in the oxygen we share in this room. "I love you, you know? And if it were you that needed defending, I would have done the same, albeit significantly less aggressively, but I would have tried to protect you, too. That's what I'm saying.

"I get it, I do. But, for us to work—to have a real shot at succeeding as a couple—we need to be on the same page with things as monumental as this. It may seem ridiculous since we have honest-to-God porn out there, but we need to be partners in all things. Don't post another explanation video, or video in my defense, without speaking with me about it first. Okay?"

Grey stares at me for a moment and his eyes search my face. For what? I don't know, but it feels like an eternity has passed before he cups my jaw and rubs his thumb against my cheeks. "Okay, vixen." With his agreement, he flips me over, pinning me beneath his large body. "I'm going to show you how much I love you now." He makes quick work of our clothes, stripping me in record time before lowering his mouth to my chest and worshiping my body.

Ava

Whenever I have butterflies in my stomach, they're attributed to Grey's hands, Grey's dick, or just Grey in general. But when I woke up this morning, the butterflies kamikaze-diving in my stomach have nothing to do with my Viking warrior and everything to do with facing the student population of Marymount University twenty-four hours after the video leaked.

Grey sensed my anxiety this morning and paid extreme care to every dip and crevice of my body in the shower. Standing in front of his bathroom mirror, my skin heats from the memory of his touch. Images flash through my mind: Grey on his knees licking into me, feasting on me like I was the most delicious thing he's ever consumed. He peppered kisses all over my abdomen and sucked on the stretch marks that decorate my skin, giving me new marks to soothe the hurt of the old ones. I didn't tell him, but I had no doubt that he knew exactly what his ministrations did to me, how much it affected me and helped ease wounds, both new and old.

With every caress, every bite, and every grip, he showed me how much he loves me.

"Vixen, if you don't get that look off of your face, you're not making it to class, again," Grey's voice snaps me back to the present. I skipped my morning Algebra class, something I'll probably regret when it comes time for finals. I look at him in the mirror, taking in the white Henley that molds to his body like a second skin and the gray sweatpants that seem to hug his dick. His backward Rockies baseball cap propels his looks from hot to fantasy-level sexy. How is this man mine?

"What look?" I ask though I know that I look like a dumbstruck idiot.

232

His eyes narrow and he approaches me, curling his hands around my waist and dragging me until my back meets his chest. Looking at me in the mirror, he says, "Like you want to suck my cock until I'm coming down your pretty throat." He presses a kiss to my pulse at my throat and I draw in a ragged breath. Trailing his hands over my body, he gently cups my neck while his other hand lowers to my thigh. I can feel him against my ass, and I grind my hips into him, seeking his hardness.

"You look fucking delicious. After your class, you're going to ride my face while I eat my dessert." He pauses, nipping my ear before continuing, "But right now? You're going to finish getting ready and then I'm taking you to class."

"Lincoln said he'll take me. We're going to the same place anyway." After everything that happened this weekend, I decided to skip my morning algebra class.

Grey's shaking his head before I finish. "No, baby. Lincoln's not taking you because you're not his woman. Now, finish getting ready, and we'll get food before we go." He releases me and swats my ass before he turns around, heading back into his room.

"Freaking overprotective tease," I mutter under my breath.

Grey's laughter booms from his room, leaving little doubt that he heard me.

—

Despite Grey and Lincoln's insistence that I get something to eat at Beans & Things, I can't stomach the thought of anything other than a coffee.

"Aves, you got to eat something. We're going to be on our feet for three hours; you're going to pass the fuck out," Lincoln scolds me. I'm surprised by his level of care; Lincoln tends to care about one person: himself. He continues, "If you pass out, you're going to fuck my grade up, and I need Chef Adrian's praise."

Ah, there it is, the apathy toward everyone other than himself. "Don't be a dick, you fucking twat," Grey grumbles, hitting him in the chest. "He's not wrong though, vixen, you need to eat something." He pushes a chocolate croissant in front of me. As good as the buttery pastry smells, it makes my stomach sour.

Shaking my head, I grab my coffee instead. "The thought of food makes me want to projectile vomit."

Lincoln's face contorts, revulsion stamped across his features. "Do not eat anything. If you throw up in the kitchen, I will kill you." He takes my croissant and tosses it in the trash behind the table we're sitting at. "If you don't fuck this up, I'll buy you a fucking Whopper or Big Mac or some shit after."

Grey doesn't seem to be paying attention to Lincoln's antics because his eyes are focused on me, trying to decipher the emotions rolling through me. "She's going home with me, and I'm feeding her after her class. Fuck off, asshole." He leans in closer, lowering his voice so that only I can hear him. "Are you okay, vixen? Say the word and we'll go back to my house and hide from the world for a few days."

I grab his hand, squeezing hard. "No, I need to get this over with. Besides, it's probably better that it's a class with Lincoln so that people will be less inclined to say something." I look up, glancing around at all of the people that are zeroed in on us. Despite Grey's video yesterday, the antagonistic and dirty looks sent my way are plentiful and wholly unwelcome. The barista that poured my coffee looked at me like I was the devil incarnate before Grey asked if there was a problem.

Clicking on my phone, I notice that there are fifteen minutes before our class starts. "Come on, guys. We need to get over to the culinary building and get our station ready before class."

—

It took five minutes to get to our building and another five minutes to convince Grey that he could not, under any circumstances, come into the kitchen to watch over me.

"If anyone gives you shit, you'll tell me? And let Linc handle it as he sees fit?" he questions, looking at Lincoln to confirm he's down to defend my honor.

"Yes, Daddy," I reply, rolling my eyes at his display of protectiveness.

"Dammit, Ava. Don't say shit like that when I can't do something about it." He grabs my hip and draws me near.

"Woah, calm the fuck down," Lincoln interrupts, grabbing me by the shoulders and pulling me away from Grey. "We've got a fucking practical to do, and no one wants to watch you two fuck. We've all seen the video and my eyes are scarred." He turns to me. "Sorry, Aves, but you're like a sister now, and I don't need to see that shit again."

I sputter out a laugh. "Dick," I yell, punching him in the bicep. Looking at Grey, I see that he looks pleased, and if I had to guess, it's because one of his best friends sees me as a sister. Shaking my head at him, I push him away. "Go, I need to get inside." I lean up and give him a quick kiss on the cheek before turning away to walk into the classroom.

I feel a hand grab my wrist and pull me. Crashing into his chest, Grey grabs my chin and tilts it upward, positioning me until I'm at the perfect angle for him. "We can do better than that, vixen," Grey whispers before his lips crash into mine. There's nothing soft or gentle about this kiss, it's a show of ownership, both his and mine. I pull away first and see that Grey's eyes are dark storm clouds. Glancing down, the outline of his dick is on full display in his sweatpants.

A wave of possession goes through me, and I have to swallow down my need to continue staking my claim. Rising to my toes, I mumble, "Put that thing away before anyone thinks they can get a free show."

Grey laughs, touching his forehead down to mine. "It's yours. If they don't know that, they're fucking stupid." I roll my eyes and pull away.

"Okay, I really need to go now. Lincoln is going to murder me."

"Fine but I'll be here when you get out. Don't fucking leave without me if you get done early."

"Yes, Daddy."

Grey growls. "Goddammit, vixen, I'm going to turn your ass red tonight."

Turning toward the room, I laugh, "Promises, promises."

—

As soon as I walk through the threshold, the happy little bubble Grey surrounded me in bursts. Making my way toward my station in the front of the room, the eyelash twins bombard me with dirty looks and faux-whispered insults.

"Did you see how desperate she looked in that video?" the one on the right says. To be frank, I distinguish them by their position at the table because they look so similar and they're insignificant to my life. "I heard that she made him post that response video. Can you say 'desperate?'"

"I would die if anyone saw me naked and I looked like that." This comes from the one on the left. "She should wear something to hold that jiggling stomach in. Gross." She punctuates her asshole comment with a shudder, as though she finds me repulsive.

What I want to say is that I'm not the one with eyelashes that look like brooms on my eyes, but I hold back. Ignoring them, and their spider-like eyes, I slide onto the stool next to Lincoln. He's staring at the baking sheets and utensils lined on our counter, seemingly lost in thought. Elbowing his side, I whisper, "So, are you going to tell me what the fuck happened with my sister last weekend?"

Lincoln freezes and his hand flexes; to someone who doesn't know him well, his reaction could be interpreted as a reflex, but after spending weeks working alongside him, I know he's panicking. Interesting.

Still looking down at our prep station, he mutters, "Nothing is going on, Ava."

"Bullshit, Lincoln. She was in the kitchen, wearing not only your sweat-shirt but also a hickey on her neck." Do they think I'm so tunnel-visioned with my drama that I wouldn't pick up on what's going on around me?

"Can you just drop it?"

"Absolutely not, now tell me what the hell was going on."

"Dammit, Ava," Lincoln huffs, sounding more like a petulant little boy than a twenty-one-year-old man. "Nothing happened. I kissed her and she freaked out, okay? We spent the night talking and then she fell asleep in the bed, and I took the floor." He lets out a long breath, visibly deflating before continuing, "That hickey? It was a burn from her iron or whatever shit you women use to do your hair. She spent most of the night talking about that bag of crusty dicks, Mitchell." Lincoln shakes his head and slams his fist down on the countertop. "Fuck that guy, Ava. The shit he put her through?

If I ever see him, I'll cut his dick off and feed it to his asshole."

I cringe at the thought of Mitchell being impaled with his own dick. "That is extremely gross and extremely graphic."

"He's a fucking asshole." The emotion behind Lincoln's words is unmistakable; he has feelings for my sister. I'm formulating my response in my head when high-pitched voices assault our ears.

"Is she trying to fuck him now? I guess she wants to be passed around like a dirty hooker," one of the eyelash twins says in a mock whisper. "Slut," she says around a cough.

Laughter erupts in the room, followed by poorly concealed whispers, and my heart sinks. Closing my eyes, I lean forward, gripping the edge of the counter and willing the taunts and jeers to bounce off me without sinking in. I know that I should say something, go back at them and shut them up just like Grey or CeCe would in this situation. But I stand frozen, shrinking, and making myself as small as possible in the front of the room.

"Oh, fuck no," Lincoln booms out, silencing the chatter. "Are you fucking slut-shaming right now? You can barely boil fucking water and have begged to suck my cock every time I see you, and you have the balls to start shit you can't finish? Cut your fucking eyelashes, you spidey fucks."

"Lincoln," I say under my breath, grabbing his arm to hold back the rest of the tirade. "It's okay."

He turns his glare on me. "Fuck no, it's not okay. They're shit-talking out of their asses because they're jealous you landed one of us." I raise an eyebrow at him, internally laughing that he somehow managed to bring up his desirability while defending me. "And the rest of you." He whips around, holding out a finger to point to the rest of the room. "If I so much as hear a single fucking word about Ava, we'll destroy you, your family, and your fucking grandchildren. Now shut the fuck up and get baking, you sorry fucks."

"Wow," I mutter. Next to me, he's shaking, a result of the adrenaline rush and anger that poured through his system.

He answers in a voice much lower than the one he just used in the class. "It's obvious that you and Grey didn't put that video out there, and his video was pretty fucking clear that you're his girl." Shaking his head, he reaches for the container of flour before continuing, "Shit pisses me off, even if you weren't part of our crew now. No one should be humiliated like that, especially not by girls that look like extras in *American Horror Story*."

"Lincoln, that's not nice," I admonish him, though he's not wrong about the comparison.

"Suck it, Aves. They're not nice, and if Grey were here, he would have ripped them a new asshole worse than I did." Lincoln grabs the scale and places a metal bowl on top, pouring the flour until the scale reads the correct grams. "Now, get your shit together. I'm not letting these lazy assholes do better than us."

As quickly as protective Lincoln came, he's gone. If he is interested in my sister, she's both lucky at his alpha tendencies and screwed by them.

—

After hours spent elbow-deep in flour and sugar in our kitchen practical, Lincoln and I finish with thirty minutes to spare. Though Chef Adrian is notoriously tight-lipped when it comes to praise, she didn't offer any criticism on the Mille Feuille pastries, or Napoleon pastries, as they're commonly referred to. Lincoln is a pain in the ass when it comes to most things, but there is no denying his skill in the kitchen and how fortunate I am to have him as a partner in the labs.

We leave the kitchen while all the other pairs are still working; our classmates don't bother looking up at our departure, probably too scared of Lincoln's threat to call attention to themselves. I don't expect Grey to be waiting for us outside of the classroom, so seeing his broad form leaning against the wall is a surprise.

Walking into his body, I ask, "How'd you know we were ending early?" I tilt my head up and purse my lips for a kiss. Grey smirks at my expression before leaning down and brushing his lips against mine.

"Linc texted me that you were almost done fifteen minutes ago." Grey reaches out and grabs the strap of my shoulder bag, pulling the weight off and slinging it over his shoulder. I look to Lincoln and raise my eyebrow; I was so absorbed in executing our final touches that I didn't even notice he had his phone out. Lincoln just shrugs, not providing any further explanation. Fingers grab mine and my attention refocuses on Grey. "Come on, vixen. I'll drive you back to your dorm." Offering a head nod to Lincoln, Grey leads me to the commuter parking lot closest to the culinary building. I open the passenger door silently, accepting Grey's help in throwing my short frame into his lifted Jeep.

He rounds the hood and slides in, starting the Jeep and pulling out of the lot carefully.

"Are you coming up?" I ask, not bothering to conceal the desire in my voice. It took a lot of willpower to not concentrate on Grey's promise from this morning. Every time I felt myself slipping into the memory of his hands on my hips and the dirty words that fell from his mouth, I would glance at the leering looks of one of the eyelash twins and be jerked right back to the present.

Grey scoffs, "Of fucking course I am, vixen." His arm stretches across the center console and grips me, wedging his hand high between my thighs. "Don't think I forgot my promise from earlier, Ava. This pussy is going to ride my face today." With deliberate slowness, he rubs his thumb over the seam of my pants, giving me just enough friction to taunt me, but not enough to get me off. I squirm in his grasp.

"Tell me, vixen, is your cunt already wet for me?" He increases the pressure of his thumb, rubbing deeper and somehow finding my clit through the fabric of my jeans and panties. "I feel the heat from you already, you're probably fucking drenched. Isn't that right, vixen?" Grey moves his hand until he's cupping my entire sex through my jeans. Squeezing, he orders, "Answer me, baby."

I slam my eyes shut and tilt my pelvis forward, pressing myself as hard as I can against his hand. "Yes, Grey," I rasp.

"That's fucking right, you are." Grey contracts his hand, gripping my center hard before letting go and retreating until both hands clutch the steering wheel. Opening my eyes, I look at him in surprise. "Get that look off your face, vixen. I'm not going to finger-fuck you while I'm driving. I need to get you home in one piece before I worship your cunt."

Biting down on my lip, I don't say anything to that, because, really, what can I say?

We're silent for the remainder of the ten-minute drive; the sexual tension has built and I'm worried that if I say something, I'm going to combust. Grey pulls into the first spot he sees and makes quick work of parking and hopping out of the car. I barely have my seat belt unbuckled before he's yanking my door open and hauling me into him.

Grey's lips find mine, firm and demanding as they work my lips apart and make room for his tongue. He leads the kiss, one of ownership and possession, and there's nothing I can do but follow him. Gripping my face, Grey tilts my head back, giving him access to my jaw and neck. Raining kisses down the column of my throat, he bites down before soothing the sting with his tongue.

I'm a panting, writhing mess before reality crashes into me. Even though we're parked in a spot away from the entrance and close to the woods, we're still close enough that anyone walking by will get a free show... again. Pulling back, I grip Grey's hair and tug him away from my neck. "Grey, not here. We need to go inside."

"Fuck," he moans, dropping his head into my chest. "You make me lose my damn mind." Leaning away, he drags me out of the car, shutting the door and locking it behind me. "We need to get to your room. Now." He lifts me over his shoulder and starts running to the entrance, eating up the distance between the parking lot and the building in record time.

"Greyson, put me down, you ogre. I can walk."

"You walk too slow," he mutters. I roll my eyes and bring my hands down to his ass. Squeezing it, I lift one hand before smacking his ass. Grey's steps falter as he walks us up the front steps of my dorm. Running his hands up my thighs, he growls before turning his head and biting me, nipping me through the fabric of my jeans.

I laugh and swat him again. Jogging up the remainder of the stairs, we pass a group of girls who stand frozen at our appearance. "Take a fucking picture," Grey mutters under his breath. His legs carry us past them and lead us up the side stairwell, through the common areas, and straight to my door.

Not setting me down, he fishes the lanyard with my keys out and opens the door.

One minute, I'm thrown over his shoulder, and the next I'm tossed like a sack of potatoes onto the bed. "Oof," I grunt as I bounce on the mattress. Leaning up on my elbows, I'm struck silent by the sight of Grey taking off his shirt and throwing it over my desk chair. I'm not sure I'll ever get over a shirtless Greyson Jansen; the contours of his muscles look photoshopped while the tattoos make him even more unreal.

Drooling over his upper body, I'm caught off-guard when he tugs off his pants and briefs. His inked legs come into view, and despite all the male perfection in front of me, I have one question slamming around my brain: when did he take off his sneakers and socks?

"Your turn," Grey growls and pounces on me, diving straight for my jeans. Reaching for my buttons, he rips them apart, tearing seams in his wake. "Hope you didn't like these, vixen," he says as he peels the ripped jeans from my skin. Throwing them over his shoulder, he stares down at me and licks his lips. Left in a pair of black panties that leave little to the imagination, I feel wet and needy and so freaking turned on by his displays of possession this weekend. What feels like hours pass as he stares down at me, not moving.

"Are you planning on touching me or are you just going to look?" I challenge, desperate to feel him against me, on me, *in* me.

He stares at me for a few more seconds before smirking and reaching out to grab the sides of my panties. "I hope you didn't like these either," he utters before ripping the black lace from my body.

Holy. Shit.

Before I can fully comprehend what he just did, Grey's laying on the bed and lifting my body until I'm straddling his chest. Still clothed on top, my naked legs and pussy are on display for him, and based on the darkening of his eyes and the tense set of his jaw, I can tell he likes the view.

"I told you I was going to eat this pussy. Now, give Daddy what he wants and get that cunt up here." He furthers his want by dragging my bare hips up until my sex is positioned just above his mouth. "Ride my tongue, vixen. Show Daddy how much you fucking want my cock." He slams me down and feasts.

There's nothing gentle or soft about how Grey is eating me—and honestly, there rarely is—and he works me over his mouth until I'm thrusting into it. Flattening his tongue, he gives me long, hard licks before circling my clit and drawing it into his mouth. Biting down, he draws my clit further into his mouth before releasing it. Pulling my hips further against him, Grey buries his face between my thighs, soaking up my wetness. I roll my hips back and forward, relishing the friction his tongue creates against me.

"That's right, fuck Daddy's face, vixen. Give me that juicy fucking pussy." He dives back in eating at me like a man starved.

I feel the telltale signs of an orgasm traveling up my spine. Rocking harder against him, I cry out, "Fuck, Grey. I'm coming." Not letting up his pressure, Grey fucks me with his tongue until I'm exploding against his mouth, coating his face.

My body twitches but Grey only stops when I collapse against him, catching myself on the headboard before I fall face-first into the mattress and suffocate him with my stomach.

"Jesus Christ," I murmur against the fabric. Pulling out from under me, Grey gets off the bed and positions himself behind me, pulling me until my back is flush against his chest.

"I'm going to need for you to hold on, vixen, because I need this cunt, and I'm not going to be gentle," he says into my neck. "You good with that?"

I nod but Grey clucks against my ear. "I need the words, vixen. Tell me that you're good with Daddy taking this pussy fast and hard."

Before Grey, the idea of a man referring to himself as "Daddy" would make me want to vomit. With Grey? I want to beg that he use my body any way he sees fit.

"Yes, I'm good with that," I reply.

"Good girl," he says before pitching me forward and burying himself inside without warning. "Fuck, look at you, taking my cock like Daddy's good little slut. That tight pussy milking my cock." He thrusts deeper, hitting a spot that causes my eyes to roll into the back of my head. "You like Daddy's cock? This is the only cock you'll ever have, vixen. No one takes what's mine." He accentuates his declaration with hard, quick thrusts, fucking me as if he'd die without my body surrounding him.

"Oh my God," I cry, leaning further into him and wrapping a hand around his neck. Grey changes his pace from quick and chaotic to slow and purposeful. Grinding against me, he circles his hips and grabs my thigh, pulling me tighter against him.

"Fuck, baby. I'm going to come in this pussy. I need you to come on my cock before that happens, vixen," he growls, increasing his pace once again. Gliding his fingers around my hip, he strums my clit, rubbing it expertly. "Fucking come for me, vixen."

All it takes is his filthy words and nimble fingers for me to detonate. Coming against him, I feel the warmth inside me signaling his release. Grey holds me against him, making sure that every drop of cum makes its way into me.

"Fuck," he groans against my neck, biting down as he spasms inside me. Gently pushing me forward, Grey doesn't pull out of me until I'm laying down on my bed. Slowly withdrawing, I feel the cum drip out of me, coating my upper thighs with our mixed pleasure. Just like the first time we came together, his fingers run over my thighs, capturing the cum that leaked out of me. Pushing it back inside my pussy, Grey growls, "Your pussy looks fucking gorgeous with my cum inside."

He pulls away and grabs a throw blanket from the foot of my bed. Dropping down next to me, Grey moves me until I'm draped over his chest and covers our naked bodies with my blanket. Running his hands over my hair, he whispers, "Relax now, vixen. I got you."

Between the stress of the weekend, the taunts of my classmates, and the hours-long bake, my body is heavy with exhaustion. I drift off quickly, blanketed by the warmth of Grey's body.

Greyson

It's been almost two weeks since the video leaked, and other than a few fucking twats that have made comments about Ava's body, there hasn't been much response since I posted my video. I'm not an idiot; I know there's something else coming, I just don't know what. Ava's handled the situation in stride, not letting the assholes affect her or her mental well-being.

I know it's been harder on her than on me; my body wasn't the one plastered all over the goddamn internet. I've checked in daily with my dad, and Ava's done the same with her parents, but so far there's been no development with the police or their investigation. It's fucking bullshit, but the asshole took precautions to conceal their identity. If I didn't know that Felicity was behind this based on her displays of jealousy, I'd think she was too fucking stupid to pull something like this off.

I'm getting my shit together for my class with Rawlins when my phone vibrates with an incoming text message. Thinking it's Ava, I grab my phone out of my back pocket and unlock the screen. My blood runs cold when I see a blocked number. Clicking on the message, I'm ready to kill this fucker, even before I read the text.

Unknown: You fucked up going to the cops, Grey Grey. I'm going to destroy your fat whore if you don't drop this investigation. You'll have no one to blame but yourself if she gets hurt.

I'm pissed about the words on the screen, but I smile to myself because the fucking idiot just revealed exactly who she is.

Grey: Nice hearing from you, Felicity. You're fucking over. Stay away from Ava, stay away from me.

Unknown: Hope you like how your whore looks dead because you'll never see that fat bitch again.

Grey: I will fucking kill you before you touch her. You fucking coward, hiding behind a phone. Grow some balls and meet me in person.

Unknown: It's her funeral. Bye-bye, Grey Grey.

"Fuck," I shout and slam my phone down on my desk. There's no doubt that the person behind the threats, the pictures, and the video is Felicity, and she all but confirmed her identity. I know the texts aren't enough for the cops to solidify a case against her, but it's a fucking start.

I grab my wallet, phone, and keys and haul ass out of my house. Ripping my Jeep's door open, I throw myself into the seat and start it up. Throwing it in reverse, I peel out of my driveway and race to Felicity's sorority house. Does she think she's going to threaten me and my girl and get away with it? Absolutely fucking not.

I make it to the Alpha Nu house in three minutes and storm up the stairs. Flinging the door open—fuck knocking—I hear the screams of women.

"Where the fuck is Felicity?" I shout, not giving a fuck if I'm scaring the shit out of these girls. For all I know, they're innocent and have jack shit to do with Felicity's crimes, but I could give a fuck.

"Greyson," a voice behind me whispers. I whip around and see Jordan standing there. While the rest of the house probably doesn't know what's going on, Jordan sure as shit does.

"Don't 'Greyson' me. Where the fuck is she?" I demand.

"Follow me, you need to see this." Jordan turns and walks toward the stairs leading to the second floor, expecting me to follow her. That's not the way this fucking works.

"Jordan, I'll call Linc and have him call your fucking parents and tell them

245

about this shit if you don't explain right fucking now. Did you fucking know what she was doing?"

She pauses on the step and shakes her head before facing me. "I swear, I had no idea. I would never do that, you need to believe me. Lincoln knows me, he knows I wouldn't do that."

"Bull-fucking-shit. You followed his ass to Paris, he knows shit about you." She grimaces and looks down, refusing to meet my eyes.

"That was a mistake," she says in a low voice. "I let Felicity talk me into that and I knew I shouldn't have. I don't even like Lincoln like that, but Felicity wouldn't listen."

"And why the fuck should I believe that."

"I get it, okay? You lump us together—everyone does. It's my fault because I followed her for the last two years and let her turn me into something I'm not. But, Greyson." She looks up at me with pleading eyes. "You need to see this. She's not here and she's supposed to be. I don't know what she's going to do next, but whatever it is, it's not good."

"Fuck," I growl and stride toward her, following her up the stairs and into a narrow hallway leading to the bedrooms. She stops in front of the first door on the right.

"This is Felicity's. We've been hanging out in the common areas or my room lately, so I haven't seen it in a while." She pauses and reaches for the doorknob. "While Felicity was in class, I came into her room to see if she took my sociology textbook. I swear, I texted Lincoln as soon as I saw it, but it read that it was undelivered. I didn't know what to do or who to call." She pushes open the door and flicks on the light.

My eyes bug the fuck out as soon as I see what's plastered all over Felicity's room.

"What the fuck?"

"I know. I had no idea she could be capable of something like this," Jordan responds. Pinned, framed, and taped throughout the room are pictures of me throughout the years—some I've seen, paparazzi photos from press events, social media posts, and other easily-found pictures. Others are candid pictures taken in secret and creepy as fuck. Printed on computer paper, my image is like a wallpaper collage. Turning around, I look behind her bed and see pictures of Ava with lines and marks over her face. Some of these pictures have fucking holes and burns over them.

On her nightstand, there's a selfie-style picture of me and Felicity from last year. In the picture, I'm looking over my shoulder, but Felicity is staring at me with a crazed look in her eyes. Her entire room is a shrine to me and a rage room toward Ava.

"Where the fuck would she go?" I ask Jordan, looking at the wall with Ava's pictures.

"I don't know. She should have been home an hour ago. We had plans to get dinner after her last class, but she never showed up. I've been calling and texting her, but there's no answer."

"Fuck," I grind out and pull out my phone, about to dial a number when I notice that Felicity left her laptop on her desk. Opening it, I see that Felicity has it password protected. "Do you know the password?" I ask Jordan.

"It used to be her birthday. I'm not sure if she's changed it, six twenty-five zero two." I type in the numbers, but it comes up as incorrect. Acting on gut instinct, I key in my birthday, seven nine zero two, and the fucker unlocks.

"Fucking stalker," I mutter under my breath. On her desktop is a folder labeled, "Greyson <3." I open it and hold my breath. Inside are hundreds of photos and videos, along with a link to an app. I click on it, and I'm brought to an app that allows users to send text messages through an unknown number. This shit was probably created for kids to prank text their friends, but Felicity fucking Dawes used it to try to destroy Ava.

With the hundreds of files in this folder, along with the creepy as fuck room, there's no doubt that she fucked up.

Pulling my phone back out, I dial a number I've grown familiar with in the last two weeks and wait for Ava's dad to pick up.

"Greyson," he greets on the second ring.

Bypassing formalities, I tell him, "I know who's behind the video, texts, and picture. I'm staring at a shitload of evidence right now."

"Goddammit. Where are you? What the hell is going on, and where is Ava?" I tell him about the text messages I received earlier, followed by the nightmare that I walked into in Felicity's room. "Ava's in class for the next twenty minutes, but I'm meeting her outside of the lecture hall to bring her back to my place tonight," I tell her dad. I don't give a fuck if he's uncomfortable with his daughter sleeping at my house, there's no way in hell that I'm going to let her out of my sight now.

"Good, she needs to be watched at all times before this girl is brought in for questioning. Once I hang up, I'll call the police and tell them about Felicity. They're going to need a search warrant to keep everything airtight. Send me a message with your exact location, and for the love of God, do not touch or tamper with anything else. As far as I'm concerned, this is an active crime scene and needs to be preserved."

"Got it."

"Call your father and let him know what's going on. I'm calling the police now, son." I hang up with Ava's dad and shoot my dad a quick text letting him know shit went down and that Mr. Gregori is handling the call with the police. Knowing my dad's schedule, I know he's filming his segment right now and won't be checking his phone for hours.

This shit is finally over, and my girl can fucking move on from this.

Ava

Thirty minutes before class was set to end, my biology professor let us out. Normally, I'd say that biology was my least favorite class this semester, but with today's early release, I feel significantly more hospitable toward the subject.

I'm already outside of the building and halfway across the quad when I realize that I didn't tell Grey that my class was let out early. When I left Grey's house before my class, he told me that he'd pick me up and we'd go for dinner afterward. Fishing my phone out of my bag, I unlock my phone and click on Grey's contact information to text him.

Ava: Hey, I just got out of class and I'm walking across campus. I'll meet you at my dorm instead so that I can freshen up before we leave. Where did you say we were going again?

Not even a minute goes by before Grey is calling me.

"Hello? Shouldn't you be in class right now?"

"Ava, get back into a building right now," Grey says with panic in his voice.

"What?" I question. "Why? What's wrong?"

"Ava, baby, listen to me. Go to the nearest populated building and wait for me. You cannot walk around by yourself right now."

"Grey, you're scaring me. What the hell is going on?"

"Vixen, I love you, and I'll answer everything when I see you, but right now, I need you to listen to me and stay calm. I'm coming to you. What building is closest to you?"

"Uhm…" I pause, glancing around the quad. "Howard Hall is closest, but I don't see any lights on inside."

"Fuck," he grinds out. "Okay, stay on the phone with me. Walk to Vernon, Dante has a class there in the lecture hall. When you get inside, slide into a row in the back."

"O-Okay," I stutter, my instincts telling me that something is very, very wrong.

"You're doing good, vixen. Is anyone around?"

I look around and notice that other than a woman sitting with her head buried in a book at one of the nearby picnic tables, there's no one around. "I see one person at one of the picnic tables outside Howard, but other than that, there's no one close by." I hear the start of Grey's engine, followed by the crunch of his tires on gravel. Grey's driveway and road are smooth, as is the parking lot by his ethics class. "Where are you?"

"I was at the Alpha Nu house." His voice is tight like he's trying to rein in his anger.

"Alpha Nu? Why would you go there? Did something else happen?" My anger starts to rise. The only reason Grey would step foot in that house is if he felt it would help me or our situation. Whatever reason he has for going there is, undoubtedly, a good one.

"Vixen, let's wait until I get there to talk about it. I'm a few minutes away from lot sixteen. How close are you to Vernon?" Lot sixteen is at least a ten-minute walk from Vernon Hall, but it's the closest parking lot to my destination.

"I'm just passing Howard, so maybe five minutes away." I pause, looking back toward the picnic tables where the woman was sitting. I don't see her anywhere. "So weird, there was just someone sitting at the picnic tables, but it looks like she left."

"Baby, I need you to start running," he pleads.

"Greyson, I doubt I need to—" I'm cut off by pain searing into the back of my head. "Fuck!" I yell, dropping down on all fours and dropping my phone on the ground.

"Ava! What the fuck just happened?" I hear Grey yelling through my phone.

Before I can pick it up, a pair of white tennis shoes step into my line of sight. Looking up, I see Felicity standing above me with a malicious grin and crazed eyes.

"Tsk, tsk. So clumsy, Ava," she taunts, shaking her head in mock concern. "Here, let me help you." Felicity lifts an object in her hands—is that a freaking bat?—and poses like a psychotic Playboy bunny. "Say, 'Bye-bye, Grey Grey.'"

"No—" I feel the smack of the bat against my head and hear the screams of Greyson coming through the phone at my side. But it's too late; the pain consumes me, pulling me under until all I see is black.

—

Grey:

"Ava! What the fuck just happened?" I yell, pressing down harder on the gas. The moment Ava mentioned a lone person sitting outside Howard, I knew, I fucking knew, she was in danger. The thud that was captured by the phone's receiver, followed by Ava's screams, will haunt me for the rest of my fucking life. I press down harder on the peddle, breaking every speed limit in this goddamn town. My blood is pumping, and I'm eating up the distance between the road and campus, fully intending to drive on the fucking sidewalk to get to her. My jaw clenches as I hear the saccharine voice of the only person stupid enough to hurt what's mine.

"...so clumsy, Ava," Felicity's disgustingly high-pitched voice assaults my ears.

"If you fucking hurt her, I'll kill you. I swear to fucking God, I will fucking kill you for this!" I yell into the car's speaker. "Leave her the fuck alone, you fucking cunt."

Her voice takes on an eerie quality, "Say, 'Bye-bye, Grey Grey.'" The call cuts out; I dial back her number but get forwarded to voicemail after one ring, letting me know that that bitch has the phone in her hand and that it's still on. Not wasting time pulling over, I tell Siri to dial Dante and blow through every fucking traffic light before I pull into campus.

"Yo, Gre—"

"Call the fucking cops and tell them to meet me at Howard Hall. That fucking bitch has Ava."

"Grey, what the fuck—"

I cut him off again. "Fucking Felicity. Call them now. My location is on, fucking track me." Two years ago, Lincoln, Dante, and I shared our locations as a damn joke and just never turned them off. Our drunken decision just saved me a shit load of time. I hang up on him and pull into lot sixteen. It's a five-minute walk from the lot but it will be a thirty-second drive if I floor it through the sidewalk.

I drive through the parking lot and aim my Jeep between two large oak trees that will give me the most direct path to Howard. I'm not a religious man, but I'm thanking God that there seems to be no one on campus right now. I shoot between the oaks and drive through the quad, not giving a shit that I'm probably ripping up the landscaping that my tuition pays for.

Fucking bill me, cocksuckers.

I stop my car in front of the picnic tables outside Howard and throw my door open. Pulling out my phone, I check my location app and click on Ava's name. As soon as we made our relationship official, we shared our locations with each other. I didn't think this shit would happen, but I'm thankful as fuck for this app.

Looking at Ava's pin, it shows that she's inside the building, less than two hundred feet from me. It doesn't take a fucking genius to realize that Felicity took her to the room where this shit first went down.

I race inside, not giving a shit about anything other than Ava.

Ava

I wake up to a sharp sting against my cheek and realize that I've just been slapped, hard. My skin burns, and the shock of the blow makes me groan and recall Felicity's attack outside Howard Hall. My stomach tenses and my head throbs; she is completely unhinged.

Batshit crazy, to put it mildly. I was on the phone with Grey when she came out of nowhere, appearing like a specter behind me before clubbing me until I lost consciousness. I have no idea how long I've been here; it could be minutes or hours. I'm fucking terrified right now. If she's crazy enough to attack me in a public place with no regard for her surroundings, there is no telling what she is willing to do to me.

I've watched enough *Law & Order* and have listened to my parents' podcast enough to know that my escape—fuck, my *survival*—depends on calming this girl down and getting her to talk.

"Wake up, you fat bitch," Felicity hisses, kicking me in the stomach. So much for keeping her calm.

I sputter a cough, trying to dispel the pain radiating throughout my body. "I'm up. Jesus, you don't need to hit me. Haven't you done enough?" I question.

"Enough? You think I've done enough, you fucking cow," Felicity says in a high-pitched squeal. "Haven't *you* done enough? It wasn't enough that you were a whore and opened your legs for *my* man, no. You had to fucking brainwash him, and he gave you lilies. That's *my* flower. I fucking told him that; he knows I love them." She sniffs, as though she's feeling something other than psychopathy. "He did it to get back at me, I know it. He's mad

I hooked up with Dylan last year, and this is him trying to get back at me. But don't worry, you'll be out of the picture soon and then he and I can be together."

I'm relatively positive that I have a concussion right now—the main cause of the pounding headache I have emanating from the back of my skull. The soliloquy that Felicity just gave me is adding to the throbbing of my head.

I have one chance at appealing to her sensibilities, if any even exist. Gritting my teeth through the pain, I try reasoning. "Felicity, you're a beautiful, smart girl." I cringe, nearly gagging on the fallacy. "Do you really want to be with a man that doesn't want you, or wants to get back at you for being with another man?" Grey would never, ever want her. When I get out of here, I'm going to kill him for hooking up with her in the first place.

She studies me, a look of distrust painting her face. I continue, "You can just let me go and I can help you. There are so many guys that would love to be with you. Don't you want to be with someone like that?" If she lets me go, I am running straight to the fucking police.

She lets out a maniacal laugh, chilling my blood. I never had a fucking chance.

"You are a fucking loser, nothing more than a warm hole to stick his dick in." She moves forward, bending down in front of me and gripping my face. Felicity's face breaks out in a serene grin before she spits in my face and slams my head into the ground.

I scream, and that just pisses her off even more. "Scream all you fucking want. There's no one here to hear you." She stands back up and walks to the desk set against a broken smart board. Working through the pain radiating throughout my body, I take stock of my surroundings: broken smart board, commercial door with no window hole or side panel, and student desks pushed to the side. Immediately, I know where we are: the classroom in Howard Hall where Grey and I were unknowingly filmed. Felicity must realize that I figured out where we are because she snorts. "Isn't it fucking poetic? You'll die in the same place you first sealed your fucking fate. I fucking warned you that he was mine and to stay away, but you didn't listen. Actions have consequences, and it's fucking time you learned what they are."

She turns to the desk and picks something up, turning around with another saccharine smile plastered on her face. "I have to say, I've been dreaming about this moment for a long time. Dragging you here cost me a nail, and you'll pay for that. If I gave a shit, I'd tell you that you need to lose weight. But do you know the quickest way to lose twenty pounds? You cut off a leg," Felicity laughs, holding up the object in her hand.

My eyes widen at the fucking machete she clutches. Where the fuck did this girl get a machete? Is she related to Indiana Jones?

Of all the ways I thought I'd die, death by a machete-wielding sorority girl was not a consideration.

"Now, which leg should I cut off first?" Her eyes glitter like she's enjoying this. Felicity advances across the room, cutting the distance between us with every step. I brace myself, knowing that unless I fight her off, I will die in this dusty room. Tears pool in my eyes, and I try to blink them away before she notices. It's no use because her gaze has been trained on me from the minute I woke up on the carpeted floor.

In a baby voice, she questions, "Oh no, is the little whore crying?" She lets out another laugh. "You should be scared, you fucking slut. I'm going to make you fucking bleed." She pounces at me, rearing her hand back, ready to strike. Before she can make contact, I roll away and scramble toward the door. Firm hands grip my ankles and drag me back, pulling me close to her.

Kicking out, I manage to dislodge one of her hands and feel my foot connect with something solid. "You fucking bitch," she screams. Not bothering to turn over to look at the damage I inflicted, I get up on shaky legs and hobble as fast as I can toward the door. Between the hits to my head, face, and stomach, I'm disoriented and unsteady on my legs. I nearly make it to the door when I feel hands tear at my head, pulling me back until I'm forced down on my knees. I claw at her, but her hold is too strong, and I can't loosen it in my weakened state.

Keeping a firm grip on my head, Felicity rounds my body and stands before me, face filled with blood and rage. Her nose is crooked and bleeding on her face, and I give myself an internal high five that I seem to have broken her perfect little nose. The crazed look in her eyes combined with the death grip she has on the machete tells me that she's about to strike. Twisting my head, I hit at her knees, attempting to make her collapse and give me the upper hand.

Anticipating my move, she kicks out and hits me in the chest, forcing me to fall back until I am lying on the ground once again. Felicity straddles me, locking her legs around my legs with surprising strength. With her body pinning me down and the pain rapidly taking over, taking me under, I breathe in a deep breath, a breath that could very well be my last.

It's a weird sensation, being aware of your impending death. There's no "if," it's a "when" and how difficult I can make it for her. Thrashing my body, I try to knock her off, or at least delay her next attack. If I can last a few more minutes, I know that Grey will find me.

We were on the phone when Felicity attacked me, and I can bet that he heard the impact of the bat and her words before she knocked me out cold. "Get off me, you fucking bitch," I yell at her, making as much movement as I can.

She laughs, the smile on her face widening at my struggle. With a speed that I don't anticipate, she slashes my abdomen and I howl in pain. She didn't cut deep, but the fabric of my shirt is cut in half, and my skin is on fire from the slash. "Oh, fuck," I cry out, stomach muscles contracting in agony.

"I didn't think I'd have this much fun slicing you open," she says, almost joyfully. "Let's see what else this little knife can do."

Before I can react, burning pain sears my pelvis as Felicity stabs me with the machete. She pulls out quickly, tearing flesh and bone. The pain is blinding, and the fight leaves my body, along with my blood. I feel myself start to go under when a roar echoes through the room, and Felicity's weight is abruptly thrown off of me.

I smile to myself, losing consciousness with the knowledge that Grey found me.

Greyson

Ava's screams detonate like bombs, bouncing and imploding throughout the deserted building. I'm racing down the hall, sprinting until I get to the last door. Instinctually, I know that's the room Felicity led her to; she's too manipulative and calculating to resist taunting Ava with this location.

I force myself to pause before throwing the door open; the last thing I want to do is give Felicity the upper hand by knowing that I'm here and that the police are, fucking hopefully, on the way. I have my hand on the door, ready to pry the shit open when the door to the building is wrenched open. I look over to see police pour into the building.

Thank fuck.

The apparent leader of the team is motioning me to get out of the way but fuck that. It's my girl in there. Turning from him, I slowly open the door and bite back a curse at the scene in front of me.

Straddling Ava, Felicity's arm pulls back before lifting, holding a fucking knife coated in blood. My vision turns red, and I rush into the room, releasing a feral growl before tackling the bitch and ripping her away from Ava.

"Ava! Baby, are you okay?" I yell to Ava while holding Felicity down. "Ava, can you hear me, vixen? Baby, answer me!" Soft groans release from Ava's mouth, but she doesn't respond. Turning to Felicity, I fucking rage.

"You fucking bitch, what did you do to her?" I slam her hands down and pry her grip open. She drops the knife—a fucking machete—and starts sobbing. I kick the knife across the room and crawl to Ava's blood-soaked body.

She's bruised and bloody and battered. "Ava, baby, answer me," I cry out. Quickly assessing her condition, I apply pressure to the wound at her pelvic bone. "Baby, just hang on. Fuck," I call out as the police rush in, guns pointed, and charge at Felicity. "Where the fuck are the paramedics?" I yell out.

Turning back to Ava's face, I lean down, whispering in her ear and praying to every religious entity that exists that she makes it through this. "Baby, I need you to hang on for me. Fucking please, vixen. Don't fucking leave me." I keep pressure on the largest open wound, but it's by no means the only lesion.

"Greyson! Grey, I did this for us! We can be together now. Please, Grey Grey!" Felicity pleas as the police cuff her and lead her, kicking and shrieking like a goddamn banshee, from the room. "Greyson, Greyson!" She chants my name.

Still bent over Ava, I vow, "I will fucking kill her. I swear to God, I will kill her for this."

A hand clamps down on my shoulder, startling me. "Son, I need to stop the bleeding," the calm voice of a man says from behind me.

"She's been stabbed, multiple times. I'm not fucking leaving her," I growl, refusing to take my eyes and hands off of her.

"I know that, but we need to stop the loss of blood. Let us do our job; it's the only way she'll have a chance of making it," the paramedic says, and fuck, he's right. I know he's fucking right. I nod my head, letting him know I heard him.

"Vixen, he's going to fix you up. I'm right here," I whisper into Ava's ear before releasing my hands, now painted with her blood. As soon as my hands lift from her wound, the blood starts seeping out of her. "Fucking do something," I yell at the paramedic.

Covering the wound with gauze, the paramedic places a gloved hand over her pelvis and the other on the pulse at her neck. "I need a stretcher," he yells, and suddenly a stretcher appears next to Ava, along with two more paramedics. Calling out, he says, "Blood pressure is dropping. We need to get her hooked up now."

Looking at me, he orders, "I need you to step away. You can join her in the bus, but we need to get her loaded and lined." I'm shoved away, replaced by two paramedics that hoist Ava onto the gurney and hook her up to oxygen. I insert myself at her side, refusing to let her out of my fucking sight. Grabbing her cold, limp hand, I walk alongside Ava as she's wheeled through the building and outside.

Like me, the police and paramedics bypassed the parking lot and drove through the manicured landscape of the campus. Unlike earlier, when Ava was fucking alone and defenseless, the quad is packed, everyone desperate for a glimpse of the drama. Where the fuck was everyone when she was being dragged across this goddamn lawn?

The ambulance is parked beside the picnic tables, and the paramedics lift the stretcher from the stand and slide her inside. I climb in after her, taking her hand and praying to a God I haven't talked to in a long time.

—

I have counted every fucking minute of every hour since Ava was loaded into the ambulance. It's been five hours and twenty-three minutes, three-hundred and twenty-three fucking minutes, that they've worked on her. Ava coded in the ambulance on the way to the hospital and had to be resuscitated; they asked me if she had a DNR, and I told them to fucking work on her.

Hearing the monitor flatline and then surge again was an out-of-body experience I never want to relive. She made it the rest of the ride and was transferred into surgery as soon as we got to the hospital.

A fourteen-minute drive, a three-hundred-nine-minute wait. Fucking agonizing.

I resorted to pacing the halls, trying to block out the cries of Ava's mom and sisters, the wails of Celeste and Serena, and the stone-faced silence of her father. It's my fault she's in here, my fault if she doesn't make it. My chest burns and I rub my palm over my heart. If she dies, this fucking organ dies, too.

When my mom left, it was her own choice because she didn't love me or my dad enough to stay. I was as upset as an eight-year-old could be, but if Ava leaves me? I'll be fucking destroyed.

"Greyson," a voice calls behind me, and I turn into the familiar embrace of my father. Clutching me to him, I finally allow myself to break down.

"She's fucking in there, Dad, under the damn knife because I couldn't keep my dick in my pants last year. I can't fucking lose her," I howl into his shoulder. "I won't fucking survive it if she's gone. It's my fault. It's my fucking fault. I should be the one on that table, not Ava."

"Greyson, she's strong. You need to have hope, pray, and believe that she will pull through this," my dad whispers into my ear. At six-foot-five, my dad is a behemoth of a man, and somehow, can still make me feel like a young boy. Pulling back, he examines me and takes stock of the blood covering my clothes. "You need to sit down, Greyson. You're no use to anyone dead on your feet." He leads me to the seat beside Ava's father. At our approach, he turns to face us, intent on joining in on our conversation.

Calling Ava's dad after getting to the hospital was one of the hardest things I've ever done. At barely five-five, he shouldn't be an imposing man, but between his stocky build and gruff attitude, he's like a legal mob boss. Hearing the cry rip from his throat over the harm done to Ava damn near gutted me.

The call to my dad didn't go much better. Because he was filming his baseball segment, I had to speak to his assistant, Penelope, who quickly got him off the air and on the phone. Breaking a clause in his contract, he left the filming location in Connecticut and drove until he made it to the hospital.

Shortly after Ava's family, Celeste, Serena, and my friends showed up, the police arrived to take my statement. With the support of Mr. Gregori, I explained the text I received and my race to Felicity's dorm room. Recounting my call with Ava, my version of her attack, and the scene I ran into at Howard Hall reduced Ava's mom to body-wracking sobs, while Celeste threatened to raise hell until Dante calmed her down. Though the police are still compiling all the evidence, the detectives assigned to the case let us know that Felicity was being charged with attempted murder and distribution of revenge porn.

I hope she rots in a prison cell for the rest of her life.

"Son, Ava is strong, you need to give her credit," Mr. Gregori says, placing his hand on my shoulder and leaning in. "You got there in time, Greyson. You gave her a fighting chance. Have faith that my little girl will pull through this," his voice breaks at the end, betraying his fear.

"Grey—" my dad begins but stops when a surgeon walks into the waiting room, asking for Ava's family. I stand up, brushing off my dad and Mr. Gregori's hands.

"We're here," I nearly shout across the packed room. Celeste looks up, clutching Dante's hand while Lincoln sits tight-jawed between Serena and Seraphina.

The doctor nods and makes her way over to us. Holding out a hand to Mr. and Mrs. Gregori, she begins, "I'm Doctor Navarro, the operating trauma surgeon. Ava is out of surgery; we were able to stop the bleeding and repair the damage done to her bladder. She will have a few complications, but this will not affect her quality of life or mobility. We will wait to go through these complications once she wakes up and we're in the clear. The next forty-eight hours are critical after surgery, and we will keep her in the trauma unit. They're weening her off the anesthesia now, and she should be coherent in a few hours. Once she's lucid, we'll bring you back to see her," Doctor Navarro informs us. Continuing, she says, "Why don't you all go grab something to eat, run home, and take a shower? When she wakes up, the last thing she needs to see is blood." She looks at me pointedly, almost in accusation.

"I'm not fucking leaving."

"Grey," my dad admonishes.

I shake my head. "No, I'm not fucking leaving this hospital without Ava."

She studies me, looking from my blood-spattered jeans to my drenched T-shirt. Whatever she sees on my face must appease her. "Very well," she replies. "I'll have one of the nurses bring you out some scrubs and show you into the room where Ms. Gregori will be transferred; there's a shower in there that you can use for the time being."

With that, she turns on her heel and walks to the nurses' station and gestures over her shoulder at me. With a nod of his head, the male nurse she's speaking with grabs a bundle and approaches our group, handing me the scrubs and instructing me to follow him to Ava's room.

I walk away from the hopeful tears of our family and go wait for my woman.

Ava

My entire body feels like it's been doused in gasoline, lit on fire, put out, and then reignited. My head pounds, and it feels like drums are beating around my skull, while my stomach burns with a pain incomparable to anything I've ever felt before.

"Mmmph," I groan, trying to reposition myself to get more comfortable, but it's no use. My body must be broken.

"Vixen," Grey's voice sounds from next to me. I slowly open my eyes, adjusting from the darkness behind my lids to the bright fluorescent lights of the room I'm in—a hospital room, it seems. Grey grabs hold of my hand, clutching it lightly. Turning to him, I wince at the movement and the pain it provokes in my skull and offer him a small smile.

"Hi," I croak, my voice sounding like a frog. "You came for me." Felicity's attack replays in my mind in a bird's eye view; the last thing I remember is Greyson tackling Felicity and wrenching her off me.

"Baby," he whispers with a suspiciously thick voice. "I will always come for you. I'm so fucking sorry." He places a hand on my face and cups my jaw, cradling it with reverence.

There's a squeal at the door, and I look in time to see my parents, siblings, and mine and Grey's friends walk in like a welcome back to consciousness committee. My mom runs over to me and drops to the foot of my bed, squeezing my calf in a gentle grip. "Ava, baby, you're awake," she says through tears. "How do you feel?"

I take stock of my injuries. "Like I got hit by a bus," I answer truthfully.

"No, just by a bat and then hacked open by a fucking machete," Bianca

262

sounds off from behind my mother.

"Bianca," my mother scolds, but I laugh. The movement quickly dissolves into a grimace as I feel the muscles in my abdomen seize.

"Oh shit," I mutter, clutching Grey's forearm to distract myself from the pain.

A throat clears from behind the group congregated by the door. A woman dressed in blue scrubs walks into the room. "Hello, Ms. Gregori, I'm Doctor Navarro, the surgeon that operated on you. How are you feeling?"

"It's Ava, and not great. But I'm alive, so that's good," I respond. Doctor Navarro offers a small smile before looking back at the group.

"I need to discuss the surgery with you, Ava. We may want to clear the room for this."

I clench my hand around Grey's arm. "My parents and Greyson can stay." I offer a sympathetic smile to my siblings and friends, but I don't want an audience for this. Celeste eyes me with watery green eyes, promising affection she rarely gives, while my sisters simply nod their heads and leave, understanding how I feel at this moment.

"Very well." She pauses until the room clears out. "The laceration on your stomach was stitched with minimal issue. We will need to evaluate you for concussion, and based on your current expression, I'd guess your head is causing quite a bit of pain. We'll bring you in for a CT scan in about thirty minutes to ensure proper brain functionality and treatment. Regarding the stab wound to your pelvis..." She looks down at her chart before continuing, "When the knife was impaled, it hit both the upper part of your bladder, as well as your left ovary and fallopian tube. We were able to repair your bladder and will remove the colostomy pouch in a week. Unfortunately, we were unable to repair the damage to both the left ovary and your fallopian tube, and they both had to be removed." The doctor takes a breath, giving me time to digest her words.

"W-what does that mean? Can I not have kids?"

She considers my questions. "Not necessarily. Because your right tube and ovary are intact and undamaged, we have every reason to believe that you will resume your menstruation cycle at a normal cadence. That means that you will continue to get your period and ovulate. The removal of a portion of your reproductive system does not mean that we removed all of your reproductive system. When you consider pregnancy"—she casts a hard look at Grey before turning back to me—"you will need to consult your primary OB. You may have difficulty with conception, since the reliance is on one ovary and tube, or you may have no issue. With these things, it's a case-by-case basis and your healthcare provider will work with you to provide you with your options."

"I..." I swallow, pulling the information deep inside myself. "Thank you, Doctor Navarro. Is there anything else?"

The first full smile reaches her lips. "No, but you have a long, beautiful life ahead of you. If you feel like you need a support group to discuss what happened to you, as well as the aftermath, the hospital has a team of psychologists that are highly recommended." Tears spring to my eyes, and I nod with a watery smile.

Doctor Navarro exits the room, leaving me with Grey and my parents. Before I can say anything, Grey squeezes my hand and begins to speak, "Ava, I know you feel like you're missing part of yourself right now—and fuck, I'm so fucking sorry—but when we're ready, we'll have a houseful of kids if that's what you want. I don't give a shit if they're ours biologically or adopted, but they're going to be there." He cups my jaw, tilting my chin upward to look into my eyes. "I know that came as a big fucking surprise, but it means nothing for our future."

The tears fall steadily down, soaking my cheeks and dripping onto my hospital gown.

My dad clears his throat, drawing our attention to him. "Ava, baby, you are alive, you are strong, and you're so damn loved. We're sending this woman away for a long, long time. We"—he pauses to rub his eyes—"we love you so much, baby girl. We're going to give you both a few minutes. We'll be back with coffee," he says to Grey before they walk out of the room.

"What if I can't have any kids?" I ask through my tears. "What if you decide ten years from now that you want to be with someone that can give you what I can't?"

"Vixen, you should know that you are everything I want. If you can't get pregnant and don't want to adopt, fuck having kids. Your brother and sisters are going to have enough for all of us," he says with a laugh, prying a smile out of me. Grey's face sobers and he grows serious. "Vixen, I can live without kids, but I can't fucking live without you."

He leans in and kisses my lips softly, silencing the thoughts parading around my throbbing head.

Epilogue

Ava:

"No fucking way are you going back to your dorm." Grey and I have been at this for hours—no, days. After being discharged from the hospital, I came to Grey's house. I couldn't argue that it would be easier for me to recover in his house, where a bathroom's connected to his room and there's more privacy than in my dorm.

But, after six weeks of Greyson Jansen as my nurse, I am going to lose my shit.

"Grey, I need to go back to my dorm," I explain calmly. "Felicity is in a psychiatric hospital until her arraignment, my body is almost fully healed, and I cannot keep staying here." After the police arrested her, Felicity's lawyer presented an insanity defense. Since the plea, she's been under evaluation at a state mental health facility.

Not having to look over my shoulder or mentally prepare myself every time my phone goes off has been a welcome reprieve.

"Vixen, why would you leave? Your parents even agreed that it made the most sense for you to stay with me," he responds with a self-satisfied smirk.

I look at him incredulously. "They meant temporarily until I'm healed. They didn't mean that I should move in with you permanently."

He shrugs. "Same thing."

"Ugh!" I scream and stomp into the bathroom. Turning the water on, I seethe. I undress, letting the fog envelop my naked body before I step into the shower. Tossing my head back in the water, I let the steam and heat soothe my annoyance with Grey. He saved me, and God knows I love him, but he's also the most annoying person I've ever come into contact with.

Hands wrap around my stomach, pulling me back until I rest against Grey's

266

body. His hand dips down until his fingers spread across the scar on my pelvic bone. When I woke up at the hospital, I met with a therapist to sort through my feelings about the attack and my future. In the weeks since the attack, I've processed what happened to me, that Felicity's mental illness was a main component in her obsession, and that she needs just as much help as I do. Will I ever forgive her? Probably not. It takes a saint to forgive the person that tried to murder them, but I can feel sorry for her and hope that she gets the help she needs.

"Vixen," Grey's voice breaks through my thoughts. "You know I don't want you to leave because almost losing you nearly killed me." He leans down, kissing the side of my head while his hand continues to caress the scar on my hip. "Besides, the doctor said we're going to have to try twice as hard to get pregnant."

I roll my eyes. "I'm nineteen. We're not trying to get pregnant any time soon."

"Yeah, but you can practice riding my cock so that we get it right on the first try." He shifts forward, letting me feel the full length of him against my lower back. I elbow him, putting distance between us before I turn around.

"Don't think that you can distract me with your elephant dick, Greyson." He raises an eyebrow but stays quiet. "I'm meeting Celeste and Serena for lunch today and going back to Serena's for a girls' night afterward." He opens his mouth to protest, but I cut him off. "Do not even think about protesting, you fuck face. I will hold out on sex and blowjobs and every sexual act if you attempt to keep me at your side."

"You're going to be the death of me, woman," Grey grinds out.

"Yeah, but you love me. So come here and kiss me." I rise on my toes and he meets me, claiming my lips in a tender kiss. Backing me against the wall, he lifts my legs and I wrap them around his waist. He doesn't take it slow or treat me like I'm half of myself. He drives in with a speed and intensity that would be alarming if it didn't feel so damn good.

"Harder," I moan, and Grey meets my demands by fucking me into the wall.

"That's right, take my cock like my good little girl," he grinds out. His hand travels from my hip to my clit, pinching down. "Come on my cock, vixen. Coat my dick in your cum," he commands while adding more pressure to my clit. I erupt around him.

"Greyson," I cry. He fucks me through my orgasm, not breaking his pace until I hear his groans and feel the warm shot of his cum inside me.

"Fucking take it all, vixen." He stills inside me, holding me against the wall while his dick softens inside me. His eyes lose the intensity they always hold during sex, turning tender with emotion. Lifting his hand, he cups my jaws and tilts my head up. "I fucking love you, vixen," he murmurs before claiming my lips.

—

Nearly three hours pass before Grey lets me out of his house. It's well past lunch by the time I make it to Serena's. Not bothering to knock, I let myself into her apartment and freeze as soon as I walk in.

On the couch, Serena is holding CeCe while she sobs, shaking from the impact of her tears. I rush over to my best friend, dropping down until I'm kneeling on the floor and clutching her knee.

"C, what's wrong? Are you okay?" I ask over her tears. I look at Serena, but she just shakes her head in confusion.

"We decided to postpone lunch after you texted and get dinner instead. She got here a few minutes ago and started crying as soon as she walked through the door," Serena explains.

"C, honey. Look at me," I coax. She slowly lifts her head and tears run down her face. Her eyes are red-rimmed, making her green eyes appear like emeralds on her face.

"I'm pregnant," she whispers.

About the Author

Lola Miles is the pen name of a thirty-something living in New Jersey with her husband, children, and dog. By day, Lola is a businesswoman, and by night, she writes smut that would make your grandmother blush profusely.

You can connect with me on:

🌐 https://www.lolamilesbooks.com

🔗 https://instagram.com/lolamilesbooks

Made in United States
North Haven, CT
24 August 2024

56525230R00154